AFTER *the* FURY

STRINGS OF FATE: **BOOK FOUR**

MELISSA J. KINCAID

LOTS OF LOVE CREATIONS

Also by Melissa J Kincaid

The Strings of Fate series:
Love, Blood & Fury
Magic, Midnight & Starlight
Fire, Fury & Chaos
After The Fury

Content Warning:
The *Strings of Fate* series is intended for New Adult to Adult audiences.
This instalment contains coarse language, scenes of battle violence, torture,
as well as sexual themes and a sex scene.

AFTER *the* FURY

STRINGS OF FATE BOOK FOUR

MELISSA J. KINCAID

After The Fury
A Strings of Fate Novel: Book Four
By Melissa J. Kincaid

Copyright © 2025 Melissa J. Kincaid

ISBN (Paperback): 9780645054897
ISBN (Hardback): 9781764048613
ISBN (eBook): 9781764048606
ISBN (Special Edition Paperback): 9781764048651

Published by Lots of Love Creations.

Edited by Carolyn Gilpin.

Commisioned art by @kalynne_art (Kalynne Pratt) including portraits of Nemesis, Krepth, Nemesis (with magic), and the three character scene of Nemesis, Krepth and Aeun.

Cover design, map and illustrations by Melissa J Kincaid.

For the ones that feel unseen, unheard, or unworthy.
You are a spark waiting to be noticed.

THE LAND of FYTHNAR
AYRITH
BORDER TOWN
WEST COURT
SCHOOL OF FATE
THE SLITHER
COLKIRK
THE WASTES
PEN
LILIDALE
MIRFIELD
THE IVORY PLAINS
FJOLL
SOUTH COURT
ERSTONIA

THE DRAGON'S TEETH
NORTH COURT
BONEMIRE
VIRIDYA
THE
HIRE DEPTHS
AMBERBOURNE
EAST COURT
TRADER'S BAY
EVERGRAVE
THE COVE
SKAALD

Pronunciation Guide

Main Characters

Nemesis Rion:	Ne – meh – sis	Ree – on
Krepth Hallier:	Kre – p – th	Hal – ee – er
Ariiaya Trillia:	Arr – ee – aya	Trill – ee – ah
Elijah Wolfe:	Ee – lie – jah	Wolf
Lorch Kruel:	Lor – k	Crew – el
Aeun:	Eh – oon	
Merrick:	Meh – rick	
Vega:	Vay – gah	
Iniq:	Ee – neek	
Tikkani Alinar:	Tik – an – i	
Emerson Alinar:	Em – er – son	
Quinn:	K – win	
Valdis:	Val – dis	
Sybell:	Si – bell	
Ghila:	Gill – ah	
Klotho:	Clo – tho	
Etropos:	E – tro – poss	
Lakhesis:	La – kes – is	
Lucada (Luc):	Luck	
Celadine Clover:	Cell – a – deen	Clo – ver
Valerie Gray:	Va – ler – ee	Gr – ay
Lyda Wild:	Lid – ah	Wi – ld

Court Families, Creatures and Towns

Freya:	Frey – ah	
Jero:	Jer – row	
Thogan:	Tho – gan	
Kadec Brolikian:	Kad – ek	Bro – li – kee – ann
Eliverus:	Ee – lie – ver – us	
Ouroboros:	Oo – ruh – bo – ruhs	
Nocturne:	Nok – turn	
Kryvern:	Cry – vern	
Fythnar:	Fi – th – nar	
Viridya:	Vir – id – ee – ya	
Ayrith:	Air – ith	

PROLOGUE

The sky darkened, though night had not yet come.

Branches split and snapped as a soldier tore through the brush, chased by screams, by the clang of steel against tearing flesh. What was meant to be a simple scouting run, a measured look at the strange pulse of magic that had unsettled every magic wielder in the kingdom, had unravelled into slaughter.

There was blood. Too much blood. *So* much blood.

The scout ran, lungs ragged, breath sawing out of his throat. He was young, far too young, but youth gave him speed. Small for his years, quick of step, his mother had said he was built like a hare – easy to overlook, almost impossible to catch once he bolted.

"Go! Ride for the castle, tell the–"

The command ended in a scream. His officer, helmet lost, eyes stretched wide with fear, vanished sideways into the brush. The sound of bone crunching, armour twisting, and a single gurgle of breath.

Numb with horror, the boy kept running, fear giving his feet wings as he vaulted a fallen log, jagged spikes of bark tearing at his palms. Leaves and dirt clung to his blood-slicked hands. Behind him, the forest erupted in chaos – branches snapping, claws tearing, voices that had once been human howling like broken instruments.

Something caught his cloak. Bony fingers raked across the fabric, tugging, ripping seams. He tore free, stumbling forward. The moans followed, thick and guttural, the sound of teeth grinding too close to

his ear.

Leathery wings beat the air, sending his hair whipping into his eyes. A scream rent the clearing, half his own, half the beast that struck. Talons plunged into his shoulders, hot pain exploding as he was lifted from the ground. His feet kicked at nothing, boots lashing empty air.

He clawed at the thing, fingernails scraping against hide like old parchment stretched over bone. The smell of rot filled his nose, a stench so strong it burned his throat.

The creature shrieked, jerking him higher, dragging him toward the droning light of the portal. It pulsed and flared like a violent cut, its song a low, grinding thrum that rattled through his ribs.

The boy's dagger slipped into his palm – training, instinct, anything to keep him alive. He drove it backward, steel crunching through brittle ribs. The thing howled, wings folding, and they plummeted.

They hit the ground with a brutal crash. Air burst from his lungs. Bones cracked, his and the creatures' both. He rolled, dazed, dragging himself forward, his broken legs trailing in the dirt. The forest swam and blurred. Ahead, the portal hung open like torn flesh, its sick blue light bleeding through the canopy.

More shapes spilled from the rift. Twisted silhouettes, claws raking earth, the gleam of silver scales and iron links. Hollow, hungry eyes locked on him.

They closed in, and the boy had no breath left to scream.

CHAPTER ONE

NEMESIS

"Have you never felt true happiness before, Nem?"

His words echoed in her mind, the question she had been asking herself since the night Nemesis Rion had learned she was Goddess-touched. The moon had hung high, draped in velvet night sky, stars winking like curious spectators as the wolf Shifter, Krepth, lay his hand against her glowing skin. The discovery of her heritage on the rooftop of Ayrith castle was still vivid in her mind, though a year of time had stretched on since.

Nem's memories were clouded, but she struggled to recall a time before that rooftop moment when she had genuinely felt happy. It was difficult to even think of a time when she had felt anything other than a simmering blend of rage, curiosity, and self-loathing. Her amnesia left her in a state of longing, yet she was unsure if her heart was holding her back, fearing the pain she might uncover.

No memories could be dragged to mind, not enough to make her skin glow again… not enough to bring forth the fire to her veins that she'd felt with *him*.

With the kingdom's master of spies.

A man who was supposed to be her enemy.

One of those she had been bred to *hunt*.

The wolf Shifter, Krepth Hallier.

Gods, so much had happened since their time on the rooftop.

War had swallowed Fythnar, with Valdis's reign causing the north to be blanketed in black ice, freezing the large body of water circling the golden castle of Ayrith. With the skies dotted with portals to another realm, horrible, eyeless, winged creatures fell to the earth like acidic rain, tearing through humans, Fae, elves and Shifters alike. The battle had been bloody, unforgiving, wretched. Valdis's experimenting with forbidden magic had nearly destroyed their nation, driven by a craving for power and an acute love for someone he had lost long ago.

Many did not make it out alive, and those who did were left with permanent wounds and scars, running deeper than flesh, deeper than bone, wounds that would never truly heal.

Without thinking, Nem found her fingers tracing the lines of her own battle scars. The puckered skin started at her hairline near one of her pointed ears, curved down over her high cheekbone, and ended just shy of her chin. Unsightly… a marring of her skin that she knew many now shared, along with the memories embedded with the wound in her flesh. A reminder of what she had survived… and what others had not.

One particular loss weighted the room where she stood and had continued to be a phantom lingering on the shoulders of those whom Nem now watched.

The late copper-haired king and son of the usurper, Lorch Kruel, was the reason they were still here today, breathing the sweet, moist air of the caverns beneath the castle. Wielding Elijah's Sword of Power, he had driven the blade through his father's heart, creating an opening for Elijah. As the tyrant was weakened, Elijah seized the chance to attempt a life bond, hoping to sacrifice himself and take down Valdis in the process.

But then Elijah's sister had taken the connection unto herself, right on the verge of death, while simultaneously utilising her Mind Wielding ability to bring Lorch to peace as they died. Instead of regaining his long dead love, Valdis lost his own son – the one he had ultimately loved the most – before losing his own life. Necromancy was a tainted magic, one that poisoned the mind, and weaved dark fates ending with death.

Love caused blindness…. it was weakness.

Since her earliest days at the School of Fate, Nem had been steeped in the Sisters' mantra: love was pain. The crumbling castle on the bluff had trained Fae assassins in the Gods' name, and Nem had never thought to question it – until she left with Ariiaya.

She saw then how love could give strength, bind hearts, inspire hope, and drive back fear. She saw it transform her violet-eyed friend, whose fated bond, gifted by the Gods, had carried her through war. Though love had aided in ending the war, it had also been the reason why it had begun.

Nem thought she was beginning to feel love, until love turned to pain.

It was the day Krepth, shadows deep beneath his eyes, confessed he could not shift. They had been on the clifftop with their friends only hours before, hands linked, remembering the one they had lost. Her touch, the touch that severed his magic, had left him defenceless, cut away from his wolf.

Nem let her fingers fall, brushing the cool metal of her armour, self-loathing a hot bloom in her chest.

Her skin hadn't glowed since he left.

Was it truly he who made her shine? Was the glow the shape of her happiness, or merely the gift the gods had pressed upon her – a gift she did not understand and couldn't control?

Often Nem wondered if things might have been different had the Gods been present in flesh, not just in spirit. Instead, they left mortals to fate and chaos. Now, they were nothing but names in dusty tomes. Weak, absent, forgotten.

She held no reverence for the bloodline that tied her to them. How could she, when their neglect had left the land in ruin?

A throat cleared across the room, drawing a sliver of her attention back from her internal musing. Drips of water pattered on the cavern floor, filling the spaces between speech as the small council gathered in the caverns below the castle. As soon as they'd begun to meet again after the battle, they had moved to the caverns to allow space for their largest member to attend.

Lysander, the King's grandfather's dragon, rested on her haunches nearby, golden eyes watching their gathering, an ancient shine in their depths. Scales shifted against one another as she crossed her claws, neck curving, nostrils flaring. The dragon's knowledge was invaluable, that of their own world and the ones beyond it.

The space had changed since Nem had last been down here, since their run in with the very first undead, Sybell's poor handmaiden, Ingrid. Beneath the huge royal blue rug, Nem knew there were gouges in the stone, remnants left by the Kryvern they'd fought here too. Now, a large circular metal chandelier hung over the heavy war table, fixed by chains from the jagged stalactites. Sconces dotted the walls, casting flicking light over the otherwise untouched and rugged natural structure around them. The waterfall raged; its boom muted to a drone by magic while sunlight attempted to chop through the water, mixing in dappled sprays across the damp cavern mouth. Unlike the last time, where the cavernous space had been damp and dark, now it held a cool, strangely intimate feel.

Nem drew her gaze to the voice in the room, a strong tenor that commanded all to it.

"Tell me where they were last seen."

King Eliverus Herington stood at the head of the war table, arms crossed over his chest in familiar stance. Draped in dark blue – the kind that clung to the edge of midnight before surrendering to dawn

– he wore the weight of his lineage stitched into every golden seam. His hair had grown, just slightly, the dark strands falling in a careful sweep over his stern brows. Eyes like molten silver swept over the council, as heavy and unreadable as ever. His beard was thicker now, though still kept in sharp order. The dragon-head crest of the North gleamed at his breast, bold and unyielding, stamped proudly where once the serpent of the Kruel family had reigned.

Magic was a consistent hum around Elijah, the sweet taste of it like a branding. His power had taken time to return, and when it had, it ingrained itself into every fibre of their city, as if burrowing under the soil of the land. Returning and making itself at home.

"To the south, just beyond the Wastes and on the border of the Ivory Plains," answered one of the council members, Yarn, a solid man with close-cropped brown hair and a beard salted with grey. He was a new member, a Fae, one whom had once headed the resistance, father to the crown healer, Celadine. Nem had heard that Cela had continued to tend to their people as healer, while telling the story of how Lorch Kruel had joined their resistance, despite the heavy prejudice he'd been taught. Rather than wallow in grief, she poured herself into reshaping the world's opinion of him. Through it all, her daughter, Mia, remained steadfast at her side, quietly learning the art of healing. The last time Nem saw her, Mia had grown nearly a foot taller, her body finally starting to catch up with the quiet, steady maturity in her eyes. For someone so young, she'd already seen and endured more than most do in a lifetime.

Nem's thoughts slid from the apothecary and her daughter as Yarn continued.

"The same location where the last were sent to investigate the strange magical pulse."

Elijah's lips thinned, brows knotting in concern.

Nem recalled the disturbance, a tremor upon the air unfelt since the end of the war. Magic had returned to Fythnar slowly, settling upon the continent as if it had never left. Those who were magically inclined felt the hum constant through the earth, in the streams, in the air. But what was felt two weeks ago was different – a jolt that sliced the peace, like a door slammed in the dead of night.

Steam cloyed the cavern air as Lysander said, *"There are dark forces in the air – tainted blood and corrupted magic."* The dragon's deep voice echoed in their minds, a strange mix of tenderness and power that Nem was still adjusting to. The beast's serpentine head tilted in the King's direction. *"This is beyond mere soldier scouts. We need more magic. We need warriors."*

"I will go."

Nem tilted her head slightly, to the ring of another voice, one which she knew almost better than her own.

Queen Ariiaya Trillia, once her life-bonded partner and still her best friend, stood beside her husband, chin held high. Her former Fury comrade had embraced the role of Queen with the same vigour she brought to any mission, stepping into it seamlessly. Despite the doubt she'd shown about ruling, her love of the land was obvious, and her love of the male beside her even more so. She was loyal, just, and fair – her upbringing had taught her to consider all sides of a story. But one thing remained unchanged: her instinct to place herself in harm's way before letting danger reach anyone else.

Today, under the speckled light of the cavern, she looked as regal as ever. She was draped in a gown of deep purple, so dark it nearly appeared black. The corseted bodice hugged her figure, accentuating her curves with elegant precision. The fabric flared out dramatically at her hips, cascading in smooth, flowing folds that swept gracefully along the floor. The rich colour and intricate design of the dress radiated both power and sophistication, as if she wore not just a gown, but an extension of her commanding presence.

The light softly highlighted the honeyed undertones woven through her dark brown hair, elegantly swept into a crown braid. A few loose curls escaped, delicately framing her face, adding a touch of softness to her otherwise regal appearance. Perched atop her brow was a simple gold coronet, drawing attention to her furrowed brows, which hinted at her fierce determination and stubborn resolve.

From what Nem had gathered from Arii, being Queen was a far cry from her previous life as an assassin. There were endless rules, protocols, and traditions to follow – an invisible web of expectations that confined her best friend. Nem could see how these constraints weighed on Arii, the frustration simmering just beneath her composed exterior. Despite being an excellent queen, the rigid structure of the role clashed with her instinct for action and freedom, leaving her feeling trapped by the very duties she excelled at. Her quickness to volunteer now wasn't a surprise to Nem .

Though Arii carried a fierce presence in all she did, it did not faze the solid, towering figure beside her. Elijah stood with his hands resting on the table, inspecting the map, his silence speaking louder than any words could. Arii tilted her head slightly, as if reacting to something Elijah had said telepathically. Her lips parted to respond, but before she could speak, one of the council members cut in.

"We cannot send a monarch to investigate a small matter like this when there is larger discourse brewing along our trade routes. The path from the south has been the harshest it's been in many years with snowstorms raging in the Ivory Plains. Valuable resources that we can only source from there are facing steep delays. Fresh water stores are delayed from the east, too, and supplies for the healing bracelets to stem the spread of Dragon Fever are also absent from the west."

Another councilman, running a finger absently along the map, eyes downcast, added, "Tensions are too high with all other courts for our King and Queen to part."

Arii was silent, though Nem could see the twitch in her tense jaw that betrayed her displeasure, even if all knew the councilman was right.

Silence hung in the air, broken only by the soft scrape of Lysander's scales against the stone as the dragon shifted cautiously.

At the end of the war, what was once off-kilter had begun to balance. The weather patterns across each court had returned to normal as the black ice melted, restoring the natural climate unique to each region. That balance had lasted until just a week ago, when anomalies began to appear once more. Heat waves scorched the northern lands, while worse than normal blizzards ravaged the south. In the east, the wet season stretched unnaturally long, and in the west, erratic currents caused chaos. All of this unfolded in unison after the strange magical disturbance.

The councilman finally lifted his head, his eyes soft beneath the steady scrutiny of violet. "You might consider a hired party. Perhaps even call upon our finest soldiers. The army is stronger now than it has ever been." He paused, his throat working as though the words weighed heavy. "If it please you, my lady."

Nem's thoughts once again drew back to Krepth, chosen as the ambassador between courts. They'd hardly spoken in the year that had passed, swept up in their duties. Yes, duties. She wouldn't allow herself to think they'd been deliberately avoiding one another. Though they most obviously had been.

Nem's turquoise eyes slid over the group which she flanked, her skin pebbling from the cold, though her discomfort was hidden beneath her armour. As the monarchs and the council continued to speak, she lifted her chin, seeking a reprieve from her thoughts, surveying the cavern ceiling, sharp and dripping like a hungry dragon's teeth. The chamber stayed cool despite the outside heat. With sconces, chandelier, and sunlight fractured by the waterfall, the amber walls revealed delicate marbling, like lakes snaking across Elijah's map.

Though it had been a year since the war ended, it felt like a small stretch of time to Nem, who relived snips of memory of the event every time she closed her eyes.

Rippling claws.

Battering wings.

Pure, blinding *light*.

Her fingers trailed her scar, pausing upon her cheek. Nem's stomach squeezed, lips parting on a breath of speech that left before her mind could catch up from the fog of memories.

"Send me."

Conversation came to an abrupt stop at her words, all eyes turning toward her. But Nem's focus remained on Arii's narrowed violet eyes as she barked, "No!" just as Yarn exclaimed, "Perfect!"

The dragon dipped her snout in approval. Lysander's golden gaze felt weighted… a strange knowing shining within. *"Send the silver one."*

Elijah moved a hand to his mate's, squeezing her fingers, before he met Nem's gaze.

"You willingly volunteer, Nem?"

The moment she'd let loose her magic to protect the people upon the bridge had been one of the only moments she'd truly felt alive. She recalled the feeling of the magic raging beneath her skin, the currents of light flowing through her veins. The surge of power she'd felt in that moment; after so long feeling lost… trapped within her hazy memories; had been unlike anything she'd felt before.

And she hadn't been able to replicate it since.

For months she'd felt displaced… not truly belonging in the regal setting of the castle, trailing her best friend like a shadow. She hadn't the desire to investigate her magic further, nor had she felt any desire to do anything but serve. To follow orders, much like her previous life.

Until now.

To the bob of Arii's throat, Nem replied, "Yes."

"We have all heard the stories of how Nemesis's light magic obliterated scores of winged beasts and undead in one charged explosion," said one of the councilmen, the note of awe not at all hidden from his voice. "A beacon in the darkness, you saved countless lives."

Heat rose to Nem's cheeks in response to the praise, feeling a knot inside at the fact that she wasn't entirely sure how she'd achieved what she did, that she wasn't sure she could do it again even if they found whatever was disturbing the balance of their land. She'd been under immense pressure, and *he* had been by her side.

Eyes of vivid green, fading to muted tones at her touch.

"Perhaps to help strengthen the relationships between our courts, each could have the opportunity to send a warrior," added Yarn.

Elijah nodded. "Allow each court to have the opportunity to investigate and act."

Yarn scooted some pieces strategically along the board as he spoke. "By sending our best warriors, one from each court, we will have a much better chance of investigating what is sending our land once again spiralling, while also using this as a diplomatic strengthening exercise."

Arii spoke around the fingernail she was biting. Even after all this time, her anxious habit hadn't dissipated. "Nem cannot go alone."

Elijah gave a silent nod of confirmation, subtly intertwining his fingers with his wife's as she brought her hand down.

The scar on Nem's cheek radiated a faint warmth, a persistent reminder of the war that had left its mark on her. It symbolised not only her past struggles but also the elusive power she had only begun to tap into.

Perhaps this mission would give her a chance to understand her abilities. Even if it didn't, it would at least serve as a welcome distraction from her thoughts.

Nem's gaze met Arii's, violet depths seemingly seeing directly into her soul.

With the council in agreeance, Elijah said, "Send word to the other courts to select a trusted warrior, while I prepare a spell to open the voids to transport them here. They will set out at dawn in a day's time."

CHAPTER TWO

NEMESIS

Nem's fist slammed against flesh, teeth raining on the tavern floorboards like loose piano keys. Anger heated her breath, perhaps from the words uttered by the mortal man, whose eyes rolled as she hoisted him off his feet, or perhaps from the fury within her, tamped down for too long.

Mrs Mulvany's tavern was a ruckus of sights and sounds. Cooking smoke from the kitchens clung to the rafters, mingled with the yeasty sweetness of spilled ale. It was busier than ever, humans, elves and Fae mingled over food and drink and memories. But unity was still building; beneath the laughter and music there was wariness, as if at any moment a careless word could peel away the fragile mortar of their peace.

Nem used the place as an escape from the castle, somewhere to be distracted by songs and people, to shoo away the beast of her quiet anxiety.

Tonight, however, her unusually short tether had snapped. It had begun simply enough – she'd been staring into her ale, watching the liquid ripple, thoughts sweeping to eyes like jade, to a dimple pressed in a smirking cheek.

A smile that both warmed her insides and set them to boil.

"Have you never felt true happiness before, Nem?"

His words haunted her, until another voice had drawn her attention.

"We sit here, drinking ale amongst those who dragged our land into ruin, with curses and dark magic. And now," the man's lips curled into a sneer, "we are expected to bow again, to an ex-assassin, a *killer*, with no royal blood, who slithered onto the throne!"

Fate had a strange way of weaving unpredictability into Nem's days, a fact she had come to expect.

"You had better still your tongue before you lose it," she now seethed, holding him away from her.

The man, eyes glassy but still feisty, clawed at her arm. "Or what, pointy ears? From one mad ruler to another, are we truly better off? We all know that magic such as King Herington's power can pull one into madness, so we are right back where we began!"

Feeling all eyes on them in the tense silence that had been filled with music a minute ago, Nem shoved him back, but he flew forward, fists swinging clumsy and wild. Without her armour, Nem felt light in her grey tunic and leathers, freer out of her royal garb. Arii had always been the one quick to spill blood but tonight Nem's emotions were heightened by the disappearing scout party and the strange shiver left upon the air by the disturbance.

She caught the blow against her shoulder, the impact hardly moving her frame as she answered with a strike of her own. Her fist cracked across his jaw again, sharp enough to rattle what teeth remained, and he stumbled against the table, sending mugs and dishes of stew crashing to the ground. Patrons were on their feet, some jeering, some urging restraint, others hungry for spectacle. Chairs scraped and toppled. The bard vanished from the stage, leaving only the discordant ring of strings as his instrument clattered to the floor.

The man roared, face red with blood, fury and shame as he snatched a knife from the table. He lunged. Nem twisted, the blade grazing harmlessly past her ribs, and with a fluid motion she wrenched his wrist aside, slamming him chest-first against the edge of the table.

The knife clattered free, skidding into the shadows.

"You know *nothing*," she snapped, cold as winter. "You know nothing of the sacrifices of our new queen!"

But still drunk on bravado, he spat blood and defiance. "Sacrifices? We have *all* sacrificed! It will be as before – humans under the magic boots of the Fae. We will all end up where we once were, slaves to magic and madness! With your murderer of a Fae Queen at the helm!"

The last shred of Nem's forced composure snapped. She slammed him to the floorboards, the thud ringing through the tavern as though the foundations themselves felt her fury. Kneeling over him, blue eyes ablaze, she struck again, fist splitting skin, the copper tang of blood filling the air.

Shouts rose around her – some calling for her to stop, others goading her on – but all blurred into noise. In that moment there was only the taste of insult, the name of her Queen and best friend sullied, and the feral satisfaction of silencing it with her own hands.

"Enough!"

The word cut through the tavern like a blade.

Nem froze mid-strike, her knuckles dripping red, as the tall figure of Mrs Mulvany barrelled into the circle that had formed. Her apron was stained with kitchen grease, her hair a frazzled halo of pink curls, but her eyes burned with authority fierce enough to quiet the room.

She planted her hands on her hips, glaring down first at Nem then at the sprawled, groaning man.

"By the Gods, I will not stand for blood spilt in my house. Not by you, Nemesis Rion, nor by any drunken fool with more bile than sense."

The man's mouth popped open as if to speak, but Mrs Mulvany silenced him with a look that could have cowed a warlord.

"And you, Torren – keep that rotten tongue in your mouth before I cut it out and toss it to the dogs. Are you truly so witless as to goad for trouble, when all anyone here wants is to eat, drink, and remember how to live side by side?"

A ripple of laughter and relief broke through the crowd, though wary eyes still flicked between Nem and her opponent. Nem's breath came heavy, shoulders rising and falling as she slowly uncurled her fists, scars hot like brands against her cheek.

Mrs Mulvany stepped closer, her voice softening though some steel remained.

"I know your anger. I know your fury. But you will not win your battles on these floorboards, Miss Rion. If you wish to defend the honour of our Queen, do it with dignity, not with brawls fit for guttersnipes."

The words struck harder than any blow. Nem swallowed and pushed to her feet. The man groaned again, bloodied but alive, and Mrs Mulvany snapped her fingers at two burly patrons.

"Drag him outside before he soils my floor any further."

As the crowd dispersed back into its clamour, the tavern's music stumbled to life again. But laughter was brittle, and glances still darted towards Nem as though she were a wolf loose in their midst. Groups drew tighter, humans to humans, Fae to Fae, with only a few daring to bridge the divide.

Nem dragged a breath through her teeth and reached for her mug, though it lay toppled, contents seeping into the cracks of the table. She cursed under her breath and straightened, only to find Mrs Mulvany beside her.

"Come," the tavern mistress murmured, tilting her head toward the bar. "You need a clearer head than the one you are brewing with ale and anger. Cohesion will take time, and though it doesn't seem it, most nights, everyone gets along. King Eliverus and Queen Ariiaya's wishes for a unified court aren't being completely ignored, young one. There will always be those who have a different opinion."

At the bar Nem sat, shoulders square, gaze fixed on the scarred counter as Mrs Mulvany poured a clean mug of spiced apple juice and set it before her.

"I am not a child, I know these things," Nem said at last, staring into the non-alcoholic beverage, her voice stubborn to her own ears.

Mrs Mulvany leaned against the bar, folding her arms. "I never said you were, nor did I question your understanding. You are carrying more than most could endure. Grief, anger, memory… they are wild things. They scratch, they bite, they break out when you least wish them to. But if you let every drunken fool drag them from you, they will spend your strength where it is wasted. You're a Queen's guard, Nemesis, you normally act like one."

Nem sighed, shoulders tight, blood drying against her knuckles. The tavern matron accommodated her brooding, even offered chances to speak about what was on her mind, but Nem was like a fortress, walls tall and composure fixed.

Nem's hands curled around the fresh mug, though she left it untouched. Her eyes lifted, cold fire still alive within them.

"He mocked what this land is fighting to rebuild. He insulted our Queen. I can't allow that."

"And so you bloodied his face," Mrs Mulvany replied evenly. "But tell me, did peace come closer for it? Or have you reminded this room how easy it is to fall back into hatred, when what we need most is healing? You and I both know our fierce Queen does not need defending from the words of drunken fools."

The words gave Nem pause. She drew a long breath, the storm in her chest tempered, though not extinguished. Mrs Mulvany sighed, softer this time, and rested her hand briefly over Nem's.

"I know you would defend this land with your life. You already have, I've heard. But sometimes, the greater courage lies in defending it with restraint. Weaving peace through patience."

Nem's gaze met hers, unflinching. "Perhaps. But there will come a time when restraint alone does not keep the peace we are trying to hold."

Nem couldn't help but feel that her words no longer described just their current predicament but also her own. She couldn't stand back and wait for things to change, for her past to be revealed. She'd decided it hours ago, under the bright, fiery gaze of her best friend. Her Queen. With the mission to occupy her, it was about time she tried to find out more about her past.

She paid her bill and nodded her thanks to Mrs Mulvany.

The tavern's noise faded behind her as Nem stepped into the night air. The door swung shut, muffling the music and laughter until only the murmur of the distant waterfall remained, its constant rush filling the silence she carried with her. Cool night mist clung to her skin, a balm against the heat still thrumming in her veins.

A sudden shadow swept across the cobbled street, vast wings cutting through the stars. The heavy beat of a dragon's flight stirred the sleepy town below, shutters rattling, dogs barking, a child's cry breaking through the night. Nem tilted her head back to follow the gleam of scales that caught the moonlight like tarnished bronze. Once, such a sight would have sent the city to its knees in terror. Now the beast arced lazily above, a guardian rather than a harbinger of danger.

Her eyes followed it until it vanished beyond the rooftops, leaving the hush of the night even heavier in its wake. She turned then, looking upward to the castle on the bluff. Once gold, its towers still bore the shimmer of faded grandeur, though now they glowed pale and silver under the moon. The sight stole her breath and twisted her chest, for it was a reminder of all that had been broken, and of what remained fragile in their grasp.

Tomorrow she would leave these walls, leave her Queen, and set out on a mission that gnawed at her mind with anxious teeth. To be parted from Ariiaya now, when the land was still tender and the crown unsteady on her brow, felt like tearing flesh from bone. Nem could only pray that her steel, her strength and her unexplored magic would be enough to keep the fragile peace intact.

Above, the stars wheeled silently, the moonlight spilling down as though the Gods themselves watched in judgement. Nem stood unmoving in the street, glaring at the dark sky, fists tight at her sides.

Drawing a breath, she turned and began the walk back toward the castle, the moonlit towers rising like both promise and warning against the night.

CHAPTER THREE

NEMESIS

"Are you sure that you want to go, Nem?" asked Arii for the second time that morning though Nem knew that her closest friend was aware that her mind was made up.

"It isn't like you to ask the same question twice, Ariiaya."

Arii twisted on her heel, morning sunlight gilding her silhouette in gold, face drawn into a scowl, fists knuckled by her sides. Nem surveyed her friend, noting the stiff set of her shoulders under her simple navy gown, the way her breath came in swift rasps. Her hair was unbound, her skin washed of the cosmetic paints she usually wore in the public eye. Now, in the privacy of Nem's personal quarters – Queen Ariiaya was just… Arii, with her anxieties plain to see.

"You look at me now in a way that I used to feel. Cold, detached… uncaring." Arii said, her voice steely, yet breathless. When Nem's gaze locked with hers, she saw fire burning bright, and love – deep, endless love. But within those violet eyes, framed by thick lashes, she also caught the flicker of fear, lingering at the edges. "We have come a long way. Don't withdraw on me now."

Nem didn't miss the way her friend's gaze lingered on her cheek, on the scar marring her skin there. Nor did she miss the way Arii watched her at times, brows creased. Worried.

Leaning against the wall with her arms crossed tightly over her chest, Nem knew that she appeared detached, even aloof. But beneath the surface, she was just as anxious about her leaving as Arii was. The difference was that over time, she had simply learned to mask her fears more effectively than her best friend.

So, she pushed from the wall, and took Arii's hands in her own, her fingers grazing the scabs of her friend's anxiety. There was a beat of silence as Nem grasped for the best words to quell Arii's fears, for she knew she was still grieving over the loss of Lorch, and all else whom they'd lost over the course of the war. Nem wasn't the best with emotion in words, only one ringing truth. "I… *need* to go, Arii."

They had once shared a life bond, forged through equal parts bravery and Arii's reckless foolishness. In those days, Nem could have sensed every emotion the Fae standing before her felt, down to the marrow of her bones. But now, all that remained was silence between them, their life bond long severed by the mating bond Arii had formed with Elijah.

There were days were Nem missed the chaos of Arii's emotions, a constant little fire in the back of her head. However, the tenseness of her jaw and the crease between her brows meant Nem no longer needed the bond to understand how her Queen was feeling.

The corner of Nem's lips quirked up.

"You have your handmaidens to keep you company. Everyone knows you don't need a bodyguard when you can easily protect yourself."

"My handmaidens despise me," Arii quipped, a pout forming. Nem stifled a laugh, recognising that Arii wasn't truly bothered by their opinions – only by the fact that their petty judgments interfered with their duties.

Arii gnawed her lip as Nem said, "They don't hate you. They fear you. There is a difference. You know you are hard to work with."

Arii did not speak, only clucked her tongue in anxious thought.

"Your former occupation as an emotionless assassin isn't entirely forgotten, despite your hand in saving the realm. But with time, they'll accept you fully, Arii. You need to allow them that time though." Nem thought back to the tavern brawl, to the bitter words of the drunken human just before her fist met his face.

Nem couldn't keep the laugh from her voice as Arii broke from her hold and charged towards the door. Her outburst didn't catch Nem off guard – Arii tended to lose her composure when it came to worrying about those she cared for. It was a familiar pattern, one driven by her fierce protectiveness and deep loyalty to her friends. Nem knew that, beneath Arii's sharp words and fiery temper, her fear for the safety of others always weighed heavily on her heart. This had nothing to do with the maids, and everything to do with Nem leaving.

What did surprise Nem was the next words to leave Arii's mouth as she opened the door and paused in the archway.

"Fine, but if you're going to go, I have one request... a promise, if you will."

Nem's stomach knotted with apprehension, eyes narrowing. She didn't need to answer, Arii would be able to see the displeasure written on her scarred face.

For Nem knew exactly what her best friend was about to say... and it would not be a request.

It would be an *order*.

Though their bond as best friends was unbreakable, a connection forged through shared trials, blood, and years of unwavering loyalty, Nem's duty would always come first, no matter how she felt. Her allegiance belonged, above all, to the one who had saved her from the brink of death. To Arii. No matter the request, no matter how difficult or personal, Nem would carry out her orders without hesitation or question. That debt bound her as strongly as their friendship.

Her duty pulled her forward now, her stomach in a tight knot, her footsteps and her Queen's echoing on the marble floors as they

headed towards the receiving rooms.

Nem swallowed, straightened her spine, steeled her expression for what was to come.

Finally, over her shoulder, Arii's chin lifted as she finally said, "You must take *him* with you."

†

Him.

Him.

Nem knew the reason for Arii's request, and it was not for added protection. The Queen knew that there was something between Nem and Krepth, and she knew that they'd been avoiding that fact for the past year.

Nem remained silent as she dutifully followed, their footfalls echoing through the once-golden halls. Ariiaya allowed her the quiet – let her stew in it – as they passed castle staff bustling about, their bows to their Queen low and reverent. After the war, most of the gold adorning the castle was taken and melted down to restore the city and help the people rebuild their lives. Where her reflection had once danced in gilded surfaces, there now stood bare, timeworn brick, the castle's bones exposed after years of wear. Yet even in its stripped-down state, the grandeur hadn't entirely faded. Polished marble tiles stretched beneath her feet, their smooth surface gleaming in the afternoon light. Sunlight streamed through the tall windows, casting a warm, golden glow that played across the hall, catching on the remaining ornate fixtures and subtle gilding, filling the space with a quiet, persistent splendour.

Arii glanced over her shoulder.

"You're angry with me."

It wasn't a question but a statement which snagged Nem's attention.

"We have a representative for the north… and the east already. It's hardly necessary to invite the Spymaster on this mission when he is no doubt already busy with his duties." Nem said, voice monotone, not allowing her friend's statement to be confirmed.

Canines flashed in a crescent moon as Arii grinned knowingly.

"Krepth's influence and knowledge are invaluable, and he won't be representing just one court, but all of them. As the master of spies, he has his paws in every court's affairs. He will oversee all of you, as he's best suited to maintain order while tensions remain high between our courts."

That wasn't the only reason. Like the Fates weaving their threads, Arii was trying to – not too subtly – force them into a situation where they would have to speak again.

Under her breath, Nem mumbled, "Of course."

"I know it's been a while since you two spoke," Arii turned as they arrived at the doors to the receiving room, and once again took her friend's hands in her own. "But he cares about you, Nem."

Nem shifted awkwardly on her feet, silver hair brushing her cheeks. She knew Krepth cared for her, and Nem was well aware that Arii understood her feelings for him as well. But things were… strained between them. Awkward. Tentative. *Strange.*

The Queen also knew the reason for the growing rift between them, and was fully aware of Nem's demigoddess powers, not to mention her reluctance to discuss anything to do with them. Or the roguish wolf Shifter.

Nem was so engrossed in her thoughts that she didn't notice when they passed the threshold into the receiving rooms adjacent to the throne chamber, nor did she hear the murmur of voices.

She hadn't even noticed that Elijah had joined them, hand clasped with his Queen's. Nem shifted into a quick bow, letting the action hide her expression. She spied Elijah's hand lift, putting her at ease.

The receiving room was hazy with candle smoke, rays of daylight cutting through to glint off the dark wood furniture. A deep blue banner bearing the Herington crest hung on the far wall, overlooking a long table cluttered with maps and paperwork. Conversations fell quiet as a small group of travellers stood to attention, offering deep, respectful bows as Nem silently took position nearby.

Arii lifted her chin as the room's focus shifted – first to her husband, then to her as she stepped forward. The courts' chosen warriors had arrived swiftly, their journey aided by Elijah's portal magic. For now, the King remained back, letting his wife study their guests.

A head shorter than Arii, the first figure was a woman with short burgundy hair, a thick fringe sweeping across her forehead while the rest was cropped close to her scalp. Her full lips curled into a smile, and thick, winged lashes framed her striking hazel eyes, almost golden in hue, as they creased with laugh lines. Her garb was a mixture of silks and leathers, a getup that was both flowery and practical for travel. Nem got the distinct impression that this western warrior – with polished brass buckles, and a confident stance, one hand on her hip and a grin flashing her teeth – was just as flamboyant as the court she came from.

The woman shifted, the clink of metal against marble catching Nem's attention. Her eyes travelled down to the warrior's feet, where an intricately crafted limb of brass and polished wood replaced her leg. There was a subtle sound of clicks and whirrs which hinted at the advanced craftsmanship of the limb, enabling it to move with fluid grace in sync with the woman's motions.

"Vega Aster of the West Court at your service, Your Highness," greeted the woman, sweeping into a bow before the King and Queen. Rounded ears and creases at the edge of her eyes hinted at her mortality, a human warrior.

"Well met, Vega Aster, welcome to the North." Arii said, offering a nod, before sweeping to the next warrior.

The man was tall, almost imposingly so, blonde hair drawn back into a bun, accentuating his handsomely rugged, harsh face and pointed ears. Thick brows angled over icy blue eyes; ones that reminded Nem of the glaciers found in the Southern Court. A short beard dusted his cheeks, a shade deeper than the hair on his head. He was dressed in thick furs and rugged leather, giving him a wild, imposing presence. With an awkward bend at the waist, he bowed, his large hands resting on the twin axes strapped to his hips. At his side rested a dire wolf, its fur a shade of corn yellow , with a white mark on its chest shaped like an arrowhead. The beast's striking blue eyes glanced up at its master, and the tip of its tail gave a subtle flick.

As the warrior leaned forward, Nem caught sight of an impressive broadaxe secured to his back, its wide blade gleaming faintly.

"Merrick Lightfoot, Your Highness," he announced, his voice was a cool timbre, like heavy fallen snow, "of the Southern Court. This here beast is Bo, my companion dire wolf." He swept a hand to the wolf, who blinked in comprehension. Merrick looked far too haggard and wild for the royal space he occupied, especially with a large beast at his side, remnants of dirt on its light paws. Nem knew they'd be feeling the Northern heat, especially in snow clothes and fur.

Nem felt a slight twinge of apprehension at the sight of the weapons, but she knew the room was encircled by guards, and the King and Queen were more than capable of defending themselves.

"Welcome, Merrick Lightfoot," Arii angled her head at the warrior's wolf, lips twitching despite her regal demeanour. "And Bo. The North appreciates your presence here."

The last warrior was familiar, her keen gaze meeting Nem's first, before skipping to the Queen, their bright green depths so like her brother's eyes that Nem felt a small pang of guilt for not checking in with Luc and his husband Emerson for the last few months. Iniq

Limus wore the woodland uniform of her kin. A moss-green tunic, perfectly suited to the tree-filled environment, matched the deep brown fighting leathers that clung to her lithe frame, a uniform worn by all those sworn to protect the forest. Over her shoulder peeked her bow, a beautifully hand-carved weapon crafted from one of the ancient trees found in the heart of Evergrave Forest. The dark skin framing Iniq's eyes creased as Arii paused before her, the air lightening ever so slightly. "It's so good to see you, Iniq. How is your brother?"

"He's faring well, Your Highness. Business is booming, though I fear it wouldn't be so without the level-headed support of his husband." Iniq responded, before clearing her throat. "Luc and Emerson ask about you and Elijah–" she caught herself, "I mean, the King, often."

"We promised to visit, and we will, soon." Arii said, her voice taking on a tender touch.

Iniq dipped into a bow as Nem surveyed their group. Each member embodied the essence of their respective court. Vega stood out with a flamboyant flair and bold confidence, a reflection of the vibrant energy of the west. Merrick, on the other hand, carried an air of calm detachment, his cool, frosty demeanour mirroring the cold serenity of the snowy south. Then there was Iniq, whose enigmatic, almost otherworldly presence shrouded her in mystery, perfectly capturing the ethereal and elusive nature of the deep forests of the east.

Then there was Nem, hovering to the side, a silent surveyor, not quite sure where she truly belonged.

"We thank you all for being here," said Arii, throwing a look back to Elijah, who inclined his head and offered a small smile. Her brow scrunched as she added, "Though we are missing an emissary–"

"Unlike the others, I wasn't offered to travel via portal, which I think is the height of rudeness."

Nem's shoulders stiffened as his voice rolled across her senses,

over the puckered skin of her scars, and down her rigid spine. A voice like honey… like a cool breeze through pine trees… a voice that was like the promise of rain on a scorching day.

A voice she'd been trying so hard to forget.

Tingles cascaded down to her toes – and they weren't unpleasant. She suppressed an inward snarl at the uncontrolled reaction that his voice brought upon her body. Nem kept her face neutral, while her insides were a frantic riot.

Krepth Hallier swept into the chamber, dressed in leathers and cloth the colour of night. Black hair brushed his forehead, the tendrils reaching further across his dark arched brows than the last time she'd seen him. And unlike then, Krepth's cheeks were ever so slightly more chiselled, his skin a little paler, but his eyes… They were the same vivid green that had ensnared her upon the rooftop in Ayrith, like a fly caught in a spider's web.

And they were fixed on her now, capturing her once more.

"You were but an hour's ride from here, hardly enough reason to use precious magic on opening a portal to get you here."

Her arms were across her chest, but there was a softness in Arii's eyes that was always there when it came to the wolf Shifter. They had grown up together, shared a home, a brief childhood – before Arii was taken to the School of Fate after her magic awakened. They were as close to siblings as two could get before blood. "That's the height of laziness, Wolf."

Krepth paused before them, hands on his belted hips. "Touche." He nodded to the members of their party, looking as if he'd just supped with them all last week.

Had he gotten taller in the months since she'd seen him last? He certainly hadn't gotten less *confident*.

"Krepth Hallier, reporting for duty." He swept into a bow, lips curling over a roguish grin as Arii stepped into his arms.

"Thank you for coming, Krepth." Arii said against his cloak.

Krepth's grin softened, eyes roaming to Nem briefly. "Couldn't ignore a summons from my Queen."

Arii pushed him back gently as Elijah approached, locking hands with the Shifter.

"We appreciate you being here. *All* of you," Elijah said, turning to the group. "You've been chosen by your courts to embark on an important mission, one that requires your collective skill and magic. Our hope is that by bringing our courts together in this, we can figure out what is threatening our peace, and in turn heal the relationship between our homes."

Elijah moved to the map on the table, hand hovering over the space south of the castle, just shy of The Wastes. "This is where the search parties were last spotted. We need you all to go there and find out what caused the disturbance."

All semblance of banter dissipated as there were muted nods around the room.

Nem's eyes stayed glued to the map, determined not to succumb to the temptation to look at the space where she knew Krepth had sidled up. She knew he had glanced at her a few times already. She *felt* his gaze, like a cool breath across the back of her neck.

"I cannot say what you'll face there, and we cannot guarantee your safety…" Elijah glanced at his wife, whose stern expression wasn't masked. "If anyone has doubts, now is the time to speak up. We will not make any of you go, if it is not your wish."

Nem's gaze finally lifted, sweeping over the faces in the room. She saw determination – and perhaps a hint of eagerness – but not a trace of fear or doubt from those chosen by their rulers. When none spoke up, Elijah continued, taking their silence as confirmation to do so.

"You'll move within the hour."

The warriors dipped into bows as Arii added, "And be careful."

Nem's lips curled ever so slightly at that. Though her best friend gave the outward impression that she was fierce and almost cold hearted, Nem knew that was far from the case. Ariiaya cared far more than she herself would ever admit.

The group dispersed, heading off to pack for the journey, but Nem stayed behind, waiting for her Queen's signal to depart. She didn't need to shift her focus to notice the dark figure lingering nearby, hands in his pockets, his attention fixed on her while Arii and Elijah conversed in hushed tones.

Had Arii just subtly lain a hand on her husband's arm, angling him away?

"Hello, Silver Moon." Krepth said, voice deep. Tentative.

The wince that curled Nem's shoulders inward was one she couldn't hide.

"Krepth," she breathed, forced.

Krepth shifted closer, enough so that she could smell his autumn pine scent. "It's good to see you."

She swallowed, suddenly hypersensitive of the scars marring her face. Her breath stuck just as her gaze lifted to his face.

Gods… he was just as she'd seen him a few months ago. Dashing in black, emerald eyes striking below his narrowed brows, lips perfect… but he was different, too. She couldn't quite put her finger on what, though. Granted they hadn't properly spoken in months, and she'd seen him in passing while they were on duty – and partially because she'd avoided him – but there was a shadow under his eyes, and an ever so slight sallowness to his chiselled cheeks. Was he eating properly? Getting enough sleep?

Nem quickly stamped down her concern. She didn't care.

"Glad you're aboard," Nem forced through her teeth, gaze lingering perhaps a touch too long on the curve of his bottom lip. Too full. Too *perfect*.

He shifted closer, hesitant, as if he were treating her like an animal on the edge of flight.

Something hummed in her chest, tingling down to her fingertips, and she tasted bitterness at the warmth gathering in her limbs. She couldn't shake the memory of how his once-bright, striking green eyes darkened and dulled the moment she touched him. Her Goddess-touched power severed his magic, a gift meant to weaken him, to give her the chance to finish him off.

Nem swallowed, sickened by the memory.

Into the awkward silence she said, "I still need to pack. Excuse me."

She did not wait for a response as the hum in her chest intensified.

Nem swerved and left too quickly from the room, missing the gentle frown falling on Krepth's face in her wake.

CHAPTER FOUR

NEMESIS

Claws caught her skin. Tearing, ripping, marring, the pain exploding across her flesh where fingers made sharp as claws cleaved like knives through her clothes.

Her power built, fighting to the surface.

Fighting for *her*.

But it wasn't enough.

Perhaps it would never be enough.

She would never be enough.

Though the power felt a part of her, it was still unfamiliar. Strange. Glowing. *Burning*. Sizzling beneath her skin as if the thin barrier were just that, a barrier, and not mortal flesh keeping in a force that yearned to be *free*.

The stench of the dead filled her nose, the sounds of their screams stuffing her ears, the flap of leathery wings throbbing around her as Nem was once again back on the bridge in Viridya, on the outskirts of the churning war, facing down the hoard of undead and winged terrors, the wails of innocent townspeople and children at her back.

"Become a sun, Nem."

She wanted to protect them all. She wanted to *use* the power strobing inside her chest, the light radiating from her skin. But she didn't know how. Every instinct told her to let go, let the power *go*, but she was afraid.

She was burning.

She wanted to *burn*.

"Burn them all."

Krepth's voice always accompanied her nightmares. Though this was a memory, one imprinted into her mind, cast unto her skin, she could never escape the pain, his voice, the blinding *light*.

"Nem?"

There was barely enough… barely enough power to stave the onslaught of the undead.

She wasn't strong enough.

Never strong enough.

"Nem," came the deep voice again, tinny, echoing across the space of her unconscious mind.

Her face hurt. Her body hurt. Her heart hurt. Nem squeezed her eyes shut as the undead swarmed around her.

Then there was a flash of pure, blinding *light*.

"Nem!" This time, the voice drew her from her nightmare, eyes snapping wide to a canopy of trees, the first rays of dawn filtering through the leaves. She shot up, palm against her chest, willing her racing heart to slow. Her fingers caught the end of the Locket of Dreaming, her fingertips grazing the curved tail of the dragon trinket. Nem always kept the necklace close, yet even after a year, it hadn't affected her the way it had Elijah's sister, Ghila. By now, Nem had attributed this to the Fae's Mind-Wielding abilities. Or perhaps it was because Nem was Goddess-touched – created with the purpose of finding the objects of power. Ariiaya had entrusted her with the last two remaining artefacts: the Sword of Power, hidden beneath her bedroll and away from prying eyes, and the Cloak of Protection, which kept her warm through the night.

Krepth knelt by her bedroll, dappled sunlight kissing his skin. Concern pinched at his brows as his hand hovered by her shoulder.

Inches from touching her.

"A nightmare, I take it?" he observed, rather unhelpfully.

Nem scoffed, letting her hair fall over her scarred cheek, a curtain between them, a confirmation nor a denial prevailing her gruff response. Reading her hunched shoulders, Krepth silently stood, clearing his throat.

"We are getting ready to move. The site of the disturbance is still a few hours away, but Iniq suggested we reach it while there's still daylight, so we can better assess it and anything else nearby that might have taken the search parties."

It was level thinking. She expected no less from Iniq. With a small nod, Nem stood, clearing away her bedroll to the sound of movement. Not glancing up, she felt the shift as Krepth moved away, the hesitation of his movement not lost on her. The air between them was awkward, and she hated it, but it was best for them both.

Birds chittered above their group, taking up residence in the trees that had begun to thin the closer they trudged south. Their party skirted The Wastes, gladly sacrificing the time it added to their journey rather than risk going through that cursed place. Nem could still recall the visions she'd seen in the mists, the horrors that it had shown each of them when they'd attempted to cross it over a year and a half ago.

"Perhaps your search parties simply ventured too close to The Wastes?" said Vega.

Nem lifted her head, only then noticing the shadow befalling her hunched form. The sun haloed Vega's outline, her hands on her hips as the woman's thick burgundy fringe hung over her left eye. She blew back the strands, adding, "Need a hand packing, Silver?"

Nem pulled the strap on her pack, perhaps with a touch more force than it needed. "No, I'm fine."

If Vega was affected by the bite to her words, she did not let it show. Her lips curled in a good-natured smile as she said, "If I know anything of people from the north, it's the lightness with which they travel. Only the bare necessities, huh?" She cast her gaze into Nem's bag. "I admire a neatly packed bag."

Nem looked at her polished brass clasps and pressed silk and leather clothing, before eying her forged limb, then skipping away.

"No need to be precious about my leg, I lost it long ago – so long that I hardly miss it anymore."

Nem stood, hefting the strap of her pack on to her shoulder. "What happened?"

"Eh, run in with a Kryvern when I was nine," Vega waved her hand dismissively, brushing off the weight of the statement. Nem suppressed a sympathetic wince. What a terrible ordeal for a child. Her thoughts touched on Elijah's past and a similar encounter that had scarred his back and severed his magic.

"It took some time to gather the gold needed for Memory, but she's come a long way from being just a simple wooden stump. She's far more comfortable now. This is the finest, most advanced technology available in the west, crafted by the most skilled artisans of my court."

Nem blinked. "Memory? You named it? I mean… her? Erm."

Vega's smile was wide, affectionate. "Though it is not the part I was born with, Memory reminds me of what I survived. When I look at her, I feel strengthened, reminded to keep going, no matter how hard things seem, because I survived once, and I can do so again." She lifted the limb, inviting the party to look closer. Nem spied cogs and levers spinning beneath the craft of the thing, allowing Vega to move her ankle.

Nem felt admiration for the human, letting that show through a small smile that pulled at the scar on her cheek, deciding she was going to like her.

"We've all survived something, and sometimes we need to be reminded to keep going." Vega said, brushing the sweep of her thick fringe from her eyes as she straightened. Nem tried not to let her words dredge up *exactly* what she'd survived.

Vega tapped her chin, "Speaking of *going*… The King's magical portals have made you folks in the north lazy. I suppose there's no need to rush when you can just step through and be wherever you want in an instant."

"I was ready to go five minutes ago," Krepth muttered, leaning against the trunk of a nearby tree with his ankles and arms crossed.

Iniq hefted her pack on her shoulder, her brown skin dappled with sunlight. "That kind of magic comes at a cost. King Eliverus doesn't use it lightly. Why do you think he didn't just transport us directly to where the last search party vanished?"

Vega shrugged and let loose a chuckle. "Perhaps it is a test?"

"I hate tests," Merrick drawled as he hefted his battleaxe, sliding it into the holster on his broad back. Bo stretched nearby, letting loose a long, yawning yowl. Merrick's imposing figure towered over Vega, casting her in shadow as he stood.

The western warrior lifted her chin, lips pursing, all confidence in the Fae brute's shadow. "Fates, they breed 'em tall in the south, don't they?"

Merrick blinked, his rugged face deadpan.

"Full of spunk too." Vega fingered the edge of Merrick's bear fur collar, "Are all southerners as talkative as you?"

Merrick brushed her off, turning away, but Nem caught the flush in his cheeks under the beautiful woman's attention. He busied himself by feeding a strip of jerky to Bo, eyes briefly flicking back to Vega as she leaned down to grab her pack.

Nem stifled a smile.

"Let's get going," pressed Iniq, waiting at a nearby junction of trees. Unlike her brother, Iniq was far more serious than Luc, with much less patience. That was good, they needed someone to keep their group on track, especially since Nem was struggling to ignore the way the dark strands of Krepth's hair curled at the nape of his neck while the rest remained straight.

Morning mist gathered at their heels, dampening the gravel path. Chilled air clung to the warmth of their breaths, the stomp of their largest companion's boots overpowering the rest. It was cooler the further they travelled south, despite the sun lifting overhead. The day was beautiful, and Nem took a moment to appreciate being back on the road again, out of the castle walls and back in her traveling attire. The leather hugged her body like a second skin, crafted so perfectly it felt weightless, yet strong enough to deflect an arrow. Golden filigree adorned the edges, with intricate dragon silhouettes pressed into the silver chest plate of her armour. Elegant and lethal.

His voice brushed over the hollow of her neck, where the Locket of Dreaming had begun to stir with heat. "Does it whisper to you, the way it did with the Herington sister?"

Cursing herself for letting her guard slip, Nem tilted her head slightly, catching Krepth in her peripheral vision. He had his chin tipped toward the sky, hands laced behind his head, lips almost puckered like he might start whistling any second. That swagger, the lazy swing of his long stride beside her, scratched at her nerves like sand against her skin.

"No," she said, flat and sure, eyes snapping forward. The trees here felt sparse, more bark than leaf, and that had always struck her as odd. Pendle was just around the bend, a farming town nestled close to the swell of the Sapphire Depths. It basked in the southern breezes, softer than the north's heat, and the land thrived in that strange balance. As long as the people kept clear of the misty border of The Wastes, then this little slice of Fythnar was almost peaceful.

"Still prefer daggers over the sword, then?" he continued, and Nem shuddered at his attempt at small talk. It felt forced... odd. Like they hadn't been friends for years. Like they hadn't shared rations beneath a burning sky, hadn't mapped out a curse-bound library buried in the spine of the mountains, hadn't watched a man shift into a dragon before their very eyes.

Hadn't survived a war that still haunted their sleep.

She scoffed under her breath, flicking a hand vaguely in his direction. "Still prefer black, then? You look like you're mourning someone. Or maybe *everyone*."

Krepth just grinned like he didn't hear the edge in her tone – or maybe he did and liked it.

Ahead of them, Vega, mid-lilt in a conversation with Iniq about spring blooms that only grew in the western cliffs, gave a soft laugh that carried back on the wind.

Bo let out a sharp bark as a shadow swept over the path, wingbeats pulsing overhead like the thrum of a giant's heart. Three dragons soared above, their hides a shimmer of yellow, tan, and smoky grey, glinting where the sun caught on scale and muscle. Fish hung from their claws, still glistening, still twitching, fresh from the Sapphire Depths.

It wasn't rare anymore, not for Nem. The sight of the beasts carving up the sky had long since become part of the rhythm of Northern life. And yet every time it made her stop. Made her look up. There was awe in her still, wide-eyed, as she watched them dip and dive, their cries echoing like wind through glass, like a language half-remembered in a dream.

"You'd wake the dead with those giant thumping steps of yours," commented Vega, folding her hands behind her head, hips swaying, angling her head towards Merrick. The man huffed, and Nem swore his footfalls became heavier.

"The dead would hear your loud, obnoxious voice first, Petal," growled Merrick, shooting Vega a glare.

Speaking of the dead had images emerging before Nem's eyes that she'd much rather forget.

Bleached bones, skeletal hands, decaying teeth gnashing inches from her face.

Her throat worked on a swallow as she banished those thoughts.

A sound left Vega, a mixture between a laugh and a snort. "Petal? Oh, my sweet warrior, at least buy me dinner before calling me pet names. If dinner isn't your style, then let us cut to the chase and kiss right now."

A shadow flickered at the edge of her vision as the two warriors argued. Nem's gaze shifted upward. The sky had suddenly become overcast.

Iniq's hand moved over her shoulder, hovering over the grip of her bow. "Perhaps you should *both* lower your voices."

"The affection of a warrior of the south is only given to those who prove their mettle." Merrick's gaze slid over Vega's silk and leather attire. "I do not spy any weapons on your person, Petal. Are you merely here to look pretty?"

Vega skipped in front of Merrick, the mechanics in her leg gently whirring as she twisted to walk backwards, the toes of their boots almost touching, eliciting a rumble from Bo.

"While perusing my *arse* earlier, did you not see the polearm on my back? It may appear small, but with a push of a button and a flick of my wrist," she mirrored the motion, causing Merrick's glare to deepen, "It becomes four times as long. Pure western ingenuity! Compact, yet deadly."

"A polearm? A blunt weapon… merely a stick to poke at your enemies."

"It has a blade! So, I can 'poke at my enemies' with a sharp end. Here, shall I give you a demonstration?" She made to reach for her weapon.

Another shadow swept across the sky, this time descending from above rather than from the trees. A bird? It had moved too quickly for her to follow. Nem's focus shifted to Krepth at the front of their group, and she wasn't surprised to see his arm already raised, fingers spread in caution.

"There's something up ahead," he growled.

All bickering ceased as the leaves of the trees ahead shuddered, before exploding with a cluster of crows. The air was filled with their sharp screeching cries as they took to the sky, clearly spooked. Beside Merrick, the dire wolf let out a ferocious, ripping snarl.

Krepth crouched, hovering a hand over some deep ruts off to the right of the road. As Nem and the others neared, she saw what had caught his attention. Signs of disturbance, raked-up soil and crushed shrubbery.

"I think we found where the last scout party disappeared," Krepth said.

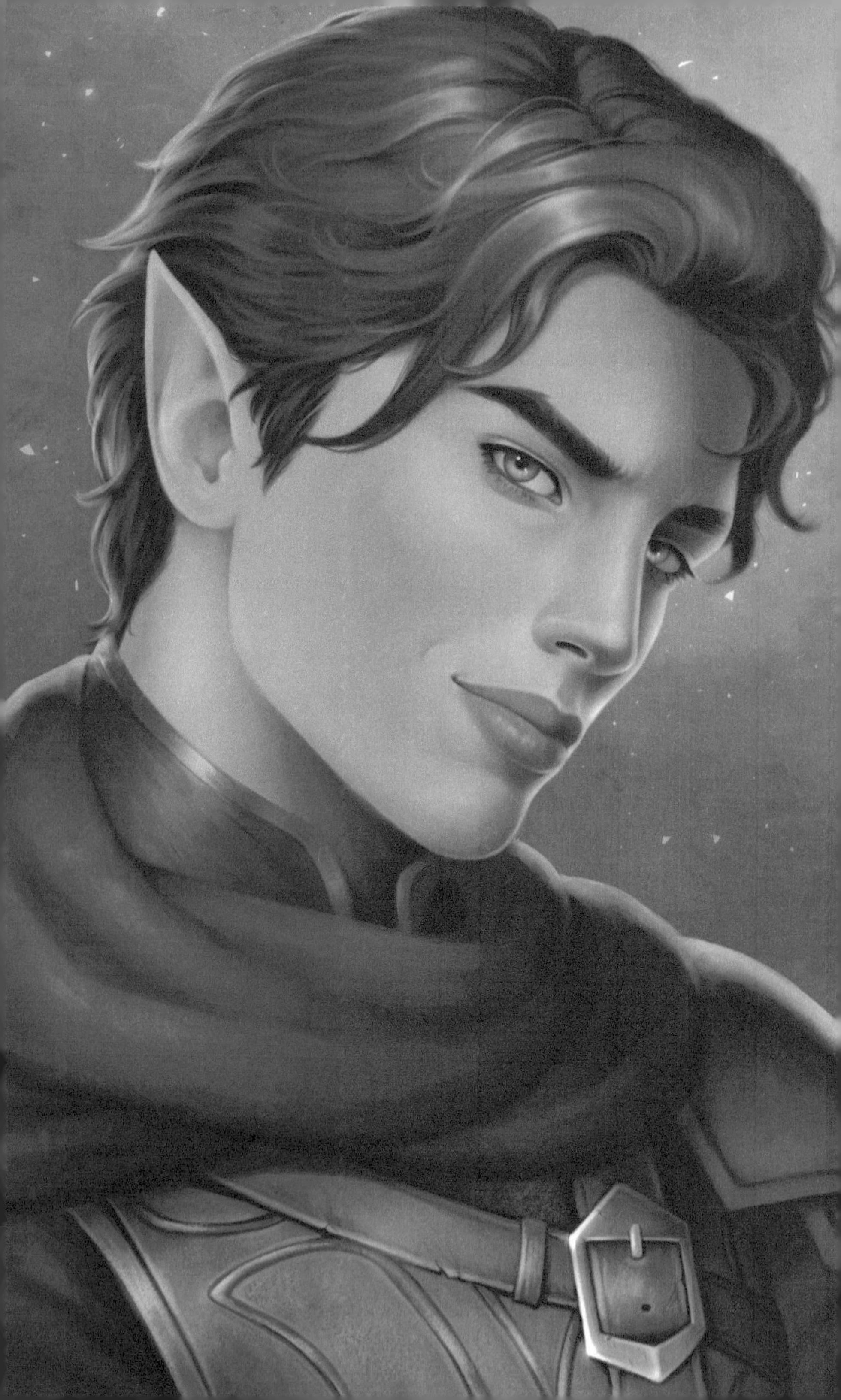

CHAPTER FIVE

KREPTH

The months that had passed since Krepth last laid eyes on Nemesis Rion had done little to quell the emotions swirling within him. Though their time together in the last year was fleeting, he still felt the same as he always felt in her presence. Curiosity, longing, *heat*. Though her gaze was cold, her demeanour towards him even more so, Krepth couldn't deny the fire that ignited deep in his stomach every time he saw her. Every time he was near her. Every time she turned her scowl upon him. He relived their kiss upon the rooftop every time he closed his eyes, recalled her breaths against his lips, relived the stunning moonlight beneath her skin.

Goddess-touched.

Created to hunt his kind.

Technically she was his enemy. So, the icy reception she delivered wasn't so puzzling.

But like a wolf longing for the full moon, Krepth wanted her – despite all that they'd discovered so far.

Perhaps he was a glutton for punishment? Maybe it was the thrill of the chase, his wolf side hungering for her like a dog after a bone. Or maybe he was a little demented inside?

Nem's striking blue eyes met his briefly, before darting away, continuing with her task – surveying the remains of the ruined cart. There was a door on the back that would have held the scout parties' provisions. She ripped free her weapons, steel glinting in the overcast light as she wedged the blade into the beam above the lock, breaking it with one strong stroke.

Krepth's body heated, one place far hotter than the rest.

Yep, definitely demented.

What further solidified that fact was the lengths he'd gone to while trying to find out more about demi-gods and goddesses, and the race of people created to retrieve the artefacts of power. He'd taken every Godsdamned contact, every set of eyes and ears within his power, to find out more. To know more about her kind, like a rabid bloodhound.

Krepth knelt, surveying the gouged gravel where the wheels of the cart had suddenly come to a halt, while his mind went elsewhere.

The walls wept in the dungeons deep beneath Bonemire, buried in the fortress' belly like an old wound. The King had no love for the place – he'd let it rot, unused, unless absolutely necessary. But Krepth, with or without the monarch's blessing, had made use of it. Quietly. Precisely. As it was meant to be used.

Bonemire, once a place used to house Valdis' armies, and the people whom he'd experimented on, was left as a reminder, a place of ghosts and shadows. The dungeons, sour with mould, heavy with the mingled scent of salt, still water and worse, had been left untouched.

Some places were meant to feel like slow death.

A man sat bound in the steelwood chair, wrists chafed, jaw clenched like it could keep secrets from leaking out. He looked thinner than the last time Krepth had seen him at court – less like a noble, more like a rat scurrying in these very tunnels.

"Strange," Krepth murmured as he stepped into the gloom. "I thought the rats would scatter after Valdis fell. But here you are. Still gnawing at what's left."

His captive's lips twitched. "You think because the war's over, the fire has gone out. But you don't understand what he stood for."

He.

Valdis Kruel.

Though it had been months since the usurper's demise, those who clung to his ideals still remained, most in secret, some with louder voices. Some hiding and manipulating, waiting to take advantage.

"I understand more than you think," Krepth said. His voice was quiet, but the edge was there, like shards of frost under silk. "I understand Valdis, just before his death, discovered the existence of a Goddess-touched. And you helped him. What do you know?"

This fact had come to light in Krepth's pursuit of information about Nem's history – that Valdis was planning to find her, and use her, along with the artefacts, to further his magical reign. Krepth thanked the Gods – reluctantly – that he'd been stopped before that had happened.

This man, with his crooked nose, pointed jaw and glazed eyes was someone who had been hired to find her, to feed information back to Valdis. And he'd been slipping around court, so close to Nem, so close to everyone Krepth cared for, that it made Krepth's stomach roil.

He moved slowly, circling the chair. "And you, Eren, you're not loyal. You're scared. You know something about what he found. Or worse... who he found."

Eren looked away.

Krepth's voice dropped to a whisper, right at the man's shoulder. "The demigods. He believed they were real. That one was in Fythnar, after so long. And he was right."

Eren's jaw twitched, but he said nothing.

"She burns like a sun, glows like a moon," Krepth went on. "Divine, but memoryless." As he spoke, he watched for the telltale signs of reaction on the man's face. Anticipated it, and without admitting... needed it.

Eren scoffed, low and bitter. "A woman."

Krepth smiled faintly, letting the misogynistic tone slide – for the moment. This man had suspected it all, but his reaction told Krepth that they hadn't figured out who it was. Krepth felt a wash of relief at that knowledge. "Gender means nothing. What do you know of the Goddess-touched?"

Saliva welled between the man's lips, and he attempted to spit, but the glob dribbled pathetically down his chin instead. "Nothin' but rumour. Besides, I won't bend to an eastern fucking Shifter freak, no matter the title he bears."

Lovely. Misogynistic and *stupid.*

Eyeing the saliva, eyes flashing, Krepth clucked his tongue, "You'll tell this freak what you know, if you know what's good for you."

"And if I don't?"

Krepth stood. "Then I'll leave you here. Not with a blade, not with poison. Just time. Time and silence and the sound of water dripping through stone. You'll go mad before the moss finishes climbing your bones."

Eren swallowed.

Cruel. Crueller than Krepth had ever thought of being.

"There is a library," Eren said at last. "In the Dragon's Teeth. Filled with knowledge... with power."

Krepth's expression remained still, but his eyes sharpened. Of course. The Library Inbetween. Thank the gods Valdis hadn't had the chance to find it.

"And the demigoddess?" he asked again.

Eren hesitated. "He didn't want to kill her. Not at first. He wanted to bring her here." His head tilted slightly. "He wanted to break her open. Examine her insides before draining her power to help usher in the beast from the crystal."

"What of the Goddess-touched now? Why do you still look for her?" Krepth was inches from Eren's sweat-beaded face, canines

bared. "The usurper is gone."

A muscle ticked in Eren's jaw, blood-red veins stark against the whites of his glassy eyes. "Ideals don't die with their makers. And the Gods aren't finished with the Goddess-touched yet."

Using Nem for her power didn't surprise Krepth. And it was clear now – this pathetic scrap of a man had nothing new to offer. Frustration ground his teeth, burning in the heat of his clenched fists.

Before he knew it, his fist smashed into the side of Eren's face, sending spit and blood flying from his torn lips.

Panting, Krepth turned, already moving for the door. "Thank you, Eren. I hope the ghosts keep you company."

He didn't slam the door, just shut it softly.

Let the dark do the rest.

The memory dusted away like sand through fingers, one of many grains building in the hourglass of his mind.

He'd spilled blood, he'd been cruel, he'd become something else in his pursuit… he'd taken lives for the chance to gather even a slither of information that would help Nem uncover more about her origins. For her sake, but also in a selfish attempt to soothe the sting of her rejection.

He did it not only in an attempt to melt a bit of that ice behind her eyes when she looked at him, but to soothe some of the anger pooled like stagnant water within his own guts. Someone had abandoned her. Someone had left her upon the shore, left her without memories… *left her.*

He wanted to ease some of the hurt he knew she felt at her abandonment. Because no matter how she felt about him… Krepth cared for Nem. The sadness he saw in her eyes when she thought no one was looking… he wanted that look *gone.* He wanted to see the timid, hesitant curl of her lips in hope again, like he'd seen atop the roof. The look of happiness and awe. Gods, he'd do anything to see that look again.

There wasn't a line he wouldn't cross to make Nemesis truly smile again.

But why? Why was that so important to him?

Krepth realised he was staring at her profile, fixated on the scar she had refused to heal with magic. It cut across her alabaster skin, disrupting the flawless smoothness of her cheek and neck. He couldn't comprehend why she had chosen to keep it, why she had endured the pain long after it could have been erased.

Krepth could still picture her standing on the bridge, engulfed in light, a flickering beacon between him, the helpless townspeople, and the advancing undead horde. His heart had almost stopped when he could no longer see her, engulfed by the dark swarm.

And then there was an explosion of light so intense that he'd shielded his eyes, just as a shudder of power took him and those around him a step back.

It was a kind of magic he'd never felt before, like heat and sparks against his skin.

Foreign… yet the lingering taste upon his tongue was *familiar*.

He hadn't time to puzzle it out, because Nem had collapsed against the cobblestones, ringed in a perfect circle of ash, blood streaking her skin, her hair.

Krepth was certain he had never run so fast in his life. He swore his heart had never faltered as intensely as it did in that moment – just like it had when one of the Fates had slashed Nem's throat back in the south.

He had almost lost her then.

He couldn't lose her.

As he'd taken her in his arms, cupped her bloody cheek and called her name, Krepth had silently cursed his inability to use his magic for healing. He hated himself then, hated that he could not do more than

shout her name and shake her shoulders, kneeling in the ash as sparks and smoke swirled around them.

When her eyes opened, the last of her magic fading from their vivid blue depths, he'd promised the Gods he'd repay them for returning her to him again.

Twice.

His debts ran deep, it seemed.

How had such a distance expanded between them since?

Nem climbed into the cart while Iniq crouched beside an empty torso of armour. "This is definitely where the scouts ended up… but where are the bodies?"

Krepth sniffed, busying himself with surveying the scene. The cart was missing a wheel, angled into the dirt beside the base of a tree. The trunk had a chunk missing, the light flesh under the bark peeking through. Had they lost a wheel and crashed? Where were the horses? Scatterings of armour and weapons lay about, shreds of cloth and wood scattered just out of sight of the road. Remnants of the search party were everywhere… but Iniq was right. There were no bodies.

"There is blood here," called Merrick, crouched beside the remains of a helmet, its gold metal specked with blood. Bo's hackles were raised; the beast's eyes cast to the trees nearby.

If Krepth were in his wolf form, he felt his hackles would be raised too.

Something felt… off.

"They just… disappeared into thin air?" said Vega, turning on the spot. "Surely not. But all evidence points to that being so."

Iniq stepped beside the southern warrior, her gaze sweeping over the blood-streaked ground. Her golden eyes shifted upward to the trees, and her stance evoked memories in Krepth of her Shifter form – a panther, dark as the night. "The air smells of violence. There was a battle here."

Nem leaped from the cart, landing lithely on her feet, gaze fixed on the trees. Bo began to growl louder, setting Krepth's teeth on edge as Nem said, "We have to go further."

Without waiting for the others to agree, she set off, storming towards the forest.

Krepth made a sound of frustration, and their party moved. "Nem, wait!"

Ariiaya was usually the one to rush headlong into danger, while Nem tended to assess the situation before acting. But this time, it looked as though something was pulling her forward, something unseen… instinctual. *His* instincts were growling for them to turn back, not to venture further, to survey the scene again. Get as far away from this place as possible.

The feeling was familiar, and he couldn't quite place where he'd felt such trepidation before.

Arguing the point would be moot, so Krepth snapped his jaw shut and followed, hands roving to the hilt of his sword, fingertips tingling. The air felt heavy, charged almost. There wasn't a sound, no birds chirping, no rustle of creatures in the underbrush. Not even the whisper of a breeze through the trees.

Dead silence.

Practiced footfalls barely disturbed the brush as Krepth's gaze drifted once more to the silver-haired figure ahead. Nem moved with a deadly elegance, her shoulders squared, hands poised near the twin crescent blades at her belt. Her ombre cloak shimmered in the fading light, just as a cover of clouds slid over the sun, casting an ominous shadow.

"There is something ahead," whispered Merrick, just as Bo once again began to growl. Deep, rumbling, chesty. A warning.

Each member of their group drew their weapons, their faces suddenly cast in blue light.

"Oh fuuuck," Vega drew out the curse as the tense sound of Iniq readying her bow vibrated through the air.

Krepth's chest tightened, and he gritted his teeth.

No… not again.

Chapter Six

Nemesis

Her chest felt heavy, her ribs constricting as her lungs struggled to expand. The silence around them was oppressive, with the distant caws of crows having long faded from the sky. Like an invisible tether, Nem was drawn through the brush, pulled along by a feeling deep in the centre of her chest, like she *had* to go this way.

A scent passed her nose, striking her senses like a baton. Rotten apples mingled with the stench of putrid meat. Violence shivered in the air, bitter copper and disturbed earth. Nem kept her daggers drawn, caution finally flooding her steps as she heard the footfalls of her companions at her back.

She didn't need to turn to see the expressions on their faces; she could feel their disdain, their disgust, their anger. Vega let out a gasp and a curse, one Nem was certain she hadn't meant to let slip. Nem's boots crunched and she glanced down, startled at the sudden change in the terrain.

At their feet were scattered bodies, their bones flayed of flesh, remnants of muscle and innards strewn across the dirt.

The scout party hadn't disappeared… they'd been *butchered*. Their armour removed; their defenceless bodies feasted upon by… Goddess knew what. The hairs on Nem's arms stood on end, a familiar hum and crackle sounding in the air, drawing her gaze up once more.

Up to a ragged tear splicing the suddenly frigid air.

A portal.

It crackled with raw energy; its edges jagged like a tear ripped through space itself. Reminiscent of those that had once scarred the skies during the war, this rift was surrounded by an aura of crackling power, revealing a glimpse into a strange world beyond. Unlike the perfect circles she'd seen before, this one looked as though a dragon's claw had slashed open the space, leaving a gaping wound between worlds.

And standing just within it was a figure, hooded, darkness lapping at their feet.

The mysterious person – perhaps male from the broadness of their shoulders – angled their head, allowing the barest hint of silver hair to slide free. Blue light strobed across a square jaw, clean shaven and pale, lips pressed in a stern line. Were they the one responsible for the deaths of all of these people? She wished she could suppress the curiosity that tangled with her disgust, the swirl of emotions stirring a faint ringing in her ears.

Krepth's hand shot out, gripping Nem's arm and stopping her in her tracks, halting a step she hadn't realised she'd taken.

"Hey!" called Vega, as the figure angled back towards the portal.

Nem's chest tightened, and the ringing in her ears intensified.

Who… who was that?

Iniq threw up her arm, halting, just as the ground beneath their feet began to shake.

Nem's glare remained fixated on the figure, a moment of time suspended between them as the mysterious man stared back, eyeless, almost faceless, cloak flapping as the Locket of Dreaming began to warm between her breasts.

Familiar. Why was the figure *familiar*?

She needed answers. For the party lost, for the north… for *herself*.

Her lips parted to call to the man, but her voice was drowned out by a sudden wailing scream.

As if that were a signal, the figure turned his back to them, just as the forest around them erupted into chaos.

Nem was momentarily fixed to the spot, eyes wide, teeth bared, frozen, as images flashed before her eyes.

Light.

Claws.

Tearing skin.

The undead penetrating her bubble of light upon the bridge – fighting their way through her magic, leaving her forever scarred… body, mind, *soul*. She'd decimated the swarm upon the bridge during the war, but barely. Nem wasn't even sure she could do it again. Her magic was a hum beneath her skin now, lazily coiled like a snake, tongue tasting the air. But it did not act.

She took a step towards the portal, body buzzing, locket turning scalding. The Sword of Power heated on her spine, it too reacting to the closeness of the portal as the figure disappeared through.

"Draw!" called Krepth, singing metal kissing the air as the undead flooded their position. They broke from the trees, crashed through from the forest beyond.

A hand fell upon Nem's shoulder, tearing her from the pull of the void.

"Nem, into position!"

Iniq's voice was firm, but there was a soft edge to it, as if she were scared of startling her from her trance. Nem reluctantly tore her attention to the fight, placing her heated palms on her weapons, bringing them free.

Their party moved into a defensive position, back-to-back as the undead swarmed like bees around them. Merrick slammed the grip of his axe against his large palm, his warrior cry mingling with the feral snarl of his dire wolf while Vega twirled her polearm.

There was but a breath of time between the swarm's arrival, and their attack. Black blood sprayed the air as weapons clashed with decayed flesh, the sounds of battle ringing in the air. Despite their overwhelming numbers, the undead fell as quickly as before, decapitated and seared by magic, the most effective methods to dispatch them.

Nem threw a glance at her companions, her heartbeat like a drum in her ears.

With lightning-fast accuracy, Iniq was shooting arrows, striking her targets in the eyes before they could even approach her by a foot. With his wolf goring everybody who approached his master's back, Merrick swung his axe and took down three at a time, the razor-sharp blade ripping through necks like butter. In a lethal dance, Vega dipped and dove, her polearm spinning as heads struck the ground like hailstones.

Nem's gaze found Krepth just as she crossed her blades over a wailing woman with half her face torn away, her exposed jaw snapping before her head separated from her shoulders. Krepth was like a shadow, black leathers soaking the blue light like a shade. His cloak flared like wings as he moved between foes, blood speckled over his cheeks like warpaint, green eyes alight like a wolf consumed by bloodlust. Nem couldn't help but stare, caught between the awe she felt for the lethal figure before her – transformed to a near-stranger in this moment of bloody beauty – and the pull of the void behind her, singing a song only her ears could hear.

Drawn to her stare, Krepth's eyes met hers, and against the suddenly overwhelming feeling to *go to him*, Nem turned her body, once again facing the crackling blue.

Nem's palms suddenly flared with pain, and she cried out, dropping her blades, just as a deafening roar split the air.

"Nem!" cried Krepth, just as a tree fell, splitting their party like a knife, crushing a few undead in the process.

Nem stared down at her palms, eyes wide, as flames of light seared her hands.

The roar rang again, as Merrick yelled, "Dragon!"

Her eyes darted from her hands to the clearing just as a streak of silver descended upon them. Wings kicked up the dirt as claws scrabbled on the trunk of a large tree. The dragon's spear-shaped head dipped low, its wings thumping in struggle. It bellowed again.

Pain. The cry was of pain.

"Is it one of yours?" called Vega, ducking the slash of an undead's skeletal hands. Nem surveyed the beast as best she could while dealing with the flaring of pain and light in her palms and the danger from all sides. It wasn't as big as Lysander – Elijah's grandfather's dragon – but it wasn't a juvenile either. Its hide was silver smattered in blood, like poorly polished metal, a colour she hadn't seen on the dragons who'd joined them in the battle at Ayrith.

The creature let loose another cry, high pitched and full of anguish.

Why was it here? Why did it not just fly away?

"Pain. Pain, stop."

Nem jolted on the spot at the voice that sliced through her head, musical, distressed. Grabbing her daggers from the dirt, she whirled, cleaving them through the guts of an attacking undead, feeling sick when she spied its scarred, pointed ears. There was Fae within these ranks, but she didn't have time to ponder where these people had been dug from. A whip tail slashed the trees, the dragon's movements jerky and wild. Vega dived onto her stomach, narrowly avoiding being taken out by the beast's tail. Again, the voice rang in Nem's mind.

"Free. I want to be free."

"No, it's not from the North. Can anyone else hear the dragon speak?" Nem called, diving beneath another pass of the dragon's tail as it took out three undead, flinging them into the nearby trees. "It's

in pain!"

Iniq whirled, using her knives since she'd run out of arrows moments ago. "Why is it here? Why doesn't it fly away?"

Despite the portal's pull, Nem broke into a sprint, racing toward the beast. As she neared, the source of its agony became clear – a collar encircled its slender neck, a chain leading to the largest tree nearby. The chain links had wrapped around the trunk several times, wedged tightly between the branches, trapping the dragon as it struggled to avoid the undead. Something told Nem that this beast had come through the portal, trying to escape its captor.

The dragon's head whipped her way, striking blue eyes wide and pupils narrowed to slits.

Nem skidded on the dirt as its jaws flew wide, the glow of white fire igniting in its throat. Dropping her weapons, she threw up her palms, cringing, light strobing from her skin as she yelled, "Wait!"

The creature halted, exhaling ash.

Nem's heart stuttered in her chest, and she heard the distant cries of her comrades telling her to stop, to get away, but she couldn't. She couldn't tear herself away from the pain of the beast, the eyes like an arctic lake, the scars like tracks slicing through the left side of its face.

Scars just like her own.

The dragon's chest expanded, then shuddered, smoke billowing from its nostrils. It did not move to fill its jaws with fire, nor did it coil its head back to strike. It surveyed her with curiosity, muscles shuddering with fear and adrenaline.

Nem kept her palms up, staring past the shake in her fingers as she said, "Let me free you."

"Nem, have you gone mad?" yelled Krepth, his voice just behind her shoulder. He sounded agitated, breathless. The clang of metal and the squelch of flesh told her that her comrades were protecting her back, remaining close despite the threat of dragon fire. There was

pleading in Krepth's voice too, and fear.

But she did not break her stare with the frightened dragon. She feared that if she did, they'd all soon be dead.

The dragon's chin lifted, eyes jumping from Nem's palms to the portal behind.

"More, more will come. Worse things."

Nem chanced a glance over her shoulder, catching the movement of dark shapes coming through the portal. Long limbs like spiders, skin like old leather, rotten teeth glinting in the flashing blue light.

Nem didn't need to be told more; the dragon's words were clear. The portal needed to be closed before she could even attempt to free it.

How? How could they close the rift without Elijah's magic? They hadn't seen Nocturne – the portal-traveling human who had aided them during the war – since it ended. If he were here, they'd be able to close it. Nem jerked back towards the dragon as it let loose a rumbling growl, lips rippling over its teeth. She watched its gaze flick from her glowing palms to the portal again, which was spilling forth even more otherworldly creatures.

The feeling returned, the one drawing her back to the tear, the one that made her skin feel as if it were on fire.

Could she have the power to close the portal?

Nem turned, and Krepth growled, "Fuck."

"I thought the thick-skulled warriors from the south were idiotic, suppose it runs in the north too, huh?" Vega laughed, slamming the blunt end of her polearm into the chin of an undead, its head snapping back, legs following suit. Nem didn't stay to hear Krepth's reply, drawn back into the fray by the pull in her chest. She dodged flying bodies and claw-tipped limbs, skidding under the tossed form of a spidery beast at the mercy of Merrick's heavy axe. The tang of copper coated her tongue, rancid, ancient blood not of this world. The smell was abhorrent, and she could hear one of her friends coughing.

Without thought, Nem threw up her palms, directing every ounce of her magic at the portal, uncaring of the consequences.

The reaction was immediate.

Light erupted from her hands, and fire scorched down her arms, forcing her head back. But a connection was tied, and she remained where she was, fixed to the earth by invisible magnets as her magic met the portal, gold streaming through the crackling blue.

Krepth bellowed her name, and she felt the brief tug of his hands in her cloak, but the sensation fell away as her mouth gaped open, eyes flaring with light as her body lit up like a lightning strike.

Skin tearing.

Undead rising from the earth, disturbed from their slumber.

A dragon's cries, its sizzling blood hitting stone, lit from within and speckled with stars.

Figures made of light surrounding one of darkness, his sadistic smile flashing from beneath a drawn hood.

A portal snapping wide, light, and then the sensation of falling.

Falling.

Falling.

Her fingers digging into sand, clutching at the grains as they slipped through, like memories she could no longer hold on to.

"Nem! Hold on!"

Strong arms encircled her, and dark strands of Krepth's hair brushed against her skin as he held her close, his back to the void, shielding her from the haunting memories. If she'd had control over her own body, Nem may have been able to stop the tears streaming down her face. But the power of the moment – the overwhelming connection – held her captive, too consuming to escape.

Amidst the chaos, a small part of her mind recognised something profound: a bond re-forming between her and the realm beyond, a link taking shape, both familiar and terrifying.

"You can do it, Silver Moon. You're stronger than whoever made that tear, stronger than whatever lies beyond it. Fight it!"

Her palms were smoking now, the pain excruciating, the burn like a hot brand being pressed to her skin. She whimpered, glowing eyes meeting his. Krepth's stare was intense, his hold tight, dark hair whipping around him. Her bright bursts hit the intense lines of his face, shadows warring with the light radiating from her skin. Magic wisps spindled around his fingers as he cupped her face, and before her eyes she saw the light leave his. Green became almost black, and her magic ignited anew, finding more from within the depths of her soul, drawing from him, drawing from the strength of his embrace, the intensity in his eyes, in his touch.

Nem's gaze darted to the portal beyond Krepth's broad shoulder, where plumes of fire traced the edge of its shifting surface. The golden light of her magic curled around it like stitches trying to close a wound, and Nem tugged, willing the thing to close.

No… she *commanded* it.

Close.

Close.

CLOSE!

With one last push, the portal screeched shut, winking from existence, leaving nothing but residual static behind.

CHAPTER SEVEN

NEMESIS

Only when the static and glitter left in the portal's wake settled on the ground did Nem allow herself to slouch against Krepth, his solid body the only thing keeping her upright. Her magic retreated as quickly as it had flared, her skin settling to pale once more.

"You did it! Now THAT is the kind of thing I was hoping to see on this adventure of ours!" called Vega, snapping her polearm closed as Merrick and Bo dispatched the last of the undead. Merrick's axe crashed down on the creature's retreating, crawling form, and he spat on its back for good measure.

"Godless filth…" he growled, wiping the bloody axe against his thigh. Bo huffed a wolfish sound of disgust.

"Are you alright, Nem?" There was a step between herself and Krepth now, and the colour had returned to his eyes, once again bright like jade stones. The idea that touching him sapped away his magic unsettled her more than she'd ever admit, sending a rattling shiver down her spine. She swallowed hard, a tingling sensation spreading to her fingertips as she picked up her fallen blades, acutely aware that every one of her companions' eyes was now fixed on her.

"I'm fine, a little drained, but fine."

"'Tis not magic I have ever witnessed." Merrick crossed his arms, his stoic façade barely concealing the questioning glint in his narrowed eyes. "There were rumours in the south of your light magic,

Nemesis Rion, but to see it with my own eyes has confirmed that you indeed exist. You're one of the Goddess-touched."

Nem couldn't meet their eyes as Vega whispered, "Can this get any better?"

A rustling sound and sudden movement behind them sent her companions whirling around as the silver dragon lifted its head, jaws parted in a pant, its wary eyes darting over them.

"Yes, suppose it can," Vega tagged on, pulling her polearm loose as the others quickly withdrew their weapons. Nem was swift, sliding between them and the dragon.

"Stop, you'll frighten her again."

"Her?" barked Iniq, bloody arrow nocked, cheek pressed against her fingers. "You said it spoke to you, telepathically I take it? The dragons in the north communicate that way too." Her gaze darted between Nem and the creature looming behind her. "You share a bond with the magic of the portal, and this dragon hails from the world beyond. But it's still a *dragon*, wild, untamed, and dangerous."

Elijah and Arii, along with countless others in the north and across the courts, continued their investigations into the dragons and their origins. Knowledge about either remained scarce and prying any information from Lysander was as futile as convincing a dragon to walk when it preferred to fly. The Ouroboros wasn't much better, offering only scraps of information when Nem accompanied Arii during her rare visits to see her father in the bowels of the Dragon's Teeth Mountains. Nem had realised some time ago that dragons were secretive creatures, hoarding their secrets like treasure.

A growl rippled at Nem's back, and her hair flew forward on her shoulders. The dragon's breath was scorching, and the ashy remnants of its exhale clung to her leathers as she turned to face it.

"That may be so, but I've learned that they are intelligent above all else. And not above reason."

Although she had kept her distance from the beasts that had returned to the north, she couldn't help but notice how swiftly her people had adapted to their presence, welcoming them as if they were a puzzle piece sliding seamlessly back into the picture of their lives. This moment, however, was the closest she had come to them – aside from her proximity to Lysander during the council meetings.

Nem could taste the tension in the air, amongst the ash and blood, and though her stomach was coiled tight, she kept her feet planted, her gaze unblinking, back straight. Dragons were proud creatures, and they respected strength. This dragon was unique, with feathers adorning her jawline, a sleek plume running gracefully from her crown down the length of her back. The blend of scales, spikes, and feathers was something that Nem hadn't seen on any of their dragons before. She studied the craters across the dragon's cheek, scars carving through her tarnished silver scales.

Whatever had hurt her had missed her eye by a hair's breadth. Nem's immediate thoughts were of the undead they'd just faced, but something told her that mere skeleton fingers weren't enough to cause such a wound to a hide that was almost impenetrable to arrows and swords. The wound didn't look fresh, either.

The dragon's chest inflated, nostrils flaring as the chain links clinked. Her head lifted slightly, eyes snapping to the shifting figures at Nem's back.

Nem lifted her hand, drawing slitted blue eyes back to her palm, a growl rising in the dragon's chest.

"You have been through hell; we can all see that. We won't harm you, I promise."

When the dragon's eyes began to shift over her shoulder again, Nem pointed to her own scars.

"We have all been scarred by those creatures in some way. This land has been peaceful, a place of safety for your kind and mine, for the past year. But the portal you came through was the first since the end of the war. Please, let me try and remove your chains, and maybe you can tell us where you came from?"

Warmth radiated near her right side, and she didn't need to turn to know that Krepth was nearby. His woodsy scent lingered in the air, but she refused to let it distract her. Her unwavering focus remained on the dragon's eyes, her hand steady and raised. The creature huffed, her body tense and unwelcoming, yet she neither unleashed fire nor launched an attack. That, at least, was a promising start.

"Merrick, approach the chains – slowly. Use your axe to break them." Nem said.

The southern warrior let loose a huff. "And let th' beast loose? You're crazy, Lightbringer." His dire wolf made a sound very much like one of agreement.

Nem reminded herself that the dragons mostly stayed in the north, making Merrick's hesitation understandable. The icy southern terrain seemed to deter the dragons, preventing the people from becoming accustomed to their presence. And even after a year of sharing her life with them in the north, Nem remained in awe.

People often feared what they couldn't comprehend, so she gave her orders with a voice that was both gentle and resolute.

"Trust me," Nem murmured, her voice steady despite the tremor in her chest.

The dragon's arrowhead-shaped muzzle dipped, slender head tilting slightly, almost curiously. Her eyes gleamed with something unreadable, a flicker of thought. Nem swallowed hard, her fingers trembling as they hovered inches from its snout, the heat of its breath searing her skin. Her words weren't just for her comrades – they were for the dragon as well.

There was a faint creak of leather and the hesitant thud of boots as Merrick yielded, yet Nem remained locked in the dragon's gaze, mesmerised by the gleaming intelligence within. It shimmered with depth, like a mirror reflecting her very soul. The dragon stayed silent, no words reaching her mind as they had before. Nem felt certain it was fear that sealed her voice, or perhaps their connection had been fleeting, a gift born of desperation, granted only in a moment of shared terror.

A low grunt and the swish of an axe marked the moment, unfolding in the blink of an eye. Merrick's axe struck, slicing cleanly through the chain links, bolstered by magic. The sharp crunch of metal sparked something in the dragon – a flicker of recognition or instinct – as the skin around her eyes stretched wide in that fleeting instant. One moment the dragon was crouched before them, the next her wings were spread, tornadoes of wind kicking up as she sprang into flight.

Nem's Fae reflexes surged to life, her hand shooting up just in time to grab the chain link snapping toward the dragon's belly. The force yanked her off her feet and into the air, leaving the startled cries of her comrades trailing in the swirling dust behind her.

Nem's arms burned with effort as her body flailed, her fingers screaming in protest under the strain of holding her weight against the relentless pull of gravity. She twisted midair, teeth clenched as she struggled to regain control. Above her, the dragon bellowed, her powerful wings battling the turbulent air currents, while Nem clung desperately, every ounce of her strength focused on hanging on.

Don't look down, don't look down.

She looked down.

The hiss she let loose rivalled the sounds from the beast above her. Never before had she been so high off the ground without a solid foothold, and she had never feared heights – always confident in her climbing skills. But this… suspended from chains around a dragon's neck, with the forest rushing away beneath her – it shattered her confidence, threatening to tear a scream from her throat. She would never admit it, especially since her best friend would undoubtedly grow insufferably proud, but she couldn't help but admire how Ariiaya rode the dragons with such fearless ease. Nem's overactive imagination showed her images of her fingers slipping, of her body plummeting to the ground, her legacy nothing but a smear over the forest below.

With no other option, Nem let out a desperate cry, thrusting one hand after the other, her fingers gripping the chain links for leverage as she hauled herself upward. She crossed her boots, wedging the links between them, inching her way up the gruelling path toward the beast's underbelly. The dragon's claws hovered perilously close, and just as Nem's fingertips came within brushing distance of the glinting silver of her scales, the wind shifted.

The dragon tilted, her massive form slipping into a sharp descent. Nem craned her neck, hair whipping into her eyes, tears springing forth as she fought against the relentless gale. Dark clouds throbbed in their path, churning like a poison tempest, and above the roar of wind Nem heard thunder boom.

Nem's mouth fell open, but her warning cry was swallowed by the deafening collision as she and the dragon crashed into the dense, churning barrier of smoke and mist that marked the beginning of The Wastes. The mists were so thick they struck her like a solid wall, flinging her upward and slamming her back against the dragon's belly. The beast let out a thunderous roar, momentarily jarred from flight, her clawed legs thrashing wildly at the unyielding air. Nem's fingers slipped, and for a terrifying moment she was falling.

Her hands found the links again, body flailing, pain radiating down her arms.

The dragon banked again, mindless and due to the mists, sightless.

And then, she twisted into a roll.

The mist lightened as Nem was flung high, momentarily greeted by a hint of promising blue sky. The chain links yanked, and she was again falling, her scream lost to the choking mist.

The dragon roared, her bellow mingling with the sudden words splitting Nem's skull.

"Get off! Get OFF! Blasted pale blighted creature! I will not go back. I cannot go back!"

The damned thing was trying to rid itself of her!

The thought ignited a surge of energy in Nem's limbs, her shock at the dragon's betrayal fuelling her with a fierce, burning anger. That anger sizzled into her hands, and with renewed vigour she climbed, scaling the dragon's neck, digging fingers into the chained collar as the beast craned its head, teeth snapping inches away. Nem curved herself inward to avoid the jaws, silently thanking the violent buffering of wind and mist. Before the dragon could roll again, she swung her legs upward, planting a boot firmly at the joint where its wing met its shoulder, using the momentum to launch herself onto its back.

"Stop! I want to help—"

The dragon plunged into a sharp freefall, wings folding tight against her scaled body. Nem's stomach lurched violently, a scream clawing into her throat before lodging behind clenched teeth. Shock gave way to raw survival instinct as fear scattered like smoke. Her fingers scrambled for purchase on the dragon's collar, nails splitting against the unforgiving metal.

The wind roared and battered her relentlessly, threatening to hurl her backward into the misty abyss. Nem could feel her body rising against gravity, but she held on, narrowing her eyes, muscles bunching as she made herself smaller, willing the wind to pass over rather than against her. For a split moment they dropped like a star falling to the earth, a shining silver blip in the churning, cursed mists.

A sound of frustration snarled from the dragon's jaws, and just as blood-red pools appeared ahead of their plummet, the beast snapped her wings out, sending them hurtling across the water, spray rising in their wake from their flight.

Panting, Nem snarled, "Stop! Please! Have you not been through enough already?"

The beast's hide shook with her growl, reverberating beneath Nem's chest. *"He will not have what is not his!"*

Nem's thoughts were a whirlwind as they cut above the red pools, thunder rumbling around them. They needed to get out of the cursed mists. Their toxicity was affecting the dragon, mingling with her anger, feeding her fears. On their journey to gain support from the other courts, this place had forced Nem and her friends to confront their deepest fears, dragging them into a dangerous, violent trance which ultimately claimed the life of the pirate, Gunner. Images of his lifeless body lay sprawled across her vision, eyes devoid of light. Suddenly Gunner's face flashed into another, one with raven black hair, sharp cheek bones and lips that usually curved into an infuriating smile, now gaping in a soundless scream.

Horrified, Nem clutched at her skull, struggling to suppress her own cry. The dragon beneath her whined, shaking her head in a mix of mourning and anger.

"This place is toxic, cursed to show you your deepest fears. We have to get out of the mist!"

The dragon's cry came softer this time, almost... broken. As they glided through the mist, wings slicing it like daggers, her struggles began to fade. That realisation pushed through Nem's own battle with the curse, compelling her to rest her palms gently against the dragon's scales, their reflective surface mirroring her own nails.

"Out... we must get... out." The dragon's voice was a whisper, a finger stroke across Nem's mind. The tremor in her words stirred something within Nem, prompting her to raise one hand and summon her magic. Her skin only warmed a touch, her light faltered, flickering

like a candle struggling to hold its flame. She clenched her teeth, the coppery tang of the mists sharp on her tongue, faintly aware of her free hand sliding against the slick silver scales.

The images renewed their onslaught… fading green eyes, a still broad chest, waxen skin… Krepth lying dead at the mouth of a violent portal as claws curled around the edges, something fighting its way through.

Flash.

Chains clattered, a massive figure loomed, obscuring the stars as the ground quaked beneath clawed feet. Twin moons loomed high in the night sky, their pale light casting an unblinking gaze over the world below, silent witnesses to a colossal awakening. Against the sprawling, ever-expanding shadow, the silver dragon appeared diminutive – a fragile speck of white swallowed by an encroaching abyss.

This vision… it was not hers. Somehow, she was seeing the dragon's fears, too.

Nem blinked through the confusion, her focus coming back to her outstretched hand, to the light spluttering beneath her skin, to the endless path of thundering mist ahead. She shook her head in an attempt to bring back some sense, but there was a connection between her and the dragon now, that much was clear. The creature had been through an ordeal, and that ordeal was shimmering in glimpses behind Nem's eyes, perhaps unwillingly thrust upon her during the dragon's distress.

Flash.

Teeth as massive as the towering bear monuments guarding the snowy gates of Erstonia gleamed in the jaws of a beast so immense it seemed endless, its colossal black form consuming every inch of her vision.

Was that the creature that had left this dragon with the scars on her face?

As she pondered, magic flowed into the palm of her hand resting against the dragon's back. Warmth and light surged through her, her skin tingling and almost burning, like touching the cooling base of a kettle. It was an odd sensation… not unpleasant but something that could leave her with burns should she continue. Light radiated beneath her fingers and Nem's eyes widened, for the light came no longer from her skin, but from between the cracks of the dragon's scales instead.

"What… what are you doing?"

Nem swallowed, the same question dashing across her slowly clearing mind. Afternoon light suddenly poured over them, golden hues setting the clearing world around them on fire. Distracted by the strange connection between them, they'd somehow angled out of the mists of The Wastes, the hazy mountain ranges of the north just visible in the distance.

Taking in a large gulp of air, Nem spoke on an exhale.

"We have much to learn about each other, but the first thing you need to know is that I don't mean you any harm. I'll vow it in whatever way you need me to, to help gain your trust."

A deep, lilting sound rode the wind as the dragon considered her words, wings acting like sails as they glided over thickening treetops.

"Aeun."

Nem rested both palms on the creature's back now, counting the last few slowing beats of her own recovering heart.

"Aeun," repeated the dragon, *"It is my name."*

"Aeun," Nem tasted the word, unfamiliar on her tongue yet no less beautiful. That one word bore the weight of trust, and Nem felt the constriction in her chest lessen ever so slightly.

"I'm Nemesis."

They glided back towards the clearing in a silence that was fragile

yet almost companiable. Nem kept her palm flat on Aeun's scales, the light she'd summoned now faded. Nem noted the way that her magic had been seemingly absorbed into the cracks of Aeun's hide like water into a sponge.

As soon as claws met earth, Nem slid from her perch, shakily falling into sturdy arms. She didn't have the energy to push Krepth away, and she was grateful for his support – though she would never admit it.

"Thank the gods you're alive!" Krepth rumbled, while the others gathered around. Merrick lifted his axe, startling Aeun, who lurched back with a cry.

"Lower your weapons!" Nem snarled, jolting backwards to position herself between them and the dragon. Her comrades quickly did so, but their looks of uncertainty remained. Aeun huffed behind her, almost as if the suggestion that she'd have harmed their friend was ludicrous.

Nem straightened her spine, eyes skipping across them.

"Aeun and I have come to an understanding."

"Aeun, that's her name?" said Iniq, jade eyes sparkling as Aeun's head dipped in a dragon's version of a bow, which Vega mirrored with her own. Even Merrick gave the beast a hesitant nod as Bo's tail began to sway.

"I apologise for my earlier behaviour," Aeun said gently. Nem translated the words from her mind to the others.

"You were bound by chains in an unfamiliar land, surrounded by the undead. Anyone would have been just as terrified in your place!" Vega said, her gaze drifting to where the portal had been – a scorched patch of grass now marked by a circle of lifeless bodies. "Now we just need to figure out how that hole opened, and who that hooded figure was."

"Can the dragon... Aeun, not tell us?" Merrick ran his fingers down his chin in thought, as Bo sneezed at his feet.

When the words met the air, Aeun was quick to speak, *"The one in the hood is unknown to me, too."* Her tone held a quiver that held Nem back from pressing for more.

Nem sighed and squeezed her brows. "She doesn't know."

"We need to head north," Krepth's eyes narrowed. "To consult the three Fates."

There was an odd edge to Krepth's tone – almost bitter. For a fleeting moment, regret stirred within her over their forced separation, a choice she had made. It struck her then how little she truly knew about the details of his past year. What had cast that shadow behind his eyes, like a dark wolf slipping through a dense green forest?

Nem couldn't argue, he had a point. The Three Fates were the closest things to Gods that their realm possessed, and if anyone could give them answers, it was them. Nem had tried in the past to squeeze questions from Klotho, Lakhesis and Etropos, but they'd been stubborn in their sharing of information, only re-solidifying what she had already been told about demi-gods – but they were a place to start. And if meeting with her old mentors didn't bring answers, then they'd venture north to the Dragon's Teeth and seek an audience with the Ouroboros.

"Regroup, tend to your wounds, and prepare to depart. We head west," Nem commanded, her voice firm as her eyes lingered on her scorched palms.

Her thoughts churned, recalling how her light magic had seeped into the cracks and scales on Aeun's back. It hadn't burned as she had expected; instead, it had been absorbed – an odd phenomenon, unlike anything she had encountered before. Even the way her magic reacted to the portal consumed her thoughts, how it connected her to the rift and allowed her to close it after the battle. All the more reason to find the Fates and demand more information about the portals… about the Gods and the silver dragon, about how her fate was seemingly entangled within them all.

CHAPTER EIGHT

NEMESIS

As the shock of their encounter with the undead and the faceless man in the hood began to dull, they pressed on. Though Nemesis tried to nudge her feelings back, her palms stung, the centres red and welted, a result of her connection with the portal and trying to keep astride Aeun.

Normally such a flesh wound would have healed within the hour, but the heated, irritated skin remained as if it were fresh, leading her to guess that the portals' magic, and perhaps *her* magic, moved differently. It was just another thing to add to the mix of her tremulous mind. The events of the last hours had left her on edge.

Nem winced, tipping her head up to the overcast sky, to the distant calls of dragons on the wind.

A shadow dropped across her path, causing her to skid to a stop. Whether it was residual adrenaline left from the fight and her flail through the misty Wastes on the back of a frightened dragon, Nem acted on blind instinct, blade suddenly in hand and spearing towards the gut of whoever had entered her path.

They were just as swift, halting her stabbing hand whip-quick with fingers on her bare flesh.

Momentum sent her silver hair cascading over her shoulders, her gaze fixated on the long fingers on her forearm, how dirt still dusted the knuckles of his lightly tanned skin, a startling contrast to her porcelain.

Krepth pinched her chin, drawing her glare up as her stomach erupted with butterflies.

Eyes dark, lips curled, black hair ghosting over his brow, he wore that look of humour she knew too well, his trademark smirk sharpened by the daylight, even as the blade pressed against the leather at his waist. He stood there, wholly unaffected by her attempt to stab him. Or worse… amused by it.

"Silver Moon," he drawled, and those two words lit a firestorm beneath her skin, sending her butterflies into a frenzy.

Nem winced, drawing her weapon back. His thumb brushed the cliff of her bottom lip – too deliberate to be accidental – fingers lingering on her chin a heartbeat longer than they should. She pulled away, but the motion lacked the force she'd intended. Her palms stung.

"All this wincing and grinding teeth will draw the flocks of hungry nearby dragons," murmured Krepth. "Give me your hands."

"I'm fine, just a few burns," she hedged, avoiding the offer of his open palm and his serious look. But Krepth was swift, catching her arm.

"Nem, listen–"

"Dragons don't even eat Fae," Nem muttered under her breath, a delayed response to his words about drawing dragons, planting her feet before shooting him a fresh glare.

Krepth blinked then shook his head, "Honestly, must you always be so damned stubborn? You're in pain, your wounds should but haven't healed yet, perhaps we should tend to your hurts rather than continue until your teeth are ground to stubs?"

The others kept going, though Vega threw an arched brow over her shoulder. Even Aeun continued on, her feather-plumed tail leaving slithering tracks on the dusty forest path. They'd removed the last of the heavy chains from her neck and the creature's head was held higher than before, free of the uncomfortable weight. But Nem could see tension in the beast's shoulders and in the fold of her wings.

"Th' dragons may scent her as the weaker of our pack, the only one with wounds sustained in the fight, leading them to strike," Merrick's deep voice, though lowered, still reached Nem's ears. "I imagine the beasts hunt like wolves."

Nem cast him a look that screamed 'honestly' over Krepth's broad shoulder. "Unhelpful, Merrick."

The group paused, and Nem shrugged her shoulders in frustration.

Vega lifted a finger in thought, "Like winged wolves! They *do* fly in packs… er, flocks, right? Makes sense they'd hunt together too – go after the weaker ones first, like any pack animal."

Aeun huffed, and a gust of hot air blasted Vega's hair off her face, leaving the western warrior blinking, stunned.

"We are far beyond mere wolves," Aeun said, craning her head toward Bo, who sat on his haunches at her clawed feet, tongue lolling. Her own tongue slid across jagged teeth. *"Besides… Fae would be too gamey. Much like wolves."*

"Please, can we get back to healing your hands?" Krepth's fingers curled around Nem's wrist, twisting her palm to the sky. Nem wrenched her gaze away, up to the tree canopy, testing her will to not look down to where his fingers prodded her sore flesh so gently.

How she didn't want to pull away, not really.

How his touch made her toes curl inside her boots.

Vega cackled, spearing a hand through her thick, heat-blasted fringe as she turned to Aeun.

"Are all dragons this sassy? I love it! Oi, could you not heal your hands with your own magic, Nem?"

"I've tried that already…" Nem's lips tightened, irritation flickering in her eyes. As if she'd simply chosen not to heal herself –

as if she'd let magic sit idle while her wounds festered.

Aeun slowly tilted her head to Vega, nostrils flaring, brow ridges rising. *"This one is... odd."*

Far too distracted now to respond, Nem kept her gaze on the speckled rays of light filtering in through the leaves, anywhere other than where Krepth's skin met hers. It took every ounce of willpower not to look down, to where he deftly tore two strips from the inner lining of his own cloak.

To where, damn it, her hands remained hovering, suspended before him.

His hands were on her wrists again, the delicate bones of her pale limbs manacled by one as he draped the cloth strips over his exposed forearms. She hadn't noticed him pull up his sleeves. Entranced, Nem hardly noticed Iniq's approach as she handed him a flask.

There was still dried blood beneath his fingernails.

When had she moved her eyes from the canopy? When had she begun staring at his hands, a golden contrast to her alabaster? Breath catching, unable to look away, her gaze finally lifted to the two intense, dark green, almost black eyes watching her as he uncorked the flask with his teeth.

Then, he poured the liquid over her hands, and Nem flinched as her palms erupted in fire.

"Ow, what the hell is *that*?" she hissed, attempting to pull away.

"Perfectly good eastern rum, luckily there isn't much left. Your wounds won't heal with magic, so this will have to do."

His grip was hard yet gentle, practiced, as he looped the first cloth around her wounded hand, before deftly twining the second. She pulled back again, a natural reaction to the feeling of fire scorching her palms, to the sparks zapping through her bloodstream at their shared touch. But he held firm.

Just as their eyes met once more, he dipped his head, caught the loose flap of cloth in his teeth and tightened the tourniquet, not once breaking eye contact.

It was the sexiest thing she'd ever seen.

Heat flushed up her neck, rosing her cheeks as he deftly tightened the second cloth with his teeth. He lingered, breath tickling her thumbs, lips curling in a sultry smile.

Damn wolf knew what he was doing to her.

Nem ripped her hands away, bristling.

"Would have held still if you'd only warned me about the rum."

Brow arched, Krepth chuckled and tipped the flask up again, forcing a frown as mere droplets came out.

"Would you have, Silver Moon? Hmm, need more whisky…"

"Yes," she whispered, staring at her wrapped hands. The sting was still biting, but there was a charged warmth to her skin that hadn't been there before. Her heart thundered, the brief moment rattling her far deeper than she'd care to admit. Someone chuckled nearby, before boots pattered the dirt again, and Aeun's huff signalled the group was continuing on.

Nem forced her feet to move, her gaze lingering on her palms.

"Sometimes I curse that fact that I don't have outward magic, that mine remains only to change my form." Krepth sighed.

"Makes no difference right now, if these wounds can't be healed with magic anyway." Nem replied, wincing at the breathlessness still touching her voice.

"True," he said as he walked on leisurely, eyes that were moments ago black now returned to their vivid, mesmerising green. "There is still so much to learn about the portals and the magic that created them." Krepth eyed her for a pause. "See anything useful while you were anchored to it?"

His words were blasé, but the heaviness in his eyes spoke otherwise – a weight not born of weariness alone, but of something knotted deeper. Curiosity. Concern. Shadows.

Her thoughts drifted, unbidden, to the year gone by, to the places the Spymaster had vanished to in silence, to the secrets he might've uncovered while the world slept and she'd stalked the halls of Viridya. Nem had always assumed it was the tangle of Valdis's influence which occupied his waking hours, the last coils of a fading tyranny still snapping at their heels. But something in Krepth's gaze gave her pause.

He had always looked at her a certain way – with a reverence that made her pulse stumble, with heat enough to make her blood sing and her palms dampen. A look that curled under her skin like fire-smoke. But now there was something more. Something searching. Something hungry.

It was not the usual smoulder of want, nor even the silent ache that so often passed between them in the hush of their fleeting, charged moments. No, this was sharper, rawer. A desperation not entirely meant for her – but perhaps for the tattered threads of memory she carried. Threads she herself could barely unravel.

"Nem?" he prompted, and she inwardly grimaced at her distracted thoughts. It was really none of her business.

"I saw flashes of things, but hardly anything I could properly decipher. It was odd though…" her voice drifted as the forest canopy parted ahead, casting thin veils of golden sunlight over the path where Aeun stepped, silver scales shimmering dully. "Some felt familiar, while others weren't my own."

He contemplated her words for a pause, eyes ahead, voice low. "The dragon? Aeun?"

Nem nodded in reply, blinking against the flash of memory.

A dragon's cries, its sizzling blood hitting stone, lit from within and speckled with stars.

It had been clear the moment Aeun stepped through the portal –

collar tight around her neck, scales caked in blood and dirt – that someone had kept her prisoner, and she had suffered for it. That much was undeniable.

What remained a mystery was the bond. It had formed the instant she arrived, as sudden and inexplicable as a thunderclap. Why? Was it simply because Nem had been the first to reach the portal? Was proximity all it took to forge something so deep?

Or was it the strings of fate drawing them together?

Fate, a thing declared unchangeable, still managed to surprise her.

Vega bumped Merrick with her hip, bouncing off his mountainous form with a laugh, their words drawn away on the wind while Aeun's head curved their way tentatively. Bo's excited yaps followed her feather-plumed tail as Iniq padded alongside, shaking her head at their banter.

Figures made of light surrounding one of darkness, his sadistic smile flashing from beneath a drawn hood.

A portal snapping wide; blinding light; then the sensation of falling.

Falling.

Falling.

Nem tasted blood, her teeth pinching at her bottom lip. She swept her tongue across the hurt and as she did, she caught Krepth watching her again, arms now crossed over his chest

Her fingers digging into the sand, clutching at the grains as they slipped through, like memories she could no longer hold on to.

"We are connected somehow, and if I had my memories, perhaps I'd understand." Her low words were heavy as she watched Aeun again.

In that moment, the dragon's head snapped up, spearing to the sky as a tinny roar split the air.

Their party halted, instantly on guard.

"Dragon?" growled Merrick, palming his axe.

The feathers ripped along Aeun's spine, rising like the hackles of a wolf.

No, it wasn't a dragon. But something else. Something she hadn't heard in a long while.

"Kryvern," Nem breathed, the word barely formed before she was already moving, her comrades close on her heels. They veered from the main path, cutting into a narrow tree line just as Aeun launched into the air, wings snapping open with startling force. Nem pushed back the panic at the thought of Aeun leaving them already – why it mattered, she couldn't say – but the moment they broke through the trees, all thought of their newest scaled companion vanished.

Before them stretched a small, weather-beaten field, and at its centre, a farm that had clearly seen better days. The main house squatted tiredly, thick wooden beams bleached by sun and storm, the tiled roof sagging under years of wear. Moss clung to the stone walls like memory. Fences ringed the property in patchy lines, some still intact and penning in skittish sheep and bleating goats, others tangled in ivy or half-swallowed by a sprawling vegetable garden, where herbs grew wild and unchecked. This was a place shaped by generations – loved, lived in.

It was the paddock that pulled them forward, the battered outbuilding nearby sheltering no peace, only chaos. A massive, obsidian-scaled creature loomed there, hunched over the ruined form of a cow. Nearby, other carcasses were scattered, the poor animals torn and strewn in the grass.

The Kryvern's roar split the air, low and guttural, sending a tremor through the earth beneath their boots.

A Kryvern. Nem hadn't seen one in months. Their kind had been driven back into the mountain passes, their numbers dwindling. To find one this far south was unthinkable.

The beast raised its head, thick jaw streaked with blood and saliva, drool slinging from its teeth as it turned. Red eyes locked on them with terrible purpose. It was a brute of a creature – its limbs thick and heavily muscled, tail long and lashing. Horns jutted from its skull, not long but dense and ridged with age. Its claws tore up the soil with every movement, wicked as boned blades. This wasn't a hatchling, or some lost straggler. This was a bull. A dominant, territorial male, and it had come looking for bigger game.

"Please! Someone help!" came a desperate shout. A man, likely the farmer, stood just beyond the paddock, waving a pitchfork in trembling hands, his face pale beneath the grime of work and panic.

Nem drew her blades. There'd be no talking this one down. Unlike the dragons, Kryvern listened to no words, showed no sign of thought other than food or fight. The only exception to this had been the juvenile Kryvern, Albert, raised by Ariiaya's father in the castle in the Dragon's Teeth Mountains. Nem had a fleeting thought of Albert, who, the last time she saw him, had grown into a lean creature with intelligent eyes. She had never felt threatened by the beast; its upbringing had made it tame, more like an oversized house cat than one of the bloodthirsty creatures now before her. She would never consider harming Albert.

But unfortunately, the only way to eliminate *this* threat was to put the beast down.

Slowly, the Kryvern began to angle their way, claws crunching bone, muscles rippling, a growl ripping through its bloodied teeth.

Vaulting the fence, Krepth exclaimed, "Never seen a Kryvern that big before. How the fuck did it get so far south?"

Iniq drew her bow, swiftly nocking an arrow. "The north is hotter than it's ever been. Perhaps it seeks a cooler climate?"

"Cooler climate? Look at that thing! I think it's been following its stomach and nothing else!" hissed Vega, swirling her polearm as the beast fully faced them now.

"Enough talking, you're pissing it off," rumbled Merrick, Bo stuck to his side, hackles raised and teeth bare.

Nem's wrapped knuckles tightened on the pommels of her blades, stinging. The burns had lessened in pain somewhat, but they were still there. "At least it isn't undead."

"Positivity, I love it, Silver Moon!" Krepth chuckled as the Kryvern's tail lashed and head lowered. Before she could think far too deeply about his choice of words, the beast launched at them, its deep resonant roar reaching a screeching pitch.

Emotions fell away as Nem locked her focus on the thundering beast, its massive form swelling before her eyes, doubling, then tripling in size as it descended upon them. It was nearly dragon-sized now.

Where was Aeun?

There wasn't time to panic over the lack of feeling from their bond, the lack of *anything* at all.

The Kryvern lunged at its first target, Merrick, who met the oncoming terror with a roar of his own. He hurled his weight into his axe, swinging it at the beast's gaping maw. The blow struck its lower jaw with a bone-jarring crack, driving the creature sideways. But it recovered with terrifying speed, its head snapping back to face the warrior once more.

Merrick twisted, narrowly avoiding the crushing bite of dagger-like teeth. His axe came down again, this time glancing off the thick, iron-hard scales of the creature's shoulder. He swore loudly, just as the Kryvern's horned skull drove into his gut. The force lifted him off his feet and flung him backwards. A moment later, its tail lashed out, catching his dire wolf and sending the beast tumbling from its flank.

It was fast. *Too fast.*

"Argh, its breath–" Vega dropped to her stomach, narrowly

avoiding a tail swipe, "–it reeks!"

Nem was coming to realise Vega rarely stopped speaking. Perhaps it kept her sharp, or perhaps it was simply her nature.

"Did ye expect the fresh mint of its last toothbrush?!" Merrick called out, voice half-smothered as he rolled away from the stomp of a clawed hind leg, dirt and grass clinging to his hair and bear-fur collar.

"Gods, this thing is huge!" cried Vega, diving.

Krepth's breathless chuckle was like a caress across Nem's senses as he retorted, "That's what she sai–" The thick of the creature's tail caught him in the stomach, throwing him back on to his arse. Nem would have laughed if the Kryvern wasn't snapping her way, claws cleaving against her magical cloak.

Out of arrows and with no time to retrieve the ones scattered about them, Iniq yanked a knife from her belt. She scowled at the blade, already knowing it wouldn't be enough. "Honestly, can you two stop with the banter for five minutes?"

"Wanna join in, Kitty?" Vega laughed, making Iniq's cheeks darken.

Instead, she flung the knife aside and crouched, braids lashing like wild snakes around her. "Fuck it."

The transformation came swift, cloaked in light. One moment, the eastern warrior stood. The next, a shadow surged from the mist – a leopard, a quarter the size of the beast, sprang onto its back. Claws dug into the jagged seams of its scales.

Nem seized the moment. She darted forward, blades drawn to a cross at its throat. But the creature thrashed, frenzied. Not even her Fae speed saved her. Its head snapped round, chin catching her face and hurling her into the dirt.

"Nem!" Krepth's winded voice came from her right, edged with panic.

The Kryvern's movements were wild, unrelenting. No opening. Nothing clean. No strike yet that could bring it down. It was hard not to compare this fight with the last, and for a split moment, Nem wished they were facing the undead. At least they were quick to fell, despite their numbers.

The Kryvern bellowed, bucking hard and tossing its head toward the sky.

A shadow swept over them.

"Iniq, move!" Nem shouted, springing to her feet.

Iniq vaulted from the creature's back an instant before something slammed down onto the Kryvern, driving it to its belly with a deep, guttural grunt. Charcoal wings thrashed in a frenzy as an unfamiliar dragon raked at the beast's hide with its rear talons.

"Oh thank the Gods!" cried the farmer nearby.

Nem had expected Aeun, yet this was not her. It was of similar size, its hide slate-grey like weathered stone on an ancient cliff face. Sweat prickled Nem's brow as she flicked her gaze to the farm.

Adrenaline scattered her thoughts like smoke in wind. She had never considered that dragons might come to defend people or land. They were intelligent, capable of loyalty, but wild animals still. Perhaps this one had simply been passing through. Or perhaps it had been fed here, a bargain of protection.

Her palms lifted, light bleeding through their cloth wraps.

Aeun's presence was gone from her mind, the space where she had lingered now as murky as dawn fog. Nem had thought she would stay, sensing the creature's curiosity about their bond. Perhaps she had been wrong.

A hacking cry tore her focus back to the fight, where the Kryvern's jaws clamped on the charcoal dragon's talons. Wings battered the air as its free claw lashed at the Kryvern's skull. Nem, fearing the dragon's talons would be torn clean away, ripped the tourniquet from a palm and thrust her hand forward.

A bolt of magic cracked through the air and struck the Kryvern's exposed underbelly. Sizzling light raced across the unarmoured flesh and the beast screeched, releasing its grip. Instead of retreating, the dragon crashed down with its full weight, pinning the Kryvern again. Blow after blow rained down, talons and teeth tearing at every opening they could find, as their crew of warriors hacked at every open opportunity. The Kryvern fought back with snapping jaws and flailing claws, a savage, chaotic dance tipping steadily in their favour.

Then the dragon's jaws gaped wide and fire roared forth, washing over the Kryvern's back like a living tide. Heat and smoke rolled over the field. Merrick whooped loud and fierce, raising his axe high.

The Kryvern's movements slowed, its cry breaking into something weak, almost pleading.

Nem almost pitied it.

Almost. Until another roar ripped through the air.

Krepth barked a colourful curse as a second Kryvern burst through the cattle shed. Wood and twisted metal rained down, missing the Shifter by inches.

Nem's forced calm shattered. Panic spiked her pulse as she skidded to a halt, eyes locking on Krepth.

Jaws gaping impossibly wide, the new Kryvern lunged at him with rabid force. Krepth spun. Nem's mouth opened to shout–

The threat was yanked skyward, screeching under talons, feathers thrashing in a storm of beating wings.

Aeun.

Nem exhaled hard and bolted after the feathered dragon. The Kryvern writhed in Aeun's grip, snapping for her underbelly but finding only air. Aeun's lips peeled back in a snarl, eyes bright as her wings billowed like sails. She halted mid-air, her roar tearing the sky.

It was enough warning for the charcoal dragon. They leapt clear as Aeun hurled her captive down into the charred, smoking bulk of the first Kryvern. The collision cracked through the field, a sickening tangle of limbs and scale.

Nem reached Aeun as she landed, the dragon's jaws opening wide in a trembling, defiant roar.

Everyone held their breath, attention on the smoking tangle of the two beasts. When they did not rise, the charcoal dragon turned to them, its golden eyes fixed on Aeun. In response to a silent conversation, Aeun's head lowered ever so slightly, brows narrowing, crinkling the scars on the side of her face.

Though the fight was over, tension still permeated the air.

"Thermata, thank you. Thank you for returning, good friend." The farmer bent almost in half in appreciation; hands pressed together before him. His pitchfork lay abandoned by the fence he had scrambled over.

The grey, Thermata, kept their gaze fixed on Aeun a moment longer before shaking its head and dipping in a nod, as close to a draconic bow as one could manage. With a thrust of powerful limbs, the dragon pushed off the grass and launched into the air, wings slicing the wind in long, deliberate beats.

Nem's shoulders eased as relief settled over them all. The farm was safe for now.

Aeun tracked the grey's ascent, feathers along the neck rippling like hackles.

"Are you alright, Aeun?" Nem asked quietly, moving to the dragon's flank. Their connection had returned, a low hum at the back of Nem's mind she would never openly admit to, yet its absence in the past moments had left her strangely incomplete. Aeun's chest vibrated with a steady rumble, answer enough.

The farmer bowed low to the group. "Thank you, thank you for defending our farm. I was not certain Thermata would return, but

she did, and I will be thanking the Gods much harder tonight." He wheezed, wiping his brow as a woman and child stepped hesitantly from the safety of the farmhouse. "The beasts roam further south more than ever. That was the largest to come against us in weeks."

Iniq, back in her Fae form, tugged her vest into place, her hair a wild tangle freed from its usual braids. "Do the King and Queen know about this?"

Nem subtly shook her head, catching the tight pull of Krepth's brows. This was news to her, but much had been happening since the disturbances lately. Nem made a mental note to notify Arii and Elijah once they reached the School of Fate.

"You have an agreement of protection with a dragon?" Vega asked, fastening her retracted polearm to the holster on her back as Merrick shielded his brow with a large hand, following the speck of the dragon riding the clouds. Bo snuffed around the still-smoking pile of Kryvern, pawing at the dirt.

The farmer straightened, catching his breath. "Aye. When her kin are in need, we give what we can spare. A lamb, a hen or two if need be. In return, she keeps the worst away from our fields and our children. It has been this way for months."

Nem exchanged a glance with Aeun, who shook a wing, but kept their gaze on the distant hills. The hum in Nem's mind pulsed once, warm and certain.

"Well," said Iniq, brushing dust from her hands, "you are more fortunate than most."

The farmer gave a faint smile. "It is no fortune, mistress, only the keeping of a promise."

"She speaks to you?" asked Nem, looking from the farmer to the dragon.

"Aye, they speak to whomever they wish, or to no one. It's the beast's prerogative."

Nem, voice lowered as the others recovered and retrieved arrows and packs, "Do you… feel her emotions?"

The farmer gave her an odd look. "Emotions? No, only her words. Quite the dry sense of humour she has. Who'd have thought it."

They parted at the fence line, the smell of crushed grass lingering in the cool air. Nem followed at the back, casting a last glance at the farmhouse and the family there, her thoughts lingering on the farmer's words. The portal had appeared so close to this tiny residence – and she shuddered to think what would happen if one opened in the heart of a town.

Perhaps it was pure luck that one hadn't yet, leading Nem to once again wonder who was opening them, and what they really wanted with their world.

CHAPTER NINE

NEMESIS

In silence they pressed on, emerging from the shelter of the pines and stepping into open fields, tracing the outer edge of The Wastes. Here the grass lost its green to a washed-out yellow hue, scattered with tall-stemmed yarrow nodding in the breeze. Keeping the wall of vermillion mist to their right, they made camp atop a rise, the vantage offering a wide view of the pale-spattered plain below. Skirting the mist-wall lengthened their journey, but it was a fair trade for avoiding the hellish bog of blood, fear and brine, and Nemesis doubted Aeun would be eager to go through that place again.

The dragon had remained silent since their run in with the Kryvern, despite Nem's gentle probing. Aeun remained relatively closed off, only offering a strand of emotion through the bond. Wariness.

So, Nem did not press, lightly fearful their newest companion would flee again.

The dragon followed, her head low, drifting just above the carpet of wildflowers, while her tail carved a slow, deliberate path through the stems. She could have easily taken to the sky, vanishing into the clouds in a blink, but she didn't. She stayed grounded, and Nem figured it was caution that tethered her to the earth, wariness of their proximity to the acrid mists.

Aeun was an odd creature, in comparison to Thermata, the dragon sentry of the farm they'd left behind. Her scales had a pearly, silver

sheen beneath the grime, interrupted here and there by plumes of soft, white, hawklike feathers that crowned her spine and fanned behind her shoulders like a royal mantle. The feathers lent her a surreal grace, a kind of delicate beauty, but they did nothing to diminish the power in her frame. Her chest swelled with each breath, scales thick like armour. Her wings were long and sinewy, every movement betraying the tension of coiled muscle. Her legs, sleek and agile, hinted at the speed she could unleash at any moment. And her teeth, gleaming and precise, like daggers. She was beautiful, yes, but terrifyingly so.

The others kept stealing glances, quick and stiff, like they expected to find teeth at their backs, despite Aeun's efforts at the farm, but Nem didn't look. She felt no need. The dragon's presence pressed softly against her thoughts, a steady thrum just behind her ear, like a chord held on a string instrument.

Nem set down her pack and dug through it for her flask. Blood still clung beneath her nails, dark against the silver. Her mind slid, uninvited, back to the battle at the portal, the glazed eyes of the undead, the way their skeletal fingers had reached for her.

A touch on her arm made her flinch. Gentle. Long fingers, olive-toned, nails chewed to the quick. Krepth. The sight jarred her. He never bit his nails. The nervous habit cut through the fog in her mind sharper than a blade, pulling her out of the nightmare.

"Are you alright?" Krepth murmured, and her cheeks heated.

A flicker of something bloomed in her chest and faded. The feeling wasn't hers.

The feeling was reminiscent of when she shared the life bond with Ariiaya. That same strange tether – thin as breath, light as pollen – danced at the edge of her mind now, not quite thought, not quite emotion. Just presence. Just... there. Ariiaya's emotions had been powerful, far less veiled that Aeun's. This one felt unpractised, almost fleeting yet fixed, like a muscle without much movement.

Nem cast a look over her shoulder at the dragon, her eyes meeting slitted blue. "I'm fine."

"Does she still speak to you?" Krepth asked, his tone casual, pressing his own waterskin to his lips.

His Godsdamned perfect lips.

Nem took her own waterskin and swished water in her mouth, swallowing loudly. "Aeun hasn't spoken since we left the forest. Before the farm." She glanced back at the beast, who was scenting the air, and glaring in the direction of the mists. "Strong silent type, unlike you."

Krepth chuckled, the sound like a breath across her neck. Orange light erupted over his profile as Vega lit the fire, and they gathered around as the sun drooped in an orange and lavender haze.

"So, those creatures... the undead ones, they were really something." Vega's voice was light, but there was a tired edge to it as she tinkered with the mechanics of her leg. "In the thick of the battle, it was easy to get lost in the swarm, their focus all over the place. But facing them with just a handful of others? It was different." She paused, the faint click of her tools filling the space. "They felt hungrier... more desperate."

"There was Fae among the hordes, too," Merrick grumbled, his voice low, almost swallowed by the mist. "Wasn't like that during the war."

Nem turned the words over in her mind, heavy as stones. She caught Aeun in the corner of her eye, curled amongst the yarrow, head lifted toward the barrier of mist. Every line of her body was strung tight; her flanks trembled, wings twitching close to her spine, ready to tear the air at the first wrong sound. A knot tightened in Nem's chest. She had only seen fragments of what Aeun had endured, the rest buried beneath the silence she carried through the forest like armour.

Nem wished, fiercely, that she could promise her safety. But the truth was rooted deeper than hope: the next void would come. She could feel it pulsing in her blood, inevitable and near, distracting her as her comrades continued to reminisce about the portal, the hooded man, and the war.

Iniq fished provisions from her pack, and while sharing around the Eastern specialty of honeyed root cakes, bread and bity cheese, Vega motioned from Nem to Krepth, brows arched.

"How'd you two meet, eh?"

Nem studied the coiled cake in her palm, eyeing the dusting of cinnamon across the golden top like snow over mountains. She hadn't had a honeyed root cake in years.

"Me and Nem?" Krepth's voice carried a flicker of surprise at the blunt question. "Ah, we grew up together. You know, assassins need information, and I was good at getting it. Though Nem would swear what we've got is strictly business, I'd argue we've been friends for years."

Unbidden, memories of her younger days stirred as Nem kept her gaze fixed on the cake. She didn't need to look up to know Vega wore a feline grin on her dirt-speckled face, she could hear it in her voice.

"Oh yeah, friends, huh? Is that all?"

Nem began to pick at a crevasse in the dessert.

"Th' Westie's too forward, too nosey," Merrick grumbled, the leather of his boots creaking as he shifted his crossed legs. "We must speak of your power. The magic you displayed back there was unlike anything I've ever seen."

Nem glanced up then, all eyes on her. Even Krepth was watching, dark brows crinkled in the middle. She waited a moment, the gentle buzz of Aeun's curiosity tickling behind her ear. Grateful to the warrior for shifting the attention from Vega's noseying, she swallowed and sat a little straighter.

"There isn't much in the history books about my kind, so my

knowledge isn't much greater than yours. I'm still discovering who… or what, I am. What I am learning though is that I am somehow connected to the world beyond the portals."

As she spoke, a large glass bottle, neck twined with waxed thread, the liquid within a golden amber, was being passed between them all. The bottle landed on Krepth, who hovered his nose over the mouth, sniffing curiously. He shrugged and took a swig.

Nem tried very, very hard not to stare at the work of his neck, the bob of his throat.

"Well, I am very grateful to know we have someone who can close the portals. Th' mission would be impossible without you," nodded Merrick, and Nem schooled her features under the warrior's praise while a little ember stoked in her chest.

While the liquor was handed around, they continued to toss ideas about what, or who, was beyond the portal, and Nem's possible connection. She tried her best to explain what she'd experienced while locked to it, what she'd seen, what she'd felt.

"So, just friends, eh?" Vega teased again, the change of topic threatening whiplash, her voice cutting through the growing buzz. "Wolf Shifter, right? Figures – he looks like he wants to eat you alive the second you turn your back." She waved her half-eaten slice of cake toward Nem again, nudging Iniq with her elbow and flashing a wink, while Iniq's cheeks flamed red.

Krepth, meanwhile, promptly sprayed his last mouthful of liquor across the fire, forcing Aeun to jolt back with a startled, disgusted expression so ridiculous that even Nem had to bite down on a laugh – despite the fierce effort it took to hide the mortified look creeping over her own face.

Bo, who'd been dosing, lifted his head and yawned wide.

Nonplussed, or perhaps ignorant, Merrick spoke around his mouthful of jerky, "Dragon looks hungry, don't suppose they eat

Fae?"

Nem's attention moved from a coughing Krepth and up to the narrowed eyes of the silver dragon.

If it wasn't for the disapproval radiating violently down the bond, Nem would have thought, just for one tiny second, that perhaps dragons wouldn't say no to a bite of a Fae.

"I'm not hungry... did we not discuss this already?" growled the beast, the sting of insult sharpening her words to a near-growl in Nem's mind. Her arrow-tip skull inclined toward Merrick, feathers bristling. *"And the dragon's name is Aeun..."* She turned, her back a wall of dismissal. *"The hairy one has the memory of a mayfly."*

All heads tilted toward the beast, surprise colouring their faces. At last, Aeun had chosen to let her words fall upon them all. Nem smiled ruefully, then deftly snatched the whisky from Krepth's fingers. She took a long sip, relishing the burn, bold spiced stonefruit and fire-charred cedar curling through her chest. She flicked her tongue against her teeth, chasing the lingering aftertaste of vanilla and malt. Her brows rose, marking it as southern instantly.

"Well, *I* don't know about you, but I think I'd be delicious," Vega chuckled, nudging Iniq again with good-natured mischief.

Iniq kept blushing, nibbling quietly at a piece of bread topped with precisely sliced pieces of cheese.

Merrick, having recovered quickly from Aeun's insult, leaned back, folding his massive arms behind his head, muscles flexing with casual menace. "I'd make you choke."

Vega barked out a laugh – too loud, too sharp – the whisky's warmth loosening the edge of the cooling night.

Emboldened, Nem cleared her throat. "Assassins of fate are cold, ruthless, heartless. So, if anyone's making you choke, it's me."

Aeun shifted, wings rustling, though she stayed coiled and watchful. Iniq nodded seriously; a Fury wasn't someone to provoke, let alone try to eat.

Then Krepth spoke, voice smooth as velvet. "Well, I know better."

His gaze caught hers and held. Nem felt the familiar pull, and the equally familiar resistance.

"I know this Fury," he said, tone soft and certain. "She's got that tough-fried outer shell – but inside? Soft as a marshmallow."

The group erupted into laughter, even Iniq chuckled, her quiet mirth bubbling to the surface. And despite every reaction Nem *wanted* to have – a sour look, a cutting glare – her lips betrayed her. They quirked. Her damn eyes softened. And for one breathless moment, all she saw was him.

Firelight danced across half of his face, that roguish grin dipped in gold. Gods, he was infuriating. But no matter how many walls she built, no matter how hard she tried, he always struck true, always found the centre of her heart.

The moment snapped like a taut string. Everything around her sharpened into focus as Vega let out a wild caw: "Merrick, is *that* your smile? Good gods!"

Merrick's face twisted, his rugged beard creasing with a grimace of a smile. But instead of retreating, like Nem expected, he threw his head back and laughed, the sound booming into the darkening sky. Aeun's head lifted, eyes wide with curiosity.

Nem didn't stand a chance. The laugh broke free of her like a secret, warm and unwilling, slipping past her lips before she could stop it.

And as the sky deepened into its blackest blue, Krepth never looked away. He just watched her – like he always did – seeing too much, seeing her, no matter how hard she tried to hide.

Their fire had dwindled to embers, the glow soft and pulsing like a dying heart. Around it, their companions slept in loose, curled shapes, snores rising and falling with the wind.

Nem, on first watch, sat apart, eyes sweeping the star-scattered horizon. Her gaze caught, as it always did, on the distant wall of mist, the red glow at its base pulsing faintly, like something alive and waiting.

Aeun's silver scales caught what little light remained, faintly luminous even in the dark. Hardly inconspicuous.

"You're certainly not a dragon of stealth," Nem murmured, stepping to her side.

The tension in the creature radiated without words, Nem didn't need the tether between them to read it. It lived in the subtle spread of Aeun's wings, bracing her against the earth. In the faint tremor of her limbs. In the low press of her ridged brows.

A long moment passed in silence before Nem spoke again.

"Why don't you just... fly?" Her voice was quiet. Not accusing, just curious. "Leave us behind?"

Aeun's head turned, just slightly. Her eyes reflected the mist's light in slivered arcs of blue. *"Where would I go?"*

Nem shrugged, arms folded against the chill. "To find your own kind."

A breath escaped the dragon – almost a laugh, almost a sigh. *"You don't know much about dragons."*

Nem thought back to the farm, to the seemingly frosty, wordless interaction between Aeun and Thermata. Feeling it still too soon in the gentle building of their friendship, Nem left her questions unanswered, sighing into the night.

"No," she agreed. "But I'm trying."

Aeun was silent, once again shifting to glance back to the mist. The space between them wasn't uncomfortable, nor was it familiar, but it was no longer completely new. Rather than press, Nem studied the side of Aeun's face, the carving in the scales, the wound not long healed.

"That scar," she said softly. "It's just like mine."

Aeun shifted slightly. *"It was given to me a long time ago, but only when I saw you did it flare up again."*

"Do you remember how you got it?"

Aeun moved again, nighttime mist curling around her limbs. *"What I do remember is that I was lucky to have escaped with a scar and not lost my entire head. Everything else is…"* She blinked towards the red wall, before moving the full weight of her gaze onto Nem. *"…mist."*

Wincing, Nem placed her hand on Aeun's flank. "I don't remember anything from before. I washed up on a beach west from here, no idea about my origins, my family, who I was before. So, I guess we have that in common?"

Aeun's nostrils flared, and her jaws opened. *"You speak as though we are strangers still, but something in you… it pulls. Like an echo in a chamber I've walked before."*

Nem blinked, startled by the weight in Aeun's voice. "An echo?"

"Yes," Aeun rumbled, her wings folding closer to her sides. *"When you touched me, the scar throbbed as if remembering something my mind cannot. There is magic in wounds like that. Old magic."*

Nem withdrew her hand slightly but didn't break the contact entirely. "You think I'm part of that magic?"

"I think," Aeun said, lowering her head until her eyes were level with Nem's, *"you're more than what you believe. And you are not here by accident."*

Nem exhaled shakily. "I've had dreams. Seen fragments. A sky split in two. A place with two moons. I've never told anyone – they'd think I'm mad."

Aeun was silent for a beat, then murmured, "Two moons… yes. My home has two moons."

Nem's breath caught in her throat. "Then it's real?"

"Either it is," Aeun said, voice tightening, *"or we are both mad. But if you've seen it, Nem, you've been there."*

Sometime later, as the sun began to rise and Nem stirred to the gentle pressure on her shoulder, the conversation with Aeun still pressed against the edges of her mind. She'd been turning it over ever since Vega had relieved her of watch, right up to the moment her head hit the bedroll and sleep had pulled her under. Aeun had said she remembered fleeing, skipping through realms to escape something… or someone. She knew where she came from, but not why she'd run. She remembered who she was, but not why that identity made her a target. And the man in the cloak… he seemed to matter to both of them, though neither could say exactly how. Aeun's memories came in fragments: some intact, most gone. Nem couldn't shake the feeling that it wasn't natural. That something – or someone – was keeping them buried. But why? What could be dangerous enough to warrant silencing the mind of a dragon?

Dawn light painted Krepth's figure in gold as he crouched by her, hand remaining on her shoulder. His jade green eyes held a look of masked concern, and the crinkle at their corners immediately had her hackles rising. "Sleep alright, Silver Moon?"

His black hair was swept back, the morning light catching on the strands like a halo, softening the sharpness of his features. His eyes – deep, unreadable – whispered things unsaid, his figure rimmed with tiny yarrow blossoms that clung stubbornly to him, as if even the wildflowers didn't want to leave. She couldn't stand it. Couldn't stand the way her pulse stuttered when his hand, large and long-fingered, rested gently on her shoulder, the warmth of it seeping through the cloth like a secret. Couldn't stand the way he looked at her... curious, a little wounded, and still, somehow, with awe.

Nem pulled her shoulder away and dropped her gaze, letting her hair fall forward like a silver veil. "Fine," she muttered, already reaching for her pack.

If Krepth noticed the cold edge in her voice, he didn't show it. He simply turned and went to help the others, quiet as ever.

The moment he left her side, a dull, hollow ache bloomed in her chest. The word she'd spoken echoed back at her, bitter and unnecessary. And the worst part, she knew the second he walked away, was that she didn't mean any of it.

She wasn't fine. The lie soured her tongue, as did her snapping tone.

Gods, she was a Goddess-touched *bitch*.

"Turned it up today, haven't they? What a glorious morning," Vega said, stretching with a satisfied groan.

The air still carried a crisp edge, a subtle bite that hinted at the season's shift, but the sky was soft with pale clouds, diffusing the light across the field of yarrow until it gleamed gold. The little flowers bent gently in the breeze, swaying in dance. In the distance, sunlight spilled over the jagged line of southern mountains, brushing the treetops in a quiet blaze, the boundary of the northern court marked not by stone or steel, but by light. Their lands were beautiful. Nem knew that. She forgot sometimes.

Iniq swung her pack over her shoulders, tugging at the straps until they settled. "The Fates aren't far now. A day's walk, if that."

A sudden rush of wind stirred the grasses as a shadow fell over them. Aeun landed with a low thump, her pink tongue flicking over her teeth. Nem felt a strange wash of relief – relief that Aeun had finally gone to hunt, and even more that she had come back.

Merrick spun on the spot, drawing all eyes to him. For the first time, Nem saw raw panic on his face, weathered features drawn. "Bo? Bo!" When an answering bark sounded and his dire wolf popped from the yarrow, his expression slid back into the stoic, grumpy southern warrior once more. "Gods, I thought th' beast had eaten ye!"

Aeun's brow ridge arched with incredulity as Bo trotted proudly back to his master, tail high and swaying. The white spearhead marking on his chest, as well as his maw, were dark with moisture.

"The burly male wounds me," Aeun growled into Nem's mind.

"Looks like they went and had a drink together," Krepth laughed, clearly amused.

Merrick crossed his arms over his broad chest. "Canteen water not good enough for you, eh?" he said, voice low and gruff, but laced with a clear note of relief – as he eyed the silver dragon.

Aeun gave a full-body shake, feathers ruffling and scales catching the light. *"The beast knew of a small stream nearby. He has a very good sense of smell, I'll give him that. Better than I."*

Nem translated the words for Merrick, and though he tried to keep his expression flat, a flicker of pride betrayed him, quiet and unmistakable.

The air about them felt light, and strangely positive as they set off from their makeshift camp, and down towards the west.

The feeling didn't linger, though. Soon, Nem felt the familiar weight of anxiety settle in her chest – a heaviness at her centre that she couldn't shake.

"Fate truly is on our side today," Vega called from up ahead, gesturing toward the lightly clouded sky, the stretch of blue just beyond. The weather was spectacular, the temperature so mild that Nem considered shedding a layer of her ensemble, not to mention they were all still caked in grime from the battle. Even Merrick had peeled off his vest, thick pale arms basking in the sunlight.

She knew she should feel better, should be heartened by the fact that they weren't far from the School of Fate, and with it, possible answers. But instead, she felt only a prickle of chagrin.

The Fates hadn't been forthcoming so far. Why should this time be any different? Because of Aeun's presence? Her bond to the portal? Her ability to close them?

Absently, Nem pressed the heel of her palm to her chest, rubbing the pressure there.

"Maybe this time will be different," whispered Krepth, the voices of their comrades bleeding to one up ahead. Aeun lumbered beside them, remaining grounded so as not cause any alarm as they neared the seaside village of Lilidale. This far west, it was more than likely that the quiet people there would not react as well to an unannounced dragon flying over their home. Though they'd once been common sight across most of Fythnar, the land was still coming to accept their return.

Nem felt the weight of Krepth's eyes on her, particularly on the hand rubbing her chest. "You alright?"

Her mind flittered back to their earlier interaction, and the feeling of guilt returned. Her voice was lighter, breathier, her gaze hesitant to meet his.

"Something doesn't feel right."

He moved closer, and she couldn't help the warm buzz that washed through her at his proximity. "Another portal?"

"No," she tasted her words, focused on them, rather than the woodsy scent of him, the pull of his dark brows, the perfect trace of his frowning lips. "No, I don't think so. It's more like… doubt."

"I don't blame you for feeling apprehensive about facing the Fates again."

His eyes narrowed, and she got the sense that he was holding back. Krepth's shoulders rolled, and he tore his gaze from her, casting it towards the thin thatch of trees ahead, as if he could see the crumbling castle upon the bluff already, giving her a view of his stormy profile. They'd just reached the edge of the field, a thinning line of trees standing like soldiers before the terrain would give way to grassy clifftops, rolling hills and a roaring ocean. They stood in the shade of the trees, and already Nem could hear waves crashing in the distance, and the sounds of the fishing village nearby.

She studied Krepth for a moment longer, but a sudden bark from Bo brought the party to a halt.

The dire wolf grumbled low in his throat, hackles raised, ears sharply forward.

"What is it, boy?" Merrick asked, hovering a hand above the beast's head as another growl rumbled from Bo.

Aeun sidled closer to her, a thrum passing through their bond. They watched the trees, surveyed the rolling fields in the distance where they'd come, and the wall of roiling mist. Nothing... there was nothing, but the feeling of being watched wasn't shaking.

"Uh, Nem? What... is that?" Vega whispered finally, her voice tinged with both awe and a hint of fear. Something caught her attention, and Nem turned her hand, squinting at her knuckles. Golden threads began to curl across her skin, like serpents chasing sunlight, their shimmering coils glowing in the shadowed light. She'd removed the cloth a short time ago, letting her pink palms breathe. The burns were sensitive flesh now, no longer bubbled and raw.

Slithers of magic curled around her elbows... magic that wasn't hers.

For a moment they all stood transfixed, watching the strings climb like vines up her arms, when Aeun fell to her belly, her limbs twisted with the same bindings of gold.

Suddenly Nem was brought to her knees.

"Nem!" called Krepth, slamming to his knees at her side, fingers reaching for the threads before jerking away, as if burned. "Fuck!"

The strings snapped tight, just as a voice stroked the breeze. "No need to seek the Fates, for fate has already found you…"

CHAPTER TEN

NEMESIS

The threads of fate held her in their grip as Nem angled her head to see Klotho emerge from the forest, flanked on both sides by her sisters. Her raven hair rippled like a silk sheet in the breeze, her golden eyes glowing with magic. Lakhesis's blood red lips pulled in a line as Etropos shifted from one foot to the other, her lips curved in a look of excitement. Nem rolled her tongue over the back of her teeth as the overpowering douse of sweet, powerful magic washed over her.

"Naturally, we'd find *you* not far from the source of a disturbance, Nemesis Rion," Klotho sneered, her strikingly beautiful face locked in its perpetual scowl.

Klotho's words were odd, for Nem rarely found herself seeking out trouble. Rather than over-analyse them, Nem instead said, "And naturally you arrive too late to do something about it. The void was closed and the threat has been eliminated."

Klotho's lips pulled back in a strange grimace, almost as if she were attempting a smile.

Etropos floated ahead, heading towards Aeun, who remained docile on her belly. Strange still that the dragon wasn't fighting the bonds. Perhaps she *couldn't.*

"Remarkable, such a unique beast!" laughed Etropos, her red hair bouncing around her shoulders as she surveyed Aeun. "Unlike any that have graced our land before." The Fate tilted her head so

far to the side that Nem was expecting her to fall over any moment. "Enchanting!"

"Let Aeun go, she was restrained when we found her, but we set her free. She means no harm and was trying to escape whoever had opened the portal." Nem jerked against the threads, tacking on, "Please, sister."

Klotho's eyes remained narrowed as they slid from Nem to the dragon. "So, the fragile barriers between realms have been pierced once more."

Nem wanted to snap that of course they already knew, that they had known the moment the portal opened, but she bit her tongue.

"And the lasting imprint it has left on the earth and air here is something we know well, for it mirrors what we sensed the day young Nemesis arrived on our shores." Lakhesis spoke at last, her voice a cold monotone that seemed to quiver in the air. Nem felt a lump form in her throat. So they had experienced this same disturbance when they discovered her all those years ago, lying weak, abandoned and memoryless on the beach near the School of Fate?

Why had no one ever told her that it was magic that had brought her to the shore?

Krepth stepped forward. "Nem wasn't the one to open the portal. Free her, now!"

Klotho lazily examined her nails, her expression one of boredom. "Spymaster, all threads of fate have a purpose. Whether they remain as they are or are woven into something new, it is fate's will that decides what comes next." As she spoke, Nem's gaze snapped back to Aeun, her heart quickening with awe as the dragon's bonds seeped into her scales. Slowly, Aeun rose to her feet, her wings unfurling, light seeping from the cracks between her scales, much like what Nem had witnessed while riding on her back earlier. The dragon was *absorbing* the magic. Etropos clapped in delight.

A surge of power coursed through Nem's arms, drawing her attention to the golden shackles that were now merging with her own skin. Her flesh smoothed, glowing with a newfound vigour, radiating from within.

She too absorbed the Fate's threaded magic, just like Aeun.

Golden eyes gleamed as Klotho's voice broke the moment. "We have much to discuss, demi-goddess. Come."

⸸

"Has anyone considered how we're going to feed such a... massive creature?" Merrick called out, tossing a piece of jerky to Bo. He glanced at the second piece in his hand, then turned his attention to Aeun, whose scaly brow lifted in response. They emerged from the thin tree line and gazed over the sloping fields toward The School of Fate, trepidation riding the wind. The silver dragon trailed closely behind them, her wing tips grazing the thinning trees. As soon as they cleared it, she stretched her slender neck, letting her wings rise.

"The barbarian needn't worry," Aeun said, her voice calm in Nem's mind. *"Dragons can go quite some time without food. During my captivity, I was given some sustenance – though it was less than I normally require. Even as a prisoner, they ensured I didn't starve."*

Merrick shrugged, handing the second piece of jerky to Bo, who devoured it greedily, as though he'd gone without food for days.

"Besides... I prefer fresh meat. Not the kind dried into leather scraps that get stuck between my teeth." Aeun huffed as Bo snuffed at her claws. The dire wolf's proximity didn't seem to faze her, but Nem did wonder mildly if Aeun might see Bo as a potential snack. As they travelled, Aeun's telekinesis grew more distinct, her speech less stilted and more coherent. Nem sensed intelligence in her, but she couldn't shake the feeling that the dragon was still young – barely

older than herself in dragon terms.

"You didn't take the opportunity to hunt earlier?" Nem pointed out, to which Aeun lifted her shoulders.

"Thought it best not to choose the wrong animal and upset a farmer, or something." Something told Nem that, from the tone of Aeun's voice, this may have happened once before.

The sound of waves crashing against the bluff reached her ears just before the salty scent of the sea did, bringing forth a strange blend of familiarity and unease. Though this place had been her home for so long, the crumbling castle walls stood as the anchor to countless memories – some marked by pain, others by triumph, blood, and friendship. Ariiaya's image flashed in Nem's mind, her wicked smile and piercing purple eyes. Nem couldn't help but think of how Arii had befriended her when she hadn't really earned it. Since washing up on the shore, Nem had carried a chip on her shoulder, a simmering anger that had no clear target, no direction – she didn't even know who she was angry with. Yet, despite it all, Arii had reached out, becoming a welcome thorn in her side ever since. To be here at the School without her felt strange, especially when they passed through the crumbling, vine smattered portcullis and into the inner courtyard, where vibrant-haired Furies paused in their tasks to watch them.

Wingbeats thumped from above, and Aeun alighted on one of the walls, causing some of the assassins nearby to draw their weapons and call with alarm. Klotho quickly ordered, "Store your weapons. This dragon is our guest!"

Parts of the wall cracked and crumbled beneath her weight, stones tumbling like rain. One Fury with purple hair nimbly skipped aside, casting an annoyed glance at their 'guest.'

"Sorry..." Aeun muttered, looking bashful.

"Place is falling apart anyway," said Vega, grinning up at the dragon before striding forward to survey their newest destination.

"So, this is The School of Fate. Got to say, I imagined this place far differently. Less… *rustic*."

"It is in gross disrepair, in need of some serious maintenance," rumbled Merrick, to which Vega shot him a look that screamed 'Do you not have a filter?!', though her own words had not been any kinder. Bo let out a sharp yap and bounded over to a nearby stack of salt-crusted crates draped in worn burlap sheets, sniffing at them curiously.

A few assassins relieved them of their bags and a familiar tall, light-haired Fae with a scowl approached. Her tattoos were stark on her wintery skin, their bold edges pulled down by her frown. "Nemesis Rion. Something shivers upon the air and of course in its wake you return."

"Tora." Nem straightened, chin lifting as her emotionless mask slipped into place, one which she donned while in the company of her assassin sisters. Well, all but one… "Odd to see you so far from the hip of Commander Sybell Kruel."

Tora's top lip quivered into a strained smile, if one could call the grimace a smile. "Your tongue remains as silver as your hair, I see." There was no anger in the Fury's tone, only amusement and a pinch of respect despite her words. "I could say the same thing of you and our Queen."

"Once again, we find ourselves in uncertain times. Yet, even amidst the unpredictability, people rarely change… only evolve." Krepth said nearby, so close she could feel the heat of him upon her back. His lips curved in a roguish grin. "You look well, Tora. Love suits you."

Tora snorted, but colour blotted her cheeks. "Wolf." She acknowledged him stiffly, sweeping some supplies into her arms as she cocked her head towards a nearby archway. "Rooms are through there. You know where."

Nem nodded in gratitude, the weight of exhaustion sinking deep into her bones. She had refused to dwell on the portal and enigmatic hooded figure; the events at the farm; or how she'd clung to a dragon's neck, fighting not to be hurled to her death within the cursed Mists. But those events were catching up to her now. Fae possessed physical strength far beyond that of mortals, their bodies crafted from something far tougher than mere flesh and bone. Yet, in that moment, Nem's mind felt sluggish, like wading through the thick mists she'd escaped. Almost a stranger inside her own head.

Tora turned and Nem followed her gaze. "The dragon… it must remain in the courtyard. It will be better protected from the sea winds." Nem hadn't realised she'd been giving Tora a look until the assassin said quickly, "The beast will be safe. I vow it."

Nem looked up to Aeun, who was already watching her with oceanic eyes. Her head dipped, a draconic nod if she'd ever seen one. *I won't be far*, Nem thought.

She trusted Tora and was confident the others of her traveling party would too, given time. Vega, nodding thoughtfully, seemed to reach that conclusion much faster – something Nem was starting to believe was just her nature. Merrick, however, shot wary glances around them, his mistrust still evident. Meanwhile, Iniq was already scanning the surroundings, effortlessly blending back into the group as they made their way to their lodgings.

As they passed the threshold, a hand touched the crook of her elbow, bringing warmth and sparks to her skin. "I know it has been some time since you returned, Nem. Are you alright?"

With bottom lip wedged between her teeth, she responded with a mild, "I'm fine."

If the return of her shortness fazed Krepth, he didn't let it show. A tiny knot of regret pinched in the bottom of her stomach again at her abrupt words, the way she spoke to him as if they hadn't been friends for years. Anxiety was an acidic beast, nestled low in her belly, spitting at every tiny piece of possible affection of kindness inched her way. Yes, it had been some time since she'd last returned. The last time she'd stood here, she'd tried to wrest more answers from the Sisters – but had left emptier and angrier than ever.

The memory rose unbidden, slipping in like a tide she couldn't hold back.

"It's maddening... they dole out information in frustrating fragments, tangled in cryptic riddles, and even then, the truth is often obscured." Ariiaya had stood beside her that day. Though she now ruled as Queen, even her newfound power had done nothing to shift the Fates' response.

"If you possess even a trace of divinity in your blood, those above and below will have their say in when and how your answers come to you. The Gods will reveal what they wish in time. That time is not now." Etropos' gaze had followed her, unblinking, unreadable, as Nem and Arii turned away. Behind the Fate, the Tapestry loomed, its enchanted ink alive, weaving untold stories across its surface. It had taunted her then, the threads of divine truth just out of reach.

When would the answers finally come?

Nem liked to think of herself as patient, steadfast, like stone worn smooth by the sea. But what was the point of patience if it bore no fruit? If waiting led only to more silence?

Now, back within the crumbling walls of her childhood home, Nem stood no wiser than she had been months ago during her last visit. But this time, she had a dragon at her side and a strange, sizzling magic in her veins that responded to the portals. She was ready to try again.

"The Fates are withholding information – whether as a power play or by the Gods' design, I can't say. But they know more, Nem. I saw it in their eyes when their magic sank into your skin."

Nem swallowed hard at Krepth's closeness, unavoidable in the confines of the narrow hallway they'd just entered. His words pulled her gaze to his, the sudden proximity sparked by a brief misstep. Krepth's sharp perception caught her off guard – a trait she often overlooked, hidden behind his usual blasé demeanour.

He was Fythnar's spymaster for a reason.

"You think they know more about my origins, and about the world beyond the portals?"

Krepth's teeth flashed, one elongated canine pinching his full bottom lip. "Silver Moon, they've been biding their time, gathering their own information. Trust me."

Nem squinted over her shoulder at him in suspicion. How could he know this? Perhaps he had spies in the school now. Perhaps he'd *always* had spies here.

"Why would they hold on to it when it could also affect what is happening with the portals showing up now?"

After her strange connection to the portal and everything she had felt during the experience, Nem was certain there was a link between her and the world beyond it. Her Goddess-touched origins extended beyond this realm, and surely, that knowledge had to be significant. The fact that she could close the portals only made it more so.

Nem pinched the bridge of her nose, the dull ache behind her eyes growing more insistent.

"You poured a lot of energy into closing that portal, and let's not forget surviving a dragon – and two bloody Kryvern. You need to rest. Recover."

He was right. She knew it. Still, the moment she sighed and turned, her thoughts scattered.

She collided with the solid wall of his chest.

Krepth's hands came up, bracing her arms. Warm. Steady. Their breaths caught – sharp and in sync – in the narrow passage between stone walls. His scent hit her first: something earthy, dark, like storms and steel and the forest, cutting through the damp air of the hall. Her pulse jumped.

She didn't move. Instead, she tilted her head back. Let her hair fall from her face. Let her lips part. Her eyes widened – an unconscious response to the heat radiating from his body, to the shadows flickering across his sharp jawline. His grip wasn't forceful, just firm enough to ground her. Through the cloth of her tunic, his touch burned slow, a low thrum under her skin.

Her chest tightened. Her heart stuttered.

She licked her lips – quick, instinctive – to soothe their dryness and caught the subtle shift in his gaze as he watched her do it.

His voice dropped, husky. "Need help settling in your rooms?"

A breath passed. Then another.

"No. No need," she said, though it sounded thinner than she'd intended. Not sharp. Not dismissive. Just... off. "I only have one pack."

Outwardly, her expression was neutral – barely.

Inside, she was *chaos*.

Heat and nerves and that flicker of want she tried so hard to ignore. His question was careful, a featherlight prod against the wall she'd kept between them. He wasn't pushing. Just... checking. Testing the lock.

She should have thought of the others, how far they'd walked ahead, what they might see if they turned around. But everything else faded. All that existed was the slow study of his eyes on her face – searching, calculating, as though she were a mystery he wasn't ready to give up solving.

"You can keep shutting me out, Nem, but that doesn't erase the part of me that wants to help you."

His words struck something deep, something that had curled in her long ago, half-starved and buried. Her breath caught.

Nem tried to look away, but his fingers slid upward, skimming the edge of her jaw, coaxing her gaze back to his. Her skin tingled where he touched her, heat spreading like wildfire beneath the surface.

Her knees felt unsteady, breath shallow as her hands lifted – hesitant – then pressed flat against his chest. The steady thud of his heart met her fingertips, maddeningly calm. Steady. As if he wasn't coming apart inside like she was.

He leaned in then, so close she could feel the whisper of his breath on her lips.

"Stop fighting me," he said, eyes dark with longing. "Just for a moment. Let me in. Let something in."

Her heart pounded. Her body ached to close the gap. But her mind – her limited memories, the shadow of her supposed *duty*, her fear – they screamed. This was what she'd been avoiding for the past year, this closeness, this vulnerability.

And yet...

Still, she didn't move. Didn't stop him when his hand curved around the back of her neck, thumb brushing the sensitive skin beneath her pointed ear, tracing the scars that ran there. Didn't flinch when his mouth hovered just above hers, not quite kissing, just waiting.

The tension pulled tight as a drawn bowstring.

Silence hung between them, heavy and close. Her fingers clenched slightly in the fabric of his shirt. She could feel the beat of him. Could taste the closeness. Every warning inside her rang like a bell, every piece of steel she'd erected around her heart, but she was tired of fighting every single instinct that said *stay*.

Nem's lips parted, barely a breath from his.

"I don't know how to not hurt you," she finally said. A confession.

His reply was a whisper, lips brushing hers with the faintest of contact. "Then *hurt* me."

"Rooms are ready. They're slightly drafty but there are extra furs and more firewood for the hearths."

Startled, Nem stepped back, blinking dumbly as Tora rounded the corner, smacking her hands together. Krepth's hands, which had been hovering, slipped easily to his sides, buried in the pockets of his pants. The Fury paused, blinked back, then cleared her throat. "Ye' know where everything else is kept. Additional bedding–" She pointedly tilted her head and rose her brows at Krepth, "and all tha'."

Nem's cheeks flamed as Tora passed them, amusement radiating from her broad shoulders.

Krepth's chuckle was smooth, sensual, promising, yet when he spoke, the words had her stomach coiling with a disappointment she'd never admit.

"Goodnight, Silver Moon."

Then he was gone.

CHAPTER ELEVEN

KREPTH

Morning came far too slowly for Krepth's liking, having spent most of the night staring at the vine-laden ceiling, tracing the roots and counting the leaves while the scent of her faded from his clothing, but not the barely-there kiss which lingered on his lips.

Now Krepth drew a deep breath of the sulphurous sea air, his gaze steady on Nem from his spot in the sun overlooking the grassy field, close to where the castle's shadow stretched. With the same care and precision she used to oil her beloved blades, she worked the cloth over Aeun's scales, methodically wiping away the grime and dried blood that clung to the dragon's silver hide. As the dirt gave way, the shimmering surface beneath gleamed like the metal of their weapons, polished and radiant. Stray strands of her hair had slipped loose from her tie, fluttering around her face as she balanced gracefully on Aeun's leg. She stretched upward, her movements steady and deliberate, scrubbing at the intricate patchwork of scales where the dragon's wing joined her sleek, powerful body.

Aeun's eyes were closed, the feathers along her skull rippling partway down the back of her neck. He had never seen a dragon with feathers before. Though they were sparse, they highlighted specific parts of her form – her jaw, spine, and tail – while the rest of her body remained predominantly covered in tough, shimmering scales. Her size indicated she wasn't quite a juvenile; her limbs were powerful, and her wings even more so. Dragon breeds were still a subject of ongoing research, with much yet to be discovered. However, from what Krepth had gleaned in his quest for knowledge, all dragons shared certain traits: they were fire-breathing creatures made of material tougher than the flames they produced. Fireproof, at least to an extent. The only discernible variation so far lay in the hues of their scales – browns, blues, reds, and blacks. Aeun had yet to breathe fire, leaving Krepth uncertain whether her distinctive hide and feathered plumes were the only traits that set her apart.

One of Nem's long canines pinched her bottom lip, a small, unconscious habit she often displayed when deeply absorbed in a task. His mind dragged back to those lips just inches from his last night, breath fanning his chin. Her focus was so intense that the world around her faded away. The gesture was endearing, softening her usually stern scowl. Strands of hair brushed against her scarred cheek and the curve of her neck. Krepth's gaze lingered, drawn to the soft skin there, his memory betraying him with the scent he once traced along that very spot. Heat stirred within him, a sensation long neglected, and he tore his eyes away, fixing them on the sky as he swallowed hard.

"I don't know how to not hurt you."

"Then hurt *me."*

The sky was overcast – as it always seemed to be here at the edge of their land, but today there was a charge upon the air that had nothing to do with the rumble of thunder in the distance. The old castle loomed upon the hill behind them like an obelisk, the grassy field they resided in lightly flattened from Aeun's talons. Had Krepth been in his wolf form, his hackles would have been raised at the static on the air.

Boots paused in the grass beside him before Iniq settled into place, drawing her knees to her chest and resting her chin atop.

"She lets you keep watch, eh?"

Krepth stroked his thumb across his bottom lip, pressing the lingering intimate heat of memory away. "The lack of stab wounds on my person should be evidence enough of that."

Iniq chuckled, a rare sound from her these days. The eastern woodland warrior was known for her seriousness, much like the woman Krepth watched intently. Yet, Krepth knew that beneath Iniq's stoic warrior exterior, she had a fondness for laughter. He had seen it often in their younger days – when they grew up together and during those nights of stolen intimacy under the moonlight.

That was before Iniq longed for more than fleeting moments, and before he had shattered her heart. Hurting her was one of his deepest regrets. It wasn't because she wasn't perfect for him – she was. She was strong and untamed, shaped by the moss and deep forests of their homeland. She could hold conversations and had an incredible sense of humour to match.

But… She wasn't… *her*.

Iniq's voice was pitched low, a hand brushing through the grass. "Do you think she and the portal are connected?"

A salty sea breeze drew fingers through his hair as Krepth's gaze shifted, finally, away from Nemesis, who had moved on to trailing the cloth over Aeun's wing.

"Undoubtedly. You saw her magic connect with it – there's no denying it. This is the first solid lead I've had in uncovering more about this mystery in the entire past year." Iniq's gaze was so intense, so *curious*, that Krepth found himself compelled to look away. He couldn't risk letting on just how deeply his own desperation ran, how much he yearned for answers that had eluded him for so long.

How much he'd done and sacrificed.

"I can see how much this means to you," Iniq whispered, words full of weight, and laced with a touch of something Krepth couldn't

quite place. "Helping her figure out herself, I mean."

He placed his hand in the grass, lifting his shoulders in a barely there shrug.

"And she hasn't spoken to you about anything of what she saw while closing the portal?"

Krepth gave her a raised brow look, and she quickly responded with, "Right," drawing on the word like a bowstring.

After a beat where all that sounded was the clash of the sea against the shore and the whip of the wind, Iniq tried again.

"I could speak to her. Female to female."

It wasn't a question, but that didn't stop Krepth's look. "That's not necessary."

"Sometimes, you just have to tell someone the truth outright, plainly and honestly, without any of this tiptoeing around it," Iniq said, her tone firm but not unkind. Krepth had little doubt that Iniq was speaking about more than just his feelings for Nem; there was an unspoken weight to her words, one that seemed to echo with the shadows of their shared history. "You've always been honest, Krepth. Painfully so."

Nem didn't need the weight of his unwanted affection. Not while she was already grappling with the revelations about her ties to the realm beyond the portal.

But he wasn't very good at keeping away from her.

Krepth angled his head, keeping his voice low, like the growl of a wolf.

"I've spilled enough blood, dirtied my hands. I don't need to tell her how I feel. It's plain to see – when she decides to look."

He wondered just how much she knew about the dangerous dance he was performing with the silver-haired demi-goddess. Only a select few knew of the devastating effect her touch had on his magic. What that meant for their relationship – if there ever was to be one.

Iniq's words were gentle, yet edged, "What have you done, Krepth?"

Memories flickered behind his eyes. Solo missions carried out in silence. Fists bloodied from interrogations. His jaw tight from hours of tense questioning. Scenes that clung to him long after the work was finished. Krepth was no stranger to these methods of gathering information, but over the past year, he'd been far more involved, far less detached.

"What anyone with my power would have done. I gathered information." His lips drew wide, a crescent flash of teeth and canines. "The only way I know how."

Iniq's lips pressed into a tight line as she stayed silent for a moment, her gaze shifting back to Aeun and Nem. Nem's eyes were narrowed, locked onto them. Krepth, unbothered, casually crossed his ankles and offered a maddening little wave. Predictably, Nem exhaled sharply, turning back to her work with renewed fervour, scrubbing Aeun's scales with noticeably more force. Krepth winced when the dragon's piercing blue eyes narrowed upon him.

Were they communicating at this very moment? Scheming how to snatch him up with dragon talons and hurl him into the sea? Or maybe they'd ignite him like a bonfire and twirl around the flames. Would Vega join the revelry, too? She struck him as the dancing type.

"Well," the soft creak of Iniq's leathers pulled him from his dark musings as she rose gracefully to her feet, stretching with an air of casual ease. Her thick, earthy hair was left unbound, dancing in the sea breeze. "You don't have to handle this on your own. *Neither* of you do." She motioned towards Nem. "We're a team, and while our mission is to learn more about the portals, we can also work together to uncover more about Nem, too."

He stood and stretched, easing the stiffness from his back. "Thank you, Iniq." Her kindness didn't surprise him, though he doubted he deserved it. Even so, he appreciated it. Iniq gave a small nod, turning back toward the castle. As she departed, she gave Nem a nod, which was met with a silent one in return.

A sudden gust of wind struck him, flattening the grass as Aeun spread her wings wide. With a powerful series of beats, she lifted into the air, soaring over their heads toward the sea. Krepth watched, hands on his hips, as she dove low, her claws skimming the waves. A flock of gulls floating on the foam scattered in a panicked flurry, their cries lost beneath her thunderous roar.

When Krepth turned back, he stifled a startled yelp, finding himself nearly nose-to-nose with Nem. Her wild, tangled silver hair framed a sharp glare that seemed to pierce right through him as she said, "You look like you're up to no good."

Krepth grinned awkwardly, rubbing the back of his neck. "Erm, no?" The word came out with an unintended questioning lilt, and he wasn't entirely sure why. Maybe it was her piercing gaze – it always seemed to do something unsettlingly strange to his insides. And... other places.

He was most certainly a little bit deranged.

"I don't believe you," Nem said, poking him square in the chest with a silver-tipped finger. "You've got *that look*."

So, steel-walled Nem was back, her cheeks no longer flushed and pink, her lips no longer parted, instead a slashing line on her face.

Krepth blinked, unable to stop the rush of warmth that shot to every nerve ending at the contact, despite her glare. "What look?"

Her lips pursed and brows drew in an adorably murderous way. "*That.*"

Krepth forced his brows to lower, and his crooked smirk to fade. "Ah."

"Look, I know that I've been avoiding you for the past few months–"

"Year," Krepth cut in. "It's been a year… but go on."

"Are you still wondering why?!" Nem growled, teeth bared as she poked him again, hard enough for him to rub at the spot.

So, their moment last night was to be forgotten, it seemed. Rather than taking it to heart, the fire that always rose when she was irritated sparked to life – and Krepth, as ever, folded his hurt into humour.

His grin was back.

"I know, I know. It's hard to do your duty as the Queen's bodyguard while distracted, I mean just look at me."

A sharp cry of frustration escaped Nem as she twisted away, but before she could storm off, Krepth caught her wrist. Skin met skin, and their touch clashed like fire and ice – her warmth against his cool fingers causing a shock to travel through him from head to toe. A familiar feeling, one he'd felt on the rooftop when they'd kissed, and when they'd danced at Emerson and Luc's wedding. Gods, those stolen moments felt like a lifetime ago. She turned, surprise flashing in her eyes before it melted into anguish.

"You don't have to explain why you've been avoiding me, Nem. I already know." He took a step closer, and with that small movement, he saw a flicker of light return to her eyes. Holding her gaze, he stared deeply, unblinking. "I know. It's because our touch severs my magic." His voice was quieter this time, but no less resolute. His gaze swept across her face, mapping the soft contours of her skin, the scars marring it, and the faint movements of her silver hair, tousled by the ocean breeze. He saw the light in her eyes sharpen as his magic faded from their shared touch. "But I don't care."

"How can you not care that the tiniest touch of my skin to yours takes away what makes you… you? Your magic." Her voice was a whisper; one he almost lost to the wind. "I'm not good for you."

"We've had this argument before, and you know how stubborn I can be," He reasoned, voice low as the surf crashed at that moment, punctuating his words. His gaze lingered on her, captivated by the way the stars seemed to dance in her eyes. He touched the tip of his finger to her chin, tilting her face up, drinking her in, scars and all. "Besides, there is much more to me than my magic. If you'd allow me, I'd show you."

"But… why? Why do you still want me?" Her question was breathless, almost weak, but Krepth knew the female before him was anything but weak. She was like a sun, and he was a moth drawn to her exquisite warmth… her brightness. Her *fire*.

"Do you really believe Fythnar's spymaster has no interest in unravelling the land's greatest mystery? That I wouldn't use every resource I've painstakingly gathered to pursue this purpose?" When her gaze wavered, threatening to break away from his, he leaned in, closing the space between them until her breath brushed against his lips. His voice softened, charged with conviction. "To help a friend uncover their past... to guide them toward a brighter future?"

"A friend…" Nem's lips snapped shut, and he could tell that the words had slipped free of their own accord. "That's all this is. A mystery you want to solve?"

"Silver Moon, you know this is far deeper than that."

Nem's lips opened to speak but before she could retort a gush of wind battered them. Aeun landed lithely on the grass a few feet away, her scales glistening with beads of seawater. She lowered her neck, her narrowed eyes locking onto them, lips twitching over the serrated teeth that held a skewered cluster of fish. With a soft chuckle, Krepth stepped back from Nem, his cloak flaring in the breeze as his hands dropped to his sides. Out of the corner of his eye, he caught Nem raising her hand, a subtle gesture of restraint.

The dragon relaxed, before throwing her head back to down her catch.

"We should head back. There are still unanswered questions that I

need to interrogate from our hosts."

Nem's brows furrowed, her expression teetering on the edge of worry. Instead of speaking, she gave a silent nod, and with an arm's length separating them and a dragon looming behind, they made their way back toward the crumbling castle perched on the bluff.

Chapter Twelve

Nemesis

A day passed by, as slowly as sap dripping on a cold winter morning.

Nem spent that day in the old throne room, seated cross-legged at the base of the Tapestry of Life, her gaze locked on to its enchanted surface, as though sheer determination could force it to yield the answers she craved. The air around her carried the mingled scents of aged books, melted candle wax and the distant tang of the sea – her only companions while her comrades were elsewhere.

Despite her anger and desperation, which had burned like a wildfire when she confronted the Fates when they'd arrived, they offered her nothing more than cryptic reassurance. "The Gods will reveal what they wish, in time, when you're ready," they had said, Lakhesis' golden eyes staring directly into her soul.

Why did they continue to delay? Why couldn't they just tell her what she needed to know? Nem's instincts hissed that the Fates knew far more than they let on – about her, her Goddess-touched origins, and the light magic that pulsed through her blood. They knew, and yet they refused to share.

Part of her wasn't surprised – the sisters had always been cryptic, withholding information like jewels. But they had shared history. They'd found her, raised her, honed her skills into what they were today. She was a daughter of fate, a loyal assassin who hadn't taken

a step out of line – until the events that had drawn her to Ariiaya's side – which seemed to have been forgiven. Did that history not count for something?

Her fingers curled on her knees, fists pressing into the cloth of her pants.

"With such significant tension building within you, it could potentially trigger a migraine."

Etropos knelt beside her, her red cloak pooling around her like a spill of blood. Nem tore her gaze from the tapestry, turning to the crimson-haired Fate at her side. Etropos' face was lit with a smile – warm and inviting. She had always been the 'friendlier' sister, though her effervescent demeanour often struck others as teetering on the edge of madness. Holding any kind of straight-lined conversation normally proved difficult with Etropos, but Nem couldn't press aside an opening to pry *something* from the Fate.

When Nem's lips parted to speak, Etropos spoke first.

"I know you seek answers, but they are not ours to give. You must wrest them from the hands of the Gods who abandoned you here."

Frustration surged in Nem like a pot boiling over, the heat of it driving her to her feet. Her fists clenched at her sides as she glared at the woman.

"Coming here was a mistake," she snapped, her voice tight with anger.

Etropos remained unshaken, her calm gaze fixed on Nem.

"Nemesis Rion," she said evenly, "you have always been the patient one among your sisters. Anger and impulsiveness are Ariiaya's hallmarks, not yours. The Gods favour a steady hand, a clear mind and unwavering loyalty. For a boat adrift in a tempest finds no safe harbor – it splinters and sinks. But if crafted with care, shaped by time and patience, might it not brave the storm and reach the shore?"

"Enough," Nem rasped, her voice trembling as the weight of

Etropos' words settled over her. They were steadier than she'd ever heard them in all her years among the assassins. Her shoulders slumped, silver hair cascading like veils around her face as her gaze dropped to the floor.

"Please," Nem whispered, her tone raw and pleading. "I only want to know who I truly am."

Cool fingers gently encircled one of her clenched fists, pulling it forward as Etropos rose to her feet. Nem flinched, startled by the unexpected touch. Her gaze darted upward and locked with golden eyes that glimmered softly, framed by a small, knowing smile. Nem swallowed hard against the dryness in her throat as the Fate carefully uncurled her fingers. Something small and light was pressed into her palm before her hand was gently closed over it.

"You'll find the answers you seek, Nemesis," Etropos murmured, her voice like a distant melody. "We once thought the Gods had abandoned us. But I believe something holds them here, binding them to this land – a spark, a tether. Their blood, their legacy… their *daughter*."

Nem's face remained an impassive mask, but inside, a tempest of emotions raged. She stood frozen as Etropos turned and walked away, leaving her alone with the weight of the words and the object cradled in her fist. Slowly, almost fearfully, Nem opened her hand. Her breath caught as her eyes fell on the glimmering coil of silver thread, delicate and shimmering, curled like a sleeping serpent in her palm.

A thread, reminiscent of the one drawn to seal the fate of the tyrant usurper king who had nearly ruined their land a year ago. Yet this one was not gold, not like the gleaming strands of the tapestry behind her. It was silver, luminous and otherworldly, as though it had been spun from the ethereal glow of moonlight encircling a midnight sky. Unique, fragile, and filled with quiet power.

Nem turned to the Tapestry of Life, gazed upon it with new eyes, as a budding emotion unfurled like a moonflower in her chest. Wonder. Familiarity.

Smooth, still calm with ever so slight a ripple.

Hope.

She moved closer, the hum of its energy vibrating through her bones with every step. Nem could taste the essence of ancient sugar – dense, radiant, and nearly overwhelming. Tilting her head, she gazed up at the tapestry, its golden glow intensified, flooding her skin with warmth like piercing sunlight. Her hand rose, fingers hovering tentatively toward the fabric, an act long forbidden to all but the Fates themselves. Whispers filled her ears, rising like tendrils of mist curling over a midnight lake, until they and the hum of the tapestry drowned out all else. The Locket of Dreaming quivered against her chest, whether in excitement or warning, she couldn't tell. Its metal grew searing hot, but Nem remained ensnared in a trance. Among the chorus of ghostly voices, one stood out – distant, familiar, female. *Aeun.* Was she calling to her? Nem's consciousness faltered; caught in a battle she couldn't win. The tapestry's pull overwhelmed her, and as her fingertips brushed its surface, the world around her dissolved to nothingness.

†

Numbness weighed down her limbs, yet somehow Nem remained upright as the world around her began to take shape. The haze cleared slowly, revealing a scene so surreal that it stole her breath. Blinking in disbelief, she felt her face slacken, her expression melting into one of awe. She stood at the base of a hill, where emerald grass rippled like waves beneath her feet, stirred by an unseen breeze. The air carried an otherworldly stillness, broken only by the whisper of movement above.

A shadow glided over her, drawing her gaze upward. She turned, her body moving sluggishly against the heaviness. Floating in the sky was a massive chunk of earth, drifting effortlessly as though unbound by the rules of gravity, smaller pieces following in its wake. Roots dangled freely from its underside, trailing into the void below. It moved with serene grace, a silent titan defying reason, and Nem could only stand frozen, a speck of awe-struck stillness in a world that seemed untethered from reality. As her gaze followed the fragments of shattered earth hanging in the air, she glimpsed hilltops resembling those from her own world in the hazy distance. Wisps of rainbow light blurred her vision, but she was certain she caught flashes of energy on each hill – portals of varying shapes tearing through the fabric of the strange place.

Her chest felt heavy, a feeling of familiarity and dread settling over her heart. Why did it feel like she'd been to this place before?

A sharp cry pierced the air above, jerking Nem's attention upward. She spun toward the incline, her body moving instinctively, her feet propelling her forward before her mind fully registered the situation. Her Fae speed carried her swiftly to the crest of the hill, but as her gaze landed on the scene ahead, her pace faltered.

Three figures loomed over a fourth, who knelt with their head bowed, their posture heavy with submission or defeat.

"You've gone too far, Ares," a voice declared, resonating with authority and cold finality. "Your thirst for power has fractured the veils between worlds, wreaking unimaginable havoc. The damage you've caused will take an immense effort and time to repair – if it can even be mended at all."

The speaker's form was shrouded in a cloak so dark it seemed to devour the very light around it. The voice was rich and dark, like the deepest brew of tea or the weightiest shadows of the night.

Nyx, Goddess of darkness.

Her raven-black hair cascaded in rippling waves nearly to her feet, writhing like serpents around her slender, cloaked body. The air around her seemed to pulse with the promise of nightfall, suffused with an ancient, unyielding power.

The figure at their feet tilted his head back in defiance, tendrils of silver hair lashing through the air like living threads of moonlight. His face was a haunting paradox of brutality and ethereal beauty, a visage that seemed sculpted by both violence and divinity. His teeth glinted sharply in a grimace across his lips, while raw, unrestrained power flickered and sputtered in his storm-dark eyes, as if barely contained. His shoulders, broad and corded with muscle, seemed carved for battle, his entire form honed to perfection for the unending trials of war.

This was Ares, God of War – fearsome, relentless, and, as she had come to learn through her travels, one of the most feared and disliked among the Gods. His reputation preceded him, stained with the blood of countless battles, his name whispered with dread by mortals and immortals alike. Yet here, in his presence, she could not deny the undeniable pull of his raw, godly power.

Another figure stepped forward; her voice as delicate as morning light kissing a waking world.

"Were it not for Athena, we dread to think of the irreversible harm you and your daughter might have wrought."

Her radiant features, as luminous as the sun itself, softened as she tilted her head, her gaze fixed on the disgraced God at her feet. Nem recognised her as Hemera, the Goddess of light.

At the words, Ares's eyes drifted down, piercing through the gap between the Goddess' cloaks, his heavy gaze landing directly upon her. A current of static energy zapped through her limbs as Nemesis stared back, the harsh square of his chin catching upon her memory.

This was the man they'd seen at the portal when they'd discovered

Aeun.

"My half-sister is a coward, a shadow reflection of what it means to be a God. Her power wanes because faith runs thin, spread too thinly across too many realms." His voice was guttural, deep like ground stone. He yanked on his bonds, the weaving of dark and light chains sizzling against his skin. "With less worlds to watch over, there would be less strain on *our* power. You've allowed *them* to stretch too far, multiplying worlds like mice in the spring."

Ares's attention shifted to the third woman, one clad in battle armour that reflected the light of his bonds, her sneer wicked sharp like a blade below her ashen blonde hair.

"You speak of eradicating entire worlds of innocents. That is not what we do, Ares." Athena held up a fist, shaking it in anger. "You have taken too much already. Soon, Zeus will have no choice but to step in, and none of us wishes for *that*."

Ares' sneered, lips turning white, "Perhaps that *is* what I want."

The peculiar winds of the place shifted, sending Ares' heavy cloak snapping in the breeze. In that fleeting moment, Nem caught sight of another figure kneeling just a foot away, previously obscured. It was a girl with her head bowed, silver hair cascading so low it brushed the grass. The strands were silken and straight – hair eerily reminiscent of the man that knelt before her. Hair that was undeniably like her own.

Nem's vision tunnelled, her breath hitching as the girl slowly lifted her head. Nem froze, staring into the face of a younger version of herself.

The realisation struck her like a thunderclap.

The girl with Ares… was *her*.

She was Ares' daughter.

Her features glowed with an almost otherworldly light, her eyes blazing like twin storms. She wore battle armour, more graceful and ethereal than anything Nem had ever donned at that age. It was strange, seeing a child wearing such attire – jarring even more so because her expression was one of stone, one of determination, one on the border of cruelty.

The vision trembled around her, her heart pounding like a war drum echoing in her ears. Somewhere, faint and distant, she heard her name, as though someone called to her from beyond this place. Yet her focus remained fixed on the events unfolding atop the bluff, everything else fading into insignificance. She was the daughter of Ares, the merciless God of war and carnage, and she had stood beside him, unleashing chaos and devastation across countless worlds. As a child, she had helped him obliterate them. As a child, her power had been so strong that even at the dawn of its awakening, she'd used it for destruction. The weight of the truth made her body throb with pain, her mind spinning as it scrambled to understand why none of it remained in her memory.

Suddenly, a terrible, ear-splitting roar shattered the air around them. It thundered with such force that the charged atmosphere seemed to vibrate, and the ground beneath her feet trembled violently. The sound was raw – a cry of rage, a wail of pain – and it emanated from something unimaginably massive, a presence that dwarfed everything around it. A shadow peaked in the cloudy maelstrom behind the hill, tips of jagged wings peeking into view. A beast so immense that Nem could only glimpse fragments of it from where she stood. Colossal, larger than anything she had ever encountered – a titan in every sense. Its skin rippled like shifting granite, its scales glowed like burning embers, and its tattered wings, formed of impossibly thick hide.

"You have tested his patience for too long, Ares," Nyx's voice rolled like thunder, deep and commanding, reverberating through the very air. "Zeus has decreed your sentence: you will reside in purgatory, a prison where neither you nor your monsters can destroy anything further."

Ares was motionless for a moment; his usual defiance replaced by a strange air of resignation. Slowly, he tilted his head back, his voice carrying a bitter calm as he asked, "And my daughter?"

Nyx's voice softened, though its authority remained unyielding. "A being of half-blood – a child of the Gods and half Fae immortal – she has endured your influence far too long. She is destined for a life far removed from the destruction you have wrought. Her memories of you and all she has done under your shadow will be stripped away. She will return to the world where she was born, the one you stole her from."

At the proclamation, the vision version of Nem startled. "No! No, father!" she cried, her young voice breaking as her face twisted in fury and anguish.

Had she wanted to be part of Ares' horrible plans? Had she wanted to destroy worlds, taking their power? It didn't sit right in Nem's stomach, though that feeling could be shock as she tried to process what she was seeing.

The bonds around Ares' limbs lifted him into the sky, his face contorting in rage. His bellows of protest were almost lost to the cataclysmic roar of the beast, but Nem heard his words as he hovered over the precipice of a huge portal, one that rippled like a red sea below their hilltop.

"No prison can keep me. You are all fools! I will break free, and when I do, you and the puny little worlds you watch over will be nothing more than specks of dust under the claws of my beast!"

Nem shivered at the threat, taking an involuntary step backward as Ares and his beast were swallowed by the fiery portal.

The three Goddesses advanced toward the vision of Nem, who stood trembling and bowed, her face pale as she struggled in vain to retreat from their approach. Hemera raised a hand, her gesture almost imploring.

"Harmonia," she said, her voice gentle yet firm. "The blood of your mother flows through your veins, and though Ares is your father, there is good within you to contend with the chaos. Harmony exists to temper the storm. You are destined for *more*, young one."

With a cry, Harmonia was lifted into the air, like her father.

"You are a beacon of power, Harmonia – a conduit of light and an absorber of chaos. Return to your home world and begin anew. In time, you will come to see that you are far more than the creation your father shaped. And when he returns, which he will… you will be ready."

Nem watched, the magic restraining her began to sink into her skin. Harmonia's eyes glowed, the air turning urgent. She was absorbing the Goddesses' magic, much like Nem had done with the Fates a few days ago.

A conduit of light and an absorber of chaos.

"Quickly," urged Athena. "Now!"

With their magic intertwined, Nyx and Hemera raised their hands, transforming the void below from a turbulent crimson to a radiant azure. This was the turning point – the moment Nem was cast into Fythnar, destined to awaken on its shores, her past erased from memory. Gasping for breath, Nem clutched her chest, watching the vision of herself as she was hurled from the cliff, swallowed by the void.

Now that the truth was laid bare, Nem wasn't sure if recovering her memory had been worth the sacrifices or the arduous quest. The weight of knowing she'd once stood as an accomplice to a villain crushed her. She felt like a betrayer, a failure – a stain on the goodness of her friends.

She tasted salt, lifting her fingers to touch the tears running down her scarred cheek.

"Nem!" A deep voice echoed around her, as the world began to warp.

Nem felt the solidness beneath her feet give way, but not before she saw the three Goddesses turn to her. Not before she saw the knowing in their eyes, and the threads of fate twining their forms.

Then, Nem was falling.

The next thing she saw was Krepth's face above her, his arms around her tight, his eyes like twin dark stones, concern etched into the roguish lines of his handsome face. "Nem, oh thank the Goddesses!"

She wouldn't tell him how wrong his words felt in that moment. Instead of speaking, she swallowed, queasiness rising with the taste of bile and vomit.

"You touched the Tapestry," whispered Tora nearby, her voice betraying just how significant an act was, her tattooed face appearing over Krepth's broad shoulder. "Then you began to convulse. I raised the alarm as you vomited on yourself. Sister, what did you see?"

"H-How long was I…" Nem pressed a palm to her forehead, avoiding the Fury's question. "How long was I out?"

Vega answered. "Only a few minutes. I was coming to see if you wanted something to eat as I don't remember you having breakfast, and you'd just collapsed–"

"What were you thinking?" growled Krepth as Nem pushed to her feet, avoiding looking at the mess she'd made. How had the vision only taken mere minutes? Everything she'd discovered – about herself, about her origins – had left her irreversibly changed. She felt as if she no longer belonged, not beneath the oppressive weight of the Tapestry, not near her friends, and certainly not near *him*.

As if sensing her inner turmoil, Krepth's face softened as he took a step back from her, "Do you want to talk about what happened?"

She did… she really, truly did. But what would he think of her afterward? She was the daughter of a God, one far from favoured, a deity who sought the annihilation of their world – and countless others – believing that mortal lives needed to be culled to enforce better control. This was far worse than she could ever have imagined.

For a brief moment, she thought of her Fae mother and wondered if she still lived. That fleeting thought shattered as the Fates swept into the room, this time unaccompanied by their usual shadows of Fury assassins. Krepth's subtle shift closer to her drew Nem's focus, her thoughts aligning like an arrow aimed for answers. Straightening her shoulders, she turned to face the sisters head-on.

"The Gods finally provided you with some answers," said Etropos, twining a red strand of hair around her finger, her face pulled in a wide, knowing smile. "Good."

Though all three sisters stood before Nem, their golden eyes fixed upon her with a new kind of glimmer, Nem fastened her own attention squarely on the dark-haired woman, the one who Nem knew – somewhere deep in her blood – had more knowledge inside than her sisters. She was the one who drew the strings from the Tapestry, the one to see the messages from the Gods first. The silver thread that Etropos had given Nem earlier now warmed in her pocket, and her chest burned with questions.

Klotho's gaze flicked from the Tapestry to Nem. Her golden eyes burned with a gravity that Nem doubted anyone else could see, an unspoken hint that Fate knew what she had seen. Their gazes met and locked, and time seemed to stretch. In the stillness, only the soft rhythm of breath and the faint rustle of fabric broke the silence, while the Tapestry of Life swayed gently on an invisible breeze.

Then Nem said into the silence, "Tell me, Klotho. What do you know of Ares, the God of War?"

CHAPTER THIRTEEN

NEMESIS

"Ares embodies the most brutal and repugnant aspects of war — slaughter and carnage driven by an unrelenting thirst for blood and pain. His obsession blinds him to the value of mortal life; to him, life and death are one and the same. He has been a constant thorn in Zeus' side, and for as long as memory serves, the Gods have struggled to find ways to keep him at bay."

Klotho pinched the bridge of her nose in frustration as they sat on musty cushions scattered across the marble floor of the throne room. Beyond the fractured windowpanes, the day had long given way to night. Candlelight flickered, casting shifting shadows over the stacks of books and catching faint glimmers of faded gold filigree, delicately painted across the crumbling archways of the ancient stone walls.

The ocean wind howled through the vine-clad cracks, filling the brief pauses between the sisters' explanations. Nem had shared the vision with the group shortly after broaching the subject of Ares, carefully leaving out that she'd also seen herself there. As if in denial of what she'd actually seen, that part of the vision lingered in the back of her mind, unresolved and raw. For now, Nem told herself, there were other questions that needed answering. She needed to know more about her father first. Understanding him might help her untangle the threads of what came next, or so she hoped. So far, she had pieced together that Ares was a chaos-driven force of destruction, delighting in plunging worlds into turmoil.

And he was now free. He had been at the portal where they'd found Aeun. No longer bound to his otherworldly prison, the question loomed: how had he escaped? And more importantly, what would be his next move?

"Ares is rebuilding his strength. He is not yet strong enough to bring his beast into this world, and it is because of you that he struggles so." Aeun's voice was soft, as if she nestled in the corner of Nem's mind. Nem had begun to grow used to her presence – a reassuring silver glimmer in the growing turmoil of her own mind.

"Because of me?" Nem thought back.

"When you set me free from his chains, you stopped his plans." Aeun said simply, not elaborating further as the hum of conversation continued outside of their mental conversation. Before Nem could ask more, her attention was drawn back to her friends.

"Some in my homeland would say that Ares represents more than just the bloody chaos of war," Merrick said, his voice a deep, gravelly timbre. He reached into the offering of food at the centre of their circle, plucking a strip of jerky with deliberate ease. As he handed it to Bo, who lay stretched out at his side, his sharp eyes flicked around the group. "They'd argue he embodies raw courage, unyielding strength, and the bravery to stand against impossible odds." The jerky found its way into Bo's eager jaws, but Merrick's gaze stayed steady, his tone as unwavering. "But even so, we're not fools. Ares is no friend to mortals, no patron of compassion. He values strength, yes, but has no patience for weakness – and even less for those who dare ask for his mercy."

"Of course, the barbarians of the south would worship a god with rippling muscles," Vega mumbled, her tone laced with equal parts sarcasm and bemusement.

The southern warrior's rugged face darkened, his brows knitting into a scowl. The flicker of offence in his eyes was unmistakable, though he quickly masked it with his usual stoicism.

"Few pray to Ares these days," he said, his voice low and measured, each word carrying the weight of restraint. "I, for one, do not."

Vega arched an eyebrow, folding her arms across her chest as the candlelight played tricks across her burgundy hair, "Really? I'd have thought you'd be first in line at his altar, asking for a sharper blade or a fiercer battle."

Nem's attention, like everyone else's, bounced from one warrior to the other. In her peripheral, she swore she saw a smile tug at Krepth's lips as he crossed his arms over his chest.

Merrick's jaw tightened. "Ares is not strength or honour. He is chaos. A god who revels in bloodshed for its own sake, without purpose or reason. If you think we of the south fight for him, then you do not understand us at all."

The two clashing was nothing new, but unlike before – when their exchanges were playful, occasionally laced with a hint of flirtatious tension – this time carried a different weight. What once held no malice now trod into charged territory, the conversation teetering between light-hearted banter and something far more serious as beliefs and convictions came under scrutiny.

Nem studied Merrick for a longer moment, spying that beneath the rugged exterior and imposing stature, there was something deeper, something she hadn't expected – a disdain not for Vega's jest, but for the God their conversation had invoked. Faith was a subject people approached in only two ways: with heart and conviction, or with disdain and a dismissive wave of the hand. With so many Gods to worship – and lately, so little sign of their presence – Nem had noticed a quiet unravelling. More and more, people were losing faith. Temples once filled with light and voices now echoed with emptiness, their crowds thinned to a trickle. Nem cast her attention briefly back at the Tapestry of Life, where its edges were stained off-colour. The spread of the stain had eased when the war ended, but Nem had spent the most of her life under its glow, and she couldn't help but notice how it still seemed to be suffering.

No wonder Ares wanted to eradicate their world. If their power came from faith, theirs was more of a liability than a source.

With the return of magic, the threads drawn from the Tapestry had begun to include those who wielded it – no longer hiding in fear of persecution. Some, unchecked, turned their magic on others. The assignments handed to the Fury assassins grew more dangerous, tangled with unpredictable power. But their ranks were shifting too: male Fae now stood among them, and younger recruits, raw, untested and *willing*, looked to the Sisters for guidance and training.

Vega blinked, seemingly caught off guard by the vehemence in Merrick's tone. "Alright," she said finally, her voice softer, though the curiosity remained. "If not Ares, then who do you fight for?"

The warrior glanced away, his scowl easing into something more reflective. "We fight for our people, our land, and the lives that depend on us. No God commands us, no matter how many muscles they flex." There was a softening of his tone towards the end, a smile in his voice.

A small smile tugged at the corner of Vega's mouth, though she tried to hide it. "Fair enough," she said, her tone lighter now. "But you have to admit, the mental image is fitting."

"I would be a liar if I did not agree." Merrick said, eyes locking with Vega's.

If the Fates cared for the turn in their conversation, they did not show it. Klotho watched the exchange intently, while Lakhesis sat motionless, and Etropos smiled, eyes distant.

Behind Nem, the Tapestry pulsed faintly, its divine energy saturating the air like an ever-present reminder of its power. The vibration seemed to hum in tune with their unease. Nem felt unsettled, as if the foundation of her own faith had been shaken. She had always prayed to Nyx and Hemera – night and day, black and white, the balance she had trusted. But now, knowing they had cast out her father – and her by extension – everything she thought she knew had been turned upside down.

They had spared her, and for that, she felt a flicker of gratitude. Yet, doubt lingered. Her prayers had always been measured, her belief steady but cautious, knowing faith varied greatly across the land. Now, she couldn't help but wonder if that caution had been a quiet intuition, a semblance of twisted support for her forgotten father.

Iniq cleared her throat, pressing a fist to her mouth before speaking. "So, Nem touches the Tapestry and sees a vision of Ares being cast into his prison, along with the Goddesses who put him there. What does it mean?"

"Ares has escaped his prison and is skirting the edge of this world until he has recovered enough power to launch a full, devastating attack. You saw him at the portal where you found your dragon–" Lakhesis' head tilted towards Nem. "He has set his sights on Fythnar to be his next conquest, and we need to prepare."

Around a half-chewed grape, Vega said, "Why here? What grudge has Ares got against Fythnar?"

Instead of the Fates, Krepth answered, "He has ties here. We need to figure out what he wants before he can get it."

Nem worked on a swallow as Krepth's heavy gaze met hers, lips pulled in a heavy frown.. His gaze told her what words did not – he knew she was withholding something, and as his brows pulled into a crease, she knew he was determined to figure it out. Like a wolf with a bone.

She would tell him. Soon. The secret weighed on her like lead, pressing heavily on her shoulders and twisting uncomfortably in her chest.

In that moment, Nem silently longed for her best friend – the violet-eyed woman who always knew how to ease her burdens. She could imagine her there, taking the weight of the secret and stretching it between them, sharing its load with quiet strength and unwavering support. Arii would have a few strongly worded things to say about the predicament they were in, and she'd sooner make the earth rumble and split before allowing Ares to destroy their world.

There was a silent question in Krepth's expression, one that twinged at her heart.

He was worried.

Nem dropped her gaze to the floor, fingers trailing the faded piping of her crimson cushion. Vibrations tingled from the material, trailing through her fingertips and into her hand.

"Let's look at the positive, here. We now know who is causing the cracks in the peace we've held for the last year. And so far, it seems we are one step ahead of Ares. That's good," Iniq said, long dark braid floating over her shoulder as she leaned forward.

Klotho lifted a hand, motioning to a cloaked scribe who had been lingering with quill and parchment in the shadows. "Send a missive to Viridya, to the west and the east, and to the twins in the south. Tell them what we know, tell them to prepare."

Fingertips tingling, Nem reached for Aeun's mind again. The connection shimmered like heat off stone. She found the dragon curled in a loose coil of muscle and scale in the inner bailey, a makeshift nest of scorched straw and weather-worn banners.

"Aeun," she asked silently, her voice a whisper through the bond. *"Does Ares want to destroy this world... or conquer it?"*

Aeun stirred, slow and deliberate. Her massive head rose, horned crown tilting toward the cloud-laced night sky. For a moment, she said nothing – only watched the stars like they were showing her a truth too heavy for words.

"What difference does it make?" she finally answered, smoke curling from her nostrils. *"Both end in death."* Aeun's words didn't just arrive in her mind – they curled around her thoughts, heavy and inevitable as a tide, dragging her deeper whether she wished it or not.

Nem frowned. The air around her grew still. *"But if I could speak to him – if I could make him remember who I am–"*

"There is no reasoning with the God of War," Aeun's growl trembled the stones beneath her. A burst of smoke flared from her jaws, and a nearby recruit – arms full of clean sheets – startled and dropped them in a tangled heap at his feet.

Nem swallowed, her hands curling at her sides. Her magic sparked, restless under her skin. She studied her palms, the creases of her hands where hints of light danced.

"When I said that you are the reason Ares has been unable to fully breach this realm," Aeun continued, her voice lowering into something older, colder, *"it was not flattery."* She turned, pupils narrowing to slits. *"It was fact. It is not* who *you are to Ares, it is* what *you are."*

"Tell me what to do," Nem whispered. "Please."

Aeun looked away from the night sky, feathers rippling, catching the firelight.

A long pause.

"There are things I cannot say," the dragon murmured at last. *"Not yet."*

Frustration twisted in the pit of Nem's stomach, but it didn't linger. Another feeling rose to swallow it whole. Anticipation.

Nem let her gaze wander across the throne room, following the ebb and flow of voices until it caught on a pair of green eyes. Krepth was watching her, unblinking, the weight of his stare a quiet promise that questions would come later. She looked away before he could read too much.

"I am sorry, Aeun."

Surprise moved along the bond like a sudden ripple in still water. *"Sorry? Why would you be sorry?"*

Nem's fingers closed into fists against her knees. The muscles in her forearms trembled with the effort of holding something in. *"I feel… responsible. For what Ares has done. For what I have just learned. I don't even know why. I just…"* She breathed through the knot in her throat. *"I am sorry."*

Aeun gave no reply, and in the quiet between them there was no coldness, only a space left open for her to fill. A pulse of understanding lingered there, low and steady, like the slow beat of a dragon's wings. Nem felt it settle into her chest, a kinship she could not name.

She thought of pressing her. Aeun had known who the figure was. Nem could feel it now, in hindsight, like a shape just out of sight in the corner of her vision. There was a sting in the knowledge that the dragon had kept it from her, a faint bite of betrayal. Yet… she understood. Trust was still something fragile between them, threads not yet fully woven. And if Aeun had told her earlier, would she have believed her? That the God of bloody war was out there, hammering on the walls between worlds?

The bond shifted. She could feel the raw edge of Aeun's recovery, the strain of having been so close to the God they now spoke of. Nem was certain he had been her captor. The feeling of it lingered in their connection, jittering through her mind like the aftershock of a storm still rumbling away over the horizon.

Aeun's thoughts tightened, drawing taut against the silence. She wanted to speak. Nem could sense it in the pause before the words that never came.

But she couldn't. Not yet.

Because there was a disturbance in the moonlit fields just beyond

their gates.

Bo let loose a soft yip, before lumbering to his paws. The sound drew the group's attention, and Nem noticed Merrick's hand moving to his hatchet at his belt as he spoke.

"Can anyone else feel that?"

Rumbling became steadier, a slight pulse at first, until that pulse blew into a full tremor that caused everyone to dash to their feet, even the Fates.

The doors slammed open, and in a whirlwind of capes and gleaming weapons as a small flourish of Furies filled the room. Surrounded by a striking cadre of assassins with vivid hair, clad in leather and light armour ready for battle, was Tora.

"Sisters, something is wrong. There is a disturbance at the gates."

"Indeed," Klotho said sharply. "A portal has just torn open outside."

CHAPTER FOURTEEN

NEMESIS

Nem couldn't shake the feeling that the portal's sudden appearance, so soon after her visions while touching the Tapestry, was no coincidence. It seemed as though her connection to it had somehow triggered the rift, that she was responsible for the contingent of creatures now threatening their crumbling fortress on the bluff.

The thought pressed down on her, stirring doubt of similar events she might have unwittingly set into motion in the past – times when she stood at her father Ares's side. Ambiguity coiled within her like a tightening fist, squeezing the breath from her resolve.

Though she now knew her origins, the deeper memories of her time at the God's side were still murky. She wasn't sure if she felt further frustrated by this, or silently grateful.

Fingers grabbed hers, snatching her thoughts for a moment. Vega smiled, blowing her fringe from her face which was set in a look that Nem knew was forced. The western warrior's pupils were shrunk in between hazel irises, the skin crinkling around her eyes.

"Time to do what we do best and strike down monsters," Vega said, following the quick paced steps of Iniq and Merrick ahead.

Krepth paused at her side, his expression of worry now switched to his usual grin. Her heart kicked a beat at the change, but she was also relieved to see his smile, even if the edges were forced.

"The perfect timing for a distraction, eh Silver Moon? Lucky for

you, my interrogation will have to wait."

Perhaps it was because she had finally learned something about her past, or perhaps it was the rising tension in the room, the promise of action coiling in the air, but she said, "I've seen the way you interrogate." Her smile curved slowly at one corner. "You'll have to try harder if you want me to confess anything."

His smile deepened, the tips of his canines catching the light, and a shiver of heat travelled down her spine.

"Oh, you haven't seen me *go hard*, Silver Moon."

The simmer in his voice sent fire low through her, a sharp pull that was all too tempting. But this was not the time for games. The weight in the air said fight, not flirt. Their eyes held in a taut, heated line, then they turned and left the room together.

The entire castle buzzed with frantic activity, a hive of chaos and urgency. Tora barked sharp orders, dispatching a squad of assassins to the walls, their crossbows gleaming with steel-tipped bolts and charged with crackling magic. Staff scrambled through the corridors, their hurried footsteps echoing as they fled toward the safety of the lower catacombs.

Meanwhile, Nem and her group moved against the tide, following the ominous sounds of shrieks and claws raking against stone, each step drawing them closer to the open-aired inner bailey. They drew to the main gates, which stood barred shut against the horrors waiting outside. The heavy barrier shuddered violently under the impact of something slamming against it, bits of rubble and old mortar crumbling to the ground.

A shadow passed over them, blotting out the speckled sky as Aeun swooped overhead, her piercing trill a stark warning.

"They're coming – be ready!"

Nem drew her daggers in a fluid motion, the amulet at her neck pulsing with energy. Her gaze locked on the gates, resolute and prepared to face the nightmare she had helped unleash.

Tora's voice rang from above. "Loose! Loose your arrows NOW!"

It happened so fast that Nem barely had time to glance at the shadow beside her. Firelight and moonlight tore across Krepth's face, across the faces of her friends, as they stood poised and ready.

My fault, my fault, Nem thought, then her inner voice was lost to a sudden BOOM.

The heavy gates buckled under the relentless weight of bodies crashing against them, limbs tangling in the chaos as the horde forced its way through the archway. A frenzied mix of undead and wolflike beasts, equally savage and bloodthirsty, burst forward.

Above, inky black winged creatures swarmed over the walls, diving with ferocious speed. Their attack was so sudden that Tora hurled herself off the battlement, landing with a bone-jarring crack on the stone tiles below. She gripped her axe tightly, spinning to meet two of the wolfen predators. The first lost its head in a single, precise arc of her blade. The second lunged, jaws agape, but before it could strike, Aeun swept through, snatching it from the air with a thunderous roar that shook the ground beneath them. Tora blinked in momentary shock, before throwing herself back into the fray.

Iniq swiftly leaped onto an old cart, shooting arrows with quick precision, attempting to thin the mass as it collided with them, taking down those who attempted to attack from the back.

Nem threw herself into the fray, all thoughts shoved far back in her mind.

"I'm up to ten! And the fun has just begun!" shouted Vega, her movements more akin to a dance than a battle. Her leg whirred, polearm flying, sweeping her opponents off their feet, before removing heads with the blade end.

Merrick's axe cleaved through an attacking undead, severing part of its already rotted face and carving away half its torso in one devastating swing as he responded.

"The more you speak, the more I want to *slice* through these undead abominations!"

"Aww, are you upset because you can't count past ten, my broody warrior? Or are you hurt that your wolf has taken down more foes than you?" Vega laughed, the cogs in her leg clicked as she dipped into a crouch, polearm flipping one janky undead man clean off his rotten feet.

Bo howled nearby, the sound almost jovial, which only seemed to make his master angrier, his foul uttering masked by the carnage in the air. Though they clashed with words, the hulking warrior instinctively guarded Vega's back, as she deflected a strike aimed at his exposed flank while his attention was elsewhere. They flowed together like water around stones, never straying far from each other, while their banter pinged back and forth like a ball game.

The creatures included the kind they'd encountered before – young and old beings missing limbs and rotten skin dangling from what was left. Winged beasts without eyes, their shrieks setting Nem's teeth on edge as she hurled herself between two, their gnashing teeth and raging wings slapping against her armour.

But the inky, four-eyed dogs were new.

Drool ran in strings from their jaws, matted fur in splotches on the skin hanging over their gangly bones. One flew at her, jaws wide, and Nem sidestepped, teeth clenched at the stench of its breath. The sights, the sounds, it all brought her back to the bridge, back to the pulse of her magic around her as a shield, the claws tearing against her skin, tears leaking down her cheeks. Faces agape, their strobing eyes alight with murderous intent as her magic – her bright, explosive magic – blew their skin, bones and wings into bloody dust.

She had felt unsteady back then, like the flickering flame of a newly lit candle – delicate, yet fierce. A fire newly forged. She'd felt… powerful, a barrel of gunpowder on the verge of detonation, a furnace roaring out of control. But at the heart of it all, as claws pierced through the sphere of light and power surrounding her – as they grazed her cheek, snagged her clothing, and scratched her skin – she'd felt alien. A stranger in her own body, a being not of this world. Fear had gripped her then, raw and primal, sinking deep into her core. Fear of *herself*.

Though she had triumphed over the horde on the bridge, the victory had left her shaken, uncertain of her magic and the devastation it could unleash.

And now, as they faced another onslaught, the battle raging around her and allies at her side, a new weight pressed down on her. The knowledge that she had once stood with the very man who might have created these horrors froze her in place. That she was *related* to such a person. Her doubt, heavy and unrelenting, bound her limbs like chains of lead.

The wolfen creature wheeled, quickly circling back, chittering like a deranged insect, claws scrabbling on stone. Its blood-red eyes streaked murderous light as it lunged again, aiming for her throat. Nem came to just in time to see a blur of black fur collide with the charging beast, their bodies slamming into a stack of nearby supply crates.

Her heart leapt into her throat as she screamed, "Krepth!"

When he emerged, in the form of his huge black wolf, Nem swallowed at the majesty of him. He stalked across the stone, his muscles rippling, catching the flicker of a spark-laden breeze. Dangerous, rumbling, *wild*.

Aeun passed above, snatching some of the undead that were attacking the Fury assassins on the battlements, a cloud of winged beasts snapping in her wake. Her pass threw up twirls of wind as Nem drew towards him.

Sparks flared around him, and then his form began to shift – pawfalls fading into the solid cadence of footsteps as he emerged human once more.

It was then she noticed: he wore nothing but his pants.

Nem's gaze swept over him unbidden. Dishevelled hair, eyes blazing with intensity. His bare chest, streaked with blood and sweat, revealed honed muscle carved by battle and the wild.

The sounds of the chaos around them came thundering back as something wailed over her shoulder. Before she could turn, Krepth's arm shot out, clasping the oncoming undead man by the throat, muscles bunching. Without looking away, he jerked his wrist, a *snap* silencing the creature's cries.

A shiver raced through her.

Gods… his body. Had it always been so sculpted? So unapologetically divine?

Krepth tilted his head, the motion more beast than man, his voice a low, wolfish growl.

"Distracted, Silver Moon?"

Her reply slipped out, unbidden and sharp. "Just keeping an eye on your back, Wolf."

His answering smirk had her knees weakening and her heart stuttering to near standstill.

She'd kick her own arse later about her stupid retort. She'd been watching his chest, not his Godsdamned *back*.

Iniq raised her arm urgently, shouting, "Nem! The portal! We must close it!"

Nem sprinted for the gates, but a trilling cry of pain brought her head up and her boots skidding on the bloody cobblestones.

Goosebumps prickled across her skin at the sound, a phantom pain seeping through the fragile bond that had formed between her and Aeun. Overhead, the dragon's shadow streaked across the ground, pursued by an even larger one. Dread crashed into Nem's chest as she stole a single, precious moment to assess the creature attacking Aeun – a winged beast far bigger than any she'd seen before, its body almost Aeun's size. Perhaps the ones they had fought until now were juveniles, and this was a full-grown adult. The beast lunged for Aeun's tail, massive teeth snapping shut just inches away. Like the others, it had no eyes, but its features were more pronounced, with spiralling horns jutting from its skull and tattered spines running down its back.

Nem sprang into motion, vaulting onto a cart before launching herself toward the battlements. She wove through the chaos of clashing bodies and flashing steel, her steps quick and sure as she raced toward the crumbling edge of the parapet. Shouts of warning were drowned beneath the roar of battle, but she didn't slow. Her muscles coiled, and in one fluid motion, she hurled herself off the edge and into the open air.

At that precise moment, Aeun swept past, her back angled toward the castle. Without hesitation, she caught Nem mid-air, the force of their momentum carrying them into a swift bank as Aeun tried to shake off her pursuer.

"You caught me," Nem gasped, leaning forward, adapting her body to her seat as Aeun angled into a sudden, steep climb. The creature in their pursuit screeched but did not relent, wingbeats thundering as it too lurched into a climb.

"I was not in need of your assistance," Aeun grunted, but Nem felt relief trickling into the bond. *"This one is stubborn and must be put down immediately."*

"Well, if you value the tip of your silver tail, let me help you before you lose it," Nem called out, her voice sharp with urgency. The castle quickly became a dark speck below, the chill of stormy clouds parting around them.

Nem twisted, gripping the prominent spine at the base of Aeun's

neck with one hand as she raised the other, unleashing a surge of magic. The blast struck the pursuing beast's head with a crackling force, drawing a shriek of pain – but it didn't slow. Instead, it lunged, teeth grazing Aeun's silver hide and ripping a few feathers from her haunch. Aeun let loose an enraged roar, the only warning Nem got before her wings tucked and they were suddenly in freefall.

Silver scraped silver as Nem's nails clawed for grip, half her body twisting painfully against the relentless wind. Aeun's head pointed down like an arrowhead, guiding their plummet, but the sheer force of air made it near impossible for Nem to press herself back against warm scales. Moisture gathered on her cheeks, whipped away in streaks as she blinked rapidly against the rushing current.

They sliced down through the clouds until they thinned, revealing the dark grassy pastures of the bluff below. The castle was a dark blot, like the centre of a target, bathed in the soft glow of dawn, while flashes of magic bloomed like fireworks around it, lighting up the castle where the fight still raged.

"Lend me your magic," called Aeun, her voice breathless as the school quickly began to double in size.

"What?" Nem cried through the whistle of wind and the shrieks of the beast still close behind.

"Your magic! Pour it into me, into my scales!" Aeun bellowed, crying out as the beast raked its teeth down her tail.

A conduit of light and an absorber of chaos.

Aeun's mental voice was a gentle yet firm stroke, *"I trusted you to release me from my binds. Now, it is your turn to trust me."*

Nem's magic had already risen, white light, surging heat and whipping chaos, making her skin radiate like a meteor. It bounced brilliantly off Aeun's scales, reflected across Nem's water-beaded leathers and armour.

Trust.

This bond between them – unexpected yet undeniably right – was still new, untested, and fragile. And yet, from the moment Nem had first laid eyes on the magnificent silver dragon, she had felt something deep and unshakable… a kindred connection, a familiarity that defied reason. Whatever it was, one truth had settle deep within her.

She trusted Aeun. And Aeun trusted her.

Nem directed her light against the scales, magic erupting from her palms like liquid gold, and before her eyes it patterned across Aeun's hide like cracks of lava, melding into the plates and feathers on her body. Energy hummed through the bond, and Nem felt heat rise under her, almost blistering.

"Hold on!" Aeun's voice rang through Nem's mind, and instinct took over. She ducked low, pressing herself against the dragon's back as Aeun twisted to face the snarling beast in pursuit, wings plastered against her body.

They plummeted toward the earth at a terrifying speed, but Nem didn't dare look, didn't allow fear to take root. Instead, she poured all she had into Aeun, her magic surging through her bones, roaring with wild abandon as it flooded into the dragon. Energy crackled along Aeun's scales, golden sparks snapping in the air like an unstable star on the verge of collapse.

Then, with a deafening roar, Aeun snapped her jaws open and unleashed a torrent of searing gold and silver fire. The blast struck the creature head-on, and its howl of agony hit Nem's ears like a physical blow. The sound was so fierce, so piercing, that she instinctively severed their connection, slapping her hands over her ears.

But it was enough. Aeun's power didn't wane. The magic-fed inferno consumed the beast in an unrelenting storm, reducing it to nothing but a plume of smoke and ash as dark as midnight.

Nem glanced over her shoulder and terror seized her chest. The ground was too close, approaching too fast. The castle loomed, so near that she could make out the alarmed faces of her Fury sisters standing on the battlements.

"Aeun!" she screamed.

With a cry, Aeun twisted sharply, wings snapping open at the last possible moment. The sudden drag caught the air, yanking them into a powerful surge that carried them just over the castle. The tips of Aeun's claws grazed a banner atop a towering spire, the fabric rippling violently in their wake.

A boom thundered at their back as the charred husk of the creature slammed into the field just shy of the castle.

Cheering sounded from the walls.

"They need you now, Silver Fury." Aeun's voice was exhausted but proud, and the same pride flared in Nem.

Sharing her magic had felt... amazing. Perhaps it had been adrenaline, the heat of the moment, but this time Nem hadn't felt apprehension, nor had memories of the bridge surfaced. This dragon, she was incredible, a marvel. She was an absorber of magic, and with it she could use a type of dragon fire that could defeat any foe.

For the first time in a long time, Nem felt hope alight in her heart, a sense of budding purpose, that she was useful to someone, even if that someone was a dragon. Her thoughts must have projected back to Aeun, because there was a smile in her voice when she whispered, *"Together, there is not much we cannot do. Now, go. Close that flame-blasted portal."*

Alighting briefly on the battlement, Aeun dipped her shoulder as Nem slid off, but as soon as her feet smacked the ground, her legs threatened to drop her. Before she could fall, strong hands grabbed her, dawn's rays haloing his lean form.

"Nem!"

Black eyes held hers, Krepth's face painted with dark blood, so dark it couldn't be his own. That thought uncoiled the anxiety in her chest – just a little.

Energy renewed in her limbs as she gasped, "I'm fine. Just getting used to riding a dragon, I think."

Heat seeped through her skin, drawing her gaze to where his large hand encircled her bicep, his olive skin striking against the pale glow of hers. When she looked up, their eyes met, and the weight in his dark gaze sent a ripple of unease through her.

He smiled, despite the discomfort their shared touch must have brought him, but there was a hollowness to his cheeks, a shadow lurking behind his usual brightness, that made her momentary elevation snuff out like a candle.

This was her doing, her power severing him from his own. It sent her heart stammering, instinct tightening its grip as her defences rose, settling into place like a well-worn shield. Krepth seemed determined not to let it show, his hand holding her firmly, canines flashing.

"Come on, Silver Moon. More creatures are coming through the portal, and we need you to close it."

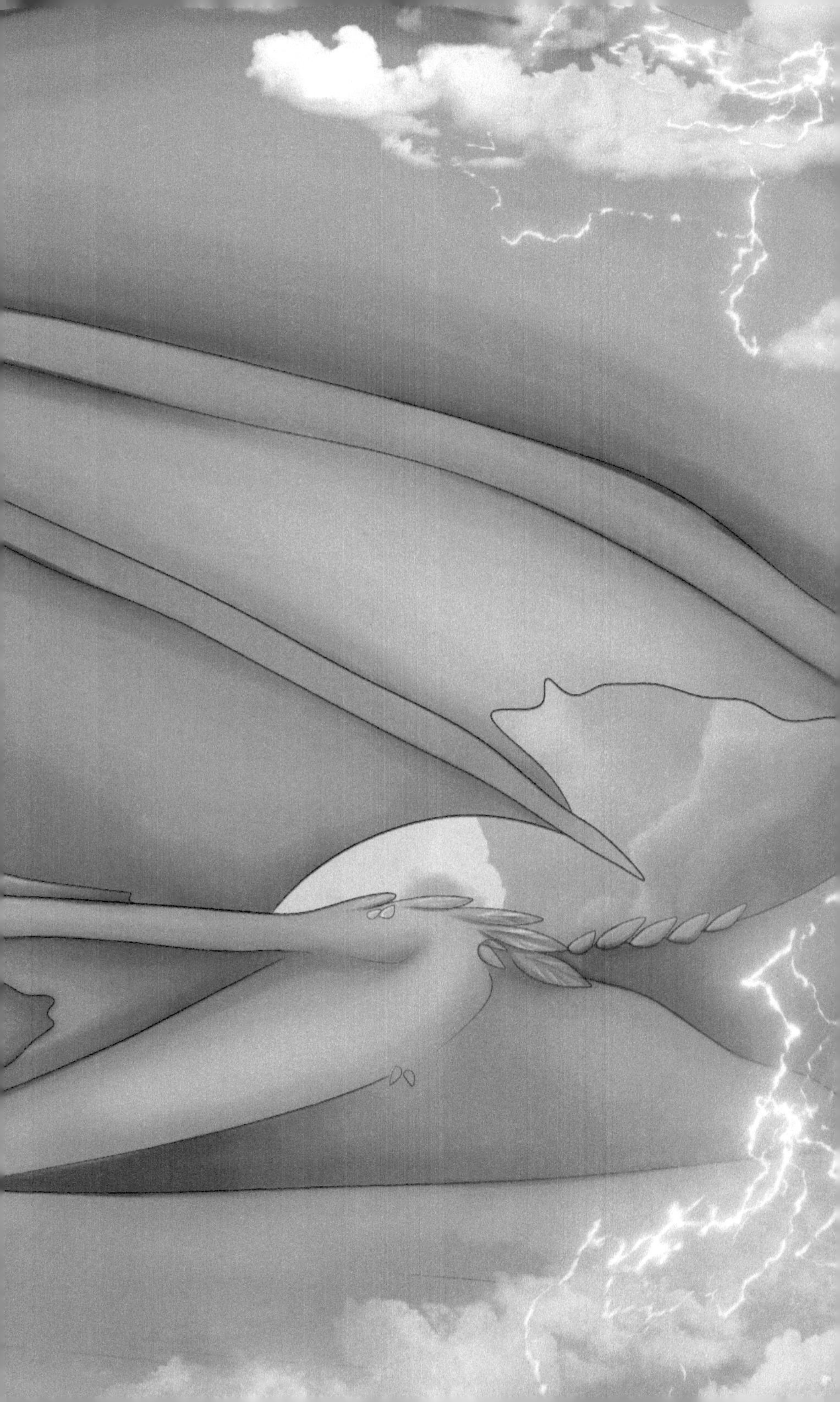

CHAPTER FIFTEEN

NEMESIS

They ran, weaving through chaos: flashes of hostile magic, the manic undead tangling with bright-haired assassins, snarling wolf-like creatures and winged abominations. Their focus was fixed on the gates ahead, the archway. Vega and Merrick now flanked Krepth and Nem, their forms glowing in her light, while Iniq held the rear, jogging backward and expertly firing arrows into the undead who dogged their steps.

The portal hovered just inches above the ground, a shimmering oval encircled by scorched and smouldering grass. Its jagged edges crackled with energy, throwing out sparks so violently that Nem had to strain to focus on the static glimpse of the world beyond.

A surge of desperation clenched her chest. That land held answers… answers she desperately needed. Was her father, Ares, there? Just beyond the flickering surface? Was that the magical purgatory the Gods had condemned him to?

Her emotions churned chaotically: anger, confusion, grief and questions clawed at her mind. Had she unknowingly played a role in the catastrophe that had nearly overrun Fythnar before? Did her presence here serve as a bridge, making it easier for her father and his creatures to invade their world? Was it because of her that he had escaped?

Nem was growing increasingly certain that the entity within the stone, the one responsible for Valdis's deranged crusade of vengeance, was none other than her father. His motivations in the vision were unmistakable – he had sought to destroy this world before. He had commanded a colossal beast, one that would have broken through into their world if not for Nocturne's intervention. The similarities were too strong to ignore.

"What are you waiting for? Close it, now!" Merrick bellowed. His battleaxe arced with deadly precision, shearing through a line of enemies lunging desperately.

"No pressure, huh, Merrick?" Nem snapped back, yanking on her sleeves.

Krepth stayed close, his presence a solid, unyielding force at her back. She could feel the radiating heat of him, like a furnace at her spine, and the weight of his sharp focus bore down on the nape of her neck. The tension in the air was palpable, an unspoken urgency hanging heavy between them. Every muscle in her body screamed for her to act, but something held her back.

A thump and a deranged scream preceded Vega's hooting voice. "Getting tired here – unlike you Fae, I don't have immortal strength to keep me going for hours." She chuckled and threw down another undead, tacking on, "Heh, the all-night mischief I could get up to!"

"Please don't start about your love life," muttered Iniq, and despite being human, the western warrior had no trouble hearing, letting loose another laugh.

Nem's brows pinched, hands raised as she fought for concentration.

"Now would be a great time to use that Goddess-gifted magic of yours, Silver Moon. I'm here, and I won't move from your side. You can do this; I know you can," Krepth said and Nem nodded in response, silently grateful.

An updraft swirled around them as Aeun soared overhead, her thunderous roar reverberating through the air and the ground beneath their feet. The winged creatures pursuing her had dwindled to just two. Banking sharply, her wingtips skimmed the tall grass, sending ripples through the field as Iniq loosed her arrows with deadly accuracy, dispatching the last of the airborne threats.

"Anytime now," Krepth uttered.

"Not you too," Nem growled back.

Aeun landed heavily nearby, the earth trembling under her weight. Her silver scales shimmered in the flickering torchlight and the portal's ethereal blue glow, though dark streaks of blood marred their brilliance. Her piercing azure eyes locked onto Nem, radiating an urgency that cut through the chaos like a blade.

"Close the rift," she commanded, her voice resonating in Nem's mind with unwavering resolve, her snarl reverberating across the physical space for all to hear. *"Before more come through."*

Krepth's brows arched pointedly, and Nem clenched her teeth.

Fine.

Heat doused her skin, and her light flared as Nem lifted her hands towards the portal. She ignored the fact that her fingers shook, that her silver nails reflected back her wide eyes, her look of uncertainty.

Her father... the land beyond the portal... the flickering thing before her held the answers she sought. Logic told her this wouldn't be the last portal to open, nor her final chance to uncover the truth. Ares was determined to breach their world, and if life had taught her one thing about the Gods, it was that their will was unstoppable. When they desired something, it was only a matter of time before it became reality.

"Nem!" a voice called out, but the cacophony of animalistic sounds from inside the portal and the chaos surrounding it drowned out everything else. Her magic surged, crackling to life. Sparks danced along her skin, and her eyes began to glow with an unearthly light.

A bubble of shimmering energy snapped into existence around

her, its iridescent surface sparking like a living shield. With a forceful will, she directed it toward the portal. When she'd closed the last one, it had simply… happened, guided by an instinct she didn't fully understand. She clung to that instinct now, hoping it would steer her again.

"Krepth," she whispered. "Stay back."

But something still held her back. Fear clawed at her throat, sharp and relentless, choking her breath. She gasped, the weight of the emotion a terrible, suffocating force. Her chest tightened as the beast of anxiety sank its claws deeper, paralysing her.

"Nem!" Krepth's voice cut through again, urgent and desperate. He was trying to reach her, sensing her distress, but the barrier of light kept him out. His presence tugged at her, his concern palpable, yet it wasn't enough to break the grip of the fear that had her mercilessly.

What if she lost control? What if she hurt her friends, standing far too close?

Suddenly, something pierced through her bubble – a flash of silver scales and glowing blue eyes. Aeun surged forward, her powerful body curving protectively around Nem. Her shimmering hide absorbed the chaotic swirl of magic that Nem struggled to control, the air around them humming with raw energy and the rippling growl rumbling from her chest.

Aeun's wings arched, creating a shelter around them as her lips curled back, her maw gaping open, her throat glowing with a rising fire. Her eyes blazed with their own otherworldly light, a magic that resonated with Nem's own. Their combined power radiated outward in an electrifying pulse, the sheer presence of the dragon pushing Nem's fear into the background, leaving only awe and a fleeting sense of invincibility in its wake.

Aeun absorbed the magic leaking from Nem's bubble, drawing it into her scales until they shimmered gold. Nem felt their connection again, as if the dragon had become an extension of her own power – a force she could command. Aeun wasn't just taking the magic; she was harnessing it, redirecting the wild energy into a secondary reservoir, ready for Nem to wield.

"Together," Aeun roared.

Together.

At the word, Nem's magic sparked anew, a forest fire raging through dried tinder. She threw her magic outward into a pulsing beam just as her mind screamed *"FIRE!"*

Aeun let loose a torrent of blazing golden fire, a mix of flame and lightning that slammed against the portal just as Nem's power did. Their combined magic coiled around the edges of the tear, intertwining with the blue sparks until the portal itself shuddered. It groaned, like a living creature resisting, straining under the force as it was compelled to yield and close.

Nem felt as if she were being torn apart, her body wracked with violent convulsions. Golden light burst from her eyes, wide and unblinking, teeth clenched as she struggled against the onslaught of chaotic visions flashing before her. They came in a blur, too fast to grasp. Fire and ice, wings and fangs. Silver scales shimmering, delicate hands aglow with the light of a thousand suns. Grass withering, soil rich with life disintegrating into ash beneath an unyielding torrent of blinding flame. The echo of laughter – childish, delighted – rang in her ears.

Then, in a sudden rush of clarity, the world snapped into focus: Nem stood alone on a hill, her arms raised high, glowing with radiant power. Before her, the world fractured and crumbled, breaking apart into ash as her form blazed brighter than the sun itself.

It was too much. Too much.

"Harmonia…" a voice crooned, as deep as a fissure in the earth, as smooth as silk. The image of a man's face coalesced, his lips curved in a smile, blue eyes and silver hair alight with her magic. "You are lost, but soon, my daughter, you will be found."

Ares.

She stood before the portal once more, the apocalyptic vision that had consumed her moments ago now vanished. In its place, the swirling portal shimmered, an outline of a figure rippling within. Ares lingered just beyond the glassy surface, his skin bathed in a storm of clashing lights, gold and blue from where Nem struggled to close the rift, and red from the hellscape he resided in. The resemblances between them, the dance of his short silver hair, the vivid blue of his eyes, the cut of his crescent smile, he was a mirror warrior image of herself, their shared blood undeniable in their features.

"Father," Nem breathed.

Ares' head cocked to the side, eyes narrowing. "You have reunited with the silver beast. Good."

Reunited? Had she met Aeun before? Conflicting emotions swirled within her, the faint hum of voices rising from the trinket around her neck. Why hadn't Aeun mentioned it?

"Look at you. You are growing into your power once more, and with the help of your catalyst, you will become the weapon I created you to be. This world, as many others, will learn your name, it will whisper across the webs of time and space, a warning. Conduit of light, absorber of chaos, breaker of bonds. Ender of worlds."

A conduit of light and an absorber of chaos.

Breaker of bonds.

Ender of worlds.

Nem's voice trembled despite her efforts to steady it, the power coursing through her – the golden fire, everything – too much to contain. "I don't understand. Why? Why use me to unleash chaos when *you* are the God of War?"

Ares sighed, as though her question was one he'd answered

countless times before. "Because, my daughter, for too long, the Gods have kept me confined, bound by their laws. They've blocked my every move, stifled my true power. I've spent ages creating demi-gods, each one a test. But you – you are different. You are the culmination of everything I've done. The perfect weapon, a vessel for chaos. You're not just a tool of destruction. You're the force that will break the chains they've placed on me."

Heart stuttering, Nem felt her world crumble. The truth weighed heavily on her: she wasn't just any Goddess-touched Fae, but one born of a violent, powerful God who had long been hindered by Zeus and the other Gods. The truth shattered the illusion she'd once held: she had not been chosen by chance but designed for a single purpose. Not for the retrieval of trinkets, as she had once believed, but for something far darker.

"You are... magnificent," Ares said, his voice low as he lifted a hand, his fingertips grazing the barrier, sending sparks and static sizzling across his skin. "Let me join you. With my guidance and your light, we could conquer worlds. You're not just a weapon; you're the beginning of the end. The spark that will ignite the bonfire of the world's destruction. Countless worlds, all waiting. There are more here, you know. More Gods exiled here, their children too, their power feared, their potential denied."

More Gods? More demi-gods like her?

Ares continued, his voice heavy with cold truth.

"Zeus ordered your dragon's kin to be slaughtered because silver dragons are volatile, unstable, and nearly powerless without a guide to fuel their fire. They claimed the dragons would be used for destruction."

Nem stole a quick glance at Aeun, her eyes catching the shimmering plumes of feathers that rippled around the dragon's serpentine head, flames bursting from her wide jaws in slow motion, her eyes aglow with an otherworldly light. Nem's gaze moved, taking in her friends, the Fury assassins, the Fates, all dotted around her now. Their clothes billowed in slow waves; eyes squinted as many shielded their faces from the radiant glow that emanated from her.

The world around Nem felt disconnected, everything moving at a different pace, as if time itself had shifted. In that moment, the space between her and Ares was a world apart from the one which enveloped everyone else. There was something undeniable about it: this moment belonged to Ares and her alone.

Nem dragged her gaze back to the portal. "Aeun is the last of her kind?"

Ares' head tipped in barely a nod.

"She has no magic unless she is given the power…" It wasn't a question exactly, but Nem needed to voice aloud the words to truly process them. "Feared because if given too much, she'd become some sort of magical ticking time bomb?"

"Does that upset you?" Ares said, voice flat despite the emotion the words might induce. "You do not need to be alone anymore, daughter. I'm here, and I will take care of you once more."

For the tiniest moment, Nem felt the part of her which had always yearned for her parents awakened, hopeful. Looking around, her gaze halted on the darkest figure nearby, held in place by what she saw.

Despite the barrier surrounding her and Aeun, Krepth had somehow broken through, his hand reaching out, just inches from her arm. His face – his strong, beautiful face – was turned toward her, and though everyone else was transfixed by the spectacle of the portal, the fire, and the blinding light, his eyes never wavered from her. The green of his gaze shimmered with her light, so vivid that she could see the shifting darkened shades within his irises, like the depths of a forest bathed in the first light of dawn. Still reaching for her, despite what one touch of her skin did to his magic.

"Have you never felt true happiness before, Nem?"

Another truth hit her with brutal clarity.

Her light. It hadn't risen from pure happiness, as Krepth had once claimed. No, it had risen because she had been siphoning his magic, taking without permission. That was why she felt energised when they touched, her body filling with sparks and light, with *feeling*, when all other times she felt almost numb.

Her heart ached. Though they constantly teetered between friendship and rivalry, Nem knew, deep down, that she cared for Krepth, despite what her actions might have suggested. She never wished to *take* from him. His magic. Or anything else.

A vision of his eyes appeared before her, so vivid, so open. There was no doubt in her mind that Krepth, the land's spymaster, would give her every ounce of magic he possessed, not just for her, but for all he loved – Arii, Elijah, and even those who had followed them across Fythnar: Tikkani, Quinn, Emerson, and Luc. The thought of her friends made Nem's chest tighten. Ares' plans cared nothing for them, or anyone who called Fythnar home. His offer, though twisted and tempting in a way, was not what she wanted.

It was the thought of leaving them behind – the idea of Krepth, her friends, being swept out of existence by the destruction Ares sought, jolted her back to reality.

"No," Nem whispered at first, barely audible, but then she said it more forcefully. "*No.*"

"No?" Ares' voice was sharp, the word a crack of disbelief.

"I will not help you conquer my home, nor will I assist you in destroying it." She gritted her teeth, her voice low and seething. "I will not let you through, or your beast."

Ares, whose expression had been soft, almost pleading, contorted into pure fury. Flames of red surged across his face, lips curling back over clenched teeth as his eyes blazed with the chaos of godly magic.

The transformation was instantaneous.

Emboldened, her magic crackling through her veins, Nem hurled her power into the portal, fighting to close it.

The world around them blurred and accelerated as she screamed, "I will die before I let you through, father!"

In a final, desperate attempt to force his way in, Ares lunged forward, his hands slashing through the glassy surface of the portal. His roar of rage was accompanied by the deafening wail of the titan that loomed behind him.

Nem jerked her arms back, and before she could even catch her breath, Ares recoiled just as the wild fissure began to shrink.

Then the portal snapped shut, Ares' rage echoing as the riot of sound was suddenly silenced.

Nem slammed to her knees, light fading from her skin and eyes. She retched as her magic retreated, seemingly just as eager to sever itself from the portal as Nem was. Hands found her shoulders, neck then face, and she tilted her head back to the full force of Krepth's concern.

"Silver Moon! Are you alright?"

In that moment, she couldn't even process the thought of their skin touching. Her heart still raced from the chance meeting with the God of War, her *father,* which had shaken her to the core. She let Krepth hold her, sinking into the brief comfort of his warmth, the wild scent of him grounding her as her emotions began to settle from the chaos inside.

Finally, mouth parched, she coughed, "Can someone else close it next time?"

His thumb feathered across her bottom lip, Krepth's relief a gust of breath over her temple as Nem pressed her forehead against his chin.

Bodies were gathering around them, and Nem gently pushed

herself up. Her gaze swept over the group, her heart racing as she searched her friends for any signs of injury. Around them, Fury assassins moved swiftly, gathering weapons and checking the bodies strewn across the grass, as dawn's rays appeared over the oceanic horizon. Nearby, Klotho, Etropos, and Lakhesis issued quiet commands, tending to their students, some barely more than children with youthful, wide-eyed faces.

To her relief, she saw no familiar, vibrant-haired casualties among them. Instead, there was an electric charge in the air – almost jubilant. The battle had been fierce, but the portal had opened in the worst possible location for the enemy. Here, the people were like tempered steel, warriors forged for moments like this. The fight wasn't a disaster; it was their calling. And they had answered it with deadly precision.

"You took your time to close the portal…" hissed Iniq, throwing her bow back into its leather holster. "What happened?"

Nem's lips opened to speak, but Krepth shifted between them, hand slightly raised. "Closing the portals is a new power, one she's still learning."

His defence of her caused warmth to spread through her chest, momentarily dousing the cold of her regret. She had taken too long, and had it been much longer, more of the minions of horror could have escaped through. Nem shivered at the thought, her eyes drifting up the slope of Krepth's bare bicep of their own accord. She wasn't sure how to explain what she'd seen, so she allowed her silence to stretch in answer for her. Iniq, blessedly, allowed her indignation to cool, her wrist dashing across her sweat-beaded brow.

"Well, it's done now. Let's hope Ares thinks again before taking on a castle full of assassins." Iniq placed her hands on her hips.

Vega chuckled as Merrick barked, "Did I miss the memo that this battle was to be conducted without shirts?"

Nem's vision was locked on the column of Krepth's neck, the glow of dawn bathing his skin, and every inch of his still bare, still very impressive, torso. Feeling flushed, she subtly looked away, to Vega who brushed a thumb across her bottom lip, eyes alight with mischievous sparks.

Nem stood, taking a reluctant yet needed half-step back while Krepth's attention shifted to Merrick, his soft chuckle like a lasso around Nem's heart.

"Not too late to strike up a last-minute shirtless wind down session," Vega mewed, brows waggling. Her humour cut through the tension, as if they hadn't just been set upon by otherworldly creatures.

Merrick's cheeks flushed with colour, before he holstered his axe with a little too much force. "Wouldn't want to show up the wolf."

"Keep your vest on, warrior," barked Iniq, surveying Aeun's still-shimmering hide for injuries. The dragon curved her head, huffing a breath, but allowed the Shifter to move closer to the shallow wound on her flank from the airborne battle. Bo snuffed at Aeun's foreclaws, tongue lolling, fur sodden in blood. Aeun trilled deeply, *"I am fine, Furry One."*

Seemingly satisfied, Bo trotted back to his master, tail high.

Tingles remained in Nem's fingertips, her eyes absently drifting to the sunrise over the crashing sea. "There will be more… Ares isn't done with us yet," she said.

"Dragon!" a voice rang out suddenly from the battlements, sharp and urgent. Nem's eyes followed the frantic gestures of the sentinel, pointing wildly out to sea. The rhythmic boom of massive wings reverberated in the air, and as her gaze locked on the approaching figure, she knew instantly that this dragon wasn't from Viridya, it was coming from the other direction.

Yet, despite its immense size and the ominous sight of its shadow stretching over the waves, something stirred within her. A deep, instinctual resonance hummed in her blood, the same pull she felt near the portals.

This dragon wasn't a threat… it was familiar. Its scales were as black as the void, its wings veined with patterns resembling glowing, charred fabric, and its body stretched longer than the average dragon. Crimson eyes, burning with intensity, gazed back, eyes that had once overseen Elijah's flight training, regarded Ariiaya's father with warmth, and spoken of a world beyond their own, a world where dragons waited, ready to answer the call to return home.

The dragon's teeth flashed in what could only be described as a draconic smile and on its back sat a familiar figure – a shock of white streaked through his dark hair, his hands raised in what might have been a friendly wave or a plea not to shoot.

Nocturne, the stranger from the land beyond.

A large object cut through the waves behind them, and it was then that Nem realised that the remains of a boat were being dragged by several ropes in the beast's talons.

Ignoring the protests behind her, Nem hurried towards the steps down to the beach, her focus locked on the figure and the colossal beast. The air seemed to hum with tension as they landed heavily on the beach, immense form dwarfing the arriving ring of people as they gathered on the sand.

"We meet again, Silver Fury," rumbled the Ouroboros.

CHAPTER SIXTEEN

KREPTH

Krepth was still struggling to steady his heart, willing his skin to lose its tension after witnessing the blinding light erupting from Nem's eyes. From every inch of pale skin that had been visible. He had watched her body seize as her power anchored her to the portal, fighting desperately to seal the rift.

Every fibre of his being had screamed to protect her, to break through the shield of energy surrounding her and Aeun, to offer his strength in her fight. But against such raw, unfamiliar magic, he felt like nothing more than a stone in a raging river – too far away to even brush a single strand of her moonlit hair.

He'd come close, pushed against the magic, against the pain; so close, yet it had felt like he was wading through wet sand.

Radiant, resplendent, a Goddess of light. Gods, she was magnificent.

Even hours later, as unusually warm beams of sunlight bathed their group , Krepth found his eyes unconsciously seeking her, tracing the curve of her neck, specked with remnants of battle still.

She was alright, thankfully preoccupied by the familiar pirates who limped up the shore as the assassins helped the bruised and battered crew of the torn-up ship.

"Valerie?" Nem called above the crash of waves, ducking under the dishevelled Captain's arm before she could collapse.

Despite looking near death, Valerie clutched her hat, waving it. "Fancy seeing you 'ere, Nemesis Rion! 'ello, wolfie!"

She coughed, and Krepth took up her other arm.

"What happened?" Krepth asked as they made their way towards the castle.

Another voice chimed in from behind as Lyda huffed into view, helping a young pirate woman with fantastically long dreadlocks. "Attacked. Was unexpected, being so far out to sea. But the portal just… tore into existence. Luckily, we were already heading away from it, so by the time a handful of winged terrors squeezed through, we were far enough away to flee."

"Not before we lost some crew. Fucking hell…" Valerie groaned. "The bloody thing was slowly growing wider as we fled. I fear how big it is now. How many more of the spawn have come through." She coughed again and they stopped to let her recover.

"This was not the reunion I'd thought we'd have after all these months. Would 'ave preferred to crack one of the expensive bottles of brandy th' King so generously let me swipe from the castle last I was there. It was on the deck of my–" Valerie looked back at the ship, wincing as the main mast chose that moment to crack and fall, the thunderous boom echoing across the beach. "–new ship."

"We are so sorry, Valerie." Nem said. "The Ouroboros and Nocturne… did they come to your aid?"

Valerie winced and nodded. "Uncanny affinity for those wretched portals, I remember. Must 'ave sensed it. I fear we'd still be on the waves, at the horrible creatures' mercy, if they hadn't have found us."

Nem and Krepth shared a look across the space between them.

The assassins found room for the pirates in the last few empty rooms of the school, the once elusive, ancient place bursting and busier than ever before.

A few hours later, beneath a canopy of golden sails set up for shade just outside the castle, in the grassy field where Aeun could join their meeting, Krepth played Valerie's words over again as his gaze found Nem once more.

She sat cross-legged on a cushion, silver hair pinned back from her face, skin fresh and clean after a bath in the school's magical healing tub. Her cheeks still carried a hint of pink from the heat of her soak, and her scars stood out as stark white lines across her cheek, her sapphire eyes fixed upon the platter of bread, cheese and fruits at the centre of their group.

He studied the crescents of her thick lashes on her cheekbones, over the blush that perhaps wasn't only to do with her bath. His mind slid back to a beam of light that had highlighted half of her beautiful face when he intercepted her in the hall a few hours ago, her hair still wet, her weathered robe cinched tight. He'd wanted to speak to her about what she'd seen in the Tapestry, and the pirates' arrival. He wanted to know what she was thinking, frustrated with the silence and bare glances she'd given him since the Ouroboros arrived.

For a moment, just after she'd closed the portal, when she'd pressed her face into his chest, he'd thought perhaps they were finally moving forward.

That she was finally ready to let him in.

Her scowl in the light of the window had told him he was delusional.

Krepth's hands found the stone window ledge as he lent in, despite the thin veil of forced outrage on Nem's face. He knew it was forced, because he could smell the delicate scent of something other than a sweet hint of juniper soap. A subtle, deeper scent that Krepth knew better than any other.

Arousal, quick and hot.

It had taken everything not to smirk, to be thrilled, so instead, he simply tilted his head, surveying her face.

"When are we to talk about what you saw through the Tapestry,

Silver Moon? Or are you going to make me work for it, as you do with all other pieces of information about your past?"

Nem's throat bobbed, her teeth pinching her bottom lip. "I never asked for your help."

He held in a groan. "We have been friends for too long for me *not* to want to help you, Nem."

"This isn't one of your missions. This isn't something you can gather information on, dissect into little pieces and trade in favours. This is… bigger than that. Far bigger than I ever imagined." Her gaze drew up to his, and he held it, determined to let her see how much he cared. Nem had always been good at reading people, and she was best handled with actions, rather than words.

She had studied him for a breath, fixed on his eyes, before she let loose a sigh. "Bigger than what is between us."

He knew she spoke of the ancient conflict between their kind. Shifters and Goddess-touched. About how she did everything she could to keep their skin from touching, despite the longing he saw in her eyes.

Nem clasped the amulet at her neck, the motion seemingly for comfort, before rolling her shoulders and taking a few steps his way.

"I heard you," he said as she attempted to push past, and his words made her pause, stiffen like a doe before a predator.

"What?" she replied, voice breathy, affected.

He turned, his fingertips itching with the urge to reach for her, to smooth away the storm of distress spreading across her face. But instead, he crossed his arms, tilting his head slightly.

"I heard what you said before you closed the portal. You've learned more about your past... about your family. Your *father*. You don't have to pull away from me, Silver Moon. You don't need to carry this burden alone."

He would keep telling her so until she finally believed it.

Nem's shoulders had drooped slightly, causing the edge of her robe to slip and reveal the subtle curve of her shoulder. A shadow danced along her collarbone, highlighting the faint outline of another scar beneath it. Gods, there were more remnants of the war etched into her skin than he'd realised, and the thought made his blood burn. Nem had always been guarded, careful with who she let in, and he'd always found himself walking a razor's edge with her.

But what had always drawn him to her wasn't just her beauty, but her unwavering strength and the loyalty that ran deeper than most could understand. He saw a vulnerability in her, that if she knew he saw, would leave him neutered. Yet, there was also a strength in her stoic demeanour that held him utterly captive.

It hadn't always been this way, this delicate dance of push and pull between them. They'd started as friends – or, at least, as friendly as a young Shifter could be with a Fury assassin. Krepth had discovered early on that he had a talent for sniffing out secrets, an uncanny knack for reading between the lines that made him invaluable. Soon enough, he became someone others sought out when they needed to hide or uncover something.

By the time he'd turned eighteen, Krepth had risen to become the land's spymaster, his network carefully built, his knowledge of the inner workings of numerous courts and factions proving essential in furthering the assassins' most perilous missions. His sharp mind and quiet presence made him a shadow in the darkness, yet a force to be reckoned with. That had brought the infamous 'Violet Assassin' to his corner of a dimly lit inn, a silver-haired, silent female standing sentry at her back.

Krepth remembered their first meeting so vividly. He'd quickly took the lead, guiding them through the bustling alleyways of Viridya's market as he directed Ariiaya and Nem towards a specific item needed for infiltrating a well-guarded, materialistic household.

Because of his shared history with Ariiaya, Krepth hadn't charged them for the information that day, glad to see his childhood friend alive and well, though hardened and honed. While Arii haggled with the stall keeper, Krepth lingered nearby, stealing a glance at Nemesis. She'd hung back, quietly keeping an eye on their surroundings. But something had caught the silver assassin's attention – a small stall with a purple sail, its neat rows of colourful soap bars emitting a whirlwind of tantalising, mixed scents. In a woven basket on the table were a few old tomes on astronomy and the stars, the tips of her fingers brushing the faded filagree on one particularly aged book.

Though Nemesis had been reluctant to speak much, Krepth had discovered that day that beneath her stoic exterior, the quiet assassin harboured a surprising fondness for scents and an even deeper curiosity about what lay beyond the stars. It was a connection they both shared, one that bridged the gap between their otherwise different worlds. As they spent more time together, they found common ground in conversations about how certain scents had a calming effect on them, and how staring at the stars was a simple yet comforting pastime that provided Krepth with solace. The exchange of these quiet, meaningful moments forged a bond between them, one that went beyond their roles as mere companions and veered into the territory of friendship. She was quietly kind, fiercely loyal, and her eyes… they were the most expressive part of her, often drawing him in completely. Though Nem wore a chip on her shoulder, one that made her chosen name feel fitting, she had a way of seeing beauty in the quiet moments. And Krepth couldn't deny the magnetic pull she had on him.

They also shared a fondness for Ariiaya, though neither of them ever openly discussed it with her. Emotions were a sensitive subject for assassins, and Krepth understood the need to tread carefully in that regard. Still, he couldn't resist pushing their buttons, delighting in the subtle hints of frustration or the fleeting spark of hidden laughter that would appear in their eyes. Nemesis was the easier of the two to crack, and there was something rewarding about seeing the faintest smile tug at her lips, especially when she'd quickly look away, as if caught off guard. It was a small, quiet victory after a long day.

Years flittered by and they continued a delicate dance, one where Krepth tried his best to respect boundaries with emotions, while also testing them. Their friendship deepened, and they spent more time together, often laying in the field just outside the forest border of Evergrave to watch the sky as it moved from afternoon to night. Often Arii was there too, the trio taking time away from their missions to relax and recoup; but sometimes it was just Krepth and Nem, and those moments felt as delicate as a fine fated string.

She'd tell him about their missions, and he'd tell her about his own, until one night they shared theories of what could be beyond the little constellations of light in the black blanket of sky. His fingers had touched hers, and after a moment of hesitation, they stroked his in return.

These meetings had became few and far between as their reputations became more severe, and Krepth had felt all the weight in that tiny touch of skin that no words could describe. He'd felt as if everything else melted away in those moments. The subtle little touches, the looks he caught when she was too slow to look away. Her carefully erected walls were lowered to him, and he had begun to believe there was possibility for more. He began to *want* more. Nem was quiet and reserved yet thoughtful and intelligent, and their conversations and banter were the highlight of his months when he finally got to see her.

Until had Krepth presented Nem with a gift, a little package wrapped in delicate blue tissue paper, tied with silver ribbon. Inside was an oval piece of soap, one that had been carved with such care that it looked like the moon plucked from the sky, imbued with a tiny hint of magic to make it glow, and the scent of the field they often spent time in. Moonlight and grass, morning dew and wildflowers. He'd thought it the perfect gift, a reminder of their shared moments.

The gift had the opposite effect.

Nem withdrew after that.

Though she appeared outwardly confident, Krepth could sense the quiet anxiety that weighed heavily on her shoulders, a burden made worse by the gaps in her memory. The uncertainty about her past and her own identity took a toll on her self-esteem. To be unable to remember where you came from or who you were before – it was something Krepth wasn't sure he could fully understand. It had a way of shutting Nemesis off from the world, making her wary of, if not entirely resistant to, acts of kindness. On top of that, her intense training as a Fury had stripped her of any connection to emotion, teaching her to sever bonds and trust no one.

But Krepth was inexorably drawn to her, chasing Nem with quiet determination, like a river carving its path.

Though she mostly resisted him, he could tell that while she was slowly beginning to explore her emotions, she wasn't entirely closed off to the idea of something more than friendship, particularly after she broke away from the Sisters of Fate in support of Ariiaya. He'd been with others over the years, hoping that those experiences might dull the fire he felt for her, but the moment her scowl and those piercing blue eyes were on him again, everything else faded into the background.

Then, atop the roof in Ayrith, they had kissed, and it was the most life-altering moment he'd ever known. In that instant, nothing else mattered. Thoughts and instincts vanished, leaving only her lips beneath his, her warm skin under his touch, her scent, the pounding rhythm of her heartbeat. It was all her, a beacon in the dark, absorbing every ounce of light from his world. For a fleeting moment, he believed she was finally letting herself relax with him, allowing herself to be happy – until her skin had begun to glow.

Nem was Goddess-touched, and she was fated to be *his* undoing.

Fate was a fucking cruel mistress; but one he was determined to defy.

Nem had seen more than what she'd told them just before the battle with the creatures from the void. He could scent the unease on her the entire time. She'd uttered the word 'Father' as light had poured from her eyes, just as the portal had snapped closed.

Father.

She finally knew something of her origins, and she was hiding that knowledge from them. Krepth was determined to uncover the reason – not for his own sake, but because, as always, he wanted to help her. Nem had simply remained silent, clutching the robe, staring at Krepth's still-soiled feet. He had whispered that he'd find her later, that when she was ready, she could talk to him about what she'd seen. Nem had nodded, turning to leave him alone in the hall.

Now, Krepth pushed aside his spiralling thoughts to return to their meeting at hand in the field outside the School of Magic.

He fixed his glare on the Ouroboros and said, "You're later than I expected, considering the magical shitshow that's been going on around here lately."

He turned to Nocturne, noting the gloves on his steepled hands. Krepth willed his heart to calm on the wake of his memories, but despite his best efforts, his gaze still travelled back to Nem.

Although Krepth had addressed the dragon Shifter, Noct took it upon himself to speak.

"We were..." he began, pausing to run a hand through his short, silver-streaked hair, before finishing in a low, rough tone, "preoccupied."

Ouro's crimson eyes darkened, even in the muted, overcast light.

"We discovered the ship after sensing a disturbance out at sea. We went to investigate, intending to circle back to Viridya afterwards. There was another portal, and unlike the ones your Queen's ravens have been reporting, larger. We have come to warn you all, and we have come to help."

Vega, chewing a slice of bread, glanced up. "How in Fythnar are we supposed to face a portal over the fucking sea?"

Merrick leaned forward, his large hand resting on his knees, his expression taut. "We are to trust a man who shifted from a dragon? What sorcery is this?"

Iniq intervened. "If we are to trust anyone, we can trust them."

That seemed to placate the southern warrior, who leaned back, arms crossing his broad chest. Merrick remained silent, considering, gaze skipping from one guest to the other while his dire wolf, Bo, gnawed a thick piece of dried meat.

"There is more," Ouro cut in, tightening his thick black cloak around his shoulders. "The portal where we found the ship is *growing*, to allow something far larger to come through. I could sense a presence beyond it, something I have only sensed once before, during the war that almost ended this land one year ago."

"You speak of the titan, do you not?" Aeun's voice was soft but sharp, her neck tilted as she fixed her gaze on her kin. Her cheeks crinkled with the glint of her teeth, scars more pronounced as her eyes narrowed. Though her words carried to the entire party, they were meant for Ouro alone. *"Ares' beast, his world-ending puppet. Is that the threat you've come to warn us of?"*

After the battle, Aeun had begun to communicate with them all, saving Nem from being a translator.

"Correct," the male affirmed, his tone betraying no surprise at Aeun's knowledge. "It will stop at nothing to please its master, and that master seeks to reclaim what he lost. But you're aware of what he's after, aren't you, *Klad'ir?*"

Krepth studied the Shifter, running the strange word through his mind, but it didn't ring any bells.

Aeun's shoulder blades shifted, the silver plumes of her crest rising in a visible sign of irritation. *"I haven't been called that in years."*

"Well, you are the last of your kind. Once upon a time, *Klad'ir* – or," Nocturne leaned in, resting his chin on his gloved hands and glancing around the group. "Aetherion dragons, were among the most feared and coveted to bond with. Your power, or rather, what you can absorb, is almost limitless." There was a note of awe in Nocturne's voice that piqued Krepth's curiosity.

And raised a shuddering feeling across his nape, instincts whispering.

Suspicion.

"And the destruction you can create with that power is just as limitless still," added Ouro, crimson gaze piercing.

"Aetherion dragons?" Vega asked, leaning forward with her hands resting on her crossed legs. "So, Ares believes he has some sort of claim on Aeun because she's... a rare magical bomb?"

"In that case, it makes sense why we haven't seen any other silver-hued dragons since the war," Iniq said, her sharp eyes flicking between Nocturne and Ouro, studying them like an owl sizing up its prey in the dark. "And you mentioned a bond. Can unique connections be formed with dragons, like a life bond?"

Krepth's gaze shifted toward Nem without hesitation, noting the slight twitch in her brow. Her expression remained otherwise unreadable. She already knew this, didn't she?

"In our land," Nocturne began, "dragons are given as eggs, usually at the birth of a royal or someone of significance – power, magic or status. They start out colourless, but as the dragon grows, the egg changes, and when it hatches, the dragon's affinity is revealed.

Aetherion dragons are incredibly rare, said to be gifted to Gods. Their power has left a bloody mark on our history; their destruction, when bonded to the wrong hands, has brought devastation to our land. Because of this, whenever one was discovered – whether bonded or wild – it was…" Nocturne paused, his eyes flickering to Aeun, who remained rigid.

"Killed," Aeun finished for him, her jaw snapping as she mentally spoke the word.

There. Krepth noted the slight twitch in Nem's scarred cheek, before her eyes abruptly lifted and locked onto his. He didn't look away, struck by the sudden, almost otherworldly glimmer in her piercing gaze.

Gifted to Gods... and perhaps demi-gods too?

Krepth pressed his tongue to the back of his teeth, the pieces of the puzzle slowly slipping into place.

Ouro spoke slowly, choosing each word with care. "One such bond exists between this *Klad'ir*... and someone here, in this realm."

"Aeun isn't bonded to Ares?" Merrick asked, his voice carrying a hint of confusion, earning him an intense glare from the silver dragon. The warrior, however, didn't seem to notice, his attention fully absorbed by the Ouroboros. Vega pinched the bridge of her nose as Merrick tacked on, "He *is* a God, correct?"

The Three Fates watched the exchange quietly, their golden eyes gleaming with knowing intent. Krepth found himself wondering how much they truly understood, and how much they had yet to reveal. If this was news to them too.

Aeun shifted, feathers bristling, *"I am not bonded to Ares."*

She snapped, but her voice lacked bite.

Merrick remained silent, thoughtful. No one asked the question again, and Krepth guessed that the puzzle was slipping into place for the others too.

"Out there, just beyond the horizon, a new disturbance brews. One far larger than the rifts you've encountered on land," Ouro said, his voice more sombre than usual. "Ares has been probing the veils between realms, searching for the thinnest points. He intends to launch his final assault over the ocean. Magic weakens in water, and though it will be a challenge, he plans to unleash his hoard despite the risks, making one last effort to set his beast loose. He knows such terrain will be a challenge for us to defend, too." Normally lilted with warmth, Ouro's voice now carried a trace of worry. "If we do not act, he will not fail this time."

Aeun's head lifted, her gaze turning westward, toward the horizon stretching across the sea. *I feel it, too.*

"King Eliverus and Queen Ariiaya have received our message about the ship, and in turn about the portal sighting," Klotho added, stabbing a delicate blade through a square of melon and tilting it to her lips. "They'll arrive at dawn, along with the heads of all the other courts. We've given them everything we know about Ares and his plans, urging them to prepare their armies for the sea. It seems Fythnar will rally together once more to fight."

"Another war," growled Merrick, hand resting on Bo's head, scratching. "And above sea no less. The peace was short lived."

Iniq stood, sweeping her hand toward Aeun. "If the dragon is what he wants, should we not simply give her to him? Wouldn't that save this world from being plunged into another war?" Her voice was calm and practical, without a trace of anger. She looked at Aeun, her lips turning down into an apologetic frown. "I'm sorry to suggest it, forgive me, but I only consider the fate of our land."

Aeun's lips curled over her serrated teeth, but the grimace was not one of threat, more as if she were holding back the urge to agree, against her own self-preservation.

"Though Ares desires the *Klad'ir*, possessing Aeun is not the only reason the God of War is drawn to your realm," Ouro said, his eyes closing as he crossed his arms over his chest.

As the conversation intensified, voices rose in a chorus of conflicting opinions, mixing with the sound of the sea, as if the waves themselves were offering their own perspective. Krepth stayed silent, watching, his mind sorting through the information he'd gathered so far. Dread weighted his stomach.

He already knew the answer.

"He is trying to get to me," Nem's voice cut through the rising tide of discussion, carrying above the crash of the nearby waves. Everyone froze, shifting their attention to her. The air seemed to hold its breath, so thick with tension that even the sea seemed to pause. "Ares wants this world because of... me."

Krepth didn't feel the surprise he expected, only a hollowing in his stomach at the weight of what Nem was revealing. He'd always known she wasn't of this realm – a Fae with ties to two worlds – but this... that she was somehow connected to the God of War. It was unexpected, yet at the same time, it made a strange kind of sense.

Nem blew out a breath, her shoulders rolling with resolve as she said, "I'm ready to tell you what I saw in the Tapestry."

Chapter Seventeen

Nemesis

Nem had expected worse.

Although she had uncovered more about her origins, she was still searching for the truth of what she truly was, and what that meant for her bond with Krepth. The Goddess-touched, or demi-gods, were said to exist for one purpose: to retrieve the objects of power. At least, that was what she had been told. Yet everything she had learned so far whispered of another design. Her skin did not merely react to magic; it devoured it, severing its source whenever she touched another wielder. Ares had wielded her as a weapon, and her banishment, coupled with the vision she had seen woven into the Tapestry, made that undeniable. But nowhere had there been mention of the objects of power, or how they might shape her existence now. Perhaps demi-gods had been bred for many purposes: destruction, chaos, protection, order. Perhaps only in this realm had they been set upon the path of retrieving artefacts.

Her recounting of the vision silenced their gathering for a time. Vega was the first to break it, whistling low. "At least now we know what he wants. Makes it easier to plan… though I'd prefer he had his eye on Merrick instead." Her tone was bright, almost playful, a spark intended to lighten rather than wound. Merrick rolled his eyes but did not contradict her, and his own words were heavy with concern as he pressed on about how they might keep Ares from laying claim to his daughter. Iniq frowned, as though seeing patterns that unsettled even her, and though she asked questions, Nem heard unease threaded through every one. Krepth alone kept his gaze fixed, unblinking, the muscles in his jaw working as he guided the discussion toward defence, resistance, survival. That much she expected of him.

Ouro and Noct agreed without hesitation. Ares did not hunger for strength alone; he hungered for dominion, and that was reason enough to end him.

What she had not expected was the agreement of the Fates. Their voices, usually divided in nuance if not in conclusion, chimed as one: the God's designs were real, and Nem stood at the centre of them. The weight of that assent pressed on her ribs long after the conversation dissolved, leaving her both relieved and afraid.

The rhythmic clash of weapons soon rose to fill the silence they left behind, steel ringing against steel in the cadence of an old song. Vega and Merrick sparred in the golden rays of the fading afternoon, the ocean stretching endlessly beyond the edge of the cliff where they trained. Its deep blue expanse typically serene, though tonight, it seemed to hold its breath. The School of Fate loomed in the distance, an ancient sentinel basking lazily in the sun's dwindling light, much like an old cat soaking up the last warmth of the day.

Yet beneath the beauty of the moment, an unshakable tension lingered. It was the hush before the tempest, the fragile silence before the world would be upended. By morning, the storm would come – and with it, their fleeting peace would be torn away like a roof ripped from its rafters.

The sulfuric breeze tangled with Nem's unbound hair as she stood on the crest, a short distance from the cliff edge, her attention fixated upon the horizon. She pulled her cloak a little tighter, the shiver tracing her spine not from the cooling breeze but the thoughts swirling through her mind. The Cloak of Protection warmed around her, humming with a now-familiar sort of magic, its lightened ends kissing the grass.

The crew of the ship were settled, some helping around the castle grounds, their wounds bandaged and their spirits higher. Valerie had seen herself to the kitchens, claiming access to their stores of wine would help heal her two broken ribs, while Lyda salvaged supplies from the wrecked ship with a handful of pirates. Nem watched them as they piled burlap sacks and barrels on laid-out canvas further up the beach, trudging back and forth through the calm, lapping waves.

"We could go now, fly out and meet Ares head on before the armies arrive."

Aeun, who stood nearby while being closely inspected by Nocturne, tilted her head towards Nem. *"But that is not what you truly wish to do, is it, Silver One?"*

No… it was not.

Nem took a deep breath. "Why didn't you tell me that you were my bonded dragon? That we've met before?" she whispered, the hurt of the secret still fresh.

Aeun's gaze remained steady, unwavering as she met her eyes. There was no point in masking her emotions – Aeun could read her with an attunement she had only known once before, when she had shared the life bond with Ariiaya.

A quiet moment passed before Aeun spoke, her voice firm, unapologetic.

"I knew your memory had been taken. What I did not know was what kind of being you had become. For years, I evaded your father's grasp, years without feeling magic – your magic – coursing through me. I was weak, a hollow shell skirting the edges of a predator's reach. And when one spends so long running, fearing, surviving in solitude… one learns to be wary of everyone. Even those they once trusted with their life."

Nem blew out a breath, grateful for the dragon's honesty. One question rose, and she asked it softly, "Did I... use you to cause destruction for Ares?"

Aeun's gaze was steady and unblinking. *"You were young when you were taken from your mother. You were impressionable, eager to fill the emptiness her absence left, and to believe the promise of a family your father offered. I do not hold you to your actions in the past."*

Nem scuffed at a clump of grass with her boot. "So... I was brainwashed by Ares?"

Aeun rumbled, glancing at Noct, who had just completed a crescent around her flank. *"In a way. But you felt remorse for the destruction you caused under Ares' command. As still do I."*

This new knowledge eased the sting of what she had seen in the visions, though a weight still pressed in her chest. "No wonder you didn't trust me when you first arrived."

Aeun had endured more than Nem could truly comprehend, and because she was Nem's, a dark regret spread through her. Nem wished she could have been there to protect her after they'd been separated. Feeling the need to move, Nem shook out her limbs as if that would ease the aches.

"Dwelling on regrets will not fortify the future. You were never cruel to me, Silver One. We are together now, and we will not *be separated again."* Aeun lowered her head as Nem approached, the beast's words igniting a fire within her heart.

"The feathers on your crown shimmer in the light," Noct observed, pausing by Aeun's left flank. His fingers rested against his chin, a slow smile spreading across his lips. "And your scales... they're like living mirrors, reflecting and absorbing the light all at once. Remarkable."

Nem's fingers tentatively smoothed against Aeun's muzzle, between the twin ridges of her nostrils, her scales cool to the touch.

"The human longs for a dragon of his own," Aeun mused privately for only Nem to hear, tilting her wing just enough to send a soft gust of air toward Nocturne. His laughter bubbled up as he swiped at his tousled hair, smoothing it back with a playful shake of his head. *"Desperation seeps from his skin, from his pores. Poor mortal."*

Nem's gaze lingered on Nocturne, truly seeing him for the first time in a long while. He looked paler than before, the angles of his face subtly sharper, as if time – or something else – had been quietly carving at him. Her eyes flickered to his hands, gloved despite the mild air. The leather was thin, supple, built for dexterity rather than warmth. Not a barrier against the cold, but a tool, a necessity. She'd never really gotten to know the man, but Arii trusted him, and that was good enough for her.

He had spoken of bonding dragons with such certainty, and yet Nem realised she had never really asked about his world, never sought to understand what shaped that certainty. The thought settled uneasily in her chest.

"Noct, do you have a bonded dragon?" The question was blunt, lacking any softness, but Nem needed to see his reaction. And there it was – subtle, but unmistakable. His brows knit together, his gaze shifting from Aeun to the restless sea. Slowly, his hands retreated into the pockets of his long overcoat, as if seeking refuge.

"I was given an egg at birth," he said, his voice quieter now. A breath slipped from his lips, his eyes lifting to the cloud-laden afternoon sky. "But mine never hatched."

A ripple of sadness drifted through the bond, quiet but undeniable. Aeun shifted a wing behind Noct in a silent gesture of sympathy. There was something different in the way she regarded him – not just with familiarity, but with an unspoken understanding, as if sensing something buried beneath his skin. Or perhaps it was simply that he, like her, belonged to the same world.

"Is that… normal?" Nem asked softly, though her heart was already deducing the answer.

Noct turned slightly, his mismatched eyes catching hers over his shoulder. The clang of training weapons rang through the air, filling the brief silence before he spoke. "Before me, it hadn't happened in over three hundred years."

Nem's throat tightened. "I'm so sorry." She shifted her weight, reaching out to Aeun, fingers brushing the soft skin beneath the dragon's chin. She wished she could remember the moment she'd been given Aeun's egg. The moment she'd hatched.

A low grumble vibrated through Aeun's chest, sensitive but not unwelcome. She leaned into the touch.

Noct merely lifted his shoulders in a casual shrug, the motion effortless, like a duck letting water slide off its back. "I've had years to accept it. It just wasn't my fate. I like to think I was meant for something else. If nothing else, it's only made me more eager to learn about them."

"It is admirable that you do not hold a grudge."

Noct's grin sharpened, a flicker of something unreadable in his gaze. "Not with the dragons… no."

Nem scratched at Aeun's neck, and her mouth opened to ask more but the sound of a loud, obnoxious curse snatched the voice from her lips.

"Frosted fucking bear fangs! You almost took my fingers off!" Merrick bellowed, shaking his hand as if to rid it of the sting, his battle axe planted in the dirt at his feet.

Nearby, Bo yipped in delight, utterly unbothered by his master's distress. The massive wolf had claimed a bone nearly the size of his own head from the kitchens, pinning it beneath his forepaws as his tail whipped furiously.

Vega's laughter rang out, as she danced a step backward, twirling her polearm with effortless grace. The weapon spun until it aligned neatly with her whirring, gilded wooden leg, a perfect extension of her fluid movements. Brushing back her thick fringe, she shot Merrick a wicked grin, breathless but triumphant.

"Too slow, southie! All those years freezing in the snow must have left your joints crusted over like forgotten stones!"

Merrick scowled, flexing his fingers with exaggerated care.

"Beginner's luck. You keep swinging mindlessly like that, and I'll be the one digging *you* out of the dirt next time," he groused, snatching his axe from the ground in a shower of dirt, wiping the blade clean while mumbling further, unintelligible obscurities.

Bo barked in agreement, though whether he was siding with his master or simply excited about his bone remained anyone's guess.

Aeun's lips curled, a ripple passing over her teeth. *"The redhead wants the snow warrior,"* she mused, her voice edged with quiet amusement. *"And though he pretends otherwise, his desire for her burns far hotter."*

Nem watched, assessing as Vega's polearm slipping effortlessly into the narrow space between the battle axe's blade and handle, stopping the strike dead. Their faces hovered inches apart, Merrick's twisted into a low, frustrated growl, while Vega's stretched into a wide, taunting grin, the gleam in her eyes daring him to push harder.

Footsteps crunched over the dirt, two figures approaching. Without breaking her stance, Vega called out, her voice light and teasing. "Hey, beautiful!"

Iniq halted beside them, hands settling on her hips, gaze flicking between the two warriors locked in their playful battle. Krepth, who'd accompanied her, headed Nem's way.

Then, just as Nem thought Aeun had said her piece, the dragon added, almost lazily, *"They both desire the Shifter female, too. And she, them."*

Nem schooled her expression into careful neutrality. Merrick's gaze slid from Vega to Iniq, his stern brows softening, lips parting, pupils dilating. Both warriors stood rooted, breaths in sync, attention zeroed. Nem's gaze flicked to Iniq, usually so composed, now betraying herself with the soft flush dusting her cheeks. Vega's attraction to both sexes wasn't exactly a surprise… but Iniq's reaction? That was unexpected.

"Vega," Iniq cleared her throat, her voice carefully even as she nodded, "Merrick. Playtime is over. We need help setting up additional tents for the incoming forces."

Vega didn't step back immediately, her polearm still locked against Merrick's axe, the playfulness in her eyes giving way to something sharper, something considering. Then, with a deliberate roll of her shoulders, she withdrew, spinning her weapon with a flourish.

Merrick snorted, retrieving his axe from where it had stalled mid-swing. "Hope the incoming forces are less demanding than you lot."

Bo barked in response, rising to his paws before clamping his jaws around the middle of his bone, tail held high as he began trotting back towards the castle.

Krepth's chuckle drew warm fingers across Nem's skin. "He hasn't met Commander Sybell yet, has he?"

"I fear not," sighed Nem.

As Merrick's dire wolf trotted ahead, the three warriors followed in its wake, their voices dissolving into the rising sea breeze. Nem exhaled, watching them go. "Standing at the edge of another war… I truly believed we had left the days of blood and ruin behind."

Krepth remained uncharacteristically silent, arms folded across his chest, gaze distant. Above them, the rhythmic beat of Aeun's wings filled the air, the gusts from her ascent tugging at their cloaks.

"Heading back now, right, Noct?" There was a tone in Krepth's voice that Nem couldn't quite read, drawing her attention to both men.

Noct's smirk deepened as he stretched. "Right, right." With an easy stride, he turned toward the castle.

Aeun's voice curled through her mind like a soft whisper on the wind. *"Spend some time with your Shifter, Silver One. Tomorrow's fate is still uncertain."*

Tomorrow's fate was uncertain, but one truth remained: blood would be spilled, magic would ignite the skies, and the battle to come would shake the very foundations of their world. By its end, their land would either lie in ruin, or one vengeful deity would be cast back into the purgatory he had clawed so desperately to escape.

Perhaps it was her shared blood with Ares that stirred the weight of dread in her chest, eclipsing even the faintest glimmer of hope. Or perhaps it was the certainty that war never came without a cost – that death was inevitable, and she was still barely grasping the depths of her magic, still barely understanding the connection she now shared with Aeun, and with Ares.

And then there was the man beside her… No longer the enemy she had once believed. Whatever lay between them remained undefined, a path uncharted, its course still uncertain.

She was no longer who she had been. Something had shifted, something irrevocable. She stood on the precipice of fate itself… either the force that would save this land or the one who would see it fall to ruin.

Her thoughts splintered as warmth curled around her fingers, grounding her in the present. She looked up, meeting eyes like cut emeralds, steady and unyielding.

Krepth's voice was barely a whisper. "Time to find out where you came from, Nem. Come for a walk with me?"

She pushed a breath through her lips, glad that a lighter note had entered Krepth's voice. He held out a hand to her, and after a brief moment of staring at his offering, his long fingers, the callused palm, she accepted, placing her hand in his.

Something shifted in the moment.

No longer an enemy… not that he ever truly was.

Chapter Eighteen

Nemesis

Fingers entwined, Nem let Krepth guide her down to the shore, where they slipped off their boots and stepped onto the cool sand. The gentle waves lapped at their bare feet, the tide a rhythmic whisper. Above them, the sun lingered on the horizon, its fiery orange glow fading into soft pinks and purples that bled into the encroaching twilight. Wisps of clouds, brushed with lavender and rose, drifted lazily, catching the last traces of light.

Where the sky met the sea, the horizon blurred into an endless, tranquil expanse, far calmer than the storm of thoughts twisting inside her. This stretch of beach, with its rugged cliffs and the imposing silhouette of the castle on the bluff, was where she had first awakened. Her past had been nothing but a void, her history a whisper lost on the ocean breeze.

Nem had returned here countless times in the years since that day, using the spot to shout her frustration to the sky, where her cries were swallowed by the sea. A place where none witnessed her pain but the ocean, which had seemingly birthed her. The memory of her fingers curling in the sodden sand, teeth covered in the grit of salt and sea, her hair limp against her young cheeks, was one which never truly left her mind.

The moment she named herself, her heart hurting, her chest filling with unexplained anger.

She'd added her surname later, hearing one of the Fates murmur the ancient Fae word for 'lost'. It'd felt fitting. Now, standing on the spot with Krepth's warm fingers curling around hers, with the knowledge of her true name, her true origins, it was hard not to feel conflicted.

She was Harmonia, a demi-goddess born of a Fae and the God of War, bred with the purpose of ending worlds with her bond to an Aetherion dragon.

Never in her wildest dreams had she imagined this to be her fate. She had once believed her parents had cast her into the sea, an unwanted burden discarded without a second thought. Or perhaps she had been the lone survivor of a tragic shipwreck, her family swallowed by the jaws of ravenous sea serpents while she alone was spared by cruel chance. Both scenarios left her bitter, angry at herself, the universe, and she'd believed her ire to be deserving, that all had been because of *her*.

She hadn't understood it at the time, but she had been filled with a quiet smoulder, an unspoken fire, and a slow-burning, all-consuming *rage*. The Fates taught her to suppress the fire, place it away lest it distract her, but never did it truly go away.

The sea had given her life, nameless and devoid of memory. With sand tangled in her hair, salt clinging to her lips, and an unbidden fury burning in her heart, she chose a name for herself.

Nemesis.

A choice that now seemed like cruel irony, as though fate had conspired to make it fit. She was this world's nemesis – its reckoning, its potential destroyer.

A conduit of light and an absorber of chaos.
Breaker of bonds.
Ender of worlds.

"Silver Moon, I can hear the grinding of your teeth over the crash of the waves." Krepth's voice was gentle, and Nem tilted her head to gaze at him, sighing out a breath when she met his dark charcoal eyes. "I know what this spot means to you. We can go, if it makes you uncomfortable," he added.

Despite her touch stealing his magic, his fingers remained firmly twined with hers.

"I'm not the one who is uncomfortable right now though, am I?" A note of bitterness she could not stop entered her tone as she ran her gaze over his face. The sea breeze swept his hair aside, leaving his open stare of her unobscured.

There was no bitterness in his expression, no pain, no anger. Only an open awe she'd seen a few times before, when she'd allowed herself brief moments to glance at him before looking away.

Nem hurried to speak, needing to fill the building tense silence with something other than the sparks fluttering through her skin from their hands. When Krepth didn't break their link, she lifted her free hand before them, turning it over as light shimmered through her skin.

"My light, this power, it is not born of happiness, or hope. It is *stolen*, a lecherous thing that takes without permission. This is far worse than I'd ever expected." She swallowed against rising emotion, considering locking it away as she'd been trained. But instead, she let the emotions stab at her insides, believing she was deserving of the pain.

"I wasn't born to retrieve the objects of power; I was born to use them to end worlds. Siphon their power to make myself stronger, until I am unstoppable. It doesn't just stop at the artefacts; it expands to other sources of magic. People, places of magic, the possibilities are endless."

Krepth was silent for a moment, watching her with that calculating way of his. "That may be what your fate was intended to be, Nem, but you know as well as I do that fate is never truly set in stone. It can be weaved, manipulated, *changed*."

He shifted, gently taking her free hand as he guided her to face him. Her hair cascaded over her scarred cheek, and she instinctively lowered her face, self-conscious. But his fingertips found her chin, lifting her gaze back to his.

"I, like the others in that castle, believe you are meant to wield the objects and your bond with Aeun to protect your home, to seal the rifts and keep Fythnar safe. That's why they were entrusted to you."

Soft voices whispered at the edges of her mind, words of encouragement flowing from the locket at her neck. Her star-speckled cloak wrapped around her in quiet affirmation. The sword remained in her room up at the castle, but she could almost feel its distant hum, responding to the flickering embers of hope which Krepth's words had ignited within her.

"Does it not disgust you that I'm the daughter of a God whose name is synonymous with blood and destruction? That I share blood with a monster – a man so dangerous the highest deities condemned him to purgatory?"

"That doesn't change how I feel about you, Nem."

"It should." She tried to pull away, but he held firm as she continued. "All I've ever done is push you away, hurt you – and I will keep doing it. Because every time we touch, I take. I take and *take*, until there's nothing left of what makes you…" Her voice faltered, cracked, then fell to a whisper. "…you. I take the very light from your eyes, the healthy glow from your skin. Like a… a leech."

Her eyes lifted hesitantly, meeting his. The way he looked at her – so steady, so certain – made her breath hitch. Though his dark gaze lacked the emerald shine and brilliance she had come to know so intimately, despite every wall she had built, something in its depths trembled. A restless force, the very wolf he embodied, pressing against the shadows, yearning to step into her light regardless.

Her next words barely bridged the space between them.

"I don't want to hurt you anymore."

Krepth blew out a breath, his hand rising to cup her face. "I want you, have done for as long as I can remember. It is not a higher power that pulls me, it's just you. Your strength, your intelligence, your allure. You, Nem. Simply you."

"But your magic–"

"Comes back after a little while. Replenishes, like when you use too much from your well. Can't Shift for a while, but it's a sacrifice I'm willing to bear if it means I get to be close to you."

She worried her bottom lip between her teeth, "I've never thought about the others, what happens when I touch them. Arii, Elijah…"

Krepth's lips quirked. "How much touching have you really done with anyone else, Nem?"

Now, come to think about it, she wasn't sure when she last touched anyone else with magic, skin to skin.

Krepth spoke while her thoughts whirled. "All the other times, before Ayrith, they were so fleeting that I don't think those moments were enough for your siphoning to really get much out of me. I simply felt like you'd chased all thought, all feeling, *away*."

"Leaving you hollow…"

Krepth moved closer. "Blissfully *silent*. You'd be surprised how much goes on in this skull of mine."

"But we aren't fated mates..." Nem murmured, grasping pathetically at reasons, not entirely sure why, keenly aware of how her beast remained alert and watchful – almost eager, but not desperate. She was drawn to Krepth, often envisioning what it would be like to be with him – countless times, she had imagined it. A world without him felt bleak and colourless, devoid of light and warmth. Nothing bound them together except history, mutual desire, and the irresistible pull of a forbidden connection.

Ariiaya had once described the insatiable hunger of her own beast the moment she met Elijah, speaking of its longing, its violence, its relentless need until the fated bond had taken hold. It had been an instinct, an undeniable truth she simply knew, of a higher power drawing fated souls together. But Nem... she felt none of that, and the realisation shattered her heart.

"There is no divine power in force, no strings of fate pulling us together, no higher power playing with our destinies," Krepth said, and Nem flinched at the confirmation, blinking as he continued. "It's just me, wanting you. Wanting the strong, incredible Fury assassin with hair like moonlight, with a gaze so piercing that I feel it hit my soul. With a face so beautiful that I could stare until my last breath. With a tongue so sharp that I'd gladly endure the sting in order to remain at your mercy. I'm beguiled by you, I'm entranced by the force of you, your quiet kindness, your love of the stars, your fierce loyalty to your friends and to our home."

Emotion clogged Nem's throat, and for the first time, she let tears silently fall. She allowed her walls to slowly lower, allowed her chest to expand with the heavy breaths that had been lodged there for as long as she could remember.

"You could strip me of everything, and I'd let you. Gladly, without hesitation. I'd give it all, every piece of me, body and soul." Krepth lifted her fingers to his lips, pressing a kiss to her knuckles. "I love you, Nemesis. Always have, always will. And I'd defy the Gods themselves, even the Fates, just to stay in your light until I fade, returning to the earth of the forest where my ancestors lie."

The conviction in his voice, the deep, resonant timbre, and the raw power surging through their joined hands shattered something within Nemesis. In that moment, she wasn't siphoning from Krepth – he was pouring his magic into her, each word pulsing with intent. Heat cascaded over her, flames igniting in her chest, yet she remained in control. It wasn't like her connection with the portals – this was different. All-consuming, yet grounding. Her skin burned with life, the warmth spilling over and illuminating Krepth's face, his smile widening in its glow.

"I love you," he said again.

She didn't hesitate. With a sudden lunge, she threw her arms around his neck, her lips crashing into his. Krepth's arms encircled her instantly, pulling her close as he parted his lips, a low groan escaping him – a sound of pure relief. His hands found her hips, curled around her lower back, as she poured every ounce of emotion into the kiss. And he took it all without pause, holding her as if the sea might reclaim her, just as it had once delivered her to them.

"I don't deserve you," Nem breathed between frantic kisses, her hands snagging in the dark mass of his hair as Krepth edged them back towards the cliffs.

"You deserve everything," he murmured back, tasting of autumn pine and the deepest of forests, wild and warm and like home.

She had been a fool – a damn fool – to push him away. To let fear build walls where there should have been bridges. She could have spent that time losing herself in him, tracing every inch of his body, unravelling the depths of his brilliant mind. She could have felt the fire in his touch, the devotion in his lips as they worshipped her skin. And now, the weight of what she'd thrown away crushed her, a regret that burned hotter than any desire she had ever known.

"I love you, too. I think I always have," she whispered against him, sluggishly realising she hadn't responded.

His answering sigh was like letting go.

As they reached the base of the cliffs, slipping into a spot hidden from the castle's view, Nem pressed Krepth against the rugged wall. Sand fell around them, clinging to his shoulders and tangling in her hair, drawing breathless laughter from them both. She had squandered the time before, but tonight, she was determined to make every moment count, to reclaim what was lost. Krepth's hand found the small of her back, pulling her closer with a boldness that left no space between them.

This could very well be the last day they had together, and by the way Krepth was staring down at her, lips parted and breath sawing through them, Nem didn't need to guess that he was on the same train of thought.

Krepth unclipped his cloak with deliberate slowness, laying it carefully on the sandy ground before guiding them both to the soft bed. He hovered over her, his brows drawn in thought, and she suddenly became aware of her hand, lifting unconsciously to the faded scar across her throat… a silent echo of the moment she had nearly lost her life, of her best friend's sacrifice. Her fingertips traced the slightly raised skin, though she wasn't sure why. Perhaps it was because, just as in that fateful moment, she now felt vulnerable again, the sensation returning under the weight of his dark eyes.

"We don't have to–" Krepth began, but Nem's hand quickly moved to cup his cheek instead.

"Make me forget," she whispered, the crash of the waves upon the shore punctuating her breathless words.

Krepth's gaze was heavy, his expression so open that Nem's breath caught between her parted lips – just before his own claimed them. He exhaled a quiet sigh. "Perhaps we can give you a new memory for this beach." His lips traced the curve of her chin, then skimmed along her jawline, each featherlight touch sending starlit shivers across her skin.

A knee guided between her legs, parting them, and Nem couldn't help the mindless roll of her hips, warmth spreading through her limbs, pooling between her legs. Her hands roamed across Krepth's back, skimming over the supple leather of his vest, frustration flickering at the layers between them. She barely had time to dwell on it before he seemed to read her thoughts.

With deliberate ease, he sat back, fingers working skilfully to unfasten the silver clasps of his black vest. One by one, they came undone, until his already slightly unbuttoned dark tunic parted just enough to reveal the enticing vee of his chest, dusted with fine, dark hair. Her mind briefly flickered back to the battle, the way his adrenaline-fueled body had looked in the firelight, the tilt of his head, the knowing curl of his lips as he caught her unabashed gaze. But now, with that same body so close, within reach, Nem was struck by an unsettling realisation, she was woefully unpractised. The thought sent heat rushing to her cheeks.

As Krepth pulled his tunic over his head, baring the full expanse of his torso to her widening eyes, a flicker of panic tightened her chest. She knew how to fight, how to wield a blade, how to spill blood without hesitation. But this? This was uncharted territory.

A low chuckle curled from his lips, dark and knowing. Her gaze snapped back to his, caught in the heat of it.

"You look like a warrior deciding on a blade before battle," he murmured, his voice all smoke and silk. "You're overthinking, Silver Moon."

Her tongue flicked across her bottom lip, hesitant, as if testing the words before releasing them. "I can't help it. I'm not… well… I haven't…"

His fingertips found the laces of her corseted vest, tugging at the woven cords. "This isn't a fight," he said, voice low, a whisper against her skin. "There are no weapons here – only lips, only hands…"

The vest parted, silk whispering over her rising chest, shifting like water yielding to stone. Then the knife-edge of his touch – quick, decisive – unfastening each delicate clasp. His fingers ghosted downward, slipping between the valley of her breasts in a motion so seamless, so practiced, she forgot to breathe.

The afternoon air, cool and electric, touched her first. Then he did – lips finding the hollow of her throat, breath warm, his dark hair brushing her chin like shadow against light.

His next words unravelled her, sending shivers dancing across her skin.

"…our tongues."

Oh, sweet goddess.

"And in this moment, my Silver Moon, we are discovering this together."

His words curled around her like a warm embrace, kindling something deep in her chest, a fire that burned through her veins. He was right. She might have been inexperienced in love, and he might have known the steps well, but this… this was uncharted. The sensations, the hesitance, the quiet thrill of it all – every touch, every breath, was something neither had ever shared in quite this way before.

They weren't just learning each other; they were creating something entirely their own.

Her beast stirred, a low, insistent hum in her core – not just hunger. *Starvation.* A deep, aching need for him, for his touch, his pleasure, for the fleeting escape from everything waiting beyond this moment. Tomorrow held uncertainty, but right now, none of it mattered.

Right now, they were only two souls, stripped of the weight they carried, the battles they had fought. Two people who had kindled love like a fragile ember over the years, feeding it slowly, carefully, until now – now, when the fire had grown strong enough to consume them. No more walls, no more restraint. Just the raw, unguarded presence of one another.

Golden light spilled across the curve of his shoulder, *her* light, soft and lingering, while a lazy drift of clouds caught the orange fire of the setting sun.

The air was cool, carrying the faint taste of salt, sand and him. She pressed a kiss to his bicep, her lips lingering, then traced the line of her nose along the strong column of his neck until his hair brushed against her scars, sending a quiet shiver through her.

His hand held her head gently as he nipped the lobe of her ear, sending a surge of heat to her limbs. A flick of his tongue had her spine arching, a curse leaking from her lips, the press of her breasts to his chest making him growl.

Krepth scooted back towards her feet, unlacing her boots and peeling away her socks. Nem propped up on her elbows and watched, breathless. The light from her skin bathed him, highlighting the vee peeking from beneath his belt, and the defined ridges of his sculpted torso.

When her eyes finally made their way to his face, he was already watching her, eyes dark. Silence stretched between them, their breaths mingling with the purrs from the ocean. Slowly, he leaned forward and hooked his fingers in the waistband of her pants, eyes filled with the words he did not speak.

"Yes." The word left her in a whisper, steady, certain.

Nem arched her hips, easing the fabric down, the cooling air licking at her newly exposed skin. The pants slipped away, forgotten, leaving her bare beneath him.

She saw it – the dark hunger in his eyes, the near-imperceptible flicker of his pulse at his throat as it bobbed, the tension in his jaw as he fought to hold himself back. He wanted her, had for so long, with the relentless need of a wolf closing in on its prey. And yet, despite the fire she knew was surging through his blood, he still moved with careful restraint, a silent offering of control. A chance to stop. A chance to turn away.

But she wouldn't. Not now.

She would not turn him away any longer.

"Come here, Wolf."

He didn't need further prompting. He crawled to her, lips parted in a silent whisper.

Glorious, dangerous, ravenous.

Hers.

His lips found her neck, teeth grazing her scars as Nem glanced at the sky, unsure when the day had melted into the muted grey of a cloudy night.

Her light spilled over the rugged enclave, gliding across the sand before reaching the sea. The foamy waves shimmered under its touch, each crest crowned in silver. As the moon climbed higher, its slow ascent bathed the world in a dreamlike haze, turning the restless ocean into fractured glass, each ripple catching the glow like a thousand scattered shards. Nem had a brief moment of clarity, enough to wonder if anyone would come to investigate the light down on the beach, but part of her – the part that sang during battle, that pressed her fears away – took that unease and buried it.

Krepth leaned back for a breath, the weight of his gaze pressing against her skin like a touch of its own. "You're beautiful, Silver Moon."

The air between them thickened, charged, his chest rising and falling in slow, deliberate breaths. A flicker of instinct whispered at her to shield herself, to cross her arm over the curve of her breasts, to hide the scars mapping her torso, the silver-dark thatch between her thighs.

But she didn't.

Instead, she tipped her head back, exposing her throat to the night, letting the breeze caress her heated skin. Grains of sand bit at her palms where they pressed into the earth. She was laid bare, vulnerable, and yet… never stronger.

"Fucking divine..." he growled, the curse edged with something almost pained, a whisper of reverence. Fabric rustled, and then the rough hairs of his legs brushed against her skin, sending a shiver through her, a quiet moan escaping her lips. "Gods, Nem, I always knew you weren't of this world. You're a star, burning bright in a coarse blanket of darkness."

The sheer devotion in his voice sent a tremor through her. Her arms moved of their own accord, hands sliding up his quivering biceps, fingers digging into his flesh, pulling him closer. Their mouths collided, breathless and urgent, her leg curling over his, pulling him closer. A sharp inhale hitched in her throat as the heat of him pressed against her, rigid and insistent. His breath tangled with hers, his hands tracing molten paths down her body, each touch searing, his tongue following, teasing, tasting.

Her thighs parted, welcoming him into the space between. Then, his mouth, hot and unyielding, found her core. The first flick of his tongue sent a jolt through her, her spine arching, eyes flying open.

The sea roared in time with her cries, one hand buried in the tangle of his hair as he swirled his tongue over the most sensitive part of her, the other planted in the sand, almost needing to be grounded. Krepth's fingers gently toyed, his sound of approval humming in her ears, his voice barely a whisper.

"You're perfect. So ready for me."

His single finger's intrusion stole a gasp from her lips but mingled with the slick pleasure he had already drawn from her body, the tender touch quickly transformed into euphoria as he discovered the strokes that coaxed the deepest moans of bliss from her. When he added another, she groaned, her entire body turning molten.

A build-up of tension low in her belly demanded more.

More.

Unbidden, she circled her hips against him, eliciting a wolfish rumble of approval, and another ripple of almost unbearable pleasure.

Then he drew the bud of her into his mouth and *sucked*.

She shattered.

Nem flew over the precipice of ecstasy with shattering force.

Relentless and unyielding, consuming her, wiping her of thought. Nem's head snapped to the side, her wide eyes blind to the silver expanse of the horizon, where the moon flared full, setting the ocean ablaze in silver fire; just as she too *burned*.

CHAPTER NINETEEN

KREPTH

The taste of her on his tongue was almost entirely consuming.

Not long after her first climax, he had traced his way up her body, pressing reverent kisses to each scar along the way. Her light was nearly blinding, but any pain it caused was drowned out by awe. She was perfection, writhing beneath him, unguarded, undone. He would endure any agony, accept his powerlessness, if only to see her like this – happy, unbound, *free*.

She surrendered to his lead, her hands roaming over him with the same eager intensity as his against her. Nem shifted to face the ocean, shoulders moving with her breaths. He knelt behind her as he stole a fleeting glance at the molten silver horizon. The misty clouds had drifted off and disappeared, leaving the looming moon to wash the bluff in silver and shadow.

No thoughts of tomorrow would intrude; only this moment mattered and how utterly, irrevocably in love with her he was. How he had been for many years. He would show her, with every sunset and moonrise they shared, no matter how many.

They were like an eclipse, his dark hand splayed across her chest like a moon blocking the rays of the sun, his magicless skin a shadow to the luminous light that burst from her. Nem's chest heaved against his palm, his fingers curling around the soft skin just below her chin as she pressed back against him, the swell of her rear eliciting a groan he couldn't control.

Krepth kissed the salt on her skin, grazed his teeth along the curve between her shoulder and neck, savoured the tiny sounds that escaped her at the firm press of his hard length against her back. The untamed part of him had wanted to bury himself inside her as soon as he'd been rid of his pants, but he knew of her inexperience. He wanted this to be perfect – for her, for them. He's waited so long, what were a few moments more?

Nem shifted against him again, until the hottest, hardest part of him slid along to where they were so close to becoming one. Her silver nails drew his head closer into the crook of her neck.

"You're insatiable, Silver Moon."

He chuckled, delighting in the shiver that his breath wracked from her body.

"Never knew I could feel this... good."

Her whisper was a breathless gasp, her chest rising and falling in time with his own ragged breaths. From his vantage point, the sight of her – soft, flushed, moonlit and utterly undone – sent a sharp pulse of fresh arousal through him.

Then she moved. Turning on her knees, she pressed her front against him, all softness meeting his hard, unrelenting shape. Her touch was hesitant, as if still discovering the right to take, but when she did, it was with a grip that brooked no resistance. And he wouldn't give any. He would let himself be shaped beneath her hands, moulded into whatever she desired.

She had always been his compass, even in absence. He had slipped through shadows with her name curled at the back of his mind, spilled blood with the faint hope of hearing her voice again. Every step had been toward this, toward her, weaving him closer, whether in a fleeting glance or an ire-laced confrontation. No matter how it came, he would take it. He always had.

All thought skittered away when her hand wrapped around his length, cool silver nails earning her a jerk. Nem inhaled a laugh, and the sound had his head tipping to the side, roguish grin twitching his lips.

"I'm at the very end of my control, Nem, and if you laugh like that one more time, I may just have to flip you and take you on your knees, like my wolf demands."

Her eyes widened, aqua depths bright with light. "Your wolf… demands it that way?"

Krepth shrugged. "He demands it *many* ways."

She traced her lips along his jaw, her palms pressed against his chest, and Krepth knew she could feel the wild, erratic hammer of his heart beneath. In answer, he brushed his thumb over her kiss-swollen bottom lip, his voice a reverent murmur.

"My Goddess must be ravished first. Your every need seen to."

She shivered, the reaction visible, tangible. "But what if I want you to let instinct take over? I want all of you, Krepth."

A shuddering silence stretched between them. He saw the slow bob of her throat, the way her lips parted, ready to fill the space – but his lack of response wasn't hesitation. It was the roaring, consuming thunder of need that rooted him in place, ensnaring him in the weight of her words.

Her hand still cradled him as she leaned in, pressing a lingering kiss to the trembling plane of his chest. "It's alright, I don't mind if–"

In one swift motion, he turned her, moving them back into their previous position. The gasp that escaped her was sharp, edged with surprise – but laced with something else. Something victorious.

Krepth's hand traced the curve of her belly, gliding lower, fingers teasing through the soft trail of hair between her thighs. "Are you sure?"

He could have sworn she murmured, "Fucking *yes*, wolf."

But the words were a husky whisper, breathless and molten, tangled in the thick, sweltering heat of her desire. When she pressed back against him, her rear sliding along his length, he almost lost all coherent thought to the wolf inside.

"Please…" she begged, her voice raw with need.

He wasn't sure how he felt hearing it. His Goddess was power, confidence – unyielding in battle, always sure of herself, always in control. Yet now, beneath his hands, she was pliant, burning with heat, radiant with something untamed. The plea wasn't just for him; it felt like a surrender to the moment itself, to the world around them, to the fire which consumed them both.

He guided himself, nudging the tip of him between her thighs.

She groaned.

Krepth swallowed hard, drawing her against him, his arms encircling her as though he could fuse her very essence into his own. She was starlight incarnate, radiant and untouchable – yet here she was, pressed to him, their bodies melding, the sheer rapture of her presence almost unravelling him. It was almost too much, almost unbearable in its beauty. Still, he held himself back, knowing the momentary pain she would feel, and so he paused, reverent, devoted, on his knees, fingers pressed into her hips in a gentle grip.

Their breaths interwove, their sweat-dappled skin burning against the cool night air, mist curling around them like ghostly fingers. From the distance, seabirds cried their mournful calls, but nothing could reach them here, in this fragile, infinite space of beach.

Perfect. It felt so achingly perfect.

Nem dropped forward, pressing herself back, her shudder of pain minute. They waited for a few heartbeats, Krepth's eyes roving the length of her back, the tiny sprinkle of hidden freckles at the intersection of her spine and shoulders that he'd never seen before, the sand-speckled curtain of her silver hair, the peak of her tapered ear.

Her scars were visible like little valleys on the map of her skin, and he traced one near the edge of her hip. A backlit map of the lingering decisions of war, of her bloody past. A wave crashed, forcing Nem to press back. Krepth couldn't stifle his groan.

"Are you alright?" he whispered, hands moving to grip her hips.

"Heavens *yes*."

Gently, he drew back, almost removing himself completely, before her sound of protest drew him forward, the sound pitching into one of surprised pleasure.

She lifted herself, her back pressed to his front, offering up the swan curve of her neck. He kissed her tenderly, brushed his nose along the lobe of her ear, breathing in the salt-and-honey scent of her hair, while his hands traced her glowing body, every raised scar, every dip and swell, like a cartographer charting uncharted land. Lightning seared through his limbs, and though his magic was absent, dancing across her shimmering skin instead, in that moment he was wholly consumed by the raw sensations coursing through his body, and the desperate need to discover how many more beautiful sounds he could draw from her trembling body.

Nem fell forward once more, arms shaking, though he knew it was not because she was spent.

She was holding back.

His thrusts began gently, in time with the crashing of the waves, then Nem pushed back more insistently until they were overtaken, slapping flesh, panted breaths, flickering light and fervent, incoherent whispers. Every nerve tingled, every thought overridden by the need to chase their pleasure.

One hand affixed to her thigh, the other wove to her front to trace gentle circles around her core, Krepth felt the instant her climax hit. Her spine curved, moonlit hair tossed like a curtain over her shoulders as he bucked, relentless, utterly overcome. The throbbing tightness wrung his own crashing end, her name a hoarse call from his lips.

They remained knelt, wordless under the moon, sand stuck to their skin, for a short time, his arms around her in an embrace as the waves rippled and crashed.

Krepth kissed her nape, guided her chin so her swollen lips met his.

"If I die tomorrow, I will not fight the Gods on their decision." His voice was breathless, gravely, as he withdrew from her and they held each other, her nails trailing his arms as they pressed her to him. "I'd die one happy man."

Nem's gusty laugh touched his lips, "And leave when we've only done this once? I'll have you countless more before we face the Gods… together, wolf."

Her words shot to his groin, and he hardened again.

Nem's smile had him swallowing a hungry groan. When her nails skimmed the head of him, he couldn't help but twist her to face him, fingers pinching her chin to inspect the curve of her lips.

"Insatiable. Nemesis Rion."

Her gentle, yet forceful squeeze, had his eyes fluttering closed. "Fuck."

Who was he to defy a Goddess?

They tangled twice more before their breaths levelled and the thick of night chilled their skin as they lay staring at the star-speckled sky. Krepth lay with one arm folded behind his head, the other a cushion for Nem's.

"What do you think will happen after tomorrow?" Nem asked, her voice barely more than a breath.

"I think Ares will push every soul in this land to their breaking point," he said quietly. "And I think, if we stand together, every last one of us, we will survive it. Changed, yes. Marked by it, no doubt. But alive, like we were the last time." He paused, mind skating to those they'd lost. "And there will be death, Nem. But it won't be yours."

Inevitable… it was all inevitable. By now, they knew war like an intimate dance, and though his words rang with determination, they felt oddly hollow, touched for once with uncertainty.

She didn't reply. Instead, she shifted, propping herself up on one elbow, her bright eyes tracing the lines of his face. "I'm going to do everything in my power to see the portals closed, and the threat of Ares gone for good. Even if it means–"

Krepth silenced her with a sudden, startling kiss. He wouldn't let talk of death taint the wonder of their night.

Inhaling her shuddering exhale, Krepth said, "Let's head back and rest. Our King and Queen will be here at dawn, and it would be nice to greet them without bleary eyes and sandy, sex-mussed hair."

She slipped on a mask he knew too well – though this one was more soft veil than stone, a temporary thing meant to keep her worry at bay. They rose and dressed, and a small laugh escaped her as he draped his arm over her shoulder.

They turned toward the rocky climb, and that sound – light, fleeting – was more precious to him than anything else in the world.

CHAPTER TWENTY

NEMESIS

Nem hadn't felt this nullified in… well, forever. Her limbs were heavy yet unburdened; her mind empty of everything except the memory of the beach with Krepth. She stared up at the vine-laced ceiling of her quarters, listening to the light snores from Vega on the cot nearby, and not even the light chill of predawn disturbed her peace. The cool air kissed her skin, raising goosebumps, her breath misting faintly as her fingers curled into the sheets. Outside, the waves crashed in their rhythmic lullaby.

So, this was bliss.

Sleep had claimed her the moment she sank beneath the layers of sheets and furs, the lingering heat of a searing goodnight kiss still burning on her lips. When she'd awoken, it had been slow, as if coming out of a deep dreamless sleep.

Nem closed her eyes, lost in the memory of dark eyes, scorching lips, and hands that knew her better than she knew herself, sure, practiced, and utterly spellbinding. Those fingers had explored her with a reverence that unravelled her, drawing pleasure so intense it left her breathless, shivering beneath the weight of whispered promises against her ear. If she had known that surrendering to him would feel like this, she would have let her walls crumble years ago.

A sleep-laced voice sounded nearby. "I thought you'd forgotten the way to your rooms." Vega yawned wide, mashing her cheek against her fist, picking sleep from the corner of her eye. "You came in late. Was tempted to send Aeun in search of you."

Aeun.

Nem tilted her head, her gaze settling on Vega's wild, mussed hair, her own expression carefully guarded. Had the dragon known what she'd been doing on the beach with Krepth? The thought hadn't even crossed her mind – what their bond might have allowed the beast to sense.

Misreading her silence as awkwardness, Vega quickly waved a hand. "No need to explain, I get it." She sat up, stretching lazily, a knowing smirk tugging at her lips. "The spymaster is easy on the eyes, and you two have history. On the eve of battle, it makes sense you'd want one last verbal spar. You and him – always with the banter. Endlessly entertaining."

Right, *verbal* sparring.

A single glance at Vega's arched brows and amused smirk told Nem she knew exactly what kind of sparring had taken place on the beach. Nem cleared her throat and lifted her chin.

"Speaking of sparring, where's Merrick?"

Vega's smirk stretched into a grin. "Outside, probably swinging that big old axe around – his weathered, barrel-chested southern frame bathed in the golden light of dawn. Hmm… we'd better get out there. We wouldn't want the King and Queen greeted first by his gruff, frowny, surly face. And he's probably growling Iniq's ear off. She's very patient, but I've seen her claws. Actually, it might be the southie who'll need saving." Vega's brows danced as she dressed.

Nem couldn't argue with both points there. Though the thought of Merrick and Elijah facing off, arms crossed, matching gruff frowns on full display, while Arii shook her head nearby, was almost enough to make laughter bubble up. Gods, her night with Krepth must have loosened something in her brain, letting humour slip through like water trickling into a widening stream. Suddenly feeling vulnerable, she shifted her mental fortress back in place, cutting off the supply of comical thoughts.

"See you down there," Vega saluted, leaving the door wide open in her wake.

Shaking her head, she swiftly readied herself.

The Locket of Dreaming swung on her chest. Rarely did she remove it, despite what she knew of the dark magic within its serpentine form, though it had remained nestled in the folds of her cloak last night. It hummed against her skin now, its whisper a promise of power. Nem's fingers traced the warm metal figure-of-eight, an unconscious habit, a quiet attempt to still the rising voices and the energy that prickled her skin like a warning.

She snatched the Cloak of Protection from the foot of her bed, its silky fabric shifting like liquid night dissolving into dawn, dusted with stars. She had never known a garment to feel both heavy and weightless at once, a comforting presence on her shoulders, carrying the quiet certainty that no mortal blade could ever break through it. Her gaze shifted to the tangle of furs on her bed, to the glimpse of a sword hilt jutting from beneath her pillow.

With a trembling breath, she reached for it, drawing forth the Sword of Power and studying its sheath, simple, yet exquisitely crafted in fine leather. Tugging it free with a metallic whine, she held the blade to the light, eyes roving the bluish, pearlescent metal. Her preferred weapon had always been the agile dagger, and Nem would be lying if she claimed the longsword didn't intimidate her – that her hesitation to wield it as her main hand hadn't stemmed from uncertainty. But as the soft dragon-scale leather settled against her palm and her nails skimmed the flat of the blade, she swung it gently, catching the morning light in a bright sweep of steel. For a moment, she stood still in the hush, in the fragile breath of solitude, surrounded by the three objects of power.

For the first time in longer than she could remember, Nemesis Rion felt the faintest candle–flicker of hope.

Until something moved in her peripheral vision.

She spun, blade slicing the air, only to meet nothing. The shadow darted to the wall, a grunt and a curse making her flinch. Silver glinted in the low light. Nem's eyes widened as Krepth slammed a red–faced Noct hard against the stone.

She sheathed her sword. "Krepth! What are you doing?"

"Knew we couldn't trust you, World Walker." Krepth's voice caressed her senses, had the hairs rising on her arms.

A gasp, "I… I can't br–"

Nem grabbed his shoulder. "He can't breathe!"

Krepth glanced back at her, eyes wide and feral. "He just tried to kill you, Nem!"

What?

Her mouth opened, but her gaze snagged on Noct's wild stare, words freezing in her throat.

"Made me do it…" His gloved hands scrabbled at Krepth's biceps, thumping weakly at his chest. Spit flecked his lips, already turning blue. "He made me!"

Nem's attention flicked to the subtle shift of those bicoloured eyes, the twitch toward the door, where a blade lay. She darted for it, scooping up the weapon.

It was strange, wholly metal, no leather bound around the grip.

She dropped it instantly with a curse as it scorched her skin.

Iron.

"I didn't want to do it! I swear it!" Noct rasped as Krepth gave him a little room, though the reprieve was short. Nem's cry of alarm snapped Krepth's temper, his forearm slammed back into the mortal's throat.

"Iron? Who the fuck sent you!"

Despite the damning evidence, Nem pressed her hand to Krepth's arm again.

"If he wanted me dead, why wait until now? Why help us in the war?" She turned on Noct. "Explain."

Gasping, sweat beading his brow, the otherworldly man gulped at the air. "Zeus… he promised me the very thing my heart longs for, in exchange for killing you. He said he'd grant me the means to keep my family safe. I was desperate. The bargain came after the war. Please, I was a fool."

Zeus? Nem's mind slipped back to her vision, to the Goddesses towering over her father. From what she had gathered, Zeus had been doing his best to hold Ares in check. Why the God of Gods would stoop to enlist a mortal man in the effort to bring the God of War to heel, she could not say. Something told her it belonged to a vast world of schemes and divine bargains that she was nowhere near ready to comprehend.

"So, you're Zeus's son?" Nem asked, stomach churning.

Noct's wild laugh was part amusement, part fear, a shimmer of the confident man she'd met a year ago peeking through.

"No, I'm not his bloody son."

He yelped as Krepth shoved him again.

"Fair questions seeing as we know *nothing* about you, or where you came from," Krepth snarled. "How can we trust anything that comes out of your mouth now?"

"I fucked up, I'm sorry!"

"You only regret it because you failed." Krepth's voice burned like venom, a whisper edged with fury, his teeth mere inches from Noct's face. "I caught the stench of your deception the moment you stepped into this place."

"If your family is in danger, Noct, we can help." Nem's voice rose

over Krepth's, sharp and steady, catching the faint flicker of hope in Noct's eyes. "You don't need to barter with a God. Stop holding back and trust us. We are not your enemies."

"What exactly did he promise you?" Krepth's grip slackened, just enough for the man to speak.

But Noct's answer was not for him, it was for her.

"A dragon."

Nem and Krepth's eyes met, a silent conversation flickering between them.

Noct's pull toward Aeun had never been subtle. He watched the silver dragon as though the sight might fill a hollow place in his chest. Only now did Nem recognise that hunger for what it was. She had heard enough fragments of his story to know his own egg had never hatched, that it had been gifted to him as a child of standing. Perhaps his kin had dragons of their own, their wings a constant reminder of what he had lost.

Her thoughts stirred to his earlier words of family, of keeping them safe. He had fought for them before, standing shoulder to shoulder when the veil threatened to tear. Without him, Ares' beast might have crossed last time. That memory left her with a thread of something, perhaps not trust, but not quite loathing either.

A horn's call drifted through the hazy window, cutting the silence in two.

Krepth eased back, though his eyes stayed hard, the promise of violence still coiled in them. "You touch her again… any of my family for that matter… and I will tear you apart."

Noct's fingers went to his throat. He bent, coughing, hair falling forward like a curtain. A shallow nod.

"Like I said," he straightened sharply, drawing in a breath. "I was a fool. Blinded for reasons of the heart. You understand, don't you, Silver Fury?"

Nem studied him a moment longer. The horn sounded again, louder now. She gave a slow nod. She did understand. Love made fools of all of them. She would scorch the earth for her own.

But understanding did not erase the fracture. She'd deal with Noct later.

And he would not dare try again. Not now.

Not with their monarchs at the gates.

Draped in her customary leathers and mail, silver dragon-scale pauldrons gleaming at her shoulders, the Sword of Power strapped across her back and the Locket of Dreaming resting over her heart, she moved down the corridor, the gradient Cloak of Protection trailing at her heels. Nem headed through the inner bailey, Krepth stalking like a shadow behind. The rhythmic thump of dragon wings, many of them, announced the arrival of the northern monarchs.

Nem stalked toward the front gates, a shadow briefly darkening the morning sun as Aeun soared overhead. Passing beneath the shouting assassins on the walls, her heart skipped a beat at the sight of a rainbow of dragons slowly descending onto the field surrounding the castle. In the distance, horns blared once more, signalling the arrival of approaching armies, banners fluttering in the steady breeze.

The north had come, along with the eastern and southern courts.

Dragon song filled the air as a massive blue beast thumped to the ground, its wings sending the grass into a wild dance. Lysander dipped her head, angling her shoulder, but Nem had no time to respond before a figure launched at her, arms embracing her tight.

"Nem!" Arii's whisper was low, almost a snarl, the sound drawing a sigh of relief from Nem.

"My Queen," Nem greeted with a smile as Arii pulled back, her violet eyes flicking over her in a swift assessment.

"All limbs intact... no new wounds..." Arii clucked her tongue, head tilting. "Your skin... you look good, Nem. Though I suspect, from the Fate's missives, we have a lot to catch up on and little time."

Krepth's smooth, deep voice skimmed the bare line of her skin, warm as the ocean's breath. It sent a shiver racing up her arms and heat coiling slow and certain in her core.

"Queenie, so good of you to join us. I hope you brought boats, though." Krepth barely had time to react before he was caught in the same crushing embrace. A strangled *oof* escaped him as Arii's arms locked around him with unrelenting force. "I know you like to skim-read your missives. They mentioned potential war in the middle of the sea." He chuckled into Arii's ombre hair.

"Bloody idiot, of course we brought boats." At her words, another blast of horns echoed from the sea. Arii's grin widened as she planted hands on hips, twisting westward to where a fleet of ships emerged against the dawning horizon.

There were dozens of them, sails high, fluttering with a vibrant mix of house crests and colours. Each ship was crafted from timber unique to its region, grown in different soils, under different skies. The entire land had banded together, pooling resources to form a formidable naval force. The variety of woods created a patchwork of vessels, each with its own character: the pale, almost sun-bleached timber of the western fleet; the rich, dark wood of the eastern court; the slate-grey, rock-like hulls of the southern ships.

Nem's eyes darted from ship to ship, barely able to take them all in. Then she saw them – royal blue banners billowing proudly in the wind, each one marked with the dragon-head crest of the North. Their warships gleamed with gilded cherry wood, dragon-scale plating stretched across their sterns, slicing through the ocean like the winged beasts they mirrored.

And still, the fleets came, crowding the horizon until not a single patch of sea remained untouched. Voices floated toward them on the wind. Stunned at how swiftly they had all arrived, Nem ran her tongue across her lips, tasting ancient sugar. Magic. Elijah had no doubt brought everyone here with portals, and the thought ought to have stirred unease, yet the magic wielded by Elijah and her father felt different.

"We brought ships, alright."

The voice was smooth, laced with amusement. Nem turned to see Arii embrace with the Prince of the West, Kadec Brolikian. His smile was wide, his hair longer than she remembered, now brushing past his shoulders. The early morning sun highlighted the dark warmth of his skin and the crinkles at the corners of his bright eyes.

"The largest fleet ever assembled in recent history," he said. "Whatever lies beyond the horizon should be trembling."

"It truly is a sight to see," Elijah said, clasping hands with the Prince as Kadec bowed low. She knew the King too well not to notice the subtle twitch at the corner of his mouth, a familiar tic that betrayed his discomfort with the formalities of his title, even after all this time. Yet his eyes sparkled under the sweep of his dark chocolate hair, his beard neatly trimmed, and without his crown and in semi-formal attire, he looked more like a refined version of the hooded ex-bodyguard he used to be.

Still, there was no mistaking the weight he carried. Power clung to him, influence built over time, magic woven into his very being. The presence of a King had always been there, undeniable and steady.

"Your efforts and presence here is beyond appreciated." Elijah angled his head, offering Nem a smile.

"Nem. Good to see you."

Nem curved into a bow and almost grinned at the look on Elijah's face. Arii, though, hooted a laugh.

"When our world is under threat, our best chance is standing together," Kadec said, having just kissed Arii's hand, nodding to both King and Queen. Around them, the sea crashed and ships groaned in the swell. "Though the times have been less than friendly of late," he added with a wry smile, "there's nothing like a good war to pull us all together."

He turned to Nem, taking her hand gently and pressing a kiss to her palm. "Miss Rion," he said with a grin, "it's good to see you again."

They hadn't shared many words before, but Nem felt it – an instinctive trust. Beneath his charm and love of revelry, there was a heart she knew was steady and good. She felt a subtle shift beside her, the barest touch of Krepth's fingers to her elbow. Though they weren't fated mates, he still had the overprotective instinct when it came to her. He'd proven this with his actions this morning – and all that she hadn't seen. The knowledge had her suppressing a smile. So, instead she nodded in reply to Kadec, her expression carefully composed as another group of warriors approached, grim-faced, clad in gear built for the fiercest storms.

"It's warmer here than I remember," Thogan said in greeting, dismounting from the back of a snow-armoured bear. His brother, Jero, let out a short laugh as he landed beside him with a heavy thud.

"Last time we were here, the north was buried under black ice," Jero said, spreading his tattooed, bare arms wide, broader now, it seemed, from long days spent in relentless training. "Everywhere is warmer than the south."

Elijah was the first to greet the Princes of the South, clasping their hands in a fierce, familiar welcome. "Jero, Thogan, you've come."

"We feel the call to arms in the earth beneath our feet, in the tremor of the air, in the scent of war on the wind. It sings to us. Of course we came," Thogan replied, his voice more growl than speech. Nem knew better than to take it as aggression; it was simply Thogan's weathered manner, shaped by brutal climates and even harsher discipline.

His brother shook his head, thick beard swaying. "We will be writing in the history books, should the south's first war fleet survive what is to come."

"If we all survive this," came a new voice, one that sounded like wind chimes drifting through midnight mist. Freya appeared, riding atop a massive antlered steer, flanked by Shifters both human and beast. Her moonlight-coloured hair was pulled into a long braid, threaded with leaves and fragments of their eastern forest home.

Surrounded now by the full presence of the court monarchs, their eyes turning – some curious, some wary – toward Nem, she felt a sudden weight press into her chest. The grandeur, the silent scrutiny, the sheer force of their gathered power… it was almost overwhelming.

A cry of gulls overhead pulled her gaze to the sky just as Aeun, having circled the assembled forces, finally descended nearby. Her silver scales caught the light in a dazzling shimmer. With her head held high, she stepped forward, blue eyes flicking from Nem to the towering figure of Lysander, then to the other dragons beyond.

It struck Nem then that Aeun might not have been around other dragons in quite some time, before their run in with the Kryvern and Thermata, and the Ourobouros, of course. And truth be told, Nem's understanding of Aetherion dragons was still far from complete. Like before, she looked wary of the others, but Nem felt a tentative hope through the bond.

As a hush settled over the gathering, Nem took a cautious step forward. She raised a hand and, in a slow, deliberate motion, swept it from her dragon to the others standing near, an unspoken gesture of introduction.

"This is Aeun," she began, as the Ouroboros and Nocturne arrived nearby.

"*A Klad'ir,*" came Lysander's voice, smooth with curiosity as her wings folded close against her blue-scaled sides. Her gaze held steady on Nem, then flicked to the silver dragon who had drawn nearer behind Nem.

Noticing Aeun's tension, Lysander's lips curled – not in warning, but in a slow, serpentine smile. *"Peace, child. You are safe among my kin."*

Aeun's posture softened, her exhale trailing like mist on a quiet morning. *"My deepest thanks."*

The tension in Nem's shoulders ebbed as well, pressure uncoiling from her spine. She should've known better than to expect anything but warmth from Lysander – or from those closest to her. Arii was already stepping forward, hand extended without hesitation.

Aeun's blue eye shifted to Nem, and at her subtle nod, she lowered her head to press her nose gently to the Queen's open palm.

"She's magnificent," Arii said, glancing back at Elijah, her violet eyes alight.

"And the greatest asset we hold in the war to come, along with young Nemesis here," Ouro added, now in human form, his dark cloak sweeping around him like a shadowy echo of the dragon wings he'd shed. Noct stayed silent beside him.

Arii's gaze held weight, and Nem saw pinched concern there. "You've got a lot to tell us, Nem."

With a long, deep breath, Nem began to offload her secrets to the monarchs.

†

Hours slipped past, and the old castle and its grounds were soon teeming with life. Tents sprang up across the grass – an impromptu city of pale canvas, worn furs, patterned linen and wooden frames. The place became a vibrant patchwork, a living tapestry of people drawn from every corner of the continent, overlooked by flocks of coloured dragons in the sky. The sea was similarly occupied, the overcast sky lending filtered light over the half-occupied warships dotted with temporary crew.

Aeun's scales pulsed warm beneath Nem's palm, alive with quiet tension as they stood upon the school's wind-swept battlement. Below, the world stirred, tents fluttering like petals in a restless breeze, but it was the sky that held their gaze. Overhead, dragons wheeled in slow, elegant arcs – bodies gleaming, wings slicing the air with cries that echoed like distant song. The sound stirred something in Aeun; feathers along her neck trembled, wings shivering with longing as her head lifted, eyes tracking the dance above with hunger.

Nem felt it all… curiosity braided with yearning, the thunder of nerves trembling through Aeun's chest. She tilted her head, catching the glint of that immense blue eye watching her.

"Go," she said softly, her voice just above the wind. "Fly with them, Aeun. It's been too long since you've felt what it means to belong. Let the war wait a while longer. There's still joy in the world, and it belongs to you too."

For a moment, Aeun was still, the slow flare of her nostrils and clenched jaw a quiet war between hesitation and hope. But through the bond, emotion surged – raw and bright and wordless.

Nem smiled, pressing both palms to the dragon's nose as Aeun lowered her head in full, eyes locked. No words needed passing between them; the moment had already said enough.

With a trill, Aeun's wings lifted, propelling her up, wind from her departure gusting back against Nem's face. A smile stretched her lips, tugged at the scars on her cheek, but Nem didn't care. The sight of Aeun joining the others, hearing their calls of greeting, sent flutters of happiness through her – a reflection of her own emotions and that which filled her silver dragon.

"I haven't seen you smile like that in… well… forever."

She hadn't heard Arii's arrival, but her voice slipped into the moment like a missing note in a familiar melody. Nem turned toward her, silver wisps of hair catching the breeze and brushing softly against her cheeks.

"That's because I haven't," Nem admitted, her gaze steady. "Even with everything that has happened over the last week and what I've learned about my past and what's to come, I'm… happy, Arii."

Her eyes lingered on her friend's face: the storm-forged set of her brow, the stubborn cut of her jaw, all softened by the quiet warmth in her eyes and the tumble of honey-kissed chocolate curls.

"You look like you're holding back a speech," Nem added, frowning.

Arii sighed, dramatically. "Now, I'm not going to launch into some overprotective tirade and say that if he so much as thinks about hurting you, I'll string Krepth's legs to Lysander's claws and have him dangled upside down until all the blood drains from his nether regions into that thick, misguided skull of his. Then I'll–"

"Arii," Nem cut in, half-laughing, half-scolding. "I'm more than capable of stringing the Spymaster up by his arse myself if it comes to that." She rested a hand on Arii's shoulder firmly. "But he won't hurt me."

Seemingly satisfied, Arii slipped her arm through Nem's, their gazes drawn once more to the restless shimmer of the sea.

"Once again, we stand on the brink of war," Arii said quietly.

"But this time," Nem finished, a faint smile touching her lips, "we have dragons."

Chapter Twenty-One

KREPTH

"Come on, she won't bite."

They stood on the bluff with the school looming like a statue at their backs. Aeun's snout hovered within Krepth's reach, lips peeled to show teeth like polished daggers, eyes as blue as the cloud-flecked sky rolling over the waves below. With teeth like that, trusting she wouldn't take a nip felt like folly. A glimmer lit her gaze, a slight lift of the scaled brows, a ripple through the feathered plumes along her head.

Definitely going to bite him.

Krepth glared, his voice taking a whiny pitch he hated. "I want to try on another one."

"There is only one dragon," Nem argued.

He bit back the pout that would earn him a sharp rebuke and instead swallowed hard. "Really, Silver Moon? An entire flock just landed with us. Besides, a wolf's paws are for land, not sky."

"I was reluctant before my first flight. So was Elijah."

He arched a brow. "You didn't get a choice, though." He still remembered the sudden way she was yanked into the sky, a split decision to help Aeun. He shivered, imagining himself hurled into the ocean, bones breaking upon impact with the sea.

Nem planted her hands on her hips, grey tunic catching the sea breeze, silver hair whipping loose about her face. Her expression told him she knew where his thoughts had gone.

"Come on, Wolf. Don't be ridiculous, Aeun won't let you fall. Besides, the others are either preparing for war or stealing a moment's peace before it starts. You at least need to try, in case the battle demands it. You must be steady on a dragon's back."

What use would he be, flailing about in the air? Krepth shot her a glare. Her lips twitched, just enough for him to notice.

She was enjoying this.

Aeun rumbled low, the sound dripping with agreement.

So much for that night under the stars softening her sharp edges. No, the fire between them still burned bright, sparking like always. Gods, he needed Elijah here, someone to back him up. Yet even in thought the King abandoned him, for Elijah would only tell him to swallow his fear and fly.

Krepth faced the dragon. "You so much as nibble me, Aeun, I swear, scales or not, I'll bite you back."

The dragon shook her head. A hot snort gusted over his fingers. He pressed them to her snout, surprised at the softness there. Her nostrils flared, drawing in his scent. Perhaps his fear.

He hated the idea but didn't linger on it. Aeun shifted, raising her head to show the saddle and angled shoulder. An invitation if ever there was one.

Nem's laugh chimed across the bluff. "Come on."

He stayed rooted.

Her fingers slipped into his, and the world narrowed to that touch. His magic ebbed, drained by her skin against his, yet instead of loss there came relief in the quiet. She tugged, and his boots left the earth as she drew him onto Aeun's back.

Straddling behind her, he had to remind himself why he was here at all.

Never in his life had Krepth imagined climbing onto a dragon, let alone riding one.

Aeun faced the ocean. Fear surged, blood roaring in his ears. Perhaps this was a mistake.

Definitely a mistake, a bad idea–

Her head dipped. Wind rose hard against them as she pitched forward.

Krepth swallowed a yell.

Weightless. For an instant the world fell away, and Krepth's grip locked around Nem's waist. He thought he heard her laugh again, bell-bright, pulling his mind from the crashing sea, from the saddle digging into his thighs, the way his legs ached from their clenching.

His stomach lurched, then dropped, gravity tearing at him as Aeun skimmed the water and shot forward, so fast the spray stung his eyes. Before he could blink it away, she banked, and his backside lifted clean off the saddle.

Nem's laugh rang out as he clung closer, chin pressed to the warm line of her shoulder. "Fucking hell."

"Hold on!" she gasped.

And then Aeun dove .

Large waves loomed, vast and snarling, their crests rearing like soldiers about to break ranks. Their roar swallowed the air as Aeun skimmed so close Krepth's breath caught. She'll pull away, she has to–

But she didn't.

Her wingtip kissed the surface, and suddenly they plunged into the curl of a wave. The tunnel closed around them, green and glass-bright, the thunder of water crashing at their backs. Spray hammered down, plastering hair across his face. He risked a glance and saw himself reflected in the crystalline wall, eyes wide and wild.

Something sparked in his chest, sunlight fracturing through the churn.

Exhilaration.

Nem whooped, a fierce, unrestrained cry, and it snapped something in him. His grip on her waist eased. His fear still clung like sea foam, but it could not choke the rush flooding his veins. He revelled in the sensations, in the scent of the ocean, mingled with Nem's soap and Aeun's draconic ash. Salt clung sharp in his nose, brine heavy on his tongue, while the faint trace of lavender drifted from Nem's hair each time the wind caught it. Strands whipped back to sting his cheek, brushing across his mouth as though teasing him with the memory of a kiss.

Beneath it all lingered the dragon's essence, a dry, smoky tang. The three scents tangled until he could not tell where the sea ended and they began, his wolf senses alight, high on adrenaline and the moment. He breathed deeper, greedy for the strange union of it. Her back was solid and warm against his chest, her heartbeat quickening beneath his palms, and without meaning to, his own breath fell into rhythm with hers. It was alive, wild, utterly unlike the cloistered castle halls and dark dungeons he had grown used to.

This was incredible.

He reached out, fingers skimming the slick wall of the wave, leaving trails in liquid glass.

Absolutely incredible.

He wasn't sure when he began laughing, but the sound bounced over the crash of the water. He laughed with abandon, let his arms splay wide, let his head tip back as water ran in little streams over his eyes, his cheeks, his chin.

Filtered fractures burst into full sunlight as they shot from the wave's mouth, darting into the curve of another mountainous wave, Aeun's wingtips cutting the water. Aeun let loose a trill, a joyous sound Krepth hadn't heard from her before.

He didn't need a bond to feel the happiness radiating from Nem, from them both. This was where she belonged, in the sky, astride a dragon bound to her heart. This was what he had hoped for her, had wanted for her so badly. This happiness. This freedom.

They left the wave and rose, climbing so swiftly into the air that he had to grip Nem's waist once more, blinking against the wind and sky.

When Aeun levelled out, he rested his chin on Nem's shoulder and let out a long breath. "Fine. You're right. This is… pretty amazing."

"The sky's a whole different world," Aeun said softly. *"Open, waiting to be explored."*

They climbed higher, breaking through the last veil of mist. They burst above the clouds, their foamy peaks glowing gold in the setting sun. It was like flying through mountains made of light.

Krepth stared, caught between awe and disbelief. He had spent his years in shadow, chasing secrets written in ink and sealed in blood, always looking down. He had forgotten there was an above. Forgotten how the sky turned, how day slipped into night, how the sun bled into stars, how darkness itself could blaze.

Krepth leaned to lay a hand against her scaled side. "Thanks for showing me, Aeun."

Aeun rumbled beneath him, steady and alive.

Krepth ran a hand through his wet hair, shook it like a dog. Nem chuckled, and he grinned.

Aeun shook her wings, water sparkling around them like diamonds. Alright, perhaps he wouldn't turn up his nose at the back of a dragon during the battle to come. Though he knew this was a taste of what riding one was like, there was no threat snapping at their heels, no urgency, no danger. That would make things more difficult, and at the thought he wished once again that he had outward magic. Being able to shift had its perks – subterfuge as a light-pawed beast in the shadows, heightened smell and natural senses, far greater than a normal Fae's. But he wished he could throw magic from a dragon's back. Now *that* would be impressive.

Fate hadn't given him such power though, so rather than dwell, he decided to appreciate the female nestled before him instead. At the power she had been granted.

"Let's make a promise to do this again, then," he said, dipping his hands through the air currents.

Nem twisted to look at him, before placing a soft kiss on his cheek. She lingered, and their eyes locked, taking the invitation, he kissed her gently, whispering, "Many times more."

The fire in her aqua gaze had his limbs heating. The promise burning there made his heart quicken, nothing to do with the blur of clouds streaking past them, the thuds of new wingbeats as a clutch of dragons joined them, wheeling in arcs above their heads.

Suddenly Nem shifted, deftly twisting to straddle before him, hands on his chest. The confidence in her open face had his breath hitching.

In a move reminiscent of their time on the beach, Nem pinched his chin, like he had to her, drawing his lips down to hers. The kiss was a subtle brush of their lips, barely enough to call it one, but everything melted away. The thump of Aeun's wings, the gusts of wind from the other dragons as they swept overhead, the colossal stretch of space between them and the ground below, the thoughts of the looming danger on the horizon. The narrowed purple eyes of his queen, should he ever put a foot wrong with the woman before him.

Though they weren't fated, Krepth's entire being hummed with a building need, one that was totally inappropriate given the company. Given they were thousands of feet up in the air, an ocean below, and a fleet of ships loaded with crew looking on. He held back, sharing her breath, knuckles trailing her jawline.

Nem's tiny gasp as his fingers grazed her scars was like a bell in the silence.

"Fuck it," he murmured against her lips, his hands tangling in her hair as their lips met. The kiss was electric, zapping currents through his body, sending fire to every limb that was previously bordering on numb. Her tongue traced his teeth, circled his own, sending all the fire directly to his groin. When her teeth tugged on his bottom lip, he couldn't help the moan that whispered through his teeth. She stroked the sensitive skin at the nape of his neck, perhaps unaware of what that tiny touch did to him. Did to *all* of him.

After a moment, and a draconic huff of a laugh from Aeun, Krepth paused, Nem's breathless gasps sheering against his lips as they stared at one another, and he swore he would never get enough of her looking like this.

His gaze drifted over her shoulder, to where a red-hued dragon soared, its head twisted towards them, mouth slightly agape. Was it… laughing at them?

"Your displays of affection amuse my kin," Aeun said, her voice warm, perhaps a little embarrassed. *"Do your teeth not… touch, or clack together? Is it not uncomfortable? Wet? Slippery?"*

"Okay, alright!" Nem laughed, placing one last kiss on Krepth's lips. "That's enough."

"You mash faces upon my back and I'm the one who needs to stop?" The dragon's wings thumped, her feathered crest wrestling as she shared an amused look with the red. The beast's tail flicked before it dove, another yellow dragon following close behind.

Krepth laughed into the air.

They were beyond magnificent, and Krepth couldn't bring himself to feel embarrassed. He'd just shared a searing kiss with his female thousands of feet in the sky, on the back of a dragon. This was the stuff of tavern songs, something to boast to Merrick about when they got back.

He wondered if Elijah and Arii had done the same?

The thought had him wincing.

"Come on, you two, let's go back." Aeun finally said, laughter in her voice as they angled back towards the sea, aimed towards the castle, bathed in the light of a tiring day.

Nem's fingers twined with his, parcelled against her stomach. "I'm proud of you, Wolf."

He was taken aback by her words, the glow in them. He hummed, watching the shoreline, the castle, the flocks of ships grow larger as they neared. He even spied a few crew members waving up at their return, their smiles bright.

He was proud of himself too. "Look at you, teaching this old dog new tricks."

Her fingers squeezed as she laughed, and he couldn't get enough of the sound.

With the warmth of her still on his lips, the afternoon sun drying them, he felt peaceful.

And Krepth was a little more hopeful, and a little less afraid.

Chapter Twenty-Two

Nemesis

Dawn's light broke cold across the waves, gilding the sea in orange as it lapped against the hull of the northern ship where Nem stood on its deck. The crew moved around her with practised precision, boots thudding against wood, sails fluttering in their binds against the whip of ocean air.

She felt him before she heard him, his presence settling beside her like a shadow stretching long with the dawn. Elijah's gaze was fixed on the horizon when he finally spoke.

"How are you holding up, Nemesis?"

Whether it was the quiet weight that always seemed to trail after her King, or the knot of doubt that had taken root in her chest – even after the warmth of Krepth's arms the night before – she could not tell. But the words came before she could stop them.

"What if I can't close this one? The portal, I mean. What if I fail?"

Elijah shifted. When she looked up, their eyes met, and in his she saw the flicker of ghosts, the echoes of battles fought and fears weathered. She recognised herself in those shadows. He knew the weight of power awakening, the uncertainty, the fear of not being enough.

"You might fail," he said at last, his voice low but steady. A salted breeze caught his hair across his brow, his storm-grey eyes unmoving. "Power doesn't promise perfection, and fate doesn't come

with guarantees." He turned back to the sea. "But you're not the same person you once were. And this isn't the same war."

He paused, his gaze thoughtful.

"You've grown into something fierce. A light against the dark. Something that burns even when the shadows try to smother it. And when you falter – because we all do – you will not be alone. That's the difference. That's the strength. You're not alone."

As the crew took their stations and began unleashing the sails, shadows rippled across the decks. A flock of dragons swept low over the sea, their tails skimming the waves in glittering arcs, cries ringing out across the water. Cheers rose from the boats below, caught somewhere between awe and exhilaration.

Among them soared Aeun, her silver hide gleaming like a blade freshly drawn, each movement effortless, radiant.

No, Nem was not alone. She had not been for a long time. But only now did she truly feel the weight of that truth, the warmth of it settling deep in her chest. She thought of the girl who had awakened on that shore, memoryless and burning with rage, and then she looked at who she was now – scarred, yes, but steady. No longer just surviving. Becoming.

Elijah's smile was faint but real. "You're allowed to be afraid. Just don't let it be the thing that stops you."

"Spoken like a true King," Arii purred, her voice velvet and edged in knowing.

The shift in Elijah was quiet but unmistakable. He leaned in, the space between them narrowing as his hand found his mate's, fingers lacing with ease, like muscle memory. His broad frame tilted subtly, instinctively – less a barrier, more a shelter.

Once, Nem might've turned away from the intimacy, uncomfortable in its nearness. But now she watched, and something settled in her chest. The way Elijah's sharp features gentled under Arii's touch, how the corners of her lips curled with quiet pride, it all spoke of battles fought not just outside, but within. Of a softness earned.

Nem thanked Elijah, to which he nodded and shared a rare smile, as others joined them.

A voice cut through the quiet. "Take it easy, Tikkani! Gods, don't make me regret letting you go to war… again."

Nem startled, breath catching as she turned toward the sound. Familiar faces were threading through the bustle of the deck – once-recruits who had travelled beside them across so many leagues. They were no longer the wide-eyed, uncertain souls she remembered, but sharpened, sure-footed beings now wholly their own. She hadn't realised the shape of their absence until their return filled it.

"Quinn? Tikkani?" she whispered, and the latter stepped into an awkward embrace.

Nem's gaze dropped to the swell between them, the sight locking her tongue in place.

"I may be pregnant, but that does not mean I cannot go to war!" Tikkani declared, grinning as she waggled her brows at Nem's stunned face.

Quinn groaned. "Ariiaya, for the love of all things sane, talk sense into her."

Arii lifted both hands in surrender, while Elijah rubbed his jaw, failing to hide his smile.

"Congratulations!" Krepth's laugh came warm and sudden, making Nem start. She hadn't heard him approach. He greeted their friends with a mix of fierce squeezes and gentler touches, though his presence never strayed far from her side.

Two more figures approached.

"Where is my girl? Where is my future niece?" Luc's voice carried over the chatter, his stride purposeful as he made for Tikkani's belly.

Tikkani planted a hand on her hip, rolling her eyes though the grin stayed put. Luc was already rubbing the curve of her tunic like it might grant him a blessing.

"Who would've thought you'd be the one making kissy faces at my stomach, Luc," she teased. "I honestly thought Emerson would beat you to it."

"I haven't had my turn yet!" Emerson elbowed his husband aside with dramatic flair, then leaned in to whisper something conspiratorial to the bump.

"Yikes, what in Nyx's tits have we wandered into?" Valerie's familiar drawl came from the main deck. She strolled into view, hat clinging on for dear life, Lyda a step behind with a smile as wide as the sea.

Laughter and chatter rose around Nem, bright and unguarded. For a fleeting moment, it slipped past her usual calm and warmed something deep in her chest. But when Krepth's fingers found hers, the weight returned. She looked at each face – familiar, beloved – and the truth settled on her shoulders like armour.

Her power was no longer hers alone. It was a promise. A shield.

And she had to be enough.

Then the horn sounded, low and resonant, carrying over the waves. Sails groaned as the crew took their stations, boots pounding the deck. To the west, thunder rolled where their fleet began its slow crawl toward the mist-laden horizon. Dark clouds swelled ahead, like the maw of some ancient beast, patient and hungry.

The three Sisters of Fate had remained on land, sending part of their force to the fleet while keeping the rest in reserve. Krepth had called them cowards at first, unwilling to face a God, but Elijah had argued that a second line of defence was no poor plan. Nem agreed.

Now, as the ship lurched forward under the pull of the wind, Nem held Elijah's earlier words close. She was not alone.

And this was not the same war.

Nem had tried to imagine what might await them in the heart of the ocean, visions shaped by the magic-laced portals they'd encountered before, perhaps something vast and oval like the rift that had split open over Viridya a year ago. But nothing… *nothing*, had prepared her for this.

The portal loomed impossibly wide; a wound carved into the sea itself. It didn't shimmer or glow; it gaped, red raw like an open burn, unrelentingly dragging the ocean down into its churning, lightless depths. The water screamed as it fell, torn from the world and devoured. This wasn't just a gateway. It was a rupture, violent, merciless, and it had seemingly no intention of closing.

Horns signalled the fleets to slow, and from her position on the prow, Nem felt the unease ripple across each vessel, across the fetid air that blasted from the tear.

The shadows of dragons whirled past, scouting ahead as Elijah motioned a signal to the flanking monarch's vessels.

Take care. Be ready for anything.

"It's like he took a hot blade and stabbed the veil between worlds," Krepth growled, leaning forward, eyes locked on the void. "Have Ares and his beast already come through?"

"I don't think so," called Nem, a shiver hitting her spine. Something deeper, colder, told her this was only the threshold. The real horror – her father's prized terror – still lurked just below the surface, watching, waiting.

Her chest burned with dread, her mouth dry. The air felt heavy, as if the world itself were holding its breath.

Then, from the abyss, something stirred.

A sound carved straight through the silence. A single, drawn-out, *anguished* cry. Not human. Not beast. Just… wrong.

"The fuck is that?" Tikkani snapped, bow already raised, arrows glinting in the dim light. Quinn was poised at her side, face grim, hands curled to fists.

Silence followed the sound, deep, unnatural. As if the entire ocean had paused mid-breath, holding still in grim anticipation.

"Silver One, something comes," Aeun warned from above, her voice sharp against the hush. The downdraft of her wings stirred the sea spray and snapped Nem's star-flecked cloak around her like a signal.

From the portal, something began to rise.

Claws burst from the void, splaying wide before slamming down, gouging into the ocean's surface like jagged rocks cresting a waterfall. The sea recoiled, churning around the portal's rim as something massive forced its way through.

A colossal, draconic snout emerged first, misshapen and unnatural. Its jaw hung crooked, overburdened with uneven teeth that jutted like splintered stone. Water poured from its brow, tracing the deep, exaggerated ridges of bones above its wide eyes. Blood red, they stared with blind, ancient malice as rot clung to it like armour, clumps of seaweed, dirt, and time-worn decay trailing from its scales.

A titan.

It heaved itself forward. Its wings, vast, skeletal things, dragged screeching against the portal's edge, scraping it wider as it fought to enter.

The people of Fythnar had never seen anything like this. Not in dreams. Not in nightmares.

But someone *else* had.

"Nocturne!" Arii screamed, her hand slicing the air as the titan's call, deep, ancient, and resonant, rippled through the sea beneath them like a living tremor. "Ouroboros!"

A black dart streaked from the sky, fast and sharp, just as the portal heaved again – this time vomiting a swarm of winged beasts. They came in a frenzy, clawing and scrambling over the titan's impossible frame, their cries sharp and jagged against the low, world-shaking groan of the behemoth.

The titan moved with glacial weight, every step a thunderclap, water exploding around it, its form too massive, too wrong to fully register. Above, the sky darkened… not with storm, but with wings. The air screamed as clouds of winged terrors burst outward, flooding the horizon in a chaos of limbs, scales, and shrieking fury.

Nem twisted as the world warped into chaos.

She leaped from the prow, thundering down the deck towards the expanse of space designed for two dragons to land. Lysander was already leaning to allow Elijah and Arii to mount, and by her side shifted Aeun, feathered crest risen in anticipation.

No fear, no mercy. Thoughts are as deadly as the blade you wield.

The old mantra of her days as an assassin rose, finding the frame of mind she slid into when entering battle.

Her thoughts were for them both, but before she could alight on Aeun's sleek saddle, a hand clasped her arm.

Nem spun to face Krepth.

Don't think.

She caught his face in her hands, holding him still as if to anchor them both in this moment. Her gaze locked onto his vivid green eyes, eyes that had always steadied her; watching as their colour dimmed, the brightness swallowed by shadow. A forest of unspoken emotion passed between them in a single, weighted breath.

Don't feel.

But oh, how she *felt*.

"Become a sun, Nem," he whispered fiercely, those same words – spoken once before – echoing back through her memory. Back to the bridge in Viridya, when she'd walked alone into the heart of a swarm of the demons they now faced again.

"Become a sun and *burn them all*."

Power surged through her, igniting where his hands touched – one resting against her scarred cheek, the other firm at the small of her back, pulling her in. The world narrowed, then vanished entirely as he kissed her, fierce, consuming, as if nothing else existed beyond those burning points of contact.

His hand moved to her heart, rested there, as Krepth gave her his magic.

And she ignited like a rapidly stoked flame.

Light tore from her skin, lancing into the low, menacing clouds like a bolt of living lightning. It strobed across the sea, flickering over the ships – a sudden, blinding beacon in the rising storm.

Lysander launched from the deck, her thundering roar like a call to arms as a rainbow of dragons rose in their King and Queen's wake.

Nem took a touch longer to burn Krepth's face into her memory, the image lit by her light, expression fierce and full of determination and hope. She pressed one last kiss to his lips before tearing away, swiftly mounting Aeun.

"Stay alive, wolf," she growled, holding firm as Aeun reared back and bellowed a war cry to the sky.

Krepth flashed that maddening, roguish smile, the one she used to want to punch and now couldn't live without.

"Who else is stubborn enough to keep being a thorn in your side?" he said, arms raised theatrically. "You'd miss me terribly."

Nem let her small smile mask the churning she felt in her gut as she gripped the saddle.

The boat lurched beneath Aeun's powerful launch, her silver form streaking skyward with three thunderous beats of her wings. Wind howled in her wake as she levelled out, cutting through the low clouds like a blade.

Nem locked her gaze ahead, on the looming titan and the horizon swarming with fiends, where the battle had already begun. She squinted as they neared, for one question burned.

Where was her father?

Where was Ares?

The titan's mournful, deep call shivered through the air as they circled from above, its lumbering movements untouched by the swarms of winged beasts wheeling around it. Scores had already broken off to assault the fleets below, the clash of weapons on scale ringing out amid the cries of beasts and humans alike. Cannons thundered in furious bursts, while magic flared like scattered fireworks, popping against the attackers diving from the sky.

Nem studied the beast, leaning into Aeun's smooth, effortless glide. Its massive wings, folded tight against its back, seemed more monument than limb, and its body was a jagged landscape of shifting plates and clustered, hardened masses. It moved as though gravity itself clung to each limb, dragging it toward the ocean's depths, yet so much of it rose above the waves that she couldn't help but wonder how much more lay hidden beneath the surface. It was draconic yet not, something so ancient that only time itself knew what it truly was.

How could they stop such a creature?

Just as doubt stabbed at her chest, Nem spotted him.

Ares.

He pulled back his hood, silver hair stark against the stone-like creature beneath him. Though small against the creature's vast head, there was nothing diminished about him. Power radiated from his very being.

His face harsh, angled to the sky.

Angled towards *her*.

Aeun let out a snarl, raw and feral, as they plunged into a dive, an arrow loosed from the heavens, aimed straight at the God below. Ares' expression twisted, shifting from icy control to something unhinged, lips widening into a smile. Nem pressed her belly flush against Aeun's back, her dragon's voice a whisper of steel.

"Strike the source, silence the storm."

Taking down Ares was their best – and maybe only – shot at stopping his titanic beast.

"Daughter!" Ares' voice cracked the sky. The titan lumbered forward, its mournful howl a constant wail in the air, as if the very ocean wept beneath its gigantic steps. With a sweeping motion, the God extended his arm toward her, eyes gleaming like molten war steel.

"Harmonia! Let us set aside our last exchange; I forgive you for denying me passage before," Ares' voice rang over the tumult, triumphant and wild. "At last we are reunited in the flesh. Fools, all of them, to think they could keep us apart. You were always meant to stand at my side. Come. Join me."

Wind whipped Nem's cheeks as her magic surged upon her anger.

"We are bound by fate, you and I. I've *missed* you, my little chaos."

Aeun banked sharply, the force pressing Nem hard into the saddle. She held fast, body steady, while her head turned, eyes locked onto him as they arched around the beast's head, the call of dragons riding the wind that carried them.

Ares' smile widened, a savage crescent that gleamed with something darker than joy. It made Nem want to turn Aeun around and put as much space between them as possible, but she couldn't flee. Not now, now ever.

"You found your *Klad'ir*," he continued, voice dripping pride and possession. "That was my gift, you know. It breathes only because I willed it. My protection kept it alive, so that eventually we would all reunite. With me, we could shake the very roots of the tree of worlds. Together, nothing could stand in our way."

Nem winced at the rising tone in her father's voice. But her voice rang out like a bell through the storm, slicing through wind and rage and memory. It was clear, fierce, unyielding.

"I'm not the child you lost, Ares. And I am not yours to command."

Aeun hovered in the tempest, the hum of her approval charging through their bond, making Nem feel bolder.

"Maybe once I stood at your side, using my magic to aid you – I don't remember. Maybe once I believed in the fire you lit in my heart. But I've walked through the ashes of your wars. I've been scarred, I've lost, I've felt the pain of the people you wish to eradicate. I've seen what your glory, what your *power*, costs."

The God's eyes flared, she could see it even from the distance spanning them, flashing between blue and red, but she didn't falter. "But I've also found what you'll never have. Love. Family. A place to call my home. I will not let you destroy this land, nor any other. We will both stand in your way, and we will not let you win."

The God's mouth opened, but his attempt at speech was quickly drowned by Aeun's roar, a bellow of defiance which allowed Nem to continue.

"I'm no longer your pawn – no longer the weapon you raised me to be. Aeun is not a piece in your plans for power. We will not help you. Not in this land. Not in any. Not ever again."

The change in Ares was instant. Whatever warmth his twisted smile had feigned now vanished. His pale hand curled into a claw around the titan's jagged spike, teeth flashing like a predator betrayed.

"You would choose this," he swept his free hand, "fragile scrap of soil, this stepping stone of a world – over your blood? Over *me*? Your only kin?"

Nem didn't need to answer, for her decision was clear. She lifted her chin and steeled her spine as Aeun roared again.

"Destruction it is then." Ares growled, face tilting back towards the sea of ships. "Watch, witness the true might of a titan, watch as your world trembles under ancient claws, burns under ancient fire. You will quickly realise you've chosen *wrong*."

As the last word rumbled from Ares's lips, the titan's mountainous hide began to smoke, plumes rising like spot fires igniting all over its body. A low, terrible sound began to build, less a roar than a rending, like the air itself was being torn open. And though they were still a good distance away, wind whistling in her ears, Nem felt it: the shift in the wind, the sudden heaviness, the icy pull of raw, ancient power.

Dread sank into her bones.

"Attack. We have to attack," Nem whispered, breathless, gripping tighter as Aeun veered into a sharp tilt. Wind screamed past them, and so did a red dragon, its roar cut short by the screech of a winged terror closing in behind it.

Aeun's response came like a whip crack. *"No. Flee. We must flee."*

Fear surged up Nem's throat, sharp and sour – like acid. What defiance she'd felt sputtered into the void of Aeun's fear, of her feeling of acute trepidation, like she knew exactly what destruction Ares' monster was about to unleash. Instead of arguing, Nem leaned down, riding the whip of Aeun's swift drop.

Then, everything shifted.

The titan *stopped*.

It loomed in sudden stillness, a mountain rearing from the sea. Flumes of fire raked its colossal hide, brilliant arcs of dragon flame lashing in coordinated strikes. Contingents swept in formation, each blast a desperate attempt to find a weakness in the living fortress. But the titan barely flinched, each strike no more than a sting, an insect bite against stone.

The sound it made was low, eerie, like wind coursing through high trees.

Then its body began to change.

The thick plates of volcanic armour along its spine stirred, lifting, spreading wide like the slow, deliberate breath of something ancient. A bathhouse venting steam. A beast opening its ribs to the storm. Air began to pull, not drift, not breeze, but a full-force suction into the yawning hollows which were opening along the titan's back. Its enormous tail rose from the ocean depths like a lash, bracing it in place.

A single yellow dragon, too slow and far too close, shrieked as the pull caught it mid-turn. It spiralled out of control, wings flailing against the vacuum, before vanishing into the abyss of one of the titan's gaping vents. Its cry was cut off, consumed by the rising thunder of the titan's power.

More followed.

Several of Ares' own winged beasts were dragged in after it, sucked into the void with a terrible finality. Bones shattered like brittle twigs, their dying screams drowned beneath the deafening hum of a force too vast to fight.

The world held its breath as the titan's maw began to open.

Gods.

Nem's eyes widened. She cast a desperate look toward the ships.

To the east, Shifters blessed with the gift of flight tangled in violent arcs against winged horrors. Queen Freya, in the form of a great white owl, tore through the sky, her talons shredding anything in her path. Even from here, Iniq's sharp cries to her troops to hold formation rang out, slicing through the chaos.

Nem's gaze snapped south. Merrick carved through the enemy with relentless ferocity, Bo snarling at his side like a creature forged for war. Cannons thundered into the sky, while eagles made of ice – conjured by the twin princes, Jero and Thogan – sent Ares' winged armies plummeting like offerings of rain into the sea.

To the west, Vega fought alongside her comrades, clashing

with beasts in a blur of magic and rose-steel. Prince Kadec barked commands from behind the front lines, his army of vibrant archers loosing flame-tipped arrows that rained down in deadly waves. The Ouroboros swept past, striking once more at the portal at the titan's pause, while Noct's magic strained against the red-ringed portal in the ocean.

And to the north, atop the great battleship, cloaked in black, Krepth stood firm. Tikkani, Emerson, and Luc fought beside him, the heart of their resistance braced against the storm. Lysander, with Elijah and Arii astride, battled the beasts aloft, magic splitting the heavens in jagged lightning that left the heaving sea glittering with static. Bright flocks of dragons wheeled and plunged upon the creatures which descended from the sky.

They were all in the firing line.

And there was no way she'd reach them in time.

Unless…

Before thought could catch up, Nem's hands flew to the amulet around her neck and the sword at her back, thighs burning as Aeun slid into a dive. The objects of power were already humming, sending a warm jolt of energy sizzling through her arms, as if they had been awaiting this moment.

Air howled around them. Aeun punched through a violent downdraft, fighting the swirling pull of the titan's orbit. Her claws skimmed the surf as wild waves crashed beneath them. Above, Ares' beasts broke their swirling formation, wings flailing, cries ragged as they scattered.

Nem kept low, teeth gritted against the sounds of airborne war. Her breath came fast and sharp as she clung to the saddle, magic roaring through her like a storm. Her hands stayed fixed on the relics, siphoning their power while Aeun dodged gouts of flame and slashing talons by a breath.

Nem didn't flinch – she *couldn't*. Her fingers stayed locked, drawing out magic like blood from a wound, even as the saddle bucked beneath her and the furious calls of the people on the ships became clearer.

Still, they were too far. The air around the titan was thick, like flying through oil, pulling them down. The gravity in the titan's orbit didn't behave. It clung. It fought.

Snarling against it, Aeun suddenly speared upward, wings blazing silver. Her scales flared with light, a signal and a challenge both. Nem felt the magic between them ignite, their bond crackling as it absorbed the surge she pulled from the relics. She twisted, staring back towards the titan, sure that one huge, blood red orb swivelled their way.

They were still too close to the ancient creature, and too far to aid their ships.

A flash of dark blue snagged her attention, drawing her eyes back to the fleet. Beneath her, Aeun whined, sensing her sudden panic.

No.

Nem's heart nearly stopped.

From the heart of the fleet, a streak of cobalt blue tore upward.

Lysander.

With Elijah and Arii clinging to her back, she flew straight toward the titan.

CHAPTER TWENTY-THREE

KREPTH

Blood. It clung to his lashes, gluing them together. Speckled his cheeks and neck. The taste of it on his lips was wrong. The creatures just kept coming, landing on the ship, tangling in the rigging, scrabbling claws tearing at the once-polished deck. Pieces of their rotten kin littered the planks. Black blood, *tainted* blood, was everywhere.

Krepth was usually an optimist. That much was clear in the savage grin carved across his face, even as his sword sliced through the horde. Had he enough magic, he'd have shifted into his wolf, but his magic was more useful with Nem, who'd looked so powerful, so *divine*, as she'd mounted Aeun's back, her skin aglow with their mixed magic.

Instead, he howled like his animal spirit, vicious and exultant, his cries rising alongside dragon calls and bursts of fire.

But when the ancient titan rose from the portal, its vast bulk staggering toward the rocking warships as though they were no more than ants in its path, even Krepth struggled to hold onto hope. Fear slicked his palms and left his jaw aching from the clench of his teeth. Hope was little more than a ragged thing clinging to his breath, his cries of encouragement drawing beasts to him rather than lifting spirits.

And when Ouroboros and Noct returned from yet another failed attempt to seal the portal, Krepth nearly howled in despair. What good was the World Walker if he could not close the cursed thing? He longed to tell the bastard to crawl back to shore, for he trusted him no further than he could hurl him. Nem's voice whispered in his mind, '*Better he remain here, lending aid. I still trust him. You should too.*'

But how could they place their faith in a man who had not long ago sought Nem's life? A man who had struck a bargain with a God?

"That is an arch titan, the highest tier of beast known in our world," called Noct, his boots hitting the deck as he dove into a roll from Ouro's back. The dragon's pass cast them all in momentary shadow.

Noct thrust out a hand, engulfing a frenzied beast in flames, fingers snapping into a complex sign as a powerful gust of wind hurled the creature overboard.

"And we need to get the fuck out of its firing line, *now*!"

Krepth swallowed his anger towards the man, realising the grudge was pointless in this moment.

He'd deal with the fucker later, if they survived this.

"Firing line?" screeched Tikkani, braid whipping her cheek as she twisted, a hand subconsciously moving to her belly. Krepth's eyes found themselves glued there for a split moment, before rising to the opening maw of the arch titan, then to the sky. The beasts were thinning…

No, they were *retreating*.

"The Ouroboros has already gone to warn the others, but we need to move our fleets as far as possible. The only good thing about a titan that large is that it's fucking slow – our only chance to survive."

Noct took the stairs two at a time, skidding to the main wheel as a panicked Emerson leapt out of his way. He grabbed the wheel and yanked it hard to the right.

"Hold on!" he bellowed, as the ship's nose tipped upward, groaning under the sudden shift in trajectory.

The crew flew to their stations, frantic to secure themselves. Quinn, Tikkani, Luc and Emerson were already strapping in – pale-faced and windblown. Valerie yanked Lyda to the bannisters, helping her comrade as Lyda's ashen face twisted in pain.

Krepth seized a rope loop on the main mast, wild-eyed in his search for Nem in the sky.

But it wasn't her that tore the curse from his lips.

It was the streak of an old blue dragon, their King and Queen riding on its back.

"Arii! Elijah!" screamed Tikkani, golden eyes rimmed with tears. "No!"

"Are they mad?" called Noct, gloved fingers gripping the wheel as the ship groaned and cut through the surging waves.

Lysander came to a hover, her mighty wings beating with a rhythm that echoed like war drums across the skies, audible even over the rush of ships slicing through the waves. Krepth knew Arii. And by now, he knew Elijah. Together, they would give *everything* to protect their people.

Even their lives.

Above the crescendo hum of the titan's awakening power, Krepth's thoughts scattered, eyes locked on the figures atop the dragon. The space around Lysander shimmered, first a flicker, then a violent *snap*, as raw magic twisted the air. Elijah sat tall, arms cast wide like a conduit drawing from the heavens themselves, while Arii leaned forward, her hands gripping their dragon's spine, head bowed in fierce focus as she poured her essence through their bond.

The sky heeded their call.

Clouds surged above, bloating and darkening until the last shred of sunlight was snuffed out. Thunder cracked like the Gods themselves were casting judgment. For a breathless moment, Krepth swore the world held still. And when the stillness broke, day was gone. The storm swallowed the horizon, drowning the last trace of day until only night and firelight remained.

Then it came. A shimmering veil swept across the horizon, magic rippling like a living current, descending fast, a wild blanket of lightning stretching to shield the sky.

The trance shattered. The arch titan's keening cry pierced the silence, rising in a scream that turned its open maw into a furnace. Fire licked up its jaws, casting molten light like lava surging through a volcano's throat.

Krepth bolted for the main deck's edge, wind ripping at his cloak as he waved frantically to the Ouroboros beginning a low, banking pass.

"Shields!" he bellowed, voice hoarse with urgency. "Tell them all to form shields!"

Ouro answered with a roar, smoke streaming from his nostrils as he shot past. Every ship had wielders, mages trained for this, but war had a way of unravelling reason. With chaos bleeding into every breath, even the obvious could be forgotten.

Magic snapped in the air, veils of it rising like shimmering blots across the fleet – an eerie calm before the storm.

Then, without warning, a violent surge of blood-red fire erupted on the horizon.

And the world fractured into chaos.

The warship lurched violently beneath Krepth. His feet flew out from under him, body flung across the deck. The breath was punched from his lungs as he slammed into the wood, stars bursting before his eyes. He tumbled, limbs tangled, until he crashed into a scatter of barrels on the quarterdeck.

Screams tore through the air, near and far, as the titan's inferno, vast, searing, slammed against the centre of their defence. Shields strained to divert the onslaught, forcing some of the destruction skyward while limbs of violent flames seared through. The column of fire suddenly surged upward, as if the beast behind it had tilted its head, momentarily distracted. Flames and molten light arched above in a roaring wave, like lava poured from the heavens, the thundering maw of a beast made of pure hell. Smaller ships vanished in an instant, consumed by the firestorm, while the sea hissed and boiled beneath them.

Dazed, shaking, ears ringing, Krepth pushed himself onto his hands and knees, retching ash and smoke as pain lanced through his ribs. Around him, the darkened sky lit up in angry reds and oranges, a smouldering wound torn open by the ancient beast's fury.

Nearby, Quinn pushed back from shielding Tikkani, his leathers and armour slick with sea spray and ash. His hands trembled, unable to fully unlatch from Tikkani's shoulders. Emerson, Luc and the pirates staggered free from a tangle of scorched wood and sodden sailcloth, faces blackened and blank with shock.

"Is everyone alright?" called Noct between ragged coughs, somehow still clutching the wheel, a line of blood trailing down one side of his ashen face. The ship creaked beneath him, scorched but afloat, the dragon scale plates glowing from the heat.

Crew scrambled in frantic motion, some shouting, some weeping, others just moving because they didn't know what else to do. A few bodies lay crumpled and still among the wreckage, smoke curling from their clothes, their stories ended in fire.

"Alright, we're... we're alright," called Emerson. "Tikkani?!"

"We're alright. Gods, what fresh hell was that? Wait... where are they?"

Krepth staggered upright, swaying, eyes dragging skyward to the scorched heavens. To the space where Lysander had been.

The space that was now empty.

Tikkani gripped his arm, nails biting through the fabric. "Where... did they...?"

His throat bobbed. No words came. The fleet was scattered and ruined across the sea, some ships nothing but floating pyres, others splintered open, barely clinging to the waves. Those on the far outskirts had fared better; still upright, fighting to hold shape. The destruction was far less than if they'd been without Elijah and Arii's shield, and Krepth didn't allow his mind to fly to what could have been.

He exhaled a lungful of thick smoke, his gaze locked on the arch titan. Smoke jettisoned from the gaping vents and cracked plates scattered across its mountainous hide, its titanic form rippling with molten heat. The very air around it shimmered, twisted by the furnace burning beneath its skin. Steam curled up in ghostly tendrils from the boiling sea while above, the sky heaved with chaos – dragons and abominations continued to tangle in a savage dance, their cries lost in the roar of fire, thunder and wind.

They couldn't survive another onslaught like that.

One more breath from the beast, and it would all be over. Them. The fleet. The land behind them.

Their home.

Gone.

Elijah… Ariiaya… *Nem*.

They couldn't be…

Gone.

"There!" cried Tikkani, stabbing a finger to the sky.

A flight of dragons dropped from the churning tempest of clouds, smoke trailing in their wake. Across the fleet, voices rose, turning to cheers as they drew closer: their King and Queen, dishevelled but alive. Beside them flew Nem and Aeun, still glowing with a divine aura, as the dragons moved to hover above the fleet. Lysander's wings beat harder, her teeth flashing in a draconic grimace. Then the Ouroboros joined them.

"Another attack of that magnitude will take time for Ares to prepare and I don't think we will survive a second," Noct called, leaping to the deck. He swept a hand toward the groaning beast on the horizon, Ares's army of winged creatures once again encircling it in a grim dance, as if held by some unholy tether. "Now is the time to strike Ares down!"

Lysander dropped to the deck, hissing in pain.

"You think we haven't been trying to do that this whole time?" Ariiaya snapped, having just finished checking Elijah for wounds. Ash smeared the King's right cheek, his hair swept aside, eyes burning with fury and rimmed with the same exhaustion Krepth felt in his own bones. Elijah could still summon more magic, Krepth knew that, but even the King's power had its limits. He might shield them again, but there were only so many times they could be shielded.

The ends of Arii's hair were singed, her skin flushed, yet she moved with that same uncaring grace, as if she hadn't come within a breath of death by fire.

Lysander hissed in pain again as Arii slid down her foreleg, quickly tending to a torn, bloody section in the sapphire-scaled armour. *"The titan was distracted, else the destruction would have been far worse."* Her serpentine neck craned toward Aeun and Nem as they landed nearby, and Krepth's heart clenched at the sight. *"It was distracted by the Klad'ir and her rider."*

Nem's skin shimmered, her eyes glowing brighter than he'd ever seen. In that moment, she looked nothing like a Fae. She looked like a Goddess. Aeun dipped a shoulder and Nem touched down beside her, silver hair whipping around her face.

"When I drew magic from the objects of power," she said, voice calm but edged with steel, "it noticed me." As she spoke, she unsheathed the sword, lifted the amulet, the cloak billowing faintly behind her.

"They reached us just in time," Elijah added, grunting as he pulled the still-heated gauntlets from his wrists. The soft clunk as they hit the deck cut the silence like a blade. "Nem added her magic to the shield right as the titan struck. If she'd had more time to direct it... it might've held stronger. But the beast definitely noticed her."

"An arch titan is near impossible to kill. In our world, we put them to sleep for that very reason," came a voice behind them. Ouroboros joined the group, now in his human form, vermilion eyes scanning each face, pausing briefly on Nocturne. "We must lure it back beyond the rift – and seal it. If what you say is true, Nemesis, you could be the perfect bait to lead it back towards the portal."

Krepth swallowed hard, the bitter taste of bile rising in his throat. Speaking of Nem as if she were 'bait' didn't sit well in his stomach, and from what he could tell, shivering from his left, Ariiaya was feeling the same rising fury. But he knew enough to realise that this was their best, perhaps only, course of action. His mind was already pacing – racing – through possibilities, none of them good. Words clung to the back of his tongue, heavy and useless. Instead, he stepped forward.

Nem was already moving toward him, her steps sure, the hem of her cloak whispering against the scorched deck. Her oceanic eyes met his, calm and unwavering, lit with a quiet fire.

"Think about this, Silver Moon."

Her voice was low but resolute. "It may be the only way. The titan is drawn to power." She paused, and the wind caught strands of her silver hair, lifting them like threads of starlight. "And *I* have power."

Krepth's breath caught. He lifted his gaze beyond her, locking eyes with Ariiaya over Nem's shoulder. His Queen stood rigid, jaw clenched tight, brows furrowed with the fury of battle – but beneath it, in her violet eyes, he caught a glint of something else. Something fragile. Something raw.

That moment when rage gave way to heartbreak, when steel gave way to sorrow.

She was bracing herself to let go.

And Krepth hated that he understood why. It was the same look she'd worn after Lorch fell.

Like the wolf he so often embodied, a creature starved, wounded, yet faced with the promise of a kill, Krepth was far too stubborn a bastard to let go. His hand rose almost by instinct, fingers brushing the scar that cut across Nem's cheek. Her skin shimmered faintly beneath his touch, otherworldly, and when her eyes fluttered shut, he felt the ache of it in his chest.

"Become a sun, Nem."

Her eyes flashed open, lips curling at the edges. She turned to the others, her voice steady.

"I have a plan. But we'll need every magic wielder we possess. All of the magic we can possibly gather." She paused, eyes sweeping across them, fierce and resolute. "Because I'll need it *all*."

CHAPTER TWENTY-FOUR

NEMESIS

Though her friends hovered close enough to touch, they left Nem space to breathe, unspoken reverence in their stillness as she lifted her chin to the sky. To the roiling, scorched clouds. To the flashes of blue battling behind them, tangled with the last embers of the firestorm. Lanterns strung about the ship cast restless light across their faces. True night had fallen, heavy and unyielding, the kind where time itself seemed to bleed out beneath the weight of storm and smoke.

She closed her eyes for a single heartbeat, letting the world rush in, the cries of dragons overhead, the distant thunder of chanting soldiers, the low, menacing hum of the arch titan and the gentle sway of the ship beneath her boots.

The air hung thick with salt, heat and static. But in that narrow space between chaos and whatever came next, she found a flicker of calm.

She clung to it, shaped it, carried it like a fragile shield into the unknown.

Beside her, Krepth stood steady, his fingers brushing hers, silent and grounding as Noct spoke.

"When you're through, I'll work with Elijah, Arii, and the Ouroboros to close the rift. It's the least I can do," he said, the last words low enough for only her to hear as he cast off his cloak.

Nem nodded, watching him go to Ouro in his dragon form,

hunched beside Lysander as they prepared for flight.

"But what about getting back?" Tikkani cried, always the one to voice what others felt better left unsaid.

Noct winced, and Quinn gently lead the elf away, his voice a low whisper.

Nem didn't let herself think of what she needed to do, or if she should feel concern that Noct would turn again. Her assassin training pulled her emotions inward, folding them neatly into the far corners of her mind.

All that remained was the sea of eyes fixed on her, the steady presence of Krepth at her side, and the friends she'd made along the way. She understood the risk ahead, the staggering truth that once she and Aeun led the titan through the portal, they might not make it back.

Krepth's shadow fell over her, dragging her out of her thoughts as he stepped into her space, close enough to touch, close enough to *hurt*. She met his eyes without hesitation, though her chest tightened the moment she did. His green gaze, so familiar, held a storm barely leashed… one of grief, stubborn hope and that quiet, desperate kind of love they'd both stopped trying to hide

His hand hovered near her cheek, hesitant in a way that made her ache. But she knew why he was hesitating. She let her eyes roam over him, memorising so much: the sharp lines of his jaw, the proud angle of his nose, the lips which had whispered promises against her skin, and the dark strands of hair that always slipped loose across his brow, just like him, never quite under control.

She reached up and touched the dimple in his chin, soft as a sigh. "You shouldn't look like this," she said, voice barely above a whisper. "Like we've already lost."

His brow twitched, and for a second, she thought he might break. But he didn't.

"I'm trying not to," he said, rough and low. "But it's hard when you're standing there looking like you might shatter too."

A bitter smile tugged at her mouth, and perhaps she was no longer master of keeping emotions completely from her face. "Well, we can't both fall apart, can we?"

"No," he murmured. "What would I do with pieces of you? I need you back whole, *glowing*, my Silver Moon. This world needs you... *I* need you. Come back to me, alright? We made a promise to explore the sky together, remember?"

That nickname had annoyed her once. Now it filled her with a tiny string of endurance. She huffed a laugh, choked and small, unable to suppress what it did to her insides. The strength of his words, the thin tremor of fear, of anger.

He didn't smile. Just looked at her like he'd never get enough time. Like he already knew how this ended, despite his words, and Nem – for all her fire – had never been one to deny the truth.

And Krepth... he'd never been one to run from it.

But this resolve... this *hope*? It was new. A fire freshly kindled in her chest, a blade reborn in the forge.

"I remember. I'll do everything I can to return. I'll push this power to its limit, use it until there's nothing left."

Krepth's face stayed unreadable, save for the faintest curl of his lips. His fingers brushed her chin, tilted her head up, a barely there touch. "And that is enough. You've *always* been enough."

Her chest tightened at his words, at the love, at the sparkle in his eyes.

"Become a sun," he whispered, voice fraying at the edges, "and burn them all."

His hand, warm and impossibly gentle, pressed against her chest, fingers splayed wide above the frantic beat of her heart, as if anchoring her to it. Her gaze never wavered, locked with his as the spark faded from his eyes, turning green flame to dim, swimming charcoal.

Something broke open inside her. Power surged in her chest like a second heartbeat, then cracked outward, racing through her limbs like wildfire.

The people around them began to close in.

Ariiaya appeared at her side without a word, her hand slipping over Nem's arm as her magic flowed through the contact. More hands and fingers began to rest on her skin, her clothes, almost anywhere they could reach.

Nem moved her eyes to her Queen, watching the light of her skin wash over her best friend's face. Arii's chin dipped ever so slightly, violet eyes speaking volumes where words fell short. She didn't need a life bond to feel the emotion rolling from her and from Elijah as he stepped to his Queen's side.

"Come back to us," Elijah murmured, voice low but unwavering. "Because I fear what waits beneath Ariiaya's wrath if you don't."

He laid a large hand on her shoulder – firm, steady, gentle – and Nem nearly crumpled beneath the force of his magic.

Her legs trembled, but she held her ground, bowing her head to her King. Her gaze swept over the crowd, a mosaic of faces, skin tones, garments, expressions, as hands touched shoulders in a living chain that led, inevitably, back to her: the rising, radiant heart of their army.

Even the distant hum of the titan couldn't shake the gravity anchoring her to the deck, to this moment. To the power lent freely by family, friends and strangers alike.

Tikkani stood with her usual fire, one hand on Quinn's shoulder, the other gently resting on her belly. Quinn's hand touched Emerson, who gripped Luc's with fierce resolve. Luc's dark hand lay over the moon-pale skin of Queen Freya, whose palm pressed into Prince Kadec's. Then to the twins, Princes Jero and Thogan, all connected.

She caught sight of Vega, Iniq, and Merrick, hands clasped, faces turned toward the light. Bo's tail tip flailed as he pressed against the leg of his master. To the left of them, the southern Fury assassin Tora with cheeks and hair marred with soot clasped Sybell's hand, the Commander's other hand pressed to her brow in a salute, the glitter of one of Elijah's curse-chasing bracelets on her wrist. Even the pirates, Valerie and Lyda, had their hands resting on the arms of unfamiliar Fae soldiers. They carried no magic, human through and through, but their presence, solid and unflinching, made her heart tighten with emotion.

Right now, it didn't matter where they came from, who they were, what titles they bore, if magic rushed through their veins. They gave their hope as one. They gave their hope to *her*, draped it over her like luminous armour.

Nem's ears rang as her eyes fluttered shut, head falling back, lips parting, arms lifting as if pulled by unseen strings. Her mind surged, waves crashing, memories clawing their way up with blistering speed.

She could smell it, the rot, the stench of the undead, thick and cloying. Bony hands stretching toward her through the shimmer of her shield, their mouths agape in silent screams. Time warped; her light slowed the world, slowed every touch, every breath.

She was there again, on the bridge during the war in Viridya. Arms wide. Soul bare. Power trembling like a newborn star, a sphere of something ancient and untested, pulsing, desperate to obey.

Desperate to *blaze*.

Claws raked across her cheek. Tears shimmered like shattered glass in the light as she choked back a scream.

Her nightmare. Her anxieties. A beast that refused to let her go.

But this wasn't a nightmare.

This was a memory reborn, one that would consume the monster of her fear, torch it in the blaze of her light. Hands rested where claws had been. Faces fixed with hope where mindless, white-eyed undead had once gnashed their teeth. Wingbeats in her ears, not of the winged terrors but of power, of dragons and magic, raw and wild, thrashing the air into a trembling sphere around her.

"Ares and his beast will wish they'd never crawled out of their hellhole," Krepth breathed.

The demons in her mind scattered like dust as she exhaled, let her chin rise, eyes snapping open to meet his.

"You're fucking magnificent."

The world sharpened into focus – on *him*.

On Krepth.

This was her purpose. This was why she had survived. Not to bring destruction or to serve a bloodthirsty God, but to protect, to light, to shape her fate around those who now believed in her.

Wings glittered as they unfurled with a thunderous snap, and Aeun loosed a roar into the sky. Her silver scales shimmered with lingering magic, catching the light until she gleamed almost gold.

And in the heart of the storm, beneath the wide-eyed stares of all, Nemesis smiled.

A real, radiant smile. One forged by hope. One born of *power*.

†

They skimmed the churning sea, the flock of dragons a vivid streak darting low, Nem's light blazing ahead like a guiding star. Thunder cracked, lightning strobed behind the clouds haloing a blood-red moon as the storm continued to rage. The air thrummed with power as dragon calls tore the air.

Up ahead, the arch titan groaned, its massive limbs dragging through the sea like living cliffs, winged beasts swirling around it.

Nem leaned low against Aeun's warm scales, eyes narrowed, wind ripping at her hair. She turned her head as flocks of Ares' creatures began to break away from their host, rabid cries rising above the wind whistling in Nem's ears.

"We will draw the flock from the titan. You just need to get its attention and lure it back towards the portal."

The Ouroboros's deep voice echoed through her mind, and with a sharp nod, Nem pressed a hand to Aeun's neck as they split from the group. The distant boom of cannon fire barely registered – already the fleet had caught some of the flock's attention, their leathery wings slapping as they scattered across the sky.

Within moments, the creatures were on them. Nem's skin sparked as Aeun jolted, only just avoiding a shrieking beast that hurtled past, crashing headlong into the sea in its frenzy. Seaspray lashed at her exposed skin and pinged off Aeun's scales as they narrowly avoided claws and snapping teeth, careening into the shadow cast by the vermillion moon as they neared the arch titan. Aeun's wingtip cut the waves as she circled, thick steam parting like cut silk as Nem tugged on the saddle horn and they swiftly rose, wingbeats in time with the drum of her heart as they slowed to a hover.

"Ares!" she bellowed.

Though the titan continued to lumber, the man on its brow turned, his skin radiant, deadly divine, his grin wide.

"Daughter! Come to tell me that you have changed your mind? I knew once you saw the power of my beast, you'd be won over." A blink, and somehow, the God's lips drew wider, eyes raking over her glowing skin. "Resplendent! Look at you, so much *power.* This world will tremble under you, and I will guide you. You are *powerful,* Harmonia, my blood, my magic, my conduit."

Nem drew the sword from her back, steel singing as the pearlescent blade reflecting her face back at her, the shocking blue of her glowing eyes, the startling brightness of her luminous skin.

She almost didn't recognise herself.

She was powerful.

She was a sun.

Set to blind, set to *burn*.

"This power is not yours. It is not mine." She pointed the sword; tip aimed at his heart. "It is *theirs*."

Lightning snapped and the red sky streaked with blue as Lysander dropped from the clouds, cobwebs of sizzling magic rocketing over the titan's head, blazing across its scales as Elijah directed his attack at Ares. Nem didn't hesitate, didn't look to see how her father fared but slapped one hand on to Aeun's scales, the other spearing the Sword of Power into the air, and with a deafening boom, lightning shot into the blade as Nem threw her magic into her *Klad'ir.*

Together they lit up the sky like an exploding star.

And the arch titan's head began to turn.

Blue streaked past, a blur against the charged cacophony of their combined power. Above it all, Ariiaya's voice rang out, clear and urgent: "Go, Nem! GO!"

Red orbs flared wide as the beast's massive jaws opened like a yawning chasm, its droning roar carrying a mournful note. A sudden whoosh – then a thunderous *thump*. The creature's ancient wings snapped open, sending tidal waves crashing across the sea.

Nem barely registered the incoherent bellows of her father, his voice raw with unrestrained fury, his commands lost on the ancient monster.

"Hold on, Silver One!" Aeun shouted, her voice cutting through the chaos.

They shot straight up, wings hammering the air as they climbed toward the churning clouds. Nem dared a glance over her shoulder and instantly regretted it. The arch titan was already rising from the sea, its massive wings dragging walls of water in their wake, tossing the fleet's boats like toys atop the swelling waves. She snapped her head forward, only to be met by a wall of churning clouds, lightning forking wildly through them.

Aeun didn't slow, she surged higher and higher, wings straining against the storm, and Nem clung tight, her thighs burning, rain stinging like needles against her skin. She could barely see more than a few feet ahead, the roar of the titan thundering behind them, closing fast. Then they broke through the cloud cover, bursting into the world above, into a star-speckled night free of the storm.

A momentary calm washed over Nem, the sky stretching wide in endless blue and black, a cosmos of stars watching, waiting. Aeun exhaled, and Nem closed her eyes, just for a breath. For that breath, they were but a speck suspended above the clouds and war below.

The wind roared in her ears as they skimmed the surface, racing the storm, until Aeun suddenly lurched. The clouds beneath them erupted in a deafening blast, and Nem's breath caught as she realised the roar wasn't the wind at all. It was the titan, surging up beneath them, its gaping maw wide enough to swallow the sky.

"Aeun!" Nem screamed, clinging on as they spun, wings rising in a spiral around them, the world a flashing blur, narrowly avoiding the thunderous boom of the arch titan's closing jaws. Aeun's roar split the sky as she swung them so violently into a dive that Nem felt herself rise from her seat, muscles screaming as she drew herself flat, as resistant to the moaning wind as she could get.

They plummeted, a falling star hurled through grey and red, the stretch of sea below no more than a shifting smear. At first she thought she saw storm clouds, but no, it was the whirling mass of winged beasts locked in savage combat with dragons. Fire flared through the veil, bursts of magic sparking like lightning across the haze. Her vision narrowed, catching on the faint, glowing orbs scattered within the storm.

More portals.

Smaller than the great rift which had birthed the arch titan, yet no less dangerous for their size. Each one tore at the world with vicious intent.

In the chaos, a thought pushed through. She hoped Noct was keeping his word, that he was fighting to close them. He had seemed truly remorseful, shaken by his own folly in bartering with a God. She could only hope his defection would not bring divine punishment crashing down upon him later.

Heat flared at her back, wrenching away her thoughts as Nem chanced a look behind, seeing the colossal head of their pursuer, far too close.

How was such a huge monstrosity so *fast*?

"You waste my time, Harmonia! Surrender or be crushed between the jaws of my pet!"

Nem's own jaws ached from clenching as they veered just out of reach of the arch titan's snapping teeth. Her thoughts swirled in a frantic storm, eyes scanning desperately. The portal had to be close. But how much longer could they keep outmanoeuvring her father?

She steadied herself against Aeun's slick silver scales, pressing her palm flat. A surge of magic pulsed through her, and golden light flickered, tracing the fractures between Aeun's scales like veins of fire. The dragon shuddered with renewed vigour, and Nem banished her anxieties, determined not to let her fears cloud them both.

She shot a glare over her shoulder again, locking with her father's as the beast surged behind them, titanic and wrathful. Its colossal head broke through the clouds as they did, ancient and crowned in smoke, flames whipping from its jaws like serpents of fire. Its roar was almost more force than sound, a sonance of dread that seemed to shake the sky itself.

Their eyes met above it all.

Ares lifted a hand. Nem's heart clenched, caught in that moment.

They dropped, falling fast toward the earth as the heavens burned behind them.

CHAPTER TWENTY-FIVE

NEMESIS

Nem swore she had seen a flash of desperation. It was a flutter against the corner of her father's eyes, thickly ringed with lashes like her own, and as bright blue as a glacial lake. Bright with manic power, ringed with red, lips stretched in a grimace that looked on the border of panic.

Perhaps Ares was not in such complete control of the arch titan as he wanted all to believe.

That knowledge lent sizzling power through her veins, just as a torrent of fire screamed past her shoulder.

Aeun's cry tore through the air as they plunged, pain flaring sharp along Nem's left arm and shoulder, leather and armour blistering under the heat. The beast's attacks came in bursts – wild, unfocused belches of flame, thrown without aim or reason.

Ares bellowed into the wind, his voice swallowed by the storm as Aeun screeched, the whistle of the gale slicing over her scales and thunder booming so loud it drowned out everything but their target below.

The portal lay open like a wound in the sea, its crackling rim steaming like an overboiled pot. Nem couldn't see what lay beyond it, and fear of that unknown locked her muscles. Her eyes streamed with tears, her sweat-slicked palms slipping as she clung desperately to the saddle. Every nerve screamed with the agony of her burns and

the sting of dragon fire in the cracks of Aeun's armour, but still she forced herself to focus – to lock her gaze forward and hold, no matter how much she wanted to collapse under the pain.

Keep going. Keep going. Keep going.

The portal grew larger.

Aeun's wings rattled, a hiss seeping through her teeth.

Nem placed her glowing hands against the sides of her neck, continuing her mantra for them both.

Keep going. Keep going. Keep–

Darkness swallowed them as they hit the portal, and the last thing Nem registered was the realm-shuddering sound of the arch titan's roar, before everything went mute.

The sensation was like falling without sound, nothing but darkness around them, the golden light of her magic blanketing them against the rolling shadows. The screaming wind was gone, and without it the tears pebbled on Nem's cheeks. Aeun keened beneath her, shaking her wings out to the peculiar weightlessness.

Until a world opened up around them, a world of red haze, a blood-red horizon, a desolate place that held an immediate feeling of sorrow.

"A severance between realms, the purgatory of restless Gods," Aeun said as they passed the threshold and shot across dry earth, red dust clouding in their wake. Shards of earth drifted in the distance; skeletons of dead trees silhouetted by a misty vermillion dawn. The same sort of winged creatures that were ravaging their world flocked in swarms, while the undead drifted in aimless masses, lost in their wandering. In the far distance, she saw the silhouettes of buildings, spindly spires and crumpled frames. Faces lifted to watch as Nem and Aeun streaked across the sky.

"With this as his home, for who knows how long… I don't blame him for wanting to be free," Nem whispered, glancing back at the dark mouth of the portal as the arch titan emerged, wreathed in fire and smoke.

Aeun banked hard, and Nem worked on plunging her hands into the roiling sea of her magic, absorbing the chaotic mix into her limbs like a sponge.

"Harmonia!" bellowed Ares, his voice crackling with fury. He seemed at the end of his ancient tether, seconds from exploding with rage. This was a man who was used to being patient, but after countless years of being so, he was now dancing on the edge of explosive madness.

"Daughter, you are testing my patience!"

"His beast tires," Aeun hissed, as the arch titan's massive claws gouged the earth, its head carving a crater before screeching to a shuddering halt. Frustration radiated from Ares as he leapt from its head, violent magic cracking beneath his feet as they slammed to the ground.

"We have but a few minutes before it rises again," Aeun added.

They had only minutes before the portal closed too, if luck was with them. Nem could already see its edges rippling, the telltale shimmer of gold magic fighting to seal it shut. She pictured her friends on the other side, battling with everything they had. If she could get close enough, she could lend her own magic, strengthen the seal too.

Nem pressed a hand to Aeun's plumage, a silent command to land. She resisted with a low snarl of defiance, but relented, touching down with a few surging beats of her wings.

Nem tore the Sword of Power from her back as she landed, stalking the distance between them as her father let loose a barking laugh.

"You're just like your mother. I see her in you – the fight, the fire, the *defiance*. The very reasons I chose her, and the reasons I *killed* her."

The snarl of Ares's words stopped Nem in her tracks.

Everything had happened too fast. The reappearing portals.

The unravelling of her family's past, the war spilling across the sea. She hadn't had the chance to learn who her mother truly was, or even if she still lived.

Now, the truth struck her like a blow to the gut. Her fire-kissed left hand pressed to her chest as if she could soothe the ache blooming there.

Dead.

Ares had killed her.

Before she could drown in the bitter taste of what that might mean, of what her mother may have endured, Nem swallowed hard, raised her sword, and levelled its tip at the centre of Ares's chest.

"I'll gut you for what you've done," she said, her voice shaking, grief and fury tangled in every word. Though she knew now that she'd not been of complete mind as a child at Ares' mercy, she felt in her heart that she'd always thought of her mother, had hoped being in Ares' good graces would earn her the chance to see her again.

Her heart broke with this new knowledge, and that she couldn't even remember trying to get back to her. Magic summoned by her anger snapped across her skin, raised strands of her hair.

Her father straightened. His silver hair rose in a ghostly arc, lifted by the snarling breath of the beast behind him.

"There it is," he said. "That rage. That thirst for blood. That part of you – that's *me*."

His expression turned her stomach. The very thought of his blood in her veins made her want to scream. Behind her, Aeun growled, turning toward the open portal.

Ares stepped closer, and now that he was near, Nem truly saw him. He was taller even than the southern warriors of Jero and Thogan's armies, with luminous, battle-scarred skin that mirrored her own.

He didn't draw a weapon. He didn't need to. With a simple twist of his palms, power flared like a second sun, thickening the air between them until it choked.

He was the weapon.

"Why did you create me?" she demanded. "What's the point of destroying entire worlds? Who's left to worship the God of War when there's nothing left?"

Ares tilted his head, an eerily familiar gesture. She swallowed the bile rising in her throat.

Dark brows drawn, he replied, "Prayer is not what sustains me, Harmonia. It is their fear, their anger, their hunger, their hatred, their spilled blood. The ashes of their obliteration. It is what fuels me, what keeps my power alive."

Of course, the hope and prayers and whispered words of mortals and immortals alike were not what sustained him.

He had tried to build an army. Demigods of unspeakable power. Children born of divine blood, yet mortal enough to slip between worlds like ghosts. Why? Because he *could*. Because he had that power. How many others, like her, were there? The possibility of such a thing in worlds unknown had her thoughts wheeling. How many others had the Gods disposed of, or thrust without memory into other realms?

"None of the others compared to you, my daughter."

Logic of his madness unravelled as Ares spoke, cutting her thoughts as another truth settled into her bones. Nem searched his face, searched the familiar contours, the features she had inherited.

This was his nature.

It wasn't reason that guided him… it was purpose. Ares had been shaped by something far older, far crueller than understanding. He was war incarnate. He would never be anything else.

There was no swaying a God from their divine design. He was destruction. A force made to oppose peace, just as night follows day and storms follow still skies. Though Nem had once dared to hope the

Gods weren't what they seemed, one truth cut through her thoughts like a blade:

Gods could not be killed.

Only contained.

"It's a shame that *they* got to you… but this has shown me that perhaps this world you have called home isn't as… insignificant as I'd first thought."

Nem's sword lowered ever so slightly with her breathy exhale, and though magic continued to sizzle through her veins, her limbs felt like lead. Seeing the tiniest slither of uncertainty in her, Ares pounced.

Magic, forged into the shape of a massive broadsword, came careening toward her, fire and ice cleaving through the hanging red dust. Nem barely dodged, her burns screaming in protest as she switched the sword to her left hand and rolled, just as Aeun launched into flight.

The dragon's bellow tore through the sky, and Nem watched her fly. Heat flared across her back as she whipped her head to one side, and suddenly he was there.

Ares.

Heat scorched her scarred cheek as Ares swept past again, golden light slicing across his sneer.

"I had such high hopes for you," he spat.

Nem braced herself, boots grinding into the dirt as her sword met his in a shower of sparks.

"No matter," he growled, "I'll take your beast and offer it to someone truly worthy of my blood."

She barely raised her blade in time. His sword came down again, clashing against hers in a shriek of metal and fury. The impact sent tremors through her arms, her spine buckling under the force. Sparks danced between them. She gritted her teeth, heels digging into the cracked red earth, but Ares was relentless.

Then his hand clamped around her throat, massive and iron-strong. The clash ended in an instant.

Air vanished from her lungs. Her blade slipped from her grasp, crashing to the ground beside her feet. She clawed at his arm, silver nails tearing skin, but he didn't flinch.

"Like prayers on a Godless night," Ares said, voice like grinding stone, "like soil with no promise of rain," he squeezed, and Nem gasped, "you fight for a dying flame. If you will not give me what is mine willingly... then I shall *take* it back."

He smiled without humour, eyes glowing with ancient power. Magic sparked in the air between them, wild and burning. Nem's breath hitched as the pressure built, his hand tightening further, his will folding over hers like a storm. Her feet left the ground as he raised her higher.

"Nem!" Aeun roared from above.

She bared her teeth, blood streaking her lips. Her fingers dug deeper, silver and red staining the God's arm. The red sun crowned him like a halo of war.

Light pulsed through her skin – and something flared inside Nem. A flicker. A refusal.

A final surge of raw, burning magic.

"F–Fuck you," she rasped, the words torn but defiant.

Light climbed her fingers, soaked into her skin, washed up her arms like rising floodwater.

Ares' gaze dropped, narrowing. He stared at where Nem's hands were buried in his flesh, where his immortal blood poured in red rivers down pale skin now flickering – dulling – compared to hers, which blazed like a lantern too full of fuel.

"You insolent little leech," he snarled, silver hair catching fire with gold. "You think you can handle the magic of a God? You think you can take from *me*?!"

His magic surged. So did she.

Nem drew, *hard*. Against the scream in her mind, the howl in her chest, agony flooding her limbs. She pulled from him just like a leech, drinking the divine, refusing to stop. Her body rebelled: skin swollen with power, eyes blurred with tears, every nerve alight with pain.

It felt like she would burst, bones cracking beneath the pressure, but she kept going, the sound of her effort climbing to a shriek only she could hear.

Ares roared, but his voice was lost in the blast.

Gold and silver fire detonated behind him, Aeun's power crashing into his back in a wave of burning light.

Nem dropped. Her feet slammed the ground and she rolled, coughing, clawing at the earth as smoke and magic and light billowed around her. Ares staggered, ablaze, his silhouette shuddering in the inferno.

She barely had a second. The dragon sliced through the smoke, wings beating like thunder. Nem snatched her sword from the dirt, fingers slick with blood, and threw her hand up, catching the underside of Aeun's saddle just as she swept overhead.

Her cry tangled with the rising chaos: the guttural screech of the arch titan recovering from its crash, its limbs grinding against the broken earth, and the furious, bone-deep roar of her father.

She hauled herself into the saddle, muscles screaming, magic boiling beneath her skin like a tidal wave with nowhere to go. Her body shook violently, every breath a war. It felt like her bones would shatter from within.

"Give me the burden, Nem!" Aeun's voice cut through the storm like a blade, fierce and unrelenting. Wings flared wide, she banked into a sweeping arc, feathers and scales catching the electric wind. *"Before it rips you apart from the inside!"* Her cry rang through Nem's mind. *"I'm your Klad'ir – bonded from the egg, forged in your*

fire, created to be the edge of your will, the shield for your heart. You don't have to carry this alone anymore. Let me bear it with you. Let me be what I was made to be."

Her eyes locked onto Nem's, burning with a desperate clarity. *"It's time we stopped surviving and started fighting. It's time we tore our way out!"*

Nem hadn't realised she was crying until she tasted tears. She didn't realise she was shaking until her eyes slid down to her hands, bloodstained and quaking.

Didn't realise she was seeing memories, once closed from her, now splashing across her eyes like a dream in hyperdrive. A woman's face, looking down on her, soft eyes the colour of honey, hair the colour of weak tea curling around her cheeks. She smiled, eyes glassy with emotion, the peak of elongated canines washed with firelight.

Her mother.

The vision was blurry, in and out of focus, before it was overtaken by one of her gazing up at the back of her mother, her arms raised, a knife in one hand. Her mother cursing, spitting, as light drenched them both. Lightning sizzled along the sky, revealing the silhouette of Ares, his hand outstretched in a fist.

Not only did she suddenly recall every memory she'd been stripped of, but in came the emotions with such startling intensity that her breath caught in her throat and her lungs struggled to draw it back.

"Silver One!"

The sensation of wings enveloped her shoulders as warmth cascaded down the bond. Nem was suddenly holding a white egg in her young palms, its pearl surface catching the filtered light of an unfamiliar world.

Another memory.

"She is different to the others," Ares said, his voice a low growl, rough with something dangerously close to pleading. There was a bite in the words, a note of defence that curled at the edge like smoke. "This one will become my legacy. She already shows such promise, can absorb power as well as wield her own. She is both vessel and weapon. Any threat to you, to our home, to *us*… will be met with fury twice-fold. She will burn them through with their own power before they ever reach Olympus."

Nem glanced up, her vision trembling with the image of another God, not quite here, not quite distant. He towered like a monolith, taller than any she had ever seen, shoulder-length hair wreathed in a strange, divine light. His severe face was carved with a thick beard, immovable as stone. He wore a drape of cloth that wrapped his frame with ancient precision, a style foreign to her eyes, as though he belonged to a world older than memory.

For a flicker of a moment, she wondered what Gods like *that* had to fear.

Zeus looked upon her with something colder than disapproval – disdain, sharp as a blade. His eyes narrowed. His arms folded across his chest like a sealed gate.

Was this where dragon eggs were sourced? Where they began their journey before being gifted to the ones who bonded with them? Or was this where Aeun's kind of egg came from? The questions swirled, but the vision version of her did not seem to care about anything else. Not the scowl which the God of Gods sent her way, not the knowledge that Ares was 'showing her off' to his brother.

None of it had mattered to Harmonia, as she stared back down at the dragon egg. Her gaze was locked, breath shallow with something close to reverence. For the first time since being ripped from her mother's arms, for the first time since her magic had exploded and torn through her like wildfire, for the first time since Ares had whispered promises of purpose, power, a place carved from chaos… she felt whole.

Though she'd taken magic before – taken so much of it – drinking in the power of others to level cities and shatter armies, it had never truly settled within her. Like a bad meal, or a bad choice. It had filled her with purpose, yes, made her feel sharp and unstoppable, but never *right*. Never whole. That feeling resurfaced now, rising through the fog.

She'd been young, impressionable, brainwashed by her father, given promises he'd no intention to fulfil. Over time he had convinced her that her mother had never truly wanted her, her mixed blood a curse in her world. A calling to a fate unbecoming of a divine. A seeker of mere objects, a lapdog for Gods long buried.

Her dragon, Aeun, was the piece of her she hadn't realised she'd lost. A piece she'd always felt devoid of, until Aeun's birth. Until they'd shared each other's magic, each other's minds. It was a bright flame in the greyness of her soul.

She hadn't been allowed a childhood. No stories whispered at night, no soft laughter from her father like the ones her mother once gave her. He'd never offered her kindness, nor compassion. When he spoke, it was always of her potential, how she could push harder, do more, become something useful. A better weapon. A finer blade.

Not once had he embraced her. Not once spoken without criticism threading his voice like barbed wire. Affection was a foreign language to him, and so it became one to her too. Until then, all she'd ever felt was anger… tight, coiled anxiety over how well she was performing, and a biting rage at herself every time Ares' lips pulled into a frown. She'd thought she didn't want to be separated from him when the Goddesses cast her into the void. But by then, that hollow ache, that constant striving, was all she'd ever known. All she'd ever been allowed to feel.

The feelings lasted only a breath. Then came the numbness. Then the sea. Then the taste of salt.

A conduit of light.

An absorber of chaos.

Breaker of bonds.

Ender of worlds.

She'd been those things. Following Ares like a hound, almost giddy on the power he gave her, her young mind twisted.

But that wasn't her. Not anymore.

"NEMESIS!" Aeun cried, as the world warped into a single focus.

Nem slammed her hands against Aeun's silver scales – and let it go.

All of it. Ares' stolen magic, the magic from the objects of power, all that she could grasp from her own pool, and what was left from her friends, the people she loved… from *him*, tearing through her like wildfire.

Not the ender of worlds.

The *protector* of them.

A Protector of worlds.

No matter the cost.

She screamed, the sound raw and full of everything she'd held back: rage, pain, power, defiance. The magic poured out of her in blinding waves, lashing the sky behind them as they shot toward the only exit from this shattered purgatory. They lit up like a star, their forms engulfed in light. Behind, the undead wailed in an unholy choir. Creatures beyond shrieked their mourning into the ash-choked air.

Ahead, the arch titan stood at full height, wings spread like a fortress wall. The portal, their escape, shimmered faintly behind it, shrunk to a slit of light, barely wide enough to squeeze through.

And before the beast stood Ares.

Just a speck against the mountain of flesh and bone behind him. Bloody, smoking and shaking, but impossibly unyielding. His silver hair rose around him; his face twisted in fury and something else…

something fractured.

He was small. But the air around him bent like stone. Dense. Unmovable.

How in all the dying realms where they supposed to get *around* them?

Aeun's voice cracked through the wind, a snapping, draconic snarl.

"Not around. Through!"

Nem folded low against the saddle, every muscle taut, her body moulded to the curve of Aeun's scales. Her eyes locked forward, narrowing through the crackling sphere of magic surrounding them. Ahead, the arch titan reared, its massive jaws yawning open, fire building like a storm inside its throat. Ares stood beneath it, a war God made small only in size.

Through.

They surged forward, aimed straight for the inferno.

"HARMONIA!" Ares' roar tore across their purgatory, merging with the monstrous bellow of his beast.

The fire came, a flood of molten fury, and Nem didn't flinch.

They shot directly into the titan's mouth, riding the edge of annihilation. The flames tore around them, gold and white and searing red, parting just long enough for them to slip between death's teeth.

A sickening crunch, bone and ancient blood spurting.

And the world exploded into white.

CHAPTER TWENTY-SIX

KREPTH

Even in the frenzy of battle, Krepth's eyes kept straying to the place where Nem had vanished into the void. His throat burned for a shout of triumph, but the fighting left no space for celebration. Ares' spawn poured on, endless, flowing from new portals popping around their watery battlefield. Humanoid undead emerged from the water, scrambling up the ship's hulls like waterlogged ants. They clambered upon the deck, weapons tangled in seaweed as they set upon the crew with mindless, murderous intent.

Steel scraped close. A rusted blade hacked wide and wild. Krepth dropped his weight, drove an elbow into the slack jaw of the corpse before him. Bone cracked, the head snapping back on its last tendon. His sword flashed, severing it clean.

Krepth's gaze flicked back to the sky, to the place where blue and black streaked from portal to portal, Elijah, Arii, Noct and Ouro snapping the voids shut as quickly as they burst open. Above them, Lysander lingered near the largest tear, watchful, while Elijah pressed his will against it once more, his magic sputtering as it tangled with the shining ring, the portal throbbing in open defiance.

Yet even so, it was shrinking, Krepth could have sworn it.

The deck shuddered with blood, spray and the trampling of boots. Too many had fallen. Those left still held, though each face was hollow with exhaustion. Tikkani's auburn hair plastered her blood-speckled cheeks, one hand pressed tight across her belly, the other lifting her blade. Quinn hovered close, every strike angled to cover her. Emerson and Luc fought shoulder to shoulder a step beyond, a second line braced against the surge.

Valerie's commands cut sharp through the din, driving the crew to hurl the dead back into the sea. The black tide slowed but did not break. Below, Lyda limped through smoke to the cannons. A heartbeat later, thunder cracked from the depths of the ship, each blast rolling over the cries of the damned.

Every last drop of magic had been thrown into Nem's well, and while Krepth did not regret giving as much as himself as possible to her, it was making things a touch more difficult.

He slammed his boot into the forehead of another undead creature as it attempted to scramble over the side of the railing. The thing yowled as it plummeted to the ocean. Krepth cast his attention out towards the other boats of the fleet, breathing hard, hoping to glimpse how the others were faring.

The undead clawed their way up the sides of all the boats like slick black ink, their bodies dripping brine, eyes gleaming with pale hunger. They spilled from the sea as though the water itself had birthed them. He knew the creatures had no need to breathe, but did that mean they swam through the depths, or trudged mindlessly across the ocean floor? The image of them, marching beneath the waves in endless silence, gnawed at him.

Almost as unnerving was the vast shadow sweeping beneath the surface, a dark mass that warped the waves above it. It drove straight toward the southerners' ship, its slate-grey, rock-like hull looming against the spray. On the deck, Krepth could just make out Merrick, Vega, and Iniq as they fought together, unaware of what hunted them. The ship groaned under the pressure of the sea, timbers creaking, rigging snapping in the salt wind.

Krepth leaned over the railing, hot, briny air slamming into his face. He didn't need to look twice. He already knew. The sea heaved, and a dragon tore past, its wings stirring the water into violent foam, heat rolling from its body in waves that singed his skin.

He flung his arms wide, voice cracking through the storm. "Ouro! Get me over there, they need to be warned!"

Banking, the black dragon returned straight away, possibly also having seen the underwater threat. Swallowing, Krepth took a few steps back, counted his breaths as Ouro came into range, then he broke into a run, brain chanting *bad idea, bad idea* even as he vaulted over the ship's railing.

Claws clamped around his middle, nearly crushing the air from his lungs.

"I will need to drop you," Ouro's voice pushed into his mind, ragged and strained. Even the dragon was feeling the weight of battle.

Krepth pressed a hand against one slick black claw that dug cruelly into his ribs. "No need to be graceful, mate."

His landing was anything but. He struck the stern deck of the Southerner's ship hard, tumbled into a roll, and came up with palms raw from ash and blood. He grabbed at his sword, lips parting to shout a warning, but an undead was already upon him. It came shrieking, jaw split too wide, arms flailing with a pair of rusted blades. Before Krepth's weapon was even clear of its sheath, the creature's head spun away from its shoulders and its body crumpled at his boots.

"'Ello, wolfie!" Vega grinned at him, her teeth white in a smile that was stretched too tight to be real. "What brings you to our humble, ravaged little ship? Not the conversation. The southies do love a good brood."

"There's something moving beneath the waves," Krepth snarled, scanning the sea beyond her shoulder. "We need to abandon ship!"

Merrick stormed towards them, Bo close at his heels.

"I will not abandon my Princes' vessel!" he bellowed. "I would rather die!"

"Where are the Princes?" Krepth shouted, eyes darting over the chaos of the deck, not sighting them.

"They're aiding Freya," Vega called back, spinning her polearm and driving it through the chest of a towering corpse-woman armed with a pitchfork. "And if you ask me, Thogan's got the hots for the eastern Queen. Hardly surprising, though. Look at her. She's stunning."

Krepth could not stop his eyes from rolling skyward.

"It is my duty to remain here, to defend this ship until the war is won or death takes me!" Merrick yelled, slamming a fist into his chest with bone-rattling force.

"Now is not the time for stubbornness, Merrick!" Iniq's voice cut sharp from near the helm, defending a southern warrior who gripped the wheel, her bow drawn tight, arrow levelled at the sea. "Something is coming."

"That is what I was trying to–" Krepth's words caught as the ship heaved beneath them. Vega and Merrick crashed together, armour clanging, while Iniq launched herself to seize Bo before the dire wolf was pitched into the surf. The deck below split with the sound of splintering timber, the whole vessel groaning as a waterlogged roar rolled over them.

Another deafening crash and the bow of the ship dropped, the fiery sky suddenly all he could see. Twisting, he groped blindly for something to hold on to, fingers skimming slick wood, but then his feet slammed into a hard surface and he was thrown onto his stomach across the railing.

Screams rose above the loud cracking of wood as a few bodies – warrior, crew and undead – fell, splashing into the churning abyss below.

Holding on for his life, Krepth stared at where the ship's bow had been only moments before. Now it was being swallowed hungrily by the sea. He craned his neck, searching desperately for the others.

Above him, Iniq clung to the stern rail with one arm while the other held tight around Bo, the wolf's panicked whines sharp against the groaning descent of the ship.

"Iniq, hold on! Where are the others?" Krepth's voice fought to carry over the gurgle and rush of water.

Her eyes found him, wide and wild, green depths flashing with fear. A shout below dragged his gaze down.

Merrick and Vega dangled from the railing just beneath his perch, knuckles white, armour scraping against the wood.

But it was not their dangling predicament that turned his stomach with dread, hair whipping into his eyes as the wind rose.

It was the vast coil unfurling beneath them, an immense azure body twisting up from the frothing, bubbling depths. The head rose sleek and terrible, jaws already spread wide, filled with seawater like a crude goblet. It surged upward toward the flailing legs of his friends.

"You have *got* to be kidding me!" Vega screeched as the sea serpent's teeth snapped inches from her boots. Cogs clattered and whirred as she yanked her prosthetic leg clear of its bite. "Blast it, Merrick! Do something, use your magic!"

Merrick's reply was breaking with the strain. "I canno'. Spent it all on the silver-haired rider! Nothin' left!"

Of course. They had not considered what came after pouring every last shred of strength into Nem. Not all the magic wielders had given, but those closest to her had. There had been no chance to recover before the battle crashed down, fiercer than before.

Come on, Silver Moon. Hurry up and end it, was all Krepth could think right then.

"Grab my hand, Merrick!" Vega called.

The beast lunged once more, its long body heaving from the water, scales slick with spray as loose planks and splintered crates tumbled against it. Nothing slowed its hunger. Merrick gritted his teeth, muscles straining, but his fingers slipped as his curse split the air.

Vega moved with sudden speed, faster than most humans had any right to be. She swung forward, prosthetic gears grinding, and caught his forearm before he was lost to the sea.

Krepth lunged to join them, narrowly avoiding a crate that shattered across the railing. He had barely drawn breath when rotten fingers curled over the ledge beside him.

"Krepth, look out!" Iniq's voice rang sharp from above.

The undead hauled itself over the railing, body dripping brine, jagged blade clenched between its teeth. Cursing under his breath, Krepth scrambled upright, boots slipping before he found his balance along the thick rail beams. He gave a fleeting, silent thanks for southern shipwrights and their sturdy design.

His sword was gone, lost to the depths when the vessel first pitched downwards. He rolled his shoulders, forcing the tension from them, and raised his fists. The sodden creature jerked upright as well, movements sharp and puppet-like. It drew the blade from between its teeth, which stayed bared in a grotesque, lipless grin.

"Come on then, fucker," snarled Krepth, the invitation spurring the thing to action, weapon whizzing with its mindless movements. Krepth ducked and twisted, the undead's blade whistling past his ear, then shoulder. He moved on instinct, every muscle burning, waiting for the tiniest break in its assault. The opening came and he surged forward, slipping inside its guard.

His hands shot up, fingers clamping around its fetid jaw. The feel of its skin was like ice straight from the grave and revulsion clawed through his stomach as he held fast. With a snarl he wrenched, bones snapping, head tearing free from shoulders in a spray of brine and rot.

The thing did not fall quietly. In its twitching death throes, it clawed at him, dead fingers like iron hooks. With a violent shove he cast it away, the limp body crashing against the serpent's glistening hide below.

Krepth lurched to the railing just as the sea serpent's jaws snapped shut with a sound that curdled his blood. White teeth flashed, the air split by a hoarse, desperate cry.

"MERRICK!"

His vision spun. Perhaps it was vertigo, perhaps raw shock, but Krepth collapsed to his knees, knuckles whitening as he clung to the rails, unable to move, unable to breathe.

The serpent's vast body now coiled around the shuddering ship, water cascading from its scales, fins along its crest rippling like banners in a storm.

And there, in its jaws, Merrick was caught, trapped from the knee down. He kicked feebly at the monster's snout with his free leg, still bellowing prayers to the southern Gods even as Vega screamed above him, her voice breaking.

Iniq's cries were lost on the violent crash of waves as the sea creature renewed its fight, blood feeding its determination.

Helplessness weighed on every breath as Krepth began to climb down, the timbers slick beneath his boots. The sea was rising fast, churning and gurgling its way up the stern. He knew with terrible certainty that soon it would claim them all.

"Don't you fucking let go, hear me, southie? DON'T YOU DARE LET GO!" Vega's voice was raw with fury and terror both, tears cutting tracks down her ash-stained cheeks.

Krepth reached them at last, dropping to the railing where they clung. He seized Vega's arms, muscles straining, but the pull beneath was monstrous, near impossible. He braced himself, taking as much of the weight as he dared before he feared he would rip her shoulders from their sockets.

"Let me go, Petal." Merrick's rugged face was white with shock, eyes gleaming silver, accent thick as river mud. "No point us both dyin'. *Live.* Sing the song of my death, sing it proud. Embrace Iniq for me, ye' hear? Yer' both beautiful." His teeth clenched around his words as he added, "And don't forge', my kill count far outstripped yours."

Krepth barely caught the words, but Vega did. A sound broke from her, half sob, half laugh, as she spat burgundy hair from her eyes. She clung on, face twisted with effort.

"You aren't fated to be food in the gut of a beast, Merrick. You're fated to plague me and Iniq until the end of our days. You don't get to die, not before we've had the chance to truly know each other. Not before we've had the chance to double your–"

A sudden streak of pale gold dropped past, so fast that Krepth mistook it for a sack of supplies slipping loose. Then Merrick's bellow tore through the serpent's roar, his voice hoarse and booming.

"BO!"

The dire wolf crashed down upon the serpent's head, his great snout spearing into the beast's eye. Bo tore at the slick flesh with a frenzy born of instinct, ripping blindly, heedless of the blood that spattered across the deck.

The serpent bucked in fury, the ship's timbers groaning and splitting beneath the strain. Its shriek split the air, forced through teeth that stayed clamped around Merrick's leg. It did not yield, not even as blood poured from its ruined eye, its grip as relentless as a rabid beast locked on a kill.

Merrick's roar broke with terror as he saw his direwolf lose hold. Bo slipped, claws scrabbling for purchase before he plummeted into the black water below.

Above them fire erupted, a torrent blazing across the sky as Ouro banked past. The flames skimmed close, forcing the serpent to thrash, but not enough to free them.

"Hold on!" the dragon's voice thundered in their minds. *"I cannot get near without burning you all or dragging the ship under faster."*

"Save Bo! Save him, please!" Merrick's voice cracked, his strength little more than a ghost now. His free leg bashed against the serpent's snout in blind desperation.

Vega, teeth bared, clung on with every shred of her strength. One arm was locked around his, her own twisting as she somehow wound her legs about his torso, ankles hooked tight to keep him anchored.

"Stop squirming, damn you!" she howled, though the crack in her voice betrayed her as the wolf vanished beneath the waves.

"Hold your fire!" Iniq's cry cut sharp through the chaos. Krepth looked up in time to see her launch herself from her perch. His protest caught in his throat as the eastern Shifter dropped like a stone, dagger gleaming in her grip. She struck the serpent's snout in a shower of spray, skidding down its ridges before seizing a hold on the jut of its brow. Her blade drove home into the beast's remaining eye.

The serpent's cry was agony itself, piercing their ears, shuddering through the very bones of the dying ship. At last, mercifully, its jaws unclenched. The coils that had strangled the vessel loosened, slipping away into the frothing sea.

And Iniq went with it.

With the crushing weight of the serpent gone, Krepth braced and heaved, hauling the dangling pair up by sheer force. Vega clung to Merrick, her voice a raw whisper against his ear.

"Don't look, Merrick. Eyes on me, alright, southie? Just me." Her fingers dug into his jaw, forcing his gaze to her face, tears mingled with saltwater and ash on her cheeks.

They found a moment's perch, lungs burning, but Krepth's attention was already fixed elsewhere. Ouro wheeled above, banking for another pass, his vast shadow cutting across the waves as he swooped back their way.

"We have to jump," Krepth barked, seizing both of them by the collars.

Merrick's mouth worked, words spilling with the tremor of shock. "Me… me leg. It's… it's gone… and Bo, where's Bo, tell me–"

"NOW!"

There was no time for doubt. Krepth hurled them forward and the two went with him, a ragged knot of bodies pitching from the splintering stern. For a heartbeat they hung in freefall, the rush of wind and spray tearing the air from their lungs, and then the sea struck them like stone.

Krepth forced himself upward, dragging the others with him, his chest screaming for air. They broke the surface in a violent gasp, Merrick dead weight between them. Together he and Vega fought the drag of the waves, hauling the man as if he were no more than a half-drowned plank, away from the corpse of the ship that groaned and sank behind them. Merrick's consciousness had left him as soon as they'd hit the water, and Krepth sent silent thanks to the Gods for that mercy.

The northerners' ship loomed above them, crew dropping over the side on ropes. When they were finally dragged up on its deck, Krepth flopped to his back, staring up at the shivering sky. Instead of cursing the sea, like he wanted to, he remembered his flight over it with Nem and Aeun, letting that memory overtake the horror.

Thoughts broke as a rough, wet tongue flew over his cheeks, making him curse.

"Bo!" he coughed, flying into a crouch as the sodden beast shook his coat, relief making Krepth lightheaded. With a bark the direwolf bounded to where Vega and Iniq remained by Merrick's side while Fae healers tended to his severed leg.

Vega's arm held Iniq close as they placed their hands on the warrior's chest, their touches turned from war to comfort. The scene was hard to watch; though Krepth was relieved to see Iniq alive, he hated to see her pure, crushing twist of grief. He'd suspected something growing between the three for some time now, and the way they tended to the man left no argument over their feelings.

Krepth stood, wringing water from his shirt while sending another silent prayer to the Gods for Merrick's recovery.

The hairs on the back of his neck suddenly stood on end, and Krepth turned to the east.

Light flashed, momentarily blinding, drawing all attention to the horizon. The yawning portal, now a fraction of its original size, suddenly screamed shut.

Krepth clutched the railing, the sudden silence deafening.

His heart, damn thing, had never lied to him. It had always known, always told the truth, even when his mind refused to listen. Instincts, sharp and silent, rang louder than reason.

Behind him, his friends voiced their sorrow.

They knew, too.

Krepth kept his eyes on the sea, now clear and still where chaos had reigned just moments ago. The storm was gone, peeled back to reveal a pale stretch of dawning sky. The last of the beasts scattered, some of the remaining dragons taking them down mid-flight, looking like gulls streaking a peaceful sky.

Where the portal once churned, only the soft smudge of retreating clouds remained, blending into the first light of morning. The ship rocked gently beneath him. No more cannon fire. No more screams. Just the sea and its quiet breath.

He stayed at the prow, unmoving. The waves lapped. Something held him there. Hope, maybe. Or something worse.

He waited. Every second stretched thin. Breath caught in his chest, as if holding it could change the shape of the world.

But he knew.

She wasn't coming back.

CHAPTER TWENTY-SEVEN

NEMESIS

"Have you never felt true happiness before, Nem?"

True happiness.

Yes… she'd been truly happy… hadn't she?

She'd known this feeling before, that strange weightlessness, but this time it wasn't steeped in rage. There was no confusion, no sorrow pounding in her chest. Her hands weren't clutching at sand, and her lips weren't cracked with salt.

Nem's cheek rested against warm, silver scales. Feathers brushed her brow, soft and steady, and beneath all that stillness, her heartbeat thumped. Calm. Sure.

Strong.

Alive.

Two hearts, side by side – hers and her dragon's.

They hung in the void, suspended in a sky scattered with stars, a quiet world where the heavens stretched both above and below, mirrored in a glass-flat plain. They drifted without sound, gliding through that strange in-between, the only two souls in sight.

Nem tried not to think too hard on the moments before. On the God-magic they'd stolen and used, the kind that burned and tore and roared. It'd protected them, while almost ripping them apart. Nor did she want to think about the way they'd cut through the arch titan's fire and driven straight through the back of its skull. She didn't want to remember the sound it made, nor the way her father had shouted her true name through the blaze.

The light had swallowed everything – white, gold, red – so much light she could hardly tell where the world ended or where it begun.

Had they killed it? The titan? She didn't know.

They hit the portal just before it shut behind them.

Now they were here. And there was no exit in sight.

And she wasn't sad. She was happy.

"Ares is back in his prison. For now, at least," rumbled Aeun, her neck curving to look back at Nem, one oceanic eye blinking slowly. *"We did it."*

Nem stroked the place between Aeun's wings. "We saved everyone, right?"

Aeun nodded, silent.

Nem pressed her tongue to her teeth, her thoughts like a returning tide… slow, heavy. "You didn't explode… how are we alive?"

Aeun's silvery hide rippled, wings stretching in a near-silent beat. *"We shared the burden. Had you forced it all into me, neither of us would be speaking right now."*

"I saw everything," Nem breathed. "Aeun, I saw my time with Ares. I saw my mother. I saw the moment they gave me your egg. I saw my power – Gods, I saw it shatter whole lands with nothing but my breath. I used you as my conduit, my reservoir, and back then… we weren't like we are now. You were my familiar… but not quite my friend yet."

Regret coiled sharp in her chest, pulling her shoulders inward.

"We were together only a short time before they tore us apart," Aeun said gently. *"But even then, you cared for me. You tried to keep me safe from Ares, in all the small ways a child could. You were never cruel. And that's how I knew you were different. That's why our bond endured."*

"I'm so sorry, Aeun." Nem swallowed. "Now we are stuck here, with no way back. It's my fault. I shouldn't have dragged you back to that world."

Aeun's feathers fluttered gently, her long neck curling as she angled her head, one blue eye locking on Nem. The starlight stuttered across her scars, casting them in silver relief, etched like old runes across her scales. Nem's magic was nearly drained, a faint shimmer still clinging to her skin, the last light between them.

"If I've learned anything," Aeun said, voice low, wings folding close, *"from the time we've shared, and the years we lost, it's this: you were never one to sit in your thoughts for long. You were always moving forward, always reshaping what was given to you. Even as a child, you hungered for more. Not more power, but more knowing. More understanding. You wanted love, and though this made you impressionable, your heart is pure. You never truly wished to use your magic for destruction; you yearned to use it for a better purpose. You'd press your hands to every new world before it had even finished forming, trying to learn it before it shattered. That fire, that drive… it came from your mother. A dragon knows these things."*

Nem stared down at her hands.

Hands that had traced Krepth's skin like a prayer.

Hands that had drawn a God's blood and magic, turning it against his own monster.

Hands that had sealed rifts to protect their home.

A pulse flickered on the horizon, a tremble in the dark, faint but insistent.

Her memories were still scattered, fogged and fractured. But instinct had never failed her. Not once. It was the one constant; curiosity edged with caution.

The darkness rippled again.

Nem exhaled slowly, pressing her palm to Aeun's scaled shoulder.

No words passed between them, just the silent current that surged when minds knew each other too well for speech.

They turned together.

She raised her hand, not fully knowing why, only that it felt right. Fingers traced a symbol in the air. Something ancient, something *hers*. Her lips curved. The ripple yawned wide, folding outward.

A portal.

As the unknown unfolded before them, her heartbeat kept whispering the same word.

Home.

Chapter Twenty-Eight

Perhaps if he threw himself into the sea, the ache in his chest would go with him. He felt the hollow, dragging weight of dead hope as Ariiaya screamed her grief at the sky. Maybe then her rage, her heartbreak, the raw fury of a sister mourning her best friend, would finally quiet. The grief that consumed his friends, too. Maybe then it would all just... end.

Never had he felt such pain; but never had he been a coward who shied from hurt.

From the prow Krepth watched, a shadow against the dawn, as Elijah folded his queen against his chest, silent and sturdy, a stone weathering her grief.

He should be consoling his friends, but he felt numb, strange, separate. Quinn soaked Tikkani's tears in his soiled tunic, holding her as Emerson and Luc embraced them on their knees on the deck. Had he been of clear mind, he would have appreciated the steady presence of Vega, Iniq and Merrick at his back, the latter sporting a heavily bandaged stump where his leg used to be and leaning on the other two for support.

But his mind was a silent resonance, a numb drone of sea waves.

The ship's crew set about preparing to sail, temporary repairs in place for the journey home.

Krepth's eyes, unbidden, were drawn to the sea.

To the roiling line speckled with seabirds, scattered and still-burning debris floating like dots, the sun rising above the glass shard horizon.

To the pulse of strange, unnatural light above the dark waves.

He narrowed his gaze, turned towards it.

"The rift is sealed, and it will take Ares some time to open one like that again," Ouro said, helping Valerie with Lyda, who winced and hopped on one leg, having broken the other during battle. "But for now, Fythnar is safe."

The sun's warmth touched the charred wood of the deck, dousing Krepth's cold skin, chasing the chill from the night away.

It reminded him of her.

"Become a sun, Nem."

"Wait." His voice was a whip crack. "Just, wait."

"Krepth, I know you're grieving; we all are. The people need to get back to land. They need to mourn their own losses, patch their wounds, go home to their loved ones. We all do." Iniq placed a hand gingerly on his shoulder, hesitantly.

The contact didn't register, for his entire being was focused on the sea.

On the rise of the sun, on the ripples of light fanning beneath the waves.

"Krepth…" Arii's voice barely rose above the wind.

"Just… wait," he murmured again.

Her hand found his, the one that had been silently carving furrows into the charred balustrade. She closed her fingers around it, firm, and pressed it to her chest where he could feel the steady thump of her heart.

"Nem… she…"

Krepth didn't answer. His eyes locked on the horizon, narrowed and burning, as if sheer will might cleave the sky and bring her back to him.

Then the air *shivered*.

"She knew what she was doing–"

"*Look*," Krepth breathed, the word a pulse, tugging Arii forward. He stepped to the prow, voice sharp enough to silence the deck. The others gathered at his back, drawn by the sudden charge in the air.

He lifted a hand to the light, shielding his eyes.

Behind his fingers, the sun itself began to split, no sound, only light tearing like golden silk. A fissure curled through it, slow and deliberate, as though some unseen blade had cleaved the day itself in two.

And then…

Wings.

Vast, radiant, slicing through the rift. A figure emerged from the light, outlined in a corona of flame and brilliance, wings aglow, silver and searing, as though the sun itself bent around them. A dragon and rider, etched in light, descending as if the sky itself had whispered them home.

"Impossible," Merrick breathed.

Vega's gasp turned into a sob as she threw her arms around his waist. He caught her, wobbling on one leg as he held her tight, his other arm drawing Iniq close, the eastern warrior's face lit gold, one hand raised toward the sky in silent awe.

No one spoke.

Not at first.

They only watched as Nemesis Rion cut through the sunlight, her silver dragon soaring a path over the crystal sea. And for a single, breathless moment, it felt as though his world had been suspended, his breath fixated, waiting just for her return. Waiting to see that she was real, and not a mirage conjured by the Gods.

Arii punched a fist to the air, crying her joy and relief as Nem and Aeun swept over their heads, ash and dust floating in their wake. Cheers erupted across the remaining fleet. Friends embraced, soldiers and monarchs alike drawn together by sheer, unfiltered relief. Laughter tangled with tears.

Elijah stepped forward, flicking a burst of gentle magic toward Aeun's feet, steadying the dragon as she dipped low, wings trembling with exhaustion. The deck shuddered under her weight, but she landed safely.

Lysander let out a roar that split the clouds, and the other dragons answered. One by one, their voices rose in a thunderous chorus that echoed across the skies.

There was no hesitation, no clearer path.

Krepth moved through the crowd, through the surge of celebration, the tangled limbs and lifted arms and jubilant noise, cutting through it all with one purpose. And when he reached her, when the chaos parted just enough, there she was.

Nem stood tall, wind lifting the edges of her silver hair, her scars like warrior's marks, her face tilted toward him. Her eyes were wide, unguarded; softer than he'd ever seen them. No walls. No mask.

The moment broke the air between them.

His hands cupped her face, surveying every inch. Her throat was raw, reddened, with fresh indentations already darkening into bruises around the shadow of the old scar. When her hands lifted to rest lightly over his, her eyes fluttering closed at the touch, he noticed the blood dried thick across her fingers and palms. She had fought hard. This would be a story whispered in halls and sung in taverns, but to him it was only a reminder of how close he had come to losing her.

Again.

"He's contained, for now," she whispered, voice hoarse and frayed. The rasp of it made him wince. He hated to think why her voice had broken so, hated to picture the moment her throat had been struck, or gripped, or worse. Yet the words themselves mattered most. Ares was contained.

That knowledge loosened something tight in his chest, let the air flow easier through his lungs, even as the last note of her warning echoed like a crack in stone. For now. The thought coiled cold in his gut, but he clung to the only truth which mattered in this moment: she was alive.

"You're alright," Krepth gasped.

"You're shaking," she shot back, heart not quite in it, as his thumb brushed across her bottom lip. Her eyes strayed past him then, drawn to where their friends stood gathered. Battered, bloodied, but still alive.

Nem drank them in, damp lashes drawing wide as she took in the shining eyes set in haggard faces, the ash that dulled every colour, Merrick's missing limb. Her brows pinched, anguish bleeding through, and Krepth gently drew her gaze back to him before it could consume her.

With her attention fixed on him once more, with the glow of light still alive beneath her skin, threads of residual magic tangling through her hair and caressing the tips of his fingers, Krepth let himself drink her in. Every line, every scar, every breath. Beyond grateful that she stood here, that she had fought her way back to him. Never more grateful for the quiet her touch gave him.

"We have a lot to catch up on, clearly. Maybe on dragon-back, on the flight home?" His smile was faint as he spoke, pulled taut by exhaustion, but relief softened it, soaking deep into his bones. Then, to gentle her heart, he added, "Everyone survived, Silver Moon."

He would have thanked the Gods, but he knew it was not their mercy which had spared her. Spared them all and spared their land.

It was Nem's own determination, her own strength, the power of hope she'd been gifted by so many here. Friends, family, strangers alike. It was thanks to her dragon, Aeun, who stood nearby, watching them with soft, blue eyes. Perhaps it was a touch of fate that had guided them to this day, not grand or merciful, but a quiet thread of design, a careful weaving of silver through shadow.

Words died in his throat as her hands tangled in his hair, pulling him to her, and their lips met in a kiss that felt like gravity, drawing everything *home*.

EPILOGUE

NEMESIS

ELEVEN MONTHS LATER

Nem was beginning to realise that this feeling – breath full in her lungs, embers steady in her chest, weightlessness in her shoulders – was something rare. Something fragile and unguarded.

Happiness, perhaps.

Love, definitely.

And exhaustion, curling at the edges like the final golden light of day.

Eleven months had passed since she had sealed Ares and his arch titan into their purgatory, and in that time, the courts had slowly begun to rebuild once again. The land's magic and weather had begun to mend. Slowly but surely.

A soft coo broke the afternoon stillness, followed by a hiccup then a full-bodied wail that scattered birds from the willow's crown. Emerson scooped the babe into his arms, cradling her with practiced ease. He whispered gentle nonsense against her cheek while his husband beamed over his shoulder.

"She really does have her mother's eyes," he said, his own shining. "As gold as the castle used to be."

Tikkani rolled her eyes, but took the child with tenderness, pressing her to her chest. Tiny fingers latched onto her tunic with determined insistence.

"And she's got my appetite," she sighed, "and her father's patience."

The baby shrieked once more, then quieted instantly under Quinn's soft touch, his hand smoothing over her crown of mousy brown hair.

Nearby, Arii lay sprawled on a blanket, her head in Elijah's lap, his fingers threading absently through her curls while his other hand rested upon hers on her stomach as they watched dragons wheel and dive around the sky-bound spires of their castle home.

In the two years since the war at Ayrith castle, they had all made it a point to gather like this, gather in Lorch's memory. Celadine, who would usually have been in attendance, had instead left them with an array of Lorch's favourite foods, while she was called away to attend a birth.

Though disappointed to miss the second gathering in what was becoming their budding tradition, she promised she would celebrate the late King's life once her duties had eased. Her daughter, Mia, had wished to remain, yet the chance to gain experience in birth was too valuable, especially with what lay ahead in the coming months. During the war against Ares, Cela and Mia had remained at the castle. Though as useful as their healing abilities would have been on the battlefield, Arii had insisted they were needed to protect those who needed to stay home.

Under the shade of the willow, Krepth lay with arms folded behind his head, eyes closed. Nem rested with her head on his thigh as the sun slipped through the branches in slivers of gold. The tree had grown tall since Arii had planted it on the hill crest, the place where she visited the graves of Lorch, Ghila and Elijah's parents.

Now the hillside had become something softer. A place for rest. For peace. A place for quiet memories to form.

"Ever thought about… that?" Krepth asked suddenly, voice half-drowsy.

Nem blinked up at the rustling canopy, pulled from her doze by the sound of his voice. "Of what?"

"Children," he murmured. "Little ones. Pups."

She sat up sharply. Her eyes narrowed. "Krepth…"

"What?" he grinned without opening his eyes. "Can't blame a man for getting clucky when his Goddess of a fiancé finally has time for him between saving the realms and closing every damned portal."

Nem huffed, but her heart wasn't in it. Of course she'd thought about it.

Especially after Queen Ariiaya's announcement that they were expecting an heir. The soft shift in her friend's expression, those violet eyes bright with new purpose, and maybe a touch of hormonal menace . It had stirred something in her.

She'd imagined it, wondered about it in quiet moments between battles. She and Krepth had spoken about it once, maybe twice. But always with the same agreement: not yet. Not while the world still teetered, not while the portals still clawed open without warning. So far, Ares hadn't shown his face, but she knew he was still out there, biding time.

She'd even solved the one thing that had made things difficult before, the siphoning that laced every touch; she'd found a way to quiet it, to let herself be close to Krepth without draining his magic or severing him from his wolf. They could be together when duty didn't pull them apart, and that knowledge had lifted some of the anxiety chest.

Though Nem was the one they turned to now, the realm's reluctant 'portal chaser', ever since Nocturne vanished after the battle at sea. More responsibility, a bit more weight, but a duty she was determined to uphold.

A purpose. *Her* purpose.

The otherworldly stranger had kept true to his word, lending his strength in closing the portals during the battle and making no further attempt upon her life. She could not help but feel a measure of pity for the man, and as her gaze travelled across their gathering, she found she understood what drove him. A passing shadow drew her eyes skyward, Aeun's gentle trill sending a shiver of warmth down her spine.

The bond and friendship she shared with the dragon was sacred to her, a part of herself she could never be without. So she understood his desire and his motives to protect his family; to have a dragon of his own for that purpose. Though he hadn't explained their troubles further, she hoped their paths would cross again.

She would not admit that part to Krepth. Though they were not fated mates, he was fiercely protective and had confessed to not liking Noct at all. It was strange, because the two were remarkably alike with their roguish smiles.

The way Krepth had worn such a smile when he had dropped to one knee, the crash of the sea behind him, bathed in the brilliant blaze of a sunset. Upon the bluff, with the School of Fate to their right, the beach where she had been found sprawled below. The smile, that roguish one she had come to know, was always used when he was masking something, whether nerves, anger or pain.

She had realised this when she saw his hands trembling, lifting a ring between them.

The ring, a simple band of silver, a quaint diamond in an almond drop, almost like a dragon's egg reflecting the moon, held in his fingers.

"Marry me, Silver Moon."

She was not even sure if she had said yes, amidst the whispers of joy, the breathless kiss they shared, the thundering, jubilant roar of Aeun nearby. The smile had shifted, wide, beaming, genuine, and it made her heart gallop. Yet there had not been a moment's hesitation, no thoughts of when, why or what if. She had not thought she could feel more whole, but she did, in his arms upon the bluff, sea breeze battering their hair and salty tears on her cheeks.

He had indeed kept his promise to create new memories where once she had none.

Nem tilted her head back now, in the shadow of the willow, looking at her fiancé, the grin she'd always loved painted across his face now. She leaned back on his chest, her nails trailing idle patterns over his forearm.

"Maybe," she whispered in reply. "One day."

They both wanted it. One day. When the world was ready. When she was ready.

But here, under the willow, in the sun, surrounded by laughter and dragons and a child with gold-flecked eyes... it was easy to imagine what that future might feel like.

Arii grinned, reaching towards their board of cakes, fruits, meats and cheeses, aiming for a dollop of soft cheese. Elijah gently changed the trajectory of her hand towards the sliced apples instead.

Now, Nem had her purpose, not one forged in prophecy or dictated by Gods, but one chosen with her own two hands. To protect the family she had found, the ones who loved her fiercely and without condition, just as she loved them.

The home she had come to cherish, not because it was written in the stars, but because she had fought for it – fought for it with the same fire she'd once given to fate itself.

For the silver dragon who danced along the water's surface, skimming claws over waves like a whisper to the wind, her call rising in harmony with her kin.

For her fiancé… the man who had never been promised to her by any divine thread, but had still chosen her, every day, with eyes like the deep forests where they would one day build a life. A quiet one, filled with new memories, and perhaps, when the world allowed it, the soft laughter of a child or two.

But until then, her path was clear.

It was her Goddess-given charge to protect this realm from whatever dared rise against it. To guard its borders, its skies, its people. Not out of divine duty, but out of *love*.

And she would.

She would fight for it again and again.

For as long as the stars burned.

Until the sun dimmed to ash and darkness, when time forgot her name, and all that remained was her light.

ACKNOWLEDGEMENTS

I can hardly believe I am here again, writing the acknowledgements for my fourth published book. It feels surreal, and I cannot properly put into words how thankful I am to have reached this point. This world has been alive and out in the wild for years now, and to still be here, sharing these stories, is something I owe entirely to you, the reader. Thank you for sticking with me through four whole books. Whether you have been here since the very beginning or whether you have only just joined me on this wild journey, THANK YOU. It means the absolute world to me.

There are so many people to thank, because I would never have made it to this moment without every single one of them. So let us begin!

First, to my husband, Greg. You have been at my side through every event, helping me plan, pack, and make each stall just right. You have restocked books, researched special editions, kept track of accounts, and somehow managed the endless invoices. You are my accountant, my quiet but steadfast fan, and my partner in every way. I honestly could not do this without you. I love you and I appreciate you more than words can say.

To my son, Eli. You amaze me every day. You were born only a few months before I published Love, Blood and Fury, and now, four years later, you walk into a bookshop, see my books on the shelves, point them out and shout proudly for the whole shop to hear, "Mum, that's your book! You made those books!" You make my heart burst. I am so proud of the smart, hilarious, cheeky little man you are becoming.

You are my best little buddy and I love you dearly.

To my parents, Lynne, Allan and Carolyn. Thank you for your endless support and enthusiasm. My love of reading is because of you, and my creativity comes from the way you encouraged and nurtured that spark when I was little. I carry that gift with me always, and I am forever grateful.

To my wonderful parents-in-law, Susan and Robert. Thank you for whisking Eli away on play dates so I could write, and for sharing in my excitement every step of the way. Your encouragement has meant the world.

To my friends and extended family who have been cheering me on since the start, thank you for every encouraging word, for buying copies of my books, and for following along with the story as it grew. Thank you!

To Katie, the queen of colour tabs, the "how did he get from here to there?" eagle-eyed BETA reader, I cannot tell you how much I value your time, your feedback, and your brilliant ideas. You have been a huge influence on this series, and I appreciate you so much. Thank you for everything.

To Alisha, my bookish best friend and wonderful sister-in-law. Thank you for your constant love for my series, for the joy you share whenever I send you a new piece of artwork or a video, and for being the best sister anyone could hope for. I love that I can fangirl with you and know you are just as excited as I am.

To my incredible editor, Carolyn Gilpin. I am so grateful that you agreed to work your magic once again on After the Fury. Your honesty, kindness, and expertise have been invaluable, as they always are. Thank you for sticking with me all these years and for helping shape these books into something stronger and more beautiful than I could have created alone.

To Kalynne (@kalynne_art on Instagram). After all these years of working together, I still stare at your illustrations in complete awe. Your art inspires me constantly, and your talent just grows brighter with each piece you create. You are a true testament to what passion and dedication can achieve. Although this series has now reached its end, you know I will always be a huge fan, and I cannot wait to return for more of your magic in the future.

To my Hype Team – Teagan, Natasha, Annee, Allie, Hope, Emma, Jodie, Lee and Usman – thank you for jumping in with such energy and enthusiasm. Knowing you were there, ready to boost my posts, cheer on my updates and give the algorithm a push whenever it was needed, gave me so much extra motivation. Your excitement for the art, the snippets, the reveals and the videos has meant everything. Also, a special mention to Kei, who suggested the name for our dragon companion Aeun, thank you, I think it suits her perfectly!

To the wonderful indie authors who inspire me and who I can turn to for advice and a chat when things get a bit curly, thank you! I'm so grateful for the many friends I've made along the way and for your trust in me as an ARC reader too. It's such a joy to be part of your journeys, and to have you as part of mine. I adore you all.

And finally, to the wonderful bookshops who have stocked my series: Dymocks Knox, A Thousand Lives Bookhaven, Novel Nook, Tales and Tomes, Nightbloom Bookstore, Arcane Books, Fables & Froth, Pixel Bound, and Pages 'n' Co. Thank you for your support and for believing in my books. Seeing them on your shelves never gets old, and I doubt it ever will.

I think I can finally say that I'm ready to leave Fythnar behind for a while, as hard as it may be. This world will always hold a special place in my heart, but it is time to let it rest without chaos and allow the characters some peace, at least for the foreseeable future. I'm excited to begin new stories that I've been quietly working on, and I hope you'll follow me there soon, into the unknown.

Until next time!

Lots of love, Melissa.

Melissa J. L. Kincaid is a fantasy author from Melbourne, Australia, who has a passion for creating worlds filled with magic, adventure, and heart. Known for her rich world-building and strong female leads, her stories often weave together forbidden love, powerful magic, and epic battles, a blend that draws in fans of both fantasy and romance.

Melissa took the plunge into self-publishing in 2021 with her debut novel, *Love, Blood & Fury*. She went on to release *Magic, Midnight & Starlight*, before bringing the trilogy to a breathtaking close in 2024 with *Fire, Fury & Chaos*. Not yet ready to leave the world behind, she returned in 2025 with *After the Fury*, a spin-off that invites readers back into the realm they had come to love.

With a background in graphic design, Melissa brings her creativity full circle by designing her own covers and book interiors, ensuring every detail matches the vision of her stories.

When she isn't writing, illustrating or curled up with a fantasy book, Melissa enjoys exploring the outdoors with her husband, Greg, and their son, Elijah Gregory, often camping under the stars.

www.lotsoflovecreations.com.au

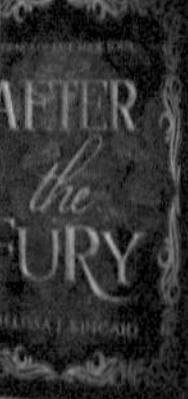

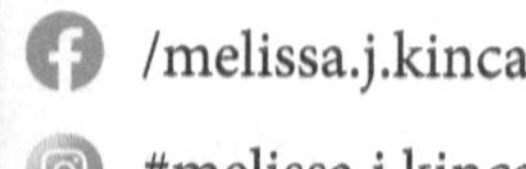 /melissa.j.kincaid

 #melissa.j.kincaid.author

 @melissa.j.kincaid.author

THE
Strings of Fate
SERIES

STRINGS OF FATE BOOK ONE
LOVE,
BLOOD
&
FURY
MELISSA J. KINCAID

STRINGS OF FATE BOOK TWO
MAGIC,
MIDNIGHT
&
STARLIGHT
MELISSA J. KINCAID

STRINGS OF FATE BOOK THREE
FIRE,
FURY
&
CHAOS
MELISSA J. KINCAID

Spin-off
STRINGS OF FATE BOOK FOUR
AFTER
the
FURY
MELISSA J. KINCAID

Melissa Kincaid
ROMANTIC FANTASY AUTHOR
WWW.LOTSOFLOVECREATIONS.COM.AU
Available in Paperback, Hardback and eBook.

SCAN ME!

Did you enjoy the story?
PLEASE LEAVE a Review!
goodreads
fable
THE STORYGRAPH
Reviews help independent authors like me reach more readers. Every review means a lot!
Scan the code to go to Goodreads.